GATHER NOW THE MIGHTY

GATHER NOW THE MIGHTY

A NOVEL BY

TREVOR GERRA

PELLETRON ★ PUBLISHING

Published by Pelletron Publishing, USA
Visit our website at www.pelletronpublishing.com

First edition: June, 2009

This fictional book was written with the intention of depicting biblical events in dramatized fashion with inspiration provided to the author solely from scriptures of the King James Bible, Old Testament. Any resemblance to other events, or persons, living or dead, is entirely coincidental.

ISBN-13: 978-0-9822170-0-9

ISBN-10: 0-9822170-0-5

Poem by Keith Gerra reprinted with permission.

(*)- King James Bible, O.T., select scriptures and paraphrases.

Printed in the U.S.A

For YUDORA, a mighty woman...

PREFACE

The idea for this book was borne out of my interest in the biblical record of "The Mighty Men of David" whose feats were so extraordinary they appear to have been supernatural. Yet, besides their mention in a handful of scriptures, there is little else known or written about these men, a fact which begs the question: Who exactly were these men called mighty and how were they able to accomplish such prodigious deeds? With this in mind, I decided to create a fictional account of these unsung heroes that would further tie them into biblical events while honoring their memory.

During the course of writing, I made every attempt to remain true to scripture and not to deviate from the historical implications of the bible. I therefore added into my tale actual biblical events and characters very purposefully, including the famous records of Joshua, Samson, and David, all of which I attempt to weave into the storyline in seamless manner and with gracious artistic license. The name of the book, "Gather Now the Mighty" is consequently representative of our protagonist's own plight as well as a description of this author's attempt to gather the accounts, in novel form, of a diverse number of mighty men mentioned in the Old Testament.

I would like to point out that being a work of fiction, the book is not meant to change history or to be added alongside scripture; the storyline is likewise not meant to offend with its mention of battles, warfare, and sometimes violent scenes, which were simply a requisite component of the tale. This book is instead merely an endeavor to stimulate our imaginations and thoughts. It is a work that was written to inspire while offering one possible rejoinder to the aforementioned question of who exactly the mighty men were.

I want to thank everyone who offered encouragement during the long course of this work, especially my family members: Yuri, Lisa, Eric, Keith, and of course mom and dad. You have each offered me your support and I am thankful for your love and your backing.

I am also happy to realize that what started out as a simple idea, mentioned to my mother over coffee so many years ago, has finally blossomed into a complete novel. I have prayed that this work would be a blessed thing and an inspiration to all that read it...

THERE WERE GIANTS IN THE EARTH
IN THOSE DAYS;
AND ALSO AFTER THAT,
WHEN THE SONS OF GOD CAME IN
UNTO THE DAUGHTERS OF MEN,
AND THEY BARE CHILDREN TO THEM,
THE SAME BECAME MIGHTY MEN
WHICH WERE OF OLD, MEN OF RENOWN...
(GENESIS 6:4)

There is a sound that goes forth
A wailing – A crying out to the souls of men

Come chase the wind
Come ride the lightning
Come dance in the fire

But in the End
Your life lay waste
At the hands of death

There is a snare hating
A trap waiting
A pit that is covered

There is a lie working
A thief lurking
A lion crouching

And lo
All do hunger and thirst
For the soul

Be careful therefore strongman
Be mindful – Where ye choose to tread

Fore there is a way that seams right
But in the end
Surely death is waiting

By Keith Gerra

TABLE OF CONTENTS

GATHER NOW THE MIGHTY

PROLOGUE

In the days of Eli the High-Priest, there was neither judge nor king in Israel. Every man did what was right in his own eyes, and even the alleged righteous, the young men of the Shiloh Priesthood, violated the sacred laws of the patriarchs. In this age of transgression, Eli discerned that God had no choice but to judicially chastise the descendants of Jacob. To their dismay, it was thus ordained that the tribal-nation of Israel was fated to undergo a tragic period of reprisal at the hand of their enemies.

The Philistines subsequently fought and defeated the spirit trodden tribes, which could do nothing but watch as the lands along Judah's western borders were conquered. Yet, even more heartrending than the bereavement that they experienced over their captured territories was the day that Israel lost its most hallowed of possessions, the Ark of the Covenant. The devastating event took place at the battle of Ebenezer, the same battle in which the sons of Eli were killed by their formidable adversaries. When the High-Priest therefore heard that his two sons had been killed and the sacred article taken by the Philistines, he fell instantly to his death; his vertebrae folding upon the steps of the Shiloh Gate. An era was over.

In the eyes of Israel, there was only one man who could rightly succeed Eli as head of the priesthood, the highest office in the land. His name was Samuel. A Nazarite from birth, it was well known that he regularly received divine revelation, and his ability to prophesy had been counted upon by the leaders of Shiloh on many occasions. After his selection, Samuel immediately reconvened the Council of Elders. In the tradition of old, these seventy men were appointed to preside over their tribesmen as representatives and adjudicators.

The Council of Seventy, as they were known, in turn elected Samuel to also fill the office of High-Judge, an esteemed designation unknown since the days of Samson. The Council then called forth the many subordinate rulers throughout Israel and convinced their tribesman to stop their worship of strange idols and make atonement for their iniquities. After many years, Israel began to obey this directive and to accept the tenets of their new leadership. It was only then that Samuel, the High-Priest and Judge, declared that the tides of war would begin to turn in Israel's favor once again.

Soon after, rumors spread of a young warrior who had supernatural strength and could wield a sword with remarkable power and skill. For two straight years he led Israel to victory on the battlefield. His distinction in combat promulgated his reputation, and he came to be known by many names amongst his tribesmen, with some calling him Josheb-Basshebeth, many calling him Jashobeam for his stalwart frame, and still others simply calling him Josheb. But no matter the name, there was one thing that he had proven certain; he was a mighty man. Consequently, as the Israelites began their final push to take back their lands east of Philistia's great cities of Ekron and Gath, the tribes were depending heavily on the abilities of this Josheb-Basshebeth. He would not disappoint...

PART 1

ANTIQUITIES

1

The thunderous sound of hard driven horses resonated over the verdant soil of the plain as the morning dew created a hazy veil of dust in the heat of the rising sun. Amidst that earth hovering cloud, a voice called out, "The battle has not yet begun!" The pronouncement was that of Josheb's as he shouted over to his father while cupping one hand on the side of his mouth.

"And it will not until we arrive," his father boldly yelled back at the top of his voice in order to be heard above the hammering of those many hurried hooves.

Including both Josheb and his father, Zabdiel, there were twelve men total from the house of Hachmon who had arrived late to the battlegrounds that day. Confident of their upcoming victory, Zabdiel now rode gallantly upon his chariot beside his son. He had insisted on waiting for the official armistice to be written up by the Council of Seventy and now carried the truce with plans to deliver it to the kings of Philistia personally. "Remember, we stop outside of their walls," he said, reminding his son of the only certain plan of battle. "For now, we will take back the lands that the Philistines gained before this conflict. The rest we'll seize another day."

Waiting on the slope of the valley ahead of them was Israel's men of war. Compared to their Philistine enemies, they were ill equipped for fighting, but what they lacked in armor, they made up for in brawn. In all, there were over 12,000 Israelites gathered from the tribes. A smaller force than what had been sent to fight during previous battles, but these were the bravest and strongest in all of Israel. Each man had proven himself worthy in combat, and certainly, to be designated as representatives of their tribesmen on this day was considered a high praised honor amongst them.

Across from these 12,000, on the adjacent hillsides, a powerful army stood. These were Philistia's heavily-armored men of Ekron and Gath whose forces, despite being utterly decimated over the last two years, still outnumbered that of Israel by more than two to one. At one time their armies were indeed much greater, but the new resolve of the young Israelites had cost them immense losses on the battlefield. In light of the situation, the kings of Ekron and Gath had already been told by the other three monarchs who concomitantly ruled the Pentapolis, which made up the united federation of Philistia, that the fight should be given up. Moreover, unless the Israelites attempted to cross into their own borders and lay siege to Philistia's lands, these other three realms expressed that they had no interest in sending more troops. Thus, Ekron and Gath were destined to fight in this conflict without the complete backing of their nation, and if they failed, this war was over.

The leaders of Israel's tribes knew the circumstances well enough and had already sent messengers with an offer of peace; if either king would acknowledge defeat, their soldiers would likewise be allowed to withdraw from the lands of Israel peaceably. But the two Philistine kings refused. Ekron's stubborn monarch had brashly torn up the proposal in the face of Israel's messenger and sent word back that there would be no surrender on the part of Ekron without a fight. Gath's corresponding answer shortly followed.

On this stage, the house of Hachmon arrived. Crowds of Israelite warriors parted for the small contingent as they made their way to the front of the ranks. There, Josheb and his father remained in the lead position for the tribe of Judah where they were flanked by throngs of their own countrymen so that each of the twelve tribes of Israel stood strong together.

Knowing that the commanders of Judah had arrived with the newly drawn up armistice, the captains of each tribe then held out their swords in succession and turned their chariots to face the Philistines. At that moment, Zabdiel looked over to his son and gave him a nod. The mighty man casually loosened the reigns of his horse and began a slow trot towards his enemy with the rest of the Israelites following his measured lead.

From the Philistines' viewpoint, the approach was nothing more than a boisterous and most unruly advance. There were no established marching positions amongst the Israelites. Some rode on horses, some walked, and in the midst of it all, there was at least one man who amusingly rode into battle on a rickety old horse-drawn wagon. The chief men of Israel themselves rode upon chariots, but these were scarce enough. The only thing in less supply amongst the disheveled bunch was the presence of armor.

After witnessing their enemy's disorderly advance, the Philistines confidently marched out in ranks: Nearly 3,000 chariots and horsemen followed the progression of over 25,000 foot soldiers, bedecked in armor and wielding iron weaponry. It was a sardonic sight in view of the fact that during all the battles of this war, the Philistines proudly considered themselves the more sophisticated war-machine.

Over a Century earlier, after Greece defeated Troy, the Greeks had likewise adopted a superior introspect, considering their own army as the most advanced in the world. Yet soon after the defeat of the Trojans, Greece was overthrown by the Philistine's barbaric ancestors, the Dorians. Claiming to be the returning sons of Hercules, the Dorian invaders surprisingly defeated and subjugated the Greeks, all the while taking pride in their unruly fighting skills and renowned ancestry.

But on this day, as Philistia faced off with Israel, these successors of the Dorians made no heedless claims of ancestry, nor did they march forth with the same shameless abandon that their predecessors once had. They left that bad-mannered role entirely to the Israelites and instead placed their confidence in a well armored line of professional soldiers who had been trained to fight with organized precision.

It must still be noted that these Philistines did not exactly lose their prideful spirit. On the contrary, every since developing their movements on the battlefield to a new level of artistry, they had gained an entirely new sense of egotism and were themselves no less fearsome than their braggart forerunners. They proved this as they marched in succession down to the valley floor, striking the handles of their spears and swords against rock-solid shields while creating a rhythmic pulsation of their strength. The din of their deeds echoed out and beyond the surrounding plains in all directions.

This imposing tactic was widely known to unnerve their enemies. But in spite of that deafening clamor, there was one who rode toward the oncoming waves of clattering iron with oblivious disregard for what that noise did connote, and his daring attitude resonated behind him through 12,000 fierce men of war. This was Josheb, and he now led the viscerally-charged advance of Israel's choice men with headstrong abandon.

The dark horse that Josheb rode upon had cast its care aside the moment its reigns were fully loosed, and as they pushed forward, at long last both Josheb and the army of Israel were able to look their enemy in the eyes. Once Jashobeam drew his sword, there was no mistaking, the battle had in truth begun.

Those Philistines whom he initially came upon were the

first to regret the chastisement of his weapon. For Josheb crushed through their iron façade with ease, proving that this was no ordinary man and that he wielded no ordinary blade.

The wealth of the mighty man's family had after all paid for his daunting sword, which was nearly twice as long as the typical bronze weapon of the day. It would have been too awkward for even the most adroit of men to competently wield in battle, but in Josheb's hand it was deft. And perhaps the biggest surprise for the armor clad Philistines this particular morning was the fact that, like every other Israelite who stood in front of them, Josheb's sword was forged with iron, not the anticipated bronze.

Israel's tribes had afore agreed to secretly pay an offensive price to the talented iron-smiths of Philistia in order to procure these weapons and assure that every Israelite man in this battle against Ekron and Gath would indeed be supplied a weapon forged with the valued heavy-metal. Hence, out of greed, the Philistine tradesmen had betrayed their own and justice was achieved. For only with iron should a warrior combat against iron.

And combat is exactly what Josheb did. He rode swiftly, passing the oncoming chariots as he swung his blade wildly with such speed and force that even those Philistines lucky enough to intercept its path by blocking it with their shields were hewn backwards and onto the ground. Alas, his enemy was soon to realize, Josheb's swing was not as wild as it appeared; it was surely calculated. Instead, it was the men of Philistia whose movements were both wild and slow to match compared to that of this mighty man.

The Philistines changed their battle stance in an attempt to steer clear of Jashobeam's onslaught, but their actions were all the more regrettable. Josheb tore apart regiments of men as they turned their backs on him, trying in vain to outrun his blade. This assault continued as he rode deeper into the Philistine ranks cutting a path behind him. He made his way first through the many footmen and then tore into the chariots. Nearing the last lines of the Philistine forces, he leaped from his horse with his sword still relentlessly swinging and planted his feet firmly to the ground.

Jashobeam's physical presence on the battlefield took an immediate effect on the Philistines. Undeniably, riding upon his horse a few moments prior he had been awe-inspiring, but the full might of this man was not fully comprehensible to his rivals until he himself stood in front of them. He was the essence of power, and the musculature of his bare-chested frame seemed to his enemy more stalwart than their own armor. This caused the Philistines to shake with fear and momentarily recoil in humbling fashion over this warrior's obvious supremacy. Their apprehension was mimicked in the actions of their horses, which refused to advance toward this son of the Eznite. When pressed with whips and jibes to move upon Josheb, the beasts defied their masters as they kicked and bucked themselves free of their harnesses. During the fracas, riders were hewn from their chariots and thrown to the ground as their cars were overturned. There would be no running this Israelite down.

Finally, one of the Philistine warriors worked up the nerve to approach Josheb on foot—sword drawn, his shield out front. But the soldier was quickly relieved of that shield as the mighty man ripped it from him and sent the Philistine away with a heel to the chest.

The acquired object was not just used by Josheb in the traditional fashion, and instead of blocking the now oncoming enemy horde with the shield, he used it to batter them. He spun around and around as he sent the Philistines flying through the air in waves. Then, after clearing a wide enough area around him, he relentlessly continued forward wielding both shield and sword as he made his way toward their backlines with an up-stir of brawn. This whirlwind of power continued whilst the rest of Israel's men of renowned followed close behind Josheb. Together they created a path, which flowed straight through Philistia's army and in effect divided its forces into two.

Having never been set down in any preemptive summit, Jashobeam's battle strategy had been completely impromptu but was nonetheless immediately understood by both armies to carry dire consequences. If the Philistine forces could actually be split, the Israelites would merely need to defend the lines on one half while the majority of their warriors could then attack the other side. This would in effect nullify Philistia's advantage of having a much larger force and set the odds in favor of the Israelites, whose warriors were much more formidable in their close combat battle skills.

As Josheb continued his barrage and reached the end of the Philistine forces, other able body warriors amongst the Israelites quickly stationed themselves in defensive posture so that the first phase of the improvised battle plan was readily accomplished. At this point, the Philistines did their best to rally and break back through the lines where their forces had been divided. But their attempts were futile, for Israel's men were too strong.

Shammah son of Agee fought that day for Israel. He was one of only a select few whose stature rivaled that of Josheb's. Under his command, a small group of men valiantly stood their ground against the onslaught of Philistines, whom they fought off with overwhelming power. A sword in each hand, Shammah punished his enemy with violent strikes, aiming distinctively while he stabbed through the dense plates of their armor. His eyes were aflame not only with the blaze of retribution for those stolen lands of Israel, but his soul burnt also with contempt over the detrimental cost of this long war and the many lost lives of his tribesmen.

Adjacent to Shammah's men were those from the house of Dodai. These brave warriors were led by Eleazar, a man long regarded as a fierce warrior. His long red locks and beard gave him the appearance of a majestic lion, and he likewise held off the charge of his enemy with the strength and ferocity of that regal beast. During the heat of battle, his grip on his sword was so intense that it melded his fingers to the handle. As a result, he swung his weapon with such force that with each strike he liberated his enemy of their own swords and sent them running away, unarmed and in retreat.

Following after the fleeing Philistines were the brothers Joab and Azahel, sons of Zeruiah. As the two had approached the battleground that day, Azahel's horse had unfortunately lost its footing and sent him toppling to the ground. But he would not be denied the honor of leading the fight alongside his brother. He instantly jumped to his feet and ran a great distance to join the fray. Azahel's resolve was outmatched only by his physical prowess, and as he ran faster and faster he astoundingly passed both his brother's horse and many of the chariots that rode before him into battle. When he arrived at the battlefront, he did not slow. Instead, Azahel drew his sword and chased his enemies down causing them to flee in a panic while begging for his mercy.

To complete the defensive line of the Israelites, situated upon a small jutting prominence of land, was Abishai, brother of Joab and the fleet-footed Azahel. To the amusement of the Philistines, he had indeed ridden a horse-drawn wagon onto the battlefield, but their delight was short lived as the destruction that would be launched from his seemingly mundane station was soon realized. For, within that simple agrarian vehicle were hundreds of iron-tipped spears, made ready to defend any ground gained by Israel. And within the grasp of Abishai, each spear soon became an unstoppable and merciless projectile that was capable of impaling through an entire line of armor clad Philistines. One in his right hand and one in his left, he launched the javelins toward his enemy in succession with ruinous speed and precision. Before this battle was over, three hundred men would fall victim to one of these spears.

Accordingly, the battle waged as these and other men of valor took the fight to the Philistines. The Israelites continued their spontaneous plan of action, turning the brunt of their tribal forces first toward one half of their enemy's army and then the other.

It was Zabdiel and the rest of the senior captains who led this second component of the battle. Zabdiel was also the first to realize that with continued pressure their enemy would be forced to fall back. With this prospect in mind, Zabdiel left his position of relative safety upon his chariot in order to join his men on foot. Like his son Josheb, Zabdiel was a mighty warrior; he was skilled in the use of the sword, and with that weapon he obstinately pushed forward.

Eventually, Zabdiel came into view of what he considered to be the final obstacle to overcome in order to end this conflict. The kings of both Ekron and Gath, along with their generals, occupied a high plot of ground under a group of olive trees in the distance. From there, they had prolonged the battle by signaling the defensive positions for their ranks of men to take. If the kings themselves could be driven into retreat, Zabdiel realized that the body of their armies would be left headless and would without a doubt collapse. He immediately yelled the orders for his men to break away from the center of combat and to charge the hill.

Yet, the well lain strategy did not go unnoticed by Philistia's kings. Upon seeing the approach of these Israelites, the Philistine command immediately signaled for a large segment of their footmen to intercept the advance. At the same time chariots, outfitted with both driver and archer, were sent to crush the brazen attack of the Israelites.

Regrettably, it seemed as though Zabdiel's zealousness had gotten the better of him. His men had promptly become inundated with incoming enemy fire as they tried to press forward against an overwhelming number of Philistine archers, and for the first time that day the Israelites were forced to give up some ground.

Still, Zabdiel fought on, swinging his sword furiously in between raising his shield to block the arrows. Then suddenly, in the midst of this furious fighting, Zabdiel looked around to notice that none of his men had been able to stand with him. He fought on alone, raising his shield instinctively as two arrows were deflected by it. Lowering the shield, he took several swipes to block an oncoming barrage of enemy swords which came at him in a cursory attack. Again, he raised the shield to block the persistence of the arrows. This he repeated several times, fighting valiantly, but as he lowered his shield once more, sword ready to jut out, he suddenly felt the severe piercing of iron through his armor. It stabbed directly into his chest shocking his senses as it was pulled out. His hand involuntarily released its grip upon his sword, and the weapon fell to the earth as pain rippled through the whole of his body. Zabdiel's shield fell next, followed by the aged body of the man.

Having landed with a thud to his knees, Zabdiel breathed out slowly, looking first toward the Philistine warrior standing in front of him and then up toward the violet sky. A wake of vultures gathered there.

It shouldn't have to end this way for such a great warrior, but there was nothing more that he could do. The fight had left Zabdiel. He closed his eyes and waited for the opponent in front of him to deliver the next blow. It would bring his life to an end. The realization hit him as he heard the faint sound of the Philistine's sword cutting through the air.

For a brief moment this brave son of Hachmon thought of nothing else, anticipating only the merciless serration upon his flesh. He grasped onto the armistice, which he still carried under the links of his bronze chained-mail. The significance of the document comforted him and reminded Zabdiel that despite the loss of his own life, his enemy's lifeblood had likewise been drained; the Philistines had already taken too many losses, and the truce would have to be honored by days end. Israel would have its land back.

The brisk sound of that iron cutting through the air towards him still resonated in Zabdiel's mind as his anticipation grew stronger. Then the choking sounds of an impaled man broke the dim hum of the reverberating timbre. Zabdiel opened his eyes.

It was not he that had suffered the fatal blow of the sword. To Zabdiel's surprise, the Philistine would-be executioner had instead landed with a thud of his own and now likewise kneeled upon his knees. From the Philistines chest protruded the handle of a sword, the same sword which had cut through the air moments prior. Zabdiel realized that it must have been hurled a great distance and at great speed, turning over and again before it finally pierced through the armor of the Philistine soldier. The handle of this sword was immediately and unmistakably recognizable as that of Josheb's. For upon it was the stamp of the tribal crest of Judah, the face of a roaring lion.

Zabdiel quickly grabbed the handle, taking the sword as a weapon for his own defense as the Philistine soldier finished his crash to the ground, but this hasty action was unnecessary. As intense as the battle had proven moments prior, it was now quiet on this plot of ground. Josheb had circled back through the Philistine forces and was successful in rallying the troops of Israel as they were being pushed down the hill. The Israelites were now overrunning the Philistines, chasing them through the fields in the distance and back to Ekron.

Zabdiel was glad to see Josheb standing beside him with a hand outstretched, and with his son's help, the wounded old warrior somehow managed to get to his feet. He then immediately removed his breastplate and clasped a hand over his chest. He had been truly fortunate, for the tight fitting hardened-leather plate had formed an immediate seal over his wound and prevented the loss of too much blood. "I am getting old," he told Josheb as he coughed up some sputum and blood and spit it out in a feisty manner. He tested his strength by walking around and inhaling deeply, all the while trying not to lose his breath.

"You need to sit down and rest," Josheb cautioned as he

watched his determined father try and walk off his pain.

"Nonsense," Zabdiel responded as he continued in the direction of the distant fighting. "I am the son of Hachmon, and I have a truce here in my hand, which I plan to deliver yet."

Arriving from the rear of the battle, the aforesaid patriarch and a number of the other elders, now happened on the scene with their chariots. "Listen to your son. He has given you good advice," Hachmon told Zabdiel as he motioned for Josheb to help the wounded man onto the chariot. "If you want to live to be as old as me, you should stay off of the field of battle. Leave that to our young men," the white haired Hachmon quipped. "Although, if I had been just a couple years younger, I may have joined you two out here today." This was more than just a slight exaggeration, and the humor caused Zabdiel to grimace and Josheb to grin. For, although Hachmon had in fact led men into battle until he was well beyond the age of his son, Zabdiel, that had been many years ago. He was now well past the age of waging war and instead did all he could to ride through the aftermath of the battles upon his chariot. It was part of his official duties as a senior member of the Council of Seventy.

As the day drew to a close, the three men slowly made their way toward the setting sun and the distant boundaries of Ekron where the last of the fighting had already taken place. It was just as Zabdiel had imagined. The armistice was inevitably delivered to the kings of both Ekron and Gath—by the house of Hachmon nonetheless.

The defiant Philistines had no choice but to accept the proviso, and for now at least, the war was over...

After the war, days of peace ensued, and because of his pivotal role in the scheme of things, Josheb was asked by the Council of Seventy to stay in the region for a while and head up a guard for Israel's regained protectorate. While honored with the elder's confidence in him, the idea of remaining in the area did not go over well with Josheb at first. Like the rest of the Israelites, he wished to return home. It would take the urging of Hachmon and Zabdiel for him to agree.

"Why would I want to stay?" Josheb questioned his father as he packed up the belongings of his camp in a perturbed manner. "This war is over, is it not? I am no longer needed here."

"You are right," Zabdiel responded. "The war is over, but future hostility from the Philistines is still possible."

Josheb momentarily paused and looked over at his father. "And what am I to do if they attack?" he retorted as he crammed his gear into his rucksack. "Am I to supposed take on their entire army on my own?"

"Of course not," Zabdiel answered back in an assuring tone. "This was once the lands of a great number of Judah's men and their families. Many have already agreed to stay and start rebuilding what was once their home. They will be under your command." He then looked over to Hachmon for assistance in explaining the situation.

Hachmon thought quickly and then suddenly responded to his grandson in an affirming manner, "These men need a leader. Who better than you, a man of Judah yourself, could command them?"

"These are not our lands," Josheb quickly pointed out. "Our home is in the heartland of Judah."

"Still you are the best suited for this task," Hachmon told him in candid tenor. "And while this area is not part of our family's personal lands, it is nonetheless within the boundaries of our tribal jurisdiction. The other tribes have come to our aid and are proud to have helped Judah regain its lands. Some have traveled from great distances, but now these men desire to return to their own tribal lands and to their families."

"And do I not have a home? Do I not have a wife and children of my own waiting for me?" Josheb asked. He was still somewhat agitated, but he had composed himself a bit after listening to his grandfather's logic.

"Yes," his father sympathized with Josheb. "Yes, of course you have a family of your own, and I wouldn't ask you to do anything that I myself was not prepared to do. Perhaps, it would be best if we both stayed. It is true; the lands that we have regained belong to our tribe. Far be it from me to forsake Judah in a time such as this. After all, if we continue to give up our tribal lands, what future will there be for your sons? What will the next generation of Judah have for an inheritance?"

Josheb knew that his father was in no condition to stay with the injury that he had sustained, and with Zabdiel's last comments he was already beginning to feel an involuntary obligation to lend a hand in the situation. "No, that wouldn't help matters. You don't need to stay in the area," Josheb insisted. "Besides, you have to get home yourself, father.

You've been away longer than I have."

Seeing that Josheb was on the brink of agreeing to the request of the elders, Hachmon continued to push the importance of the issue, "You and a small force of men should be able to readily hold the area while proving to the Philistines that we won't be trifled with. The majority of us, from both Judah and the rest of the tribes, will be able to return home immediately. This would give the tribes a real sense of closure by ensuring them a sense of accomplishment and the feeling that this war is indeed over. Not only would the elders appreciate your sacrifice, but the whole of Israel would owe you a debt of gratitude."

Josheb thought about the situation for a moment. He took a deep breath and asked his next question in a less aggravated tone, "How long would I be needed to stay on?"

Knowing his son well, Zabdiel began to chuckle in a lively manner as he tried to cheer him up, "Don't sound so downcast. You will be here for a few months at the most. I promise."

The discussion was accordingly finished, and Josheb was assigned as the leader of a relatively small but reliable group of men. As Hachmon and Zabdiel left, they each assured Josheb that supplies would be sent out. Once again, they each reiterated that this was a momentous occasion. "The elders already have plans to meet with Samuel," Hachmon explained.

"We must somehow develop a plan, which will provide a more stable future for this loose knit conglomeration, which we call Israel," Zabdiel added. "This war has already proven that as a combined federation, we can defeat even the most powerful of our adversaries."

Josheb and his assigned men were subsequently left alone. As a shrewd leader, the young warrior had them move to a strategic location in the area and set up a proper camp right away. Next, he assigned everyone individual responsibilities.

After this, he sent out scouts, which returned with reports on the numerous landmarks within the outlying countryside. Their accounts of the region helped Josheb form a rough sketch of the surrounding topography in his mind. This knowledge would be invaluable in establishing posts for the men, and it would also help him make quick decisions during any sort of future confrontations with the Philistines.

Half of the men were then sent out with a few rations to stand watch throughout the area. Josheb wanted a well placed guard, which would rotate back and forth between the main encampment and their outlying posts. These watchmen were thus spread-out on the borderline of Philistia, from Ekron down towards Gath. Josheb told them that they were not only to report on the Philistine's activity around the cities, but he also wanted to be alerted if there were any troop movements between the two capitals.

To be sure, Josheb kept them all very busy for nearly an entire month by being as thorough as possible in his direct- ives. A tight schedule was likewise quickly developed around the camp and in short order things were running smoothly. When Josheb was finally satisfied with the daily rotations and that the Philistines had no immediate plans to regroup and attack, he let the men relax a little.

Hence, as night began to fall on the twenty-eighth day of their encampment, they built a large fire and sat around it for some warmth and long deserved rest. It had been their first relaxing afternoon and evening spent in quite some time, and the tranquility was appreciated. One of the men even played a consoling song on a flute. The quietly piped music along with the crackling warmth of the fire unexpectedly lulled Josheb to sleep.

That night, he had a dream. Through the white clouds he soared. He could not see his own body but intuitively under- stood himself to exist in the form of some sort of winged creature, a bird of prey perhaps. His eyesight was keen, and he could sense a healthy vibrancy in his body and limbs. The wind whisked past him as he dove into the white mist and then descended below the clouds to get a better look at the valley.

The haze gave way to a blue forefront as he happened upon a group of hills. Next, the green and yellow foliage of the plains came into view and he effortlessly maneuvered onward through the air flying swiftly along the expansive stretch of a valley. This could very well have been the same setting as the recent battle that he had engaged in. Yet this scene was peaceful and lacked the presence of any army.

He circled the area taking in the majestic scenery before hearing a peculiar noise droning in his ears at a dull, intermittent pace. He dropped lower, tilting his ear in order to pick up a better comprehension of the strange sound. It grew louder. The call of some kind, it was guttural and alerting. Then, as he turned and approached a distant knoll, the source of the noise became apparent. It was the forewarning whelp of a lion.

Josheb climbed the sky, dodging the florid peak of a prominent crag as he passed the creature, which had imprinted its body pattern several times over into the lush shrubs on the top of the summit. Poised and confident, the lion let out an incessant bawl over the distant gorge. It appeared to be directing its bellow to a specific locality out on the remote plane.

Josheb turned his gaze in the same direction and noticed that there was something occurring in the center of a meadow ahead of him. He continued on his course, curious to discover what was unfolding. There was, in the center of the serene grasslands, a large tree, and around that tree stood a group of men. He encircled the site, keenly spying out the scene as though he was indeed an eager bird of prey waiting to nourish itself on the remains below. From his birds-eye-view, he could ascertain that the men were there in an attempt to bring down the tree.

At first, their choice of tools appeared somewhat unusual.

They not only wielded axes, but they also stood with swords and whips ready as if they must first subdue the entity before it could be brought down. Then, after taking a closer look, Josheb decided that the men's cautious approach was not so peculiar after all. There was something noticeably sinister in the trunk and branches of that tree below. And even though its ashen bark and barren appendages confirmed enough of its lifelessness, the lofty height of the tree, along with the expansive reach of its hovering limbs, hinted at the likelihood of it becoming a worthy adversary should it ever be disturbed.

The whips cracked through the air and then around its prominent branches. The men then pulled down with all their might and attempted to stake and tie off their ensnared quarry. All at once, the wind picked up in a torrential current, and thunder rumbled in the distance as clouds rapidly arrived, swathing the sky above. Then the whelp of the lion grew ever louder over the breadth of that isolated plain, and the branches of the tree began to sway in the wind as one of the men approached its trunk, axe in hand. As the rocking of those branches increased with the speed of the wind a strange thing then occurred. The limbs of that tree began to flail about in life-like fashion. They now not only swung with the coaxing of the breeze, but instead, they seemed to move with a will all their own. Suddenly, a large root broke out from its earthen grave and came to life as it struck out towards the axe wielding man causing him to dodge backwards and fall to the ground.

The bray of approaching horses abruptly woke Josheb from his strange dream as the heaping ashes of the fire sent whisking smoke out into the cold morning air. To his surprise, the light of day was upon him. Josheb realized that he must have been very tired to have actually spent the entire night out by the fire without waking to return to his tent. From the calm reaction of the men in the camp and the lack of any warning from the night watchmen, he figured that the noise of the arriving horses could only mean one thing; the supply-wagons had finally made it. The mighty man stood up and shook off his drowsiness with a yawn and a stretch. Then he yelled out to the arriving outfit, "We were beginning to run quite low on our provisions."

The man out in front of the group, responded, "Yes your father figured as much." Bringing the horses to an abrupt halt in front of Josheb, he assumingly wagged a finger at the mighty man. "You would no doubt be Josheb-Basshebeth."

"I am," Josheb answered back.

"I have heard much about you. Your father sends his greetings," the trail leader said in an affable manner despite a weary look about him. "It has been a long journey for us," he continued explaining as he jumped down from his cart and immediately began to unload the supplies. "I am Jair by the way."

"Let my men do that," Josheb told him and then promptly gave a signal for some of the camp members to unload the cart. He was intrigued by the man's hastiness. "You must be very tired after your trip. Did you come from Beth-Shemesh?"

"All the way from Ramah," came the response to the surprise of Josheb.

"Ramah? You and your men traveled through the night then?" Josheb inquired.

"The trip took a few days," Jair informed him with a pleasant smile. "We camped during the nights. I saw the smoke of your fire at daybreak and followed it here."

"I see," Josheb replied. "And my father personally arranged for you to bring these provisions for us? What was he doing in Ramah?"

"You haven't heard? Well, I guess not. Being out here, you wouldn't have," Jair reasoned in an enthusiastic tone.

"I haven't heard what?" Josheb asked in an inquisitive manner.

"Do you mind?" the man questioned, pointing toward the burning embers.

Josheb gave an affirming nod and Jair walked over to the

fire-pit as his men and those from the camp unloaded the supplies. He stood there for quite some time taking turns holding his hands out to the heat and then rubbing them together. He then breathed heavily into his cupped palms and then repeated the action all over again several times.

Jashobeam soon tired of the man's lengthy routine and delay in the announcement. He asked his question again, "What is it that I haven't heard?"

Jair seemed to bask in the suspense of the moment as much as in the warmth of the fire's remnants. "Are you ready for this?" he asked with a cunning look in his eyes.

"Yes, what is it?" Josheb said.

Jair shook his head and smiled, apparently caught up with the thought of what he was about to say. He then stroked his chin with his fingers and palm, stared at the twinkling cinders, and responded, "It really is some amazing news."

"Tell me already man!" Josheb insisted beginning to become perturbed with Jair's drawn out pronouncement.

"Alright, alright, but maybe you should sit and—"

"—Say what you have to say."

This last order from Josheb was spoken in a very somber tone, which seemed to pacify the moment and finally elicit a pertinent response from Jair. "Israel is to have a king of its own," he said, absorbing the sudden surprise on Josheb's face in a satisfied manner.

"Israel is to have a king?" Josheb repeated.

"A king to rule over all twelve tribes," Jair added excitedly. "The Council of Seventy have gone to Samuel and demanded that a man be chosen from one of the tribes and appointed as our king…"

With the thrilled response from the camp over word of a king, Jair and his men changed their plans of immediately returning home. They instead stayed for the rest of the day, conversing with the members of the post over what little details they knew of the situation. By the time Jair's group had left the next morning, there was still much talk over the topic of a sovereign power in Israel. The buzz continued well into the afternoon as the men alternated duties with those out in the field. Josheb was the only one in camp that had remained somewhat calm and neutral over the matter. The others chattered on non-stop over whether a king was right or wrong for Israel.

As their conversations persisted past supper and into the late afternoon, Josheb wandered out onto the plains alone. He walked for quite a distance to the brow of a small hill and looked out at the horizon. "Hail, king of Israel," he said aloud in order to hear what the notion would sound like from his own lips. The wistful warrior shook his head as he continued to deliberate the situation. "What would it be like to be king?" he thought to himself. To have that authority was inscrutable, and to be the very first king in Israel's history was all the more daunting a prospect. Yet, the twelve tribes had grown to a sizable populace, and perhaps it was time for a king. The elders were surely acting in the best interest of Israel by demanding such a thing.

Drawing his sword, Josheb swung it over the tall blades of grass in one direction and then the other. The motion created a wave of bending stems that bowed twice and then stood upright. He then looked at the handle of his sword and the face of the lion upon it. Turning the weapon ever so slightly, its blade glimmered ephemerally as a ray of sunlight broke through the clouds for a brief moment. "Was this what he was born for, to wield a sword and to wage war?" Josheb silently pondered. Then he quickly closed his eyes to forget about such notions. His strength was surely a gift from God. He should not question such an endowment. After all, he had been given authority because of his physical aptitude. Opening his eyes, he realized where his privilege would eventually lead him? Josheb thought of this future. It was mundane really. He would no doubt be put in charge of a regiment of the king's men, assuming an army could effectively be put together of course. And because of his family's influence, he would probably even get to remain within close proximity to his home. This was not such a bad prospect. There were plenty of men who would count themselves lucky to only have to worry over such trivial problems.

This last thought made Josheb think of an alternative fate for himself. What if things did not turn out so fortunate? He considered where his so called privileged life had gotten him so far. He was literally left out in the cold, in a no man's land, far away from those that he loved. Was this the path of the mighty, to take on the yoke of others? Once again he grasped his sword and briskly swung it to forget about such thoughts. But this time he let the blade come into contact with the tall grass. It whisked delicately through each stalk sending vestiges of the meadow up into the air where it was carried away with the breeze.

Just then, a voice called out from behind Josheb, "The Philistines are approaching!" He turned, and immediately asked which direction the advance came from. His horse was brought to him, and he now rode swiftly, troop in tow, to the west. Approaching across the plain from the opposite direction was indeed a small contingent of Philistine soldiers. As they came close, the mighty man drew his sword but then noticed that his enemy was not poised for battle. Instead, they stopped in the distance, their shiny armor glistening as the clouds swept the sky and the sun set at their backs. They seemed to talk something over between them and then quickly turned, riding off in the direction from which they had come.

"Should we follow?" one of the men questioned.

"Let them go," Josheb answered. "They were merely checking our response, and now they will return to their king and give him a report." The mighty man was correct about the alacrity of the Philistine's report to the King of Ekron, but what he did not know was that he was indeed recognized by his enemies. Because of that distinguishable sword of his, the

Philistines had remembered him and reconsidered their advance. His mere presence had been the real reason they had turned around without so much as drawing their own swords.

"A king must know all that goes on within his own realm as well as the activities that take place throughout the surrounding borders," Josheb said on the ride back to camp. Being somewhat still preoccupied with the elders' notion of a king for Israel, he was thinking out loud more so at the moment than speaking to his men. His wonderment was understandable, for, as the nonstop discussion around the camp had proven, a ruling king in Israel was certainly a grandiose idea. And the concept had not only mystified him and his men, it captivated the entire populace of Israel.

3

Despite the fact that most of the inhabitants of Israel were eager to witness the crowning of a king, there was at least one man who had a negative view of what a monarchy would mean for the tribes. When the High-Judge Samuel first met with the elders, to hear their plea for a king, he rebuked their ungracious attitude with an offended tone, "For the first time in many generations we have a legitimate prospect of peace between us and the Philistines, and this is how you respond? Your contempt for our success is evident by your imprudent request to abruptly change our structure of leadership, to change the very essence of what has already made us a distinctive and prosperous nation."

Josheb's grandfather, Hachmon, had been present during that meeting along with the rest of the seventy Council members. He tried his best to be considerate of Samuel's admonition while at the same time offering the High-Judge some reassurance concerning the Councils viewpoints. "Samuel has truly led us through this time of uncertainty," Hachmon admitted, speaking both to Samuel and the Council of Seventy. "As our priest, he has offered sacrifices unto our God for our iniquities. As our Prophet, he has directed our path, and as our High-Judge, he has adjudicated over this once disbanded Council, organizing us into an effective administration. In all three capacities, he has been our consummate leader, and today we truly stand victorious and at peace with our enemies as a result of his leadership."

"Yes, but what is to happen when Samuel is gone?" a voice of dissent spoke out from amongst the elders. "Who will lead us then? Samuel will not live forever and we surely cannot rely on his sons. For, they do not walk in his ways." This last comment caused a feeling of uneasiness to manifest throughout the room, changing the once civil atmosphere to a more antagonistic one.

Hachmon desired to offer more words to buffer the last comment, but before he could speak, Samuel responded, "I have long suspected that my sons have strayed in their ways." His comment was followed by a long silence and there was now a marked transformation in his voice, which sedated any further hostile comments from the Council. His attitude was at once changed from authoritative to that of a sincere and humble contemporary of those in the room.

The reason for this was simple. The two men in question had long ago been appointed by their father to senior judge-ship positions over the southern region of Israel. Samuel had raised them to be upright and had hopes that they would do him proud by becoming respected and honest arbitrators, but from the beginning of their appointments they had engaged in illicit acts. And it had become common knowledge that the two judges could easily be bribed. Samuel had heard rumors of their dishonest practices for quite some time, but now the Council was confronting him with the unsavory issue. Realizing the reproach that his sons had brought upon him, he continued in a reticent tone, "But I have overlooked my sons' less than exemplary lifestyles out of my own hopes that the rumors of their wrong doings were unfounded. And even if those ill reports were true, I had hoped that they would one day turn from their inappropriate behavior in redemption before the Lord. In short, I have been blinded by my love for them. Who amongst you will fault me for this?"

Small pockets of sympathetic murmurs spread throughout the room and then quickly died out as Samuel continued, "Nonetheless, far be it from me to allow blame to continue upon my house. I am prepared to dismiss the idea that the likes of my sons can rise to any true prominence. I will take your request for a king before the Lord." Samuel hung his head low for a short while, but then a spark of duty compelled him to look out to the room of elders and speak his mind once more, "But let me just say one last thing. Up until this point, your God, the Creator of the heavens and earth, has been your king. What other nation can declare such distinction? I tell you that today you have forsaken the sovereignty of your God in favor of the rule of man." With this last reproof, Samuel left the Council.

The report of that meeting had not reached the ears of many, but Josheb had learned of it even as he was stationed out on that lonesome plain. Hachmon and Zabdiel both made the journey out to personally deliver the next shipment of supplies and visit Josheb. During their talks, Hachmon recounted the entire story for his son and grandson along with the goings on before and after the Council's meeting with Samuel.

"After the treaty at Ekron was accepted, the Council of Seventy all met informally," Zabdiel said recapping the precursory details. "This was well before the meeting with Samuel. And as we looked at one another we recognized that each tribe had grown strong. More importantly, we understood that if we could completely unify under one central authority, we would likewise become even more powerful. We saw it as an historical concept and the next logical step in our existence as a nation. Thus, we took our demands to Samuel. Appoint us a king, we declared, so that under his rule, neither Philistia nor any other nation can ever again succeed in their attempts to overrun us. It was decided beforehand that if Samuel completely objected, we would bring forth that unfortunate subject of his sons and their illegitimate actions. I didn't agree with using such tactics, but my sentiments were in the minority."

Hachmon cleared his throat and requested that some water be brought to him before he finished with his narrative. After quenching his parched voice—a result of the dry climate of the area—he continued in a stately tone, "Consequently, as I have already explained, the harsh subject regarding the corruption that Samuel's sons were engaged in was hastily brought forth at the Council meeting. I will have to admit that this tactic did seem to have a convincing effect on Samuel, and as he left the assembly that day, somewhat downtrodden, we knew that he had no choice but to yield to the rest of us. For, the Council was never in more agreement over any issue. And knowing that we had succeeded in our objectives, we then declared with one voice that we would soon be a nation of sophistication, a prideful country united by a king and respected by other great nations."

"And did Samuel finally agree to allow for a king?" Josheb questioned.

"Not before he cautioned us on the demanding nature of a king," Hachmon remarked in solemn tone. "He told us that a king would over tax us and amongst other things that a king would also take our men off to war."

Both Josheb and Zabdiel were troubled over this last statement. Zabdiel questioned his father's seemingly lax attitude, "Does the Council not heed this warning? After all, wasn't it you that took up for Samuel as you announced to the Council that he rightfully holds title as our great prophet?"

Hachmon explained the Council's sentiments once more, "Of course. The Council has considered the words of the prophet, but we see his warnings for what they truly are, only one possibility of things to come. Since he has sincerely cautioned us on the matter, we will reciprocate by taking every necessary precaution to guard against the risk of such problematic issues arising. The Council has therefore already decided that we will remain in session during the entire process of instituting a monarchy and retain much of our current authority and governing powers. The king will not hold absolute authority until his legitimacy can be fully established."

Over the next several months, Josheb continued to receive word on the developments taking place in central Israel. Through various conversations he had with Jair, whenever the supplies arrived, and as a result of a few more visits from his father, he learned all the details of the events as they unfolded. A man was soon chosen to reign as king over Israel. A Benjamite by the birth, his name was Saul, and by all accounts he did indeed have the appearance of regality despite also having a seeming lack of experience as a leader.

The elders and judges along with many of the wealthy Israelite families hastily joined together to champion the young Saul in spite of the foreboding words of Samuel concerning the problematic rule of kings. They quickly helped gather taxes from their tribesmen in the form of an agreed upon percentage of the countries projected grain harvests, vineyards, and livestock. Storehouses for the latter were quickly constructed by tradesmen who were paid in kind from the goods of the very stockrooms, which they had built. Those staples would continue to be collected as taxes throughout the year and act as the king's main depository to run the country and to pay for the underpinnings of a royal administration. The latter was of course accomplished with the help of the Council of Seventy who organized a collection of gold and silver in the form of a one time donation from the eager families of Israel in support of their king.

Proper armor was bought from both Philistine and Amorite sources so that the king could be provided with an able-bodied army. Troops were sourced out directly from each of the tribes' local militias at the request of the Council and at the discretion of the tribal elders with the subsequent agreement that every one of the tribes would send forth groups of their militias in rotations to serve in the king's army throughout the year. Complete with standardized armor and weaponry, the king's soldiers were also to be given a salary for their service.

The fortress at Gilgal, already recognized as one of Israel's most splendidly built structures to date, was reinforced and made ready to temporarily house both the king and his army. It quickly saw the added construction of higher walls and new gates as well as a grand hall in which royal banquets and national ceremonies could be held.

There were plenty of proud citizens who offered their services to aid the king at Gilgal. Men gladly plowed fields around the region, the land of which had been granted the king by the Benjamites along with the bestowment of the fortress. Others served as royal blacksmiths, woodcarvers, weapon makers and scribes. Women from the region meanwhile lent their help within the walls of the fortress working as perfumers, bakers, and cooks.

It honestly appeared that things were beginning to shape up rather quickly for the newly formed sovereignty of Israel and the remainder of the collected gold was allocated for the building of a legitimate capital city that would eventually replace the fortress at Gilgal and serve as the country's hub. The latter was a grand project, one which Josheb would soon take part in, one that in the scheme of everything else would soon altar the course of his imagined role...

The mighty man sat against a rocky knoll eating his first decent meal in two days. Several months had passed since the crowning of King Saul and supplies for the camp had been arriving increasingly late. Luckily, Josheb had adopted the regular habit of rationing food, which allowed his men to sustain themselves on meager provisions for quite a while—upwards of three weeks on some occasions. Thankfully, their troubles were much shorter lived this time around, and the latest shipment was delivered a little less then a week late. It came with the surprising arrival of a large contingent of the king's soldiers. With an abundance of supplies presently at hand, Josheb therefore now ate enthusiastically not noticing a group of the soldiers approaching him.

"On your feet, follow me!" one of the men instructed him.

Josheb looked up in a perplexed manner. "Surely he wasn't addressing me," he thought to himself and went back to eating.

"I said on your feet man!"

Josheb looked up again. "Are you talking to me?" he asked, slightly agitated over the abrupt interruption of his long awaited meal.

"Yes Josheb-Basshebeth, quickly, follow me!" the soldier demanded.

Josheb stood up and hesitantly followed the troop of men. He was escorted out past the south side of the camp and into a wooded area where an ornamented tent had been set up. The man who had addressed him earlier gave him another order, "Take your sandals off and leave your weapons. Enter and do not speak until you are spoken to."

Josheb was perplexed but did as he was told. As he entered the tent, he heard a strong voice, which was decidedly fitting to the person that it belonged to; a strapping man with long graying braids and beard stood in front of him. "Our nation has been united under a king for only a short time. The pageantry can not be overdone at this point," the man said as he looked down at Josheb's bare feet. "My name is Samuel. Do you know who I am?"

"You are the High-Judge of this nation. Some say you are also a prophet," Josheb replied.

"Yes, two roles, which compliment one another quite well at times. Still, I am not the All-Knowing," Samuel explained as he took a seat. "Although, I do know of your father; is he not the Eznite who sits in the gate at Bethlehem?"

"Yes, I am from Bethlehem, son of Zabdiel, son of Hachmon the Council elder."

"Very interesting," Samuel replied as he picked up a staff and held it out for Josheb to take. Josheb slowly reached out and took it in a puzzled manner. Samuel continued, "That staff was forged over one hundred and fifty years ago. Solid bronze, it comes from Greece. I want you to try and bend it." With that instruction, Josheb bent it with ease into a half moon as if it were a pliable twig in his powerful grip. "Impressive my young friend," Samuel said as he stood up and walked over to a long chest made of Acacia wood. After opening it, he took out another staff and brought it over to Josheb. With a skeptical eye, the prophet then handed it off to the mighty man. "Bend that one," Samuel told Josheb who admiringly looked it over. It was ornately carved in a fashion that gave him the impression that it was much older than the one that he had just destroyed. He inspected the intricate carvings and monikers that adorned it from end to end. "Bend it," Samuel instructed once more.

Josheb shook his head and replied, "It would be a shame to ruin such a magnificent piece." With that, he handed it back over for Samuel to take.

The prophet reached over and gladly took it back. "This staff is from Egypt and is nearly five hundred years old," he informed his guest. "It belongs to the age of Moses, when the people of Israel were slaves. You couldn't bend it if you tried."

Josheb looked amazed. "Forged by God to be unbreakable?" he uttered in amazement.

"No, my young apprentice," Samuel responded. "It has merely calcified and hardened over the years. With too much pressure, it would crumble like stone. I said it belonged to the age of Moses, not to Moses himself."

Josheb stood in silence, now feeling a little idiotic after Samuel's marked correction to his apparently silly assumption concerning the staff. With a little agitation in his voice he then questioned Samuel in a patronizing fashion, "Then what is your point, oh wise one?"

"My first point, do not jump to conclusions. My second, you have indeed passed my test. By questioning my orders, you have shown discernment and respect for something that you appreciated and saw as valuable. On the road that lies ahead you will have to use such discernment to guide you, but you can't always count on your own understanding. Over the coming years, I will hopefully teach you to look to God for this."

Josheb looked puzzled. "What do you mean?" he asked. "Am I not to return to my post then?"

"Tell me, young Josheb, what have you sacrificed over the past two years?"

Josheb gave a direct answer, "I am a mere 23 years of age,

and I have served this nation with my sword for the past two with the utmost dedication. In that time, I have only seen my wife and children on a handful of occasions. I love them very much, but I have sacrificed my time with them and traded it to witness the horrors of war. I have fought fearsomely and done horrible things to mine enemy. I have made both friend and foe afraid of me because of my fierceness in battle. And I have done these things with a sincere purpose, that we may one day establish a stronghold in the midst of our enemies and that the God of Israel may be honored by our victories."

"Ah, you have served your purpose well. What would your wish be then?" Samuel asked. "Would you like to see your wife and children more often, and return to the quiet life that you once knew?"

"How would that be possible?" Josheb implored.

Samuel responded with an exciting prospect, "Your grand-father has requested and I have arranged, if you so desire, for you to leave any future fighting to the king's newly appointed army. The soldiers that brought you to me have already been told that they will be taking over your post immediately. And you are being offered the opportunity to leave this place in order to live with your family while working for the king in Gibeah. It is there that Saul intends to have a palace built, which will serve as a proper center for his administration."

Josheb was thrilled with what Samuel had to say and immediately accepted the offer. He was given time to travel home in order to gather his family and was to subsequently meet up with Samuel in Gibeah, along the Central Benjamin Plateau. The reunion was joyful. For Josheb had not seen his wife, Sora, or his two young boys, Eli and Sham, for nearly a year. As they made their way to their new destination, he shared the cheerful news with his family of how he had received favor from God in all his endeavors and how he had been honored with this new position. Once in Gibeah, they found that Samuel had already arranged for their housing at the newly built southern end of the city. He had also left instruction that Josheb was to spend a few days with his family before reporting in for further word on his new assignment.

"Have you found your dwellings suitable?" Samuel inquired on their second meeting, which took place at the magnificent building site of what was already becoming known as the City of Saul. Progress was being made at a burgeoning rate, and a great wall had already gone up around the entire perimeter of the city along with the completion of several impressive centrally located buildings. The foundation of the king's palace had also been completed, and some of the massive stone walls, which would ensure its defense, were now being erected.

"I have been given so much," Josheb announced. "I am amazed that six months have hardly passed since I was engrossed in battle with my enemy. Yet today, I stand in the peaceful hub of this nation's great future. Truly, I slept in a magnificent manner last night, comforted by the presence of my family."

"This is the beginning of your service," Samuel said in a promising manner as he led Josheb around the various construction sites.

"This palace of the king's will truly be a magnificent structure," Josheb declared as he walked up a small flight of stairs to a mammoth stone column and appreciatively patted its solid construction. There were two such rows of these stone columns, each stretching far up into the sky in support of an open-air-ceiling and guard tower. Directly between these two rows of columns, a wall was being erected. "Where do such splendid building-materials come from," Josheb questioned.

"We will get to that in due time," Samuel explained. "Meanwhile, let me show you where the actual palace is being erected."

Josheb gave Samuel a bewildered look. "You mean this isn't the palace?" he asked in amazement. "But it is by far the most remarkable structure that I have ever witnessed. Those columns look sturdier than the oldest cedars of Lebanon."

"The façade that you stand in front of is the entrance to the court that will one day house and host the assembly of the Council," Samuel clarified. "Here the Council of Seventy will deliberate, and on the far end of the courthouse will be a modern prison. This grand structure will stand as a represent-ation of Israel's pursuit to uphold God's Justice and laws." After explaining this, Samuel led Josheb a short distance to the site of the royal palace. There, Josheb was introduced to many of the people who made up the army of workmen responsible for constructing the city's magnificent structures. "Most of these men have been individually selected to help with this building project because they are considered the finest of artisans and craftsmen," Samuel explained. "They are the best at what they do, and their expertise is what will distinguish the palace as a dwelling fit for kings."

"How long will it be before the king inhabits this great structure? And where does he stay for now?" Josheb inquired.

"The king will remain at Gilgal. It served as Joshua's first hub and is thus suitable for Saul's makeshift headquarters until the completion of the palace. These men work night and day to usher in that occasion."

Josheb listened intently to Samuel and soon began to wonder what his role could possibly be in the scheme of this superb operation.

"Perhaps, you are wondering what your contribution will be to this undertaking?" the prophet asked, seeming to have read his thoughts. "Your purpose here is two fold; you will work and you will learn."

"Sounds easy enough," Josheb replied. "I am no stranger to hard work."

"Ah yes, but what of the second task?" Samuel questioned. "Are you acquainted with your potential? Are you ready to obtain that sort of knowledge and turn it into wisdom? Are you ready to learn your purpose in this life and of your destiny? I can teach you all these things."

Josheb thought Samuel's questions were strange. Still, he was interested in what the prophet was offering. "And how does one learn of his own destiny?" the mighty man asked.

"By looking at your past, and then to God; by this, Josheb, you will learn of your future."

"But, I know of my past. I have led a simple enough life," Josheb stated.

"Yes, but do you know the past of your predecessors and of your country, Israel? This is the past of which I speak. And it is also what I will help you to understand," Samuel proposed as they came to a gate, which was located on the perimeter of the city. He then pointed out to a basin in the distance and gave Josheb instructions, "If you follow the road that leads through this valley you will eventually come to a stream. Turn there and follow against the flow of the stream until you come to a large cave. That is where you will meet me tomorrow, and I will finish explaining your first purpose for being here. As far as the second purpose, your training has already begun." Whilst they departed, Samuel gave one last instruction, "Pack enough supplies for a three days stay, and leave early in the morning. It is quite a distance." With that, Josheb happily went home to his family.

The next day, he rose early as instructed, said goodbye to Sora and his boys, and started on the trip down through the valley. At one point, he made a wrong turn, and in spite of a hurried pace it took him the better part of the morning to find his way back to the main road that led to the stream that Samuel had spoken of.

Once he was finally in view of the cave, half the day was gone. To Josheb's surprise, Samuel was already there waiting for him. Along with Samuel, there appeared to be approximately three to four hundred men at work chipping away at the hillsides and the valley floor. They were a rough bunch, with hardened looks. It seemed as though they had made this rock quarry their home, for there were smartly built huts carved out of the sides of the smaller caves that surrounded the area. As Josheb made his way up through the camp, the men ceased working for a brief moment and looked him over in a scrutinizing manner. Josheb peered back at them with his own daunting stare, which instantly turned most of the gazes back to their previous tasks.

"I see that you took your time in getting here," Samuel called out from the mouth of the large cave located high up at the furthest end of the excavation site. His voice echoed through the valley.

"I had no idea that it would be so far," Josheb said as he made his way up the final slope where Samuel had now taken a seat. "When did you leave?"

Josheb hardly believed it when the old prophet told him that he had left that same morning. "I am not going to even ask," he thought to himself.

Aware of Josheb's confusion, Samuel told him to take a seat as the operation that he saw before him was explained, "This quarry is just one of the many that are currently supplying the stone building blocks for the palace. We have exhausted all of our closer resources, but regardless, our concerted efforts are effective and we are still making great progress."

Josheb looked around to see that as some of the workmen extracted blocks of stone from the hillsides, others then chiseled and shaped them to form the final blocks.

Samuel continued, "The blocks are simply moved atop logs by others who travel out here from the city every three days to retrieve them. It is a measured and time honored process, but now that you are here it will be much faster."

"I appreciate the confidence," Josheb responded. "But I am just one man. What kind of difference can one man make in such a grand endeavor?"

Samuel smiled and nodded his head as he sat on the lofty ledge of the quarry. He spoke to Josheb in an edifying tone, "Listen now to the story of what one man can do when he lives for God and walks in all of His ways. Listen now to the history of our people. Listen now to antiquities...

* * *

...After the great flood, the earth was populated so that all the kings and patriarchs could trace their lineage to one man. That man's name was Noah, and through his lineage, Abraham was born in Ur of the Chaldeans. This one man, Abraham, would likewise become the father of many nations. And he did become wealthy and powerful, eventually settling in the land of Canaan east of the Mediterranean. There, because of his wealth, he controlled all the interests of those lands as a king properly should.

Yet, Abraham claimed no title. He instead attributed all of his blessings to God. To recognize such loyalty, God, the Creator of the heavens and earth, made a covenant with that one man and promised him all the lands of Canaan as far as his eyes could see. Abraham would enjoy it while he lived, and his descendants would return to it making it a nation of their inheritance. Following this promise from God, Abraham begat Isaac, and Isaac begat Jacob. And God did give privilege and favor to both Isaac and then Jacob, because akin to Abraham these men were loyal—honoring of Him.

Thus, Jacob received title amongst men directly from the Lord in the form of a new name, Israel, which quite literally means 'The Prince of God.' Jacob's nobility was therefore established, and by divine privilege this one man's blessing was passed on to twelve others, his sons. And these twelve sons of the patriarch Israel eventually left the land of Canaan in the time of a terrible famine to enjoy a noble life in the region of Egypt. This was the result of one man, their brother Joseph, who had himself received favor from the Lord and was willing to therefore share his blessings with his family. The twelve sons became great families there in Egypt, and their children's children grew into twelve great tribes, including the two tribes of Manasseh and Ephraim, which descended from the house of Joseph. But after many years, these tribes were no longer favored in the land of the Pharaohs.

Their wealth and foreign status eventually caused enmity against them, and their descendants were made slaves by a new generation of Egyptian rulers. But God divined that the sons of Jacob, the tribes of his prince Israel, should not be captives in Egypt forever. Instead they were to one day realize their noble inheritance in the promised land of Canaan. Thus, God once again raised up one man for this task, the patriarch Moses.

And Moses led the Israelites in an exodus from Egypt and into the wilderness beyond the Red Sea. There, God established order amongst the children of Israel. He gave them their laws and had Moses appoint judges who would preside over the disagreements that took place within the tribes. These men were hence the rulers of their tribesmen, and amongst them were many officers and judges creating a hierarchy within the Israelite community. And at the very top of this order of officials, a Council of Seventy Elders ultimately ruled the tribes alongside Moses, the foremost man in all of Israel. And the spirit of God was upon him and the Seventy.

But soon the generation of Moses became disobedient to the commands of the Lord. When God told Moses to send twelve spies, one from each tribe, out of the wilderness and into the land of Canaan, ten of them returned with intimidating reports of great walled cities and giants that now inhabited that land. But two of the spies had a good report of a great land of milk and of honey. They insisted that the promise of their inheritance awaited them. Still, the Israelites ignored the two and instead heeded the words of the ten. They were sorely afraid, refusing to go into battle against such great enemies. They professed that they would have rather died in Egypt or in that very wilderness, which they currently were traveling through.

And therefore, God granted that generation of Moses their desires and let them die in the harsh wilderness. After forty years of wandering, every man over the age of twenty who had heeded the negative report of the ten spies and originally refused to enter Canaan had indeed past away. The exceptions to this were of course the two spies who had given a good report of Canaan. And one of these two men was Joshua. This one man led the younger generations of Israel in a conquest over the land of Canaan where to this day the tribes have settled upon their lands of promised inheritance.

On his death bed, Joshua said these words '(*) –One man of you shall chase a thousand: For the Lord your God, He it is that fighteth for you, as He promised you. Therefore take careful heed to yourselves that you love the Lord your God...'

*　*　*

...These are very powerful words, Josheb," Samuel explained as he finished his lesson. "So take heed, Hebrew. For what you have said is true. You are just one man, yet you are the right man for this task."

5

After recounting these ancient histories of Israel to Josheb, Samuel stood up and directed Josheb to follow him further into the cave. There, in the dim light of the grotto, was a long lead crate similar in design to the wooden one that Samuel had previously retrieved the old calcified staff from when the two first met.

"Another exercise to test me and perhaps make me look foolish, no doubt," Josheb thought.

"Not a test," Samuel stated in his clairvoyant manner, as he reached into the box and pulled out a strange instrument. It was some sort of apparatus, which appeared to have possibly been purposed for agriculture. Yet its sickle like blade had at its distant edge a greenish hue that seemed to radiate and reflect the light of the torches within the cave. "Take this," Samuel said as he handed the tool off to Josheb. "Now this is older than you can fathom. It is adorned with the shamir, the gem of the ancients." Samuel led Josheb out of the cave and down to the stone foothill. "Now concentrate your strength and strike the rock with the ancient tool."

Josheb was eager to see what was to unfold, and with that instruction, he grasped the device with two hands and raised it directly over his head. "Not a test, huh?" he said as he concentrated on the point that he would strike, and with all the strength that he could muster, Josheb violently swung the curved instrument down toward the solid wall of the hill. He was sure that his blow would shatter the integrity of the shamir, but instead, with a deafening crack, like lightning striking from the heavens, it plowed through the stone and sliced deep into the hillside. With the menacing blast, each of the quarry workers looked up to see that Josheb had sunk all but the wooden handle of the instrument into solid stone. A number of the men ran over to see the achievement.

The crowd of men stood in disbelief as they murmured words of astonishment. "Impossible, the man is supernatural," was the concurrence of everyone who had witnessed the event. Josheb himself stood back in disbelief as Samuel then called all the men together. As they congregated, some of the men immediately pulled the instrument from its position and struck it upon the rock, but it simply bounced back at the lot of them. Then, Shammah, the biggest and most obstinate of them all, who had actually been in charge of the men until Josheb arrived, stepped forward. He grabbed the handle and swung it over his head until his back arched and the tip of the sickle nearly touched the ground behind him. Shammah came back at the quarry wall with a strike that momentarily had everyone convinced that the results of his feat would equal that of Josheb's. But this time the shamir was left only slightly embedded into the stone. And because the force of the blow had not been quite enough to cut a wide gouge, it resulted in the blade bouncing back and forth against the tightly formed fissure. A terrible vibration then worked its way from the point of the blade to the handle and then through the hands and arms of Shammah. With his entire torso quivering violently, he quickly let go of the still quaking instrument and let out a humiliating gasp. All of the men of the camp responded by roaring out with laughter over the humorous site.

After the amusement had subsided, Samuel spoke up, "Josheb, show us again. Strike the rock with the shamir."

As he walked back to where it was entrenched, Jashobeam reached out with one hand and released the lodged instrument from the stone. He then repeated his earlier actions and drove it through the hillside with relative ease. The workers once again began to murmur as Samuel turned to the mighty man and instructed him, "You are to take charge of these workmen and see to it that the city will be built." With this last instruction, accompanied by the convincing display of Josheb's strength, everyone including Shammah became instant believers in the fact that Josheb was indeed the right man for the job. Samuel bid everyone at the camp goodbye and upon leaving told Josheb to divide his time between managing the quarry and visiting the city, where he could be with his family as well as oversee the unloading of the stone blocks from this and all other quarries in the area.

For nearly an entire year, Josheb did a fine job of working the quarry and supplying material for the construction of the city while avidly directing his hardworking group of men. They came from all walks of life. Some, like Shammah and Josheb, had come from noble families while others shared a more dubious past. But regardless of their histories, all of them were artisans adept to performing fine masonry work. A first-rate working relationship based on mutual respect was quickly struck up between them and their mighty leader, Josheb.

"I remember you. You led us at the battle of Ekron," Shammah had told Josheb at the end of the first day that the mighty man had arrived into camp. Everyone then listened intently as Shammah recounted the tale of Josheb's strength in battle against Philistia.

"Yes, and I remember you as well," Josheb had responded back to Shammah, which furthered the delight of the men. "You are quite the ambidextrous swordsman."

Shammah then gladly obliged everyone's request for him to give them a display of his skill as he took two heavy picks, one in each hand, then twirled and spun them around his head and torso with amazing speed. His antics impressed even the mighty Jashobeam.

From that day forward, Josheb would spend three days at the quarry where he would personally wield the curious shamir. Then he would leave Shammah in charge as he would help deliver the massive stone blocks to the city and spend four days with his family. Josheb had often times asked Samuel where the strange instrument had come from with its mystical shamir gem. Yet, Samuel never gave him a direct answer. The prophet seemed more pre-occupied with ensuring that Josheb was keeping it safe, that he was storing it properly by covering it with wool, and that he always set it on a bed of barley bran within its lead box. "It is not for ceremonial purposes that the instrument is stored in this manner, but rather for practical reasons," Samuel explained. "The shamir can and will shatter any object it comes into contact with for an extended amount of time. Save placing it in lead, there is no other way to store it." For quite some time that is all that Samuel would disclose concerning what he knew of the shamir.

But one day, out of the blue, the prophet finally gave Josheb a terse summary of the gem's origins. "Its derivation is somewhat mysterious even to me," he said with an enigmatic voice. "Having been raised in the Shiloh Temple, I was introduced to the instrument at a young age. The malevolent sons of Eli, many years my senior, often told me far fetched stories of its source. To this day, I truly do not know whether or not their claims were told in earnest or in mockery. Nonetheless, despite their constant pranks, when it came to the shamir they always spoke in a reverent and sincere manner.

The shamir, as was told by Hophni, the eldest of Eli's sons, was created by God at the beginning of days. In addition, it is supposedly not the only gemstone of its kind. There are various others, but they are truly rare. And besides being valued for their aesthetics, they have always been expressly treasured by men for their ability to cut other stones. Therefore, being such a rare yet practical commodity, the shamir stones have caused much enmity amongst men, both king and commoner alike.

The first pharaohs of Egypt were especially interested in getting hold of them in order to use the shamir gems as tools in their ever increasing architectural endeavors. They bargained, stole, and fought for them while continually scouring the earth to locate these rare stones. By the end of its eighth dynasty, it was believed that Egypt had indeed acquired possession of all the shamir gems known to exist in the world, along with their coveted power. Hophni alleged that many years later when Moses fled Egypt during Israel's great Exodus, he opportunely absconded with one of the prized gems. And with that very gem, the one that you now work the quarry with, the great-prophet purportedly wrote the commands of the Lord upon tablets of stone."

Josheb listened keenly to the story of the shamir questioning only the matter of how it had come atop the sickle shaped instrument. "Ah yes, to understand that, you will have to understand the histories of the judges," Samuel explained. "This is precisely where we left off on your last lesson. If you remember, Joshua had led the major conquest through Canaan, but the Lord told Joshua that there was much more fighting to be done in order for Israel to claim its complete inheritance...

* * *

...Before his death, Joshua apportioned the promised lands of Canaan to each tribe, both the lands which had already been taken by Israel and those still inhabited by other populaces. He told them to fulfill their destiny by continuing the fight. And as I have already told you, Joshua prophesied on that day that any one Israelite would have the ability to chase a thousand of his enemies into retreat. But this was a conditional envisage. For, Joshua also told them that this would only come to pass as long as Israel continued to love their God and to serve Him in sincerity and in truth.

Sadly, over time, Joshua's foreboding words were forgotten, and Israel turned from their Lord, even after He had delivered them from slavery and led them to the land of their inheritance. Not only did they forget what the Lord had done for them, but they did not adhere to His commandments. Instead of continuing their conquest of those lands, they attempted to make peace with the inhabitants of Canaan. Thus, they dwelt amongst their enemies, allowing their cultures to become entwined. Before long, the Israelites were worshipping the idols of their enemy. These last acts in effect lost them the espousal of God and nullified the power of the Israelites.

They were no longer an overwhelming military force. Instead, Israel's tribes often found themselves overthrown by the very people whom they had spared and dwelt amongst. And without God's backing or the leadership of a divinely appointed patriarch, neighboring kings rose up against Israel during these times of susceptibility, subjugating them and demanding tribute of them. But God had not completely forsaken Israel. He thus decided to raise up a deliverer, a devout person, to act as a shepherd and to delegate authority over the tribes. This person would settle all the civil unrest that arose throughout the nation and act as High-Judge over their foremost disputes. This High-Judge was also responsible for leading the Israelites into battle against their oppressors. This was accomplished with the aid of other men who God likewise endowed with His spirit. As in the days of Moses, these men were chosen and numbered, a Council of Seventy Elders to help rule the nation. And with their help, along with the headship of their High-Judge, Israel did reestablish itself as mighty amongst its enemies.

Yet, this was only the beginning of a destructive pattern for God's chosen people. As the time of the judges progressed and one High-Judge after another led and governed them,

Israel cyclically fell into periods of transgression. These eras of setback, whence they would practice idolatry, would bring conquering enemies to their lands causing the tribes to once again call out to their God for deliverance. Sadly, this trait, this inherent attribute of disloyalty and doubt, is a cursed affliction not only of this nation, but of humankind. And it will continue to bring stern reproach from the Lord until the day that all prophecy is fulfilled.

But I digress. I was telling you about the shamir. Yes, well in the days of the High-Judge, Ehud, Israel gathered all of its forces on its eastern borders in an attempt to drive out the Moabites, who had tyrannized them for eighteen years. But alas, this deployment of their forces on the east left them vulnerable to a surprise attack by their western enemies, the Philistines.

Indeed, the Philistines began such an assault by gathering a small group of a thousand men to attack the bordering town of Beth-Shemesh. What they were not counting on was being met by Shamgar, son of Anath. Now Shamgar was a mighty man, but being from the tribe of Levi, he did not go into battle against the Moabites. Instead, like his father before him, he had been passed down the duty of tending to the shamir along with various other objects of value held by the priesthood. But, when Shamgar heard of the oncoming attack by the Philistines, and understood the vulnerability of Israel, he fashioned the shamir onto the sickle end of a broken oxen's goad and went into battle single handedly against the Philistines. He knew very well the power of the shamir, and on that day this seemingly commonplace cleric fended off that entire force of Philistines, bringing down six hundred of their men with his weapon before sending the remainder of them into retreat.

When the Philistine forces returned to their homeland with the report of their losses, their kings halted their original plans of an all out attack on Israel. They questioned themselves, asking if just one Israelite could rain such destruction upon their men, what could and entire army of Israel's forces be capable of? Shamgar's actions are hence remembered amongst those of the High-Judges to this day, because his valiant feat once delivered the whole of Israel from certain devastation..."

* * *

Over the next few months, Samuel continued his account of the High-Judges giving Josheb a detailed description of their heroism and of all their great deeds. From Othniel to Samson, their chronicles were recounted until Josheb was familiar enough with each one of their lives that he felt that he knew them personally. Samuel ended his antiquities with the story of his own life and how he himself had become the High-Judge of Israel, "...There was no strong ruler to step in after Samson, and the authority of the High-Judgeship was eventually usurped by the Shiloh Priesthood. Under the lax governance of High-Priests, such as Eli, Israel had once again become a loosely knit nation. So when I took on the commission of High-Priest, I likewise took heed of what had made our nation successful in the past and appointed a formal Council of Seventy Elders in an attempt to hold the country together..."

Josheb made sure that he diligently carried out Samuel's instructions on how to keep and store the shamir along with all of his other duties. The men that worked for him came to trust him during this time for his integrity, admiring the way that he smartly managed the excavation site while working relentlessly himself. No one could keep up with his maddening pace of cutting the stones from the quarry, which by itself was producing nearly as many materials as all of the other quarries combined. Shammah would receive a good chuckle from all of the men as he would often try his hardest to keep pace with Josheb, but even he would eventually tire out and have to take a long break.

Josheb loved his work. And when he wasn't at the quarry or directing the stone bearers who transported the cut stones, he was at home playing with his two sons and lavishing attention on his beautiful wife. But, as the construction of the palace drew to a close, Josheb started to spend more time away. He wanted to ensure that it was his own quarry that supplied the finishing stones for the palace and that they were in time for the upcoming New Moon Festival. On his return home one day, Sora spoke to him in a concerned voice, "You have been working too hard. You need to get some rest."

With delight in his voice Josheb gave Sora some good news, "The fortress is almost complete, and when it is, I will not be working so much. I have been offered a prominent position as the captain of the king's guard."

"So you will be able to spend all of your nights at home?" Sora excitedly questioned.

"Yes, I will. And that is not all, we have been offered quarters in the palace as part of the arrangement!" Josheb likewise responded.

"Daddy, daddy," the voices of Josheb's two young sons interrupted his good news as they ran in and jumped on his lap.

"We missed you daddy", Eli exclaimed as he looked up and petted the face of his father. At five years old, he was the older of the two boys.

Sham, whom was only three, latched onto Josheb in his normal fashion after climbing up onto his lap. He quickly began to go to sleep and closed his eyes with a look of contentment on his face but was quickly snatched away by Sora. "Boys, your dad is tired and he needs to get cleaned up and get some rest," she told them in a stern voice.

Josheb stood up as the sound of horses hooves beckoned his departure. "Actually, that should be Shammah now. I have to go back to the quarry for another day or so," he regrettably announced.

His words were accompanied by looks of disappointment by everyone in the room as Sora briefly contended, "But you just got back." Yet, she gave in a bit easier than usual in light of the announcement. "Just promise not to overdue yourself."

"I promise," Josheb said as he quickly gave each of the boys hugs and lavished his wife with kisses. Like always, he told Eli and Sham to take good care of their mom and assured them one more time, "I will be back soon. After the king arrives and the New Moon Festival is celebrated, we will have no more of these sad partings."

Before reaching the boundaries of the city, Shammah gave Josheb a pat on the back and directed his attention over to their periphery. Samuel was busy directing men who were loading supplies onto a carriage. "You shouldn't have gone to all the trouble of sending extra supplies with us just because we have been working so hard," Shammah shouted in a joking manner. "We can wait a few more days to celebrate our accomplishments."

"Actually these supplies are for my own journey," Samuel called back. He quickly scaled the side of the carriage as the workers finished loading the provisions. The prophet then made his way to the two men and happily informed them of his plans, "I am on my way to greet the king with the news that the palace will be ready for the festival. I will make my way eastward toward Gilgal and meet up with King Saul. We will subsequently head back here accompanied by the army. All the arrangements have been made for the king's entrance into the city, and I would like you to personally see that the final stones are delivered back here." These last words were directed towards Josheb. "After everything is set in place, you will head out and meet us on the northern road and will likewise ride in with the king's procession."

With that, Samuel went his way while Josheb and Shammah traveled to the quarry. When they arrived, the sun was almost down, but the men were still hard at work. He ordered them to stop for the day and to gather around. He saw this as a good opportunity to talk to the men for the last time as their leader. "It has been a productive year," he began in an earnest voice. "I am proud to say an uneventful one in terms of argument and discord amongst us. Most of the men have already told me that they will be leaving here in a few days to look for another commission and to hopefully begin work soon on another project. Although we will be here for another day or so, I just wanted to let everyone know right now that you are all fine men, and it has been an honor to work alongside each and every person here. I wish all of you the best in your future endeavors." As Josheb finished with his address, the men reverently stood before him with a genuine sense of appreciation for his leadership. They continued to exchange goodbyes, and by the close of the evening, the men had each stepped forward, one by one, to pay their respects.

Over the next two days they finished everything up and then waited for the loaders to arrive from the city in order to carry the last of the stones back. Yet, the men didn't show. Josheb immediately thought it was strange. They had never been late before. It was the same rotation every week since he had taken charge. A crew of men would arrive from the city with their logs, and Josheb would help in the process of lugging the stones back to Gibeah.

As they went to bed for the second time with nothing to do except wait, Josheb became very uneasy. Then, as the sun rose the next morning, his worst fears were realized.

One of the stone bearers arrived without the remainder of the working party. He was bleeding profusely from a wound to his shoulder and seemed disoriented. The men helped carry him into the coolness of a small cave and gave him some water as they tended to his wounds. Josheb was called immediately. As he arrived, the injured man was explaining what had happened.

"They attacked us in the night," he said in a frail tone. "All of them are dead. They killed everyone."

"Who did they attack?" Josheb demanded. "Have they killed the stone bearers?"

"No," the man said with fear in his eyes. "The Philistines attacked outside the southern end of the city and slew everyone, all of the workers from the region along with their families." He began to cough violently and was quickly given some more sips of water. "They have destroyed most of that part of the city along with the work that was put into it. They stopped only outside the fortified walls of Gibeah. I was barely able to escape and make my way here. I knew this was the closest place that I could find refuge."

"It's impossible," Josheb said in denial. "How would they make it that far into our lands?" And then it occurred to him. It wouldn't have been so difficult. There was only a small guard in charge of protecting both the palace and the outlying areas while the city was under construction. Spies sent out by the Philistines could have easily scouted out a route through the hills and gained access to the region.

"My horse, bring me my horse!" Josheb yelled. No sooner had it been brought to him, the mighty man had disappeared in a surge of dust as he traveled toward the main road, which led to the city. He pushed the horse to the point of exhaustion as he made the trip. After arriving on the outskirts of town, he saw smoke rising throughout the pillaged region. It was thought that the palace would mean a new future for the young nation but it was not to be. Before it was completed, it was already a target for hostility.

As Josheb drew nearer to Gibeah and onto the final stretch of road, he noticed someone approaching ahead. Coming closer, he suddenly recognized the figure. It was Zabdiel, his father. With this last realization, Josheb slowed his horse to a trot. His father's attendance could only mean one thing, and all at once Josheb knew that his family's fate had been sealed. He watched his father hurry out toward him, quickly dismount his horse, and stand waiting in the middle of that pebble filled, dusty road.

"Stop your horse, son," Zabdiel's told him. His voice echoed tranquilly in Josheb's ears, resounding delicately over the repetitive beat of his horse's measured steps. Josheb did not look at his father nor did he stop the horse as directed. Instead, he gazed forward in the direction of the city and the place that he had called home for the past year. He directed his horse to ease ever forward to that location as his eyes remained steadfastly fixed ahead. "Stop," his father calmly beseeched him one more time as Josheb attempted to steer his horse around the man. Suddenly the only sound in

Josheb's ears was that of his own racing heart as he realized that his father had grabbed hold of the reigns and brought the horse to a halt. "You needn't return home, Josheb," the voice of Zabdiel uttered to his son who sat motionless upon the horse. "Come down from there," he continued, "there is a shade tree in the distance where we can sit."

But Josheb didn't want shade or rest. He wanted only to get to the city, to see that his family was alright, and to hold them in his arms. He coaxed his horse forward with a jibe of his heel, but it was no use; his father still held the reigns. Josheb attempted to seize them, but there was really no deliberation in his actions. All the while, his silent gaze never waned. He made one last ditch effort for his father to let him go as he urged his steed onward. This resulted in a momentary struggle between the three of them until finally Zabdiel pulled his son clean off of the confused horse. It instantly ran off down the road toward Gibeah, leaving the men behind. Zabdiel then embraced his son and reluctantly told Josheb what he already knew to be true, "They are gone, the three of them killed during the raid."

The mighty man wilted. Had his father not held his son up, Josheb would have crumpled under the weight of those tragic words. Zabdiel's strong arms held fast to his son as he continued to hold Josheb up in a consoling clinch. The strength eventually returned to the shaken man and as the shock of the moment subsided, Zabdiel let him go. Josheb immediately turned around and took a few steps. He cried out on the point of madness; "No!" he screamed in outrage and sorrow. Then he collapsed to the ground, kneeling there in agony. He wept with such grief that he felt as though his body would never have the strength to stand again. The burning in his throat felt as though it had been slit open, and his chest was so heavy, he thought that he would suffocate and die in that very spot. But the mighty man was eventually able to muster his spirit and stand to his feet. Fortunately, his father was there to console him as Josheb asked about his beloved family, "Tell me, father. In what condition did you find them?"

"I was already on my way to pay you and your family a visit when I received word of the raid," Zabdiel said as he placed his hand on the shoulder of Josheb. "I am thankful only that I arrived here before you." He paused and took a deep breath before solemnly continuing, "I have already told you that you needn't go home, at least not until my orders can be carried out. I have made the arrangements for the proper care of their precious bodies."

Josheb understood, and asked no more questions about this unbearable matter. For, although he had seen the mangled remains of many such victims and witnessed the massacres that so often transpire during these type of raids, to see his own family cut down in such a manner would have been too much for him to endure. He knew all this from the moment that he saw his father riding out to meet him.

Later that day some of the men from the quarry arrived in town to check up on Josheb. He and his father had returned to his home, and were now making the final arrangements for Sora and the boys to be transported to their family's lands. It would be their final resting place.

"We have heard of what has happened," Shammah told him. "All of the men from camp have come and are waiting along with perhaps another thirty or forty men from the northern part of the city. We will fight, if you will lead us." He further informed Josheb that he had already learned that the Philistines had attacked in the early morning hours, and after a day and a half of ransacking the southern end of the city, they headed off in a southwestern direction. "No doubt toward their homelands," Shammah explained. "They are a day ahead of us and we will be tremendously outnumbered, but this will be the only chance that we have to retaliate. King Saul and his soldiers will not arrive for three more days, and the Philistines who carried out this massacre will have long reached their own lands by that time."

"Gather the men and start heading in that direction

straight away," Josheb instructed in an ominous tone. "I will meet up with you soon enough." Josheb then left his father in charge of transporting his family and immediately rode to the quarry. Remembering Samuel's account of how Shamgar the judge had devastated his enemy, he headed directly for the lead box that housed the shamir with a similar plan of action. He had wielded it many times as a relentless tool, and he would now use it as an adjudicating weapon against the Philistines.

He caught up with his men on the outskirts of Debir and was told by Shammah that local herdsmen had seen troops from Ekron passing through the area earlier that day. When scouts reported that they had spied the Philistines up ahead, Josheb did not wait for any further report. He took off in their direction with the face of a heated lion on the heels of its prey. He rode swiftly, followed closely by his men until he saw his enemy's camp in the distance. The Philistines themselves, with an encampment of over three thousand men, were immediately incensed, becoming enraged after being alerted to the fact that a small cavalcade of men were riding furiously toward them. They brandished their weapons and made ready for battle.

Josheb was the first to arrive on the scene. And with the knowledge that the shamir had readily sunk its teeth through solid stone, he plowed directly through their lines, swinging crushing blows to the men in his wake. The shamir did truly make an equally devastating weapon against the armor of the Philistines as it had the stone floor of the quarry, and their soldiers were quickly cut down in their tracks as Josheb dismounted his horse and attacked the heart of their forces. Shammah and the rest of the men arrived behind the mighty man and with equal determination fought against the Philistines.

As they witnessed the bludgeoning barrage brought on by the men of Israel, the Philistines began to retreat in panic. But Josheb and his men gave chase and trampled down every last one of their fleeing enemies. By the time that the battle was finished, over eight hundred men had personally felt the mortal strike of Josheb's avenging shamir. The men of Israel then made there way back toward Hebron and were met by a patrol belonging to the king's army. The report of their successful retaliation soon made its way throughout the whole of Israel while Josheb was summoned to smartly report to Samuel who had returned to Gilgal with Saul.

After a slight reprimand from Samuel over his imprudent use of the shamir and at his own request, Josheb was granted permission to join the ranks of the army. He was made captain over a company of men, and King Saul subsequently declared his battle-feats spectacular, recognizing the man as mighty. Jashobeam would thus spend the next three years leading his men into raid after raid against the Philistines until one day Samuel again summoned the young captain to report before him.

Josheb arrived to Gibeah, which had since seen the rebuilding of its southern region. Accompanying Josheb was Shammah who had stayed with the mighty man through the entire endeavor and had become a much celebrated warrior himself. The two arrived to stand before the prophet while the rest of their exhausted company was given a needed break. Samuel addressed Josheb in an inquisitive yet mild manner, "You have been granted your request and have been turned loose against your enemy whom you have struck fear into with an unrelenting onslaught of violence. I have heard of your vicious war manners and have called you here today to question what, if anything, you have learned over the past years?"

Josheb thought about the question and then stated that he would forever feel the sorrow over his loss, yet his anguish and animosity had been somewhat quenched by the fight that he had taken to the Philistines. "I have fought, and I am tired," the mighty man proclaimed. "My anger has been doused with the blood of my enemy, and I am content with the hurt that I have dealt them. In my exploits, I also have realized that no matter how many of my enemies fall at my hand, I do not have the power to obtain an immortal recompense."

"You have learned much," Samuel answered back. "And you are correct; you can seek remuneration from your enemy but must ultimately leave justice to your God. That being said, I see you have been emancipated from the hatred that could have very well consumed you. And I likewise have a new commission for you. The elders of Judah have begun to make complaints over the war blunders of King Saul. Save your success, the rest of his army has suffered many losses over this past year. Our newly formed nation is quickly growing restless as raids on our northern and eastern borders have increased dramatically. These are becoming very dangerous times and many of the tribal elders have beckoned their sons to return home where they can provide protection for their own lands. I have likewise spoken with your grandfather over an alternative commission for you, and he has agreed that it would be an upright gesture on your part to accompany me during this time and head up my personal guard."

Without hesitation Josheb declared his intentions, "I do not wish to abandon the efforts of this nation. Still, to save my own sanity and for the benefit of Israel, I am prepared to relinquish my military office to Shammah, my second in charge, and accompany you."

Samuel was pleased with Josheb's quick decision and declared to him, "Josheb-Basshebeth, son of Hachmon, you will accompany me as my ornament, and your name shall hereby be called Adino."

The former Josheb-Basshebeth, known those many years as Jashobeam and various other war-names, therefore took on the new name of Adino along with this latest charge as Samuel's custodian in humble fashion. For, the time spent with the prophet was uneventful in regards to battle, and although stories of Adino's past feats would still circulate widely, his new role caused the mighty man's significance to fade into obscurity.

Spending the better part of the next fifteen years at Samuel's side, he was not to draw his sword with true intent even once in all that time. As the years past, his muscles thus began to ache with restive anticipation, and his crusading appetite longed to be satiated. But this yearning would not last indefinitely, because the nation of Israel, in due course, would again require his sword...

PART II

POLITICUS

And so it was, during the twentieth year of Saul's reign, the foundation of his kingdom was to be shaken. He had just returned from a fierce battle with the Amalekites and Samuel was now hot on the trail of the king with intentions to deliver a grave message. According to their sworn duty, Adino and a band of choice warriors, trained by the mighty man himself, accompanied the prophet as his guard from Ramah to the rolling hill-country of Carmel, south of Hebron.

As they neared their destination, Adino suddenly sensed the skulking eyes of men in wait. His steed, vigilant and instinctive as its rider, slowed its trot as the mighty man carefully perused the surrounding woods. Meanwhile, waiting in the heavens, two vultures circled, taking turns giving hungry, piercing calls. Their small shapes reflected down below in the gleam of Adino's blade as he drew it slowly from its sheathe. He looked upwards toward the blue. Then, ominously, one of the two black speckles shook a feather to the earth. Adino had been casually leading his small group through these tranquil canyons for most of the day, but his laxity was aptly heightened by the presence of those scavengers up above. He sped his advance and then deliberately reached his sword out into the air as he watched the falling quill split in two across his blade.

Putting away the weapon, he motioned for his men to take caution as he continued to examine the upcoming rocky peaks, which had rapidly begun to encircle their approach. He then crouched low and rubbed the neck of his horse—a familiar command for it to travel stealthily. An especially thick tuft of forest lay ahead in the foreground, its foreboding darkness begging his attention. He took notice.

Within the shadows of that wooded area a cautious body made a calculated, almost imperceptible move. Yet, Adino quickly picked up on it and immediately realized that he had perhaps led his company of men into a trap. A smile sprouted across his face. As always, Adino was relying on his ability to anticipate a stalker's next move, and if a tussle lay ahead, he would not hesitate to end it in a hurry with the wrath of an avenging angel. Suddenly, he saw movement to his right, but alas it was to his left. He turned and gave a quick nod of his hooded head signaling his companions to keep up as he quickened the pace of his horse with a jibe of his heel and headed directly towards the tree canopied high ground.

Adino thought of the marauder's plot of ambush. It could be accomplished easily enough. To hide and wait for some innocent passerby group to rob and perhaps even kill was a conspiracy that many a bad men had profited from. But today these stalkers would lament their insidious improvisation. As Adino contemplated all of this, one of his companions caught up with him and overtook his lead. This maneuver was a reminder to him that they were in a hurry to get to their destination.

The mighty man seemed to comply as he followed the new trail leader off of their current path and in a direction which would take them around the foreboding trees. Then abruptly, Adino changed his mind as all at once he caught the shaded outline of not just a few but a horde of men dodging into the foliage. Both in his periphery and in the hills up ahead, he could see a slew of shadows, which instantly quickened his pulse and tightened his skin. This was no small raid.

The Eznite brought his horse about and in a measured trot headed back towards what he anticipated to be the hub of the ambush, the dark woods that his squad had purposefully avoided just a few moments prior. In a restless manner, his entourage followed suit. Then, as they drew closer someone called out from the darkness of the forest, "Come closer, slowly, and show your faces!"

Adino gladly complied. Once he was within close proximity to the thick leafed trees, he rigidly planted his weapon into the root hardened soil with a sharp flick of his wrist before dismounting his horse. Always on the guard, he then stepped in the way of his attendee and removed his hood revealing his chiseled profile and long black hair, which over the years had grown down the length of his muscular back. It now flowed in braids, a sign of his piety. For, sometime during his many years serving under Samuel, he had taken on the practice of his teacher and adopted the vows of the Nazarite.

An intimidating figure appeared upon the fringe of the woods and held his hand up in the air. Archers simultaneously materialized from the surrounding hills and rocks, taking steady aim at Adino and his group of men. Complete with a portentously adorned helmet, the man then emerged fully from the foliage and stood opposite Adino. His body was a bastion, donned from head to heel in murky armor. It was obvious that he was a high ranking military officer, but his robust breastplate was also fractured in various areas suggesting that he had seen a fair share of fighting. He stood his ground for a short while and merely watched as Adino grabbed his sword and returned it to his cloak. With his belli-cose warrior's gear standing in sharp contrast to the robes that the mighty man now unassumingly wore, the soldier deliber-ately walked up a small knoll and stood above Adino with the intent to intimidate. "State your name and purpose for traversing the king's corridor," he ordered in a hurried tone, which begged for a similarly fashioned reply.

Undaunted, Adino answered in a contrastingly casual and composed voice, "I am sorry, but I could not understand you through your cog. Could you speak up a little, please? Or else remove your helmet?"

The man felt a bit silly for having to repeat himself, but after recognizing Adino's clothing and appearance as that of a cleric's, he indubitably removed his helmet to show his own stern and clever face. He began to repeat his orders, but before he was able to utter a complete response, Adino asked a question of his own, "—Do you have good reason for ordering us around? We are on a communal passage not a military one. Shepherds have used these trails to lead their flocks from —"

"—That is not what I asked of you sir," the man interrupted feeling as though he was losing control of the situation along with his patience. "I told you to identify yourself and also the reason why you are following the same route as the king's army. Now, for a second time, please answer me. Why are you traveling this route?"

Adino remained calm and collected. "Yes, I actually heard you the first time," he admitted in undercutting fashion, "but still, I have to ask, why are we being harassed for traveling on a commonly shared trail through our own countryside?"

In a put out manner, the battle clad man was compelled to explain himself, "My name is Abner. I am carrying out the orders of King Saul and maintaining guard of this route, sir. I am a general in his majesty's army and by questioning my authority you might as well be questioning an order of Saul himself. Is that your intention, man?"

"Not at all," came the cool response.

Ignoring Adino's obviously impertinent attitude and using his own last words as self assurance, the general leaned forward and spoke through his teeth, "Do you wish to find out how we deal with those who second guess the orders of the king?" He walked down to Adino, reached toward the handle of his sword, and gave a conceited smirk. "I will take your weapons for the time being."

Then suddenly, in a surprising move, Adino tossed his robe over his right shoulder revealing a comprehensive glimpse of his menacing and stalwart physique. He subsequently grabbed the general's hand and intercepted its advance. The grip was so powerful that it brought the unassuming man to one knee. Adino then quickly drew out his massive sword and aimed its apex towards Abner's throat.

Just as the bowmen prepared to unleash their arrows, the general was able to peer around Adino's powerful frame. From his new found cowering point of view, he caught a quick glance of an austere figure standing behind the mighty man. "Samuel!" he gasped in a relieved breath, and with his free hand, he gave the signal for his men to lower their bows. He spoke hastily to Samuel in a gasping voice, "I thought you were someone else, prophet. You nearly got yourself killed."

Adino immediately released his grip on the general and gave an audible, "Hmmf!"

Samuel then made his way between the horses and slipped around the craggy hillside toward Adino and Abner. He spoke in a strong voice, "Forgive my companion, general, but Adino is just acting on his duty to protect me. I told him that we may run into some trouble as we traveled today." Patting Adino on the shoulder, Samuel grinned displaying his straight teeth and friendly eyes. At roughly twice the former man's age, he still appeared remarkably young and at the moment seemed to be at the peak of life. In a display of his own prowess, he quickly grabbed the sword from Adino's hand twirled the weapon twice around like a baton and gracefully returned it to the sheath on its owner's hip. All the while, he maintained an eager and polite grin.

Adino displayed an ever so slight smirk of his own as he perused the king's soldiers who now, on hearing his name, advanced from their hideouts to shake hands and praise his reputation. The smirk soon became a beam after he realized just how many soldiers there were throughout the surrounding area. The mighty man was undoubtedly thinking of the outcome of the near fight between them and the fact that he had done his best to provoke General Abner simply for a thrill.

Abner gulped down his smugness as he realized whose clenches he had been in. He glanced at the amazing physique of Adino and the size of his sword. "Your actions are perfectly understandable, my good man," he said as he tried to inconspicuously rub his now sore hand in an attempt to get the blood and some feeling back into it. Looking back at Adino, he inquired, "You are the mighty warrior once called Jashobeam?"

"Yes, that would be me," Adino said in a confident tone as he shook hands with the last of the soldiers who had come out to greet him. "But I haven't heard anyone call me by that name in many years."

"Well Adino, I have certainly heard of your reputation and it appears that it is likewise fondly known throughout the ranks of my men," Abner pointed out. "Indeed, you were once a soldier yourself. Yet, you no longer fight for the king. Why is that?"

Samuel answered for his companion, "Adino serves a different purpose now." He then changed the subject abruptly, "But tell me, why are you acting in such a cautious manner, general? Are you in retreat? Were you not successful in defeating your enemy, the Amalekites?"

"You have traveled too far up these hills," Abner affirmed. He motioned for Samuel and Adino to have a seat on some logs that were propped up within an improvised stronghold amidst the thick brush of the woods. Before he proceeded to answer Samuel's question, he wanted to make sure that the two men were good and comfortable. "Let me get some fresh water and something for your men to eat before I explain the strange occurrences of this past week," he said, motioning for some water and victuals to be brought to them. Only after all the men were finished eating did the general continue with his lengthy answer to Samuel's question, "Israel's strength over our enemy was most amazing—our foot soldier's alone numbered an astounding 200,000 plus as we went to battle against the Amalekites. Our conquest was swift and decisive, and with the strength of God on our side we felt that we could have taken on any army the world over. From the moment that we had our first and oldest enemy in our site, we knew what we were to do next.

The king's plan had been explained to us weeks beforehand; once we met up with the Amalekites, we were to make our move to crush them. The order stated that nothing was to be left alive, not soldier, woman, child, nor animal. The supposed decree of the king was that anyone who violated the plan would themselves be put to death. Then a strange thing happened. Just as things were going according to Saul's orders, we were suddenly told to stop our fighting. Even without the utter demise and complete sacking of Amalek, the king ordered us to let go the small remaining army of the Amalekites who were now in retreat. Then he immediately sent me and the rest of the officers to select the spoils of war. Later, word went out that Amalek's king, Agag, had been captured and was to be escorted back here to Carmel, alive."

Abner, who was now easily confiding his story to the prophet, paused for a moment before continuing in a perplexed tone, "Then King Saul made his way to this rocky peak, where you no doubt intended to find him today." Pointing up through the valley, the general spoke in a solemn manner, "But Prophet, if you travel to the top of these hills, you will find neither King Saul nor his captive, Agag. You will instead find our soldiers erecting a monument in Saul's honor and in his image. Under the king's orders, they have been working day in and day out since his departure to construct such a thing. And while Agag has been secretly taken down to the fortress at Gilgal, King Saul has falsely put out the word, hoping it would be leaked to the spies in question, that he would be staying here in Carmel for the next month in order to oversee the project. So now you can perhaps understand how I mistakenly thought that you were a small group of spies from Amalek, come to find their captive King.

Samuel listened to all that Abner had said and after a short pause spoke with a sad, prophetic countenance, "It is fitting that Saul avoided passing by Ramah, an effort to forestall seeing me and to avert having to hear my judgment for his acts, no doubt. But in going so far out of his way to dodge me, he has appropriately made his way back down to Gilgal. For Gilgal was the place of his coronation, and in a significant manner, it will soon become the place of his judgment. According to God's will, Saul was to wipe clean from the face of the earth every last Amalekite, but he has chosen to instead tempt fate. I had already forewarned the king before he went into battle that if he did not heed the voice of God and destroy every last one of the Amalekites, they would rise up again, and he would die at too early of an age because of this. Perhaps the power to control his own destiny was too much for him to bear. And he has chosen a small plunder over the will of his God. He has chosen trifling goods and spoils of war over his own life. He is doomed."

No sooner had Samuel finished his words, there then came a torrent of fiery arrows. These fell to the earth like rain, penetrating through the armor of many of Abner's men and piercing into their soft flesh. It was their enemy, the Amalekites. Having been reduced to a seemingly insignificant number, they had nonetheless regrouped and banded up with a regiment of Philistines. The Philistines sought the stolen treasures and goods taken by Saul's army—the worth the Amalekites undoubtedly exaggerated in order to secure the alliance of their momentary allies—the Amalekites themselves had come for their king.

As a barrage of arrows released their destructive flames onto the camp, Abner's men scurried about to find defensive positioning. In the midst of it all, Adino grabbed the arm of

Samuel and led him further back into the protection of the dense trees. As he ordered his men to stay with Samuel, Adino drew his sword and prepared to head back out, but the prophet stopped him. "No Adino, this is not your fight today," Samuel asserted. "In order to end this, we must make it to Gilgal and to King Saul. You must get me there quickly."

Adino made his way back to the front of the camp where Abner stood shouting orders to his men over the blazing shrubbery surrounding them. "Is there any way out of this valley besides the way that we came?" he questioned.

Abner took the time to quickly answer while still remaining watchful on the unraveling situation in front of him, "Yes, make your way up to the crest of this rocky knoll and to a dried up creek-bed. There is a path that leads back down on the opposite side of the range." With a disappointed look on his face, he then questioned Adino's motives, "But aren't you going to stay and help us? We could use your sword, my friend." Then his expression changed once again, and he spoke in a grave manner, "You know, my men say that these Philistines have giants, which fight for them."

Adino gave the general a perplexed look and then responded in a dismissive tone, "It has been some years since I met the Philistines on the battlefield, but I never saw or heard of any giants?"

"Still, it is rumored that they have giants on their side!" Abner replied back. "My men are fearful of their legends. They are said to have been bred to become fierce warriors and that they cannot be defeated in battle."

Discounting the general's grim attitude, Adino patted Abner on the back and talked to him in a bolstering manner, "Listen, if you come across one of these so called Philistine giants just try to remember one thing; he is only a man."

This last comment seemed to reassure the general, and while letting out a nervous chuckle he tried to cover up his trepidation, "I didn't say that I myself believe these rumors." But despite his claim, he once again asked Adino's intentions,

"So you won't be fighting with us today?"

Adino smiled, "I would love to stay, but I have more pressing matters to tend to." In a compromising gesture he then called his group of men over. "I want you to stay and fight under the general's command until I return for you," he told them all.

Abner looked over at Samuel who stood with an anxious look about him. He then stared back at Adino's valiant men. Nodding in an understanding manner, and happy to have these impressive warriors, the general accepted their assistance and responded to Adino in kind, "Go, we will cover you."

With that, the general gave the signal for all of his archers to synchronically set their arrows aflame and answer their enemy's barrage with waves and waves of earth-scorching destruction of their own. And so, under a blanket of flaming arrows, Adino and Samuel made their escape.

By the time Samuel and Adino had arrived into Gilgal, the celebration over King Saul's victory was already going on its second day. Just as the sun was setting, they approached the fortress. Samuel thought of Adino's role in the upcoming encounter with the king. "Saul has grown jealous of the status of certain men and is at odds with the likes of your grandfather and the rest of the elders," the prophet warned as he glanced over at his companion. "He would no doubt be distracted by your presence. I need his undivided attention during this meeting. Thus, I would rather you stay out in the antechamber when we get to the fortress."

Adino was surprised at Samuel's decision. "But what purpose do I serve, but to protect you?" he asked. "What if there is trouble?"

"The God of Israel is my protector," Samuel answered. "I have let you misconstrue your purpose for accompanying me for some time, but now you might as well know the truth. When you agreed to act as my escort, you thought that it was I that needed protection, but it was in fact you that was in need of being watched over. I have thus kept you close to me as a precious ornament, so that you would not stray into the hands of evil, and so that you would learn to continually seek God and His purpose in your life. You have without a doubt been set aside to one day carry out a very important commission. This was revealed to me the first day that I saw you."

"Then what is it? What is this commission that you speak of?" Adino asked.

Samuel remained silent for a while as they walked. Then, after seeing King Saul's inscription on the entrance to the fortress at Gilgal, he spoke again in a staid manner, "Adino Ben Hachmon, your true purpose and destiny will soon be revealed."

Adino thought silently over the proclamation of Samuel. Neither of the men uttered a word until they had reached the entrance of the king's assembly hall. From outside, they could hear the commotion that accompanies revelry and celebration. "Who is behind these doors?" Samuel immediately asked one of the guards stationed in the antechamber. It was always an easy task for the High-Judge to elicit information from the king's men.

"The king is, of course," the soldier timidly replied.

"And who else?" Samuel questioned.

The man did not hesitate to impart what he had witnessed over the past few days, "The king arrived three days ago and began plans for celebrating what he has been calling his greatest victory. He then locked himself up in his chambers and did not come out until yesterday. That was when he called for the king of the Amalekites to be released from the jailhouse and brought to the feast."

Adino spoke up, "You mean to say that King Agag is in there with him now?"

"Yes, he has been tied to a chair, and he has been fed nothing but strong drink for two days. He sits in his own excrement as King Saul dances around him and proclaims himself ruler of all the earth."

Samuel, bowed his head for a quick moment, and then directed Adino, "Give me your sword."

Adino thought that he had heard wrong. "What's that you say? My sword?" he warily questioned.

"Quickly, and remember to stay here," Samuel came back. "It is time that I re-assume my role as the High-Judge of this nation."

Adino reached down and pulled out his finely crafted, razor sharp sword, which gave a reverberating shrill as it was pulled from its sheath. As he handed off the weapon, the mighty man watched Samuel measure its considerable size and weighty quality within his firm grasp. Then Samuel simply turned and entered the hall. Adino would forever remember the strange sight: The aging prophet walking into the grand hall while wielding the massive sword. As the doors closed, Samuel lowered its tip to the ground and let the sharp tip of the weapon etch a line in the marble floor behind him.

Complying with the prophet's directive, Adino remained in the antechamber where he crouched down next to the wall beside the soldier who stood guard. He could hardly believe what had just happened. It was no surprise that the guard did not question the High-Judge carrying the large sword into the king's feast. Everyone in the land knew Samuel and his authority. Nobody would suspect that he would attempt to do anything to the king, who was himself appointed by Samuel through divine directive. But still, Adino wondered; why did he ask for the sword? Was Saul to die this day at the hand of the prophet? What if Samuel was wrong and he actually needed help? These questions came to Adino as he heard the celebrating in the adjoining room abruptly stop. The entrance opened, and Adino stood up as most of the participants filed out. The doors then closed instantly behind them.

As the last of the crowd quickly exited the fortress, the mighty man crouched down once more and rested with his back leaning comfortably up against the wall of the antechamber. He took in a deep weary breath as he tried to hear what was unfolding; hardly able to make out the muffled voice of Samuel's from that of Saul's, he tilted his head back against the wall of the adjoining room to get a better listen. Then unexpectedly, his weariness got the better of him, and as he closed his eyes in concentration, he immediately drifted off into a dream, the same reoccurring dream that he had intermittently experienced over the years.

He was flying, again over the plains. The subconscious memory of his past dreams set precedence for this one, and in his mind, there was not even a moment of confusion about who he was. Thus, having no recollection of anything else, he was all at once a powerful bird of prey; he had always been so.

Instead of gliding aimlessly over the valley scenery as in previous episodes, he headed instinctively toward that ominous site in the distance amongst the storm clouds. He arrived swiftly on the scene, passing the hills and the bellowing lion as he circled above the group of men and the sinister tree. For the first time, the scene was slightly different. The storm had grown worse with deafening thunder and intense lightning, which struck the earth with bursts of white flares. The tree itself was now much larger and darker then ever before, and it became more threatening by the moment as it broke free from the whips that had once bound it. The men were likewise more desperate to subdue it, but their attempts to inflict damage upon it were hopeless. Each time they approached, its boughs harassed them and struck out at them with murderous intentions. Thus they retreated and could only look on as the tree's branches flailed triumphantly in the wind.

Adino was suddenly awakened from the strange episode by the opening of the chamber doors. Out stepped Samuel. He exited in the same manner that he had entered, with the sword dragging behind him. Adino jumped up and quickly took the weapon from the prophet who held it out for him to take. As Adino put the blade back into its sheathe, he noticed fresh blood dripping down its fringe. Samuel said nothing but instead continued his measured stride out of the king's fortress and toward the city gates.

Adino questioned what had just happened, "What was said in there? What is going on? Are you alright?"

As they walked, Samuel kept his silence. Then, once they were completely out of the city, he finally spoke, "Today the kingdom has been torn from Saul."

"What are you talking about?" Adino questioned again. Thinking the impossible he spoke aloud, "The king couldn't be—"

"—The king is dead", Samuel finished Adino's thought. "I smote him, and he is dead." The prophet spoke in a manner which conveyed that justice had been carried out.

Adino was thinking of a thousand things all at once. "But, what does this mean that you have killed the king? Are you to be hunted for sedition? Will there be civil war now?"

Samuel stopped and reasoned with the confused Adino, "You have far too many questions. You can relax. Saul lives and is unscathed by the sword for the time being." The prophet then explained what had taken place back in the king's banquet room; events had unfolded in an entirely different manner than what Adino imagined.

...As the doors of the hall had closed behind him, Samuel perused the drunken men and women around the room. Some were still caught up in the throws of revelry, others were completely passed-out in their chairs when all of a sudden the prophet got their attention by simply letting the shrill sound of Adino's sword scrape the ground and resonate its irritating shriek. This sobered the crowd immediately, and the prophet needn't have said a word to the king's guests who instantly recognized his grave intentions. Everyone quickly filed out of the room.

Samuel then proceeded past Agag, who was tied to a chair in the center of the room, and approached King Saul's table. It was cluttered from the remains of the feast that had taken place over the past two days. Saul himself sat with his head face-down on the table as he muttered some unintelligible words over and over. Samuel's entrance, followed by the emptying of the room, had gone on completely unnoticed by him. He rocked back and forth oblivious to his surroundings for another quiet moment. Then suddenly, he noticed the silence. Saul slowly looked up to see Samuel standing in front of him wielding the sword of Adino.

"Marvelous," Saul exclaimed. "You have come, prophet. I have done all that God has required."

Then the prophet's voice abruptly rang out above the king's as he began to utter judgment over the folly of Saul and his unpardonable decision to spare the Amalekites, "What is this that I hear and see? Could it be the king of your enemy who sits amongst your celebration? Is it possible that the spoils of war pervade this place? (*)- What meaneth then this bleating of the sheep in mine ears, and the lowing of the oxen which I hear."

Saul rose and began to offer his excuses, "You must listen to me. I did not"

"—You did not carry out your duty as the King of Israel! You did not heed the voice of your God!" Samuel continued. Saul tried to follow up with additional excuses, but his voice was drowned out as Samuel repeatedly rebuked him, "I have been deemed not only a prophet but the last of God's governing High-Judges. And as the mighty judge Samson, was given great strength by the Spirit of the Lord, I rely upon that strength to deliver unto this nation justice and deliverance from its enemy."

Then suddenly, with true warrior-like vigor, Samuel amazingly raised the cumbersome sword of Adino's high into the air. He turned, and with five remarkably quick and unforgiving blows, he hacked apart the body of King Agag who sat unassumingly in their midst. Samuel then turned to leave as Saul ran up and grabbed him by the fringe of his robe, which tore off in the king's hand as he tugged on it. The prophet authoritatively rebuked the king, "(*)- The Lord hath rent the kingdom of Israel from thee this day, and hath given it to a neighbor of thine, that is better than thou." And with that, he made his exit.

"…So you see," Samuel finished his summary of events for Adino, "it was King Agag that felt the merciless edge of your sword today. And for the time being, the Amalekites will have no king to retrieve and no one to assemble them."

Accordingly, with a feeling that justice had been served, the two composedly returned to Samuel's home in Ramah.

Saul sat on his throne, mulling over Samuel's last words of rebuke. After the prophet and Adino had returned to Ramah, the king had likewise left that fortress of reproach in Gilgal and immediately returned to his grand palace in Gibeah, a locale where he could regain some self-esteem. This city, after all, was the center of his regime and its great edifices were testimony of his power. "My kingdom will never be torn from me," Saul thought to himself.

That last act of admonishment from the prophet had pushed the king even further into a state of panic over what had become his greatest fear, the loss of his authority amongst the people. For quite some time, even before this last incident with Samuel, the king believed that others were conspiring against him. He was especially haunted with thoughts that the elders as well as certain members of the priesthood had become seditious traitors.

His customary court of advisors attended him in complete silence. It had been this way for days. Like a wounded animal that must not exert itself, the king remained listless as he licked the wounds affronted upon his pride by Samuel.

After contemplating his next move at great length, Saul finally came to a decision. "It's time to act," he said aloud as he motioned over a nearby soldier. The predominant feature of the man that the king had beckoned, besides his substantial size and balding head, was a large scar that began on his forehead and extended down the length of his face to his jawline. This was the captain of his guard, a man reputed to be a ruthless enforcer. The king whispered some orders into the captain's ear concerning some changes that he wanted made within his administration. "...I will be waiting in my chambers. Send in those whom I have summoned," the king said, finishing a list of detailed instructions as he began to massage his temples with both hands. Saul then made a hasty exit perceptibly grimacing in pain as his court bowed low to him.

A shrill howl of the wind rushed through the halls of the palace as two unsavory characters arrived later that day— Doeg, a skeleton of a man both in appearance and in character, was Syrian born and had likewise recently served as the king's ambassador to the regions of both Syria and Ammon; along with him was a cloaked woman from the town of Endor.

"What was that?" Doeg questioned as the two made their way up the northern turret on their way to the king's chambers. He was responding to a faint, almost ghostlike howl, which now made its way through the cavernous expanses of the tower that they climbed. "It sounded like the voice of a banshee."

"A keen ear you have," the woman responded. "What you hear is indeed the voice of torment."

As they approached the king's quarters, the howl became a shriek and then a bawl. But it suddenly stopped as a guard pushed open the doors to Saul's room. Everything was now silent as Doeg bade the woman to enter ahead of him. Once inside, the two found it very dark and quiet except for the sound of heavy breathing, which resonated throughout the room.

"Come, help me out," Zephaniah immediately instructed.

Doeg followed behind her and was astonished to discover that the king was listless and lain out on the floor. As Saul shivered violently, they led him off of the cold, stone tiles and assisted him to his bed. The woman removed her hood and quickly drew out a small flask for the king to drink from. She pressed it to his lips as she brushed back his hair with her fingers.

Doeg was again surprised at the familiarity that this woman had with the king and also with her mesmerizing beauty, which was highlighted by dramatic eye make-up and long silky hair that stretched down half the lank of her slender frame.

Saul slowly sipped down the elixir but remained in a confused state. As the king seemed to gradually come around, Zephaniah administered a few more doses. All the while, Doeg impetuously lead a one-sided conversation. He spoke at length to Zephaniah in a soft, hurried tone, seemingly nervous over the condition of the king. The woman from Endor finished tending to Saul as Doeg ended his impulsive chattering "...You know, I have heard of you. You are Zephaniah, the necromancer. Some would consider you a witch."

"And what is it that you know of witches?" she asked in a pensive voice.

Doeg answered her in a serious tone, "They are ugly with warts and snakes for hair."

The two looked at each other, somberly at first, and then simultaneously, they broke into anxious laughter over the melodramatic tension in the room.

"What have you found that is so amusing?" King Saul asked in a weak, perturbed voice as he awoke from his stupor and broke up their awkward banter.

"Nothing, my king," Doeg quickly responded. "I was just concerned over your well being and glad to see that you are alright."

"Of course I am alright now that Zephaniah is here. I just needed to lie down," Saul retorted as he sat up and began to rub his temples again. "Sometimes when I meditate on a matter for too long, I become thoroughly fatigued. She knows to bring the proper concoctions in order to get the life back into my tired body. Only my queen, Ahinoam, knew how to soothe me with such remedies, but she is gone these many years, passed during the birth of my youngest. "

"Truth be told my lord, Doeg was just questioning my reputation as a necromancer," Zephaniah said as she put away her brew.

"Ah, I see. You are quite knowledgeable of the rumors that are circulating," Saul conceded. "But despite what you may have heard, Doeg, this woman is not a malevolent host. It is true that Zephaniah is more than a mere medicine woman. But her ability to see as a prophetess can be used as a benefit. For her prowess as a diviner is unmatched as far as I am concerned."

"Of course, of course, I have heard that she is perhaps the foremost oracle in the land," Doeg admitted. "Except for Samuel, that is."

The king gave a scornful look. "Yes, but Samuel's strengths derive from another well. And that is the reason that I called for the two of you," he explained. "I will need you to form a union of sorts. Doeg, I am creating a new position just for you. For now on you will hold the title of my 'Supreme Advisor'. As for you Zephaniah, your knowledge of medicinal herbs has recently been an undeniable benefit to my health. You will join my court of advisors as well, immediately acting as my personal physician and heading up a curative regiment to help me through the stressful days that lie ahead. My sovereignty is in perilous risk of being compromised, and I need the both of you in times such as this."

"Your royal court? Her?" Doeg asked in a judgmental tone. "But you have a throng of counselors my king. What is that she can provide that is not already being—"

"—I am being attacked!" Saul responded in an abrupt voice, but he quickly regained his composure. "I have been warned by the spirits."

Doeg gulped down his trepidation before responding, "Is it possible that you speak of hearing from—"

"—Is it possible to hear the voice of God?" the king pontificated in a thunderous intonation. "That is fast becoming the question in this day and age. No, I have not heard that voice for quite some time. Yet there are indeed other spirits that come to me, to warn me and to protect me."

"They are evil then," Doeg offered. "We must not invite their deceptive influence by allowing this woman—"

"—Silence you fool!" Saul commanded in a maddened tone. "She is here for a sincere purpose, and if you are too mindless to see that she is needed, perhaps I should reconsider my offer to you."

"No, please that won't be necessary," Doeg cowered. He quickly sputtered out his next thoughts, "I am ready to do your bidding as your Supreme Advisor, and with your permission I truly do have a number of new ideas to share, which I believe, once executed, will allow for a more efficient sovereignty along with increased power for you, your majesty. I have learned much from studying the rule of your neighbors."

This last statement aroused the king's interest, but before he could acknowledge Doeg's proposal, there was a knock on the door. The scar face captain of the guard entered, followed by Jephthah, currently Saul's lead advisor.

"Ah, Jephthah, I am glad you could join us. It seems that you should be present for our little meeting," the king remarked without looking at the man.

Jephthah gave a perplexed look after considering the company that he was now in. He furled his brow and cleared his throat before responding, "My king, how can I serve you today?"

"That is exactly the topic that was at hand before you came in," Saul explained as he walked over and put a hand on the shoulder of Doeg. "It seems that with you leaving, there is a need to find someone to replace you. Doeg here has come to my attention as the best possible candidate."

"But, I don't understand," Jephthah retorted.

Saul continued, "You see, I need someone that will be loyal and act on my orders without question. Someone with," he paused briefly and looked at Doeg and then back at Jephthah, "someone with new ideas that can pump new blood back into my regime." Jephthah began to break out in a cold sweat as he tried to remain composed. "Oh, that reminds me," Saul persisted. "Were you able to quell that problem that has arisen within the ranks of the priesthood?" The king walked back towards the foot of his bed as he waited for the response.

"Their talk of you has proven innocent my king," Jephthah said nervously. "It is just one of their methods of teaching the people. They practice object lessons using you as an example in order to inspire. I've explained to you already that I have looked into the situation. No one has committed any sort of treasonous act as you first feared, my lord. Everything is under control."

King Saul leaned against his bedrail then turned with an amiable smile, which he extended around the room to each of his guests. He settled his gaze upon the scarred face of the captain of the guard. Then he spoke in a patronizing fashion as he raised his brow and tilted his head, "That is why I hate to see you go, Jephthah. Your wisdom is truly profound."

Oblivious to the king's disdain, Jephthah regained his composure and responded with a proud gawk toward Doeg and Zephaniah, "I was going to mention to you a little earlier that if you are referring the trip I am taking back home, I will really only be gone for a short time. There is no need to worry about replacing me for so little—"

—The sound of Jephthah's voice was suddenly stifled as a rag was forcefully stuffed into his mouth by the captain of the guard. A gunny-sack was then thrown over his head. The doors burst open and in marched two soldiers who quickly shackled the man's hands and feet. Jephthah was left helplessly wriggling about as he attempted to yell out with no avail. The captain stood calmly awaiting his next orders. He peered languidly at the king, who simply returned his flat gaze with a disgusted expression.

"Throw that miserable worm into the prison and do not let me hear him spoken of again," Saul immediately ordered. "The thought of his impertinence sickens me." The king then turned to Doeg who now stood in shock as he tried his best to ignore the image he had of the terrible fate that awaited his contemporary in prison. "Now, back to the topic at hand," Saul said in a calm manner as though nothing out of the ordinary had occurred. "You have told me that you are ready to do my bidding, Doeg. Before we commence, you need to understand that this new position of Supreme Advisor will require your utmost loyalty along with the ability for you to take charge of certain situations. Have you any questions?" Doeg said nothing but instead, still stunned, stood silent and merely nodded his head as Saul spoke on, "Good, then let us make plans for dealing with those menacing priests along with the rebellious tribe leaders. For I know who is with me and who is against me in this land. The spirits tell me their folly. The voices tell me their names. Jephthah's name was offered just this morning."

"Yes, and you have dealt with him appropriately," Zephaniah offered as the captain of the guard helped the soldiers lug Jephthah's portly body from the room. All the while, the subdued man continued to struggle and tried to utter some words in his own defense as he was carried off. But with the rag and the sack being used to successfully restrain him, Jephthah's voice was nearly inaudible.

"I am happy to see that I can rely on at least one person to side with me," Saul said as he smiled at Zephaniah. "Now, before we were so rudely interrupted, you were saying something very interesting, Doeg. I would like to know more about where your loyalty lies and to hear these new ideas of yours, my new Supreme Advisor."

Doeg stood motionless for a moment, second guessing whether or not he could actually speak openly with the king about his proposals.

"Tell me what you were going to say!" the king barked, snapping Doeg out of his confounded state.

"Oh yes, yes," Doeg quickly responded deciding that it would be better to speak up than to remain silent and appear weak. "I was saying that I have learned much from studying the likes of the King of Damascus and his methods of ruling."

"This should be interesting," Zephaniah said in a sarcastic tone as she walked over and took a seat.

"Indeed it shall," King Saul remarked in a sincere voice. His attitude contradicted that of Zephaniah's for the first time that afternoon. "You see Zephaniah; there is a reason that I have decided to put Doeg in a position of authority. My old lead advisor, Jephthah, albeit a clever man, did not have the experience that my new Supreme Advisor has. Doeg has visited many other kingdoms and has devoted his life to the pursuit of worldly knowledge. He is brilliant and perfectly suited to advise me during these uncertain times. I will gladly entertain his ideas—" The king then suddenly cut his words short as he stumbled awkwardly towards his bed in order to lie down.

It appeared that the concoction that Zephaniah had given him was taking full effect on his senses, and his mood had changed rapidly. The king made it clear that he no longer desired to continue the discussion as he lay there in silence with his eyes closed and his hands discourteously clasped over his ears. Only after Zephaniah once again went to his side and administered him another swallow from her flask did he speak again. "I am unable to concentrate enough to continue this discussion," he complained in a tired, dismissive tone. "Doeg, you will present your ideas in front of my entire court at a later time. For now, I am weary and need my rest." As soon as Saul had finishing saying this, he then fell fast asleep. Hence, Doeg and Zephaniah happily left that bedchamber. They spoke quickly and surreptitiously to one another as they likewise schemed amongst themselves over their new found favor with the king. All of a sudden, Doeg stopped himself short as he once again heard the disturbing whisper of the wind and what sounded like footsteps down one of the corridors. "Who is there?" he questioned as he looked down the dark hall.

"You will get used to all the strange noises of the palace," Zephaniah said in an assuring voice. "I know that it took me a while."

"I could swear that I heard someone walking down there," Doeg answered back, still cautiously inspecting the darkness. He then shook off his uneasiness and turned to Zephaniah. "But perhaps you are right. It is probably just my imagination..."

10

Several days after that first meeting the two new advisors promptly appeared before the king and his court. After their official introductions, Saul spoke up, "I am the ruler of this nation, am I not?" He stared across his throne room to the only other space that signified authority. It was the empty seat of Samuel, always vacant except for in times of grave circumstances such as when the nation prepared to go into a major battle. The king continued, "So why are there still those who dare to oppose and contradict my authority?"

Picking up on his connotation, Zephaniah of Endor made a declaration as she climbed the small flight of stairs that led up to Samuel's elevated rostrum and stood behind the vacant seat of the prophet. "You are the high majesty of this land and of this room, King Saul. There should not be another seat parallel to yours," she cried, and with that she stretched out the palm of her hand. Then, with a quick flash of her wrist, Zephaniah shocked the horde of advisors currently present at the king's court. For, even though it appeared that she hadn't made direct contact with the heavy wooden chair, it astonishingly flew off of its platform and was sent violently tumbling down the stairs. Once it reached the ground, it continued to roll across the room as though it were being thrust by an unseen force. It finally came to a stop as it crashed into pieces against a distant wall. Zephaniah subsequently walked down and picked up one of the splintered parts as the crowd began to murmur over her strange powers.

Not to be outdone, Doeg quickly climbed to the top of the stairs, stood on the position where Samuel's seat once occupied, and made an announcement, "We should build a statue of you in this spot, your Highness, in recognition of your absolute and austere authority over this court and of the nation."

"Don't bother with the flattery, Doeg," the king said in a rigid tone. "Just get on with what you have been brought here today for, your proposals; tell us what you have learned about the art of ruling the people. How I can repress the power of the elders, subdue the voice of the priesthood, and more importantly, how do I go about vanquishing Samuel's authority and office of High-Judgeship?"

"My king," Doeg spoke up and then cleared his throat. "Regarding the first problem that you touched upon, the issue of the elders of Israel—"

"—What about them?" the king's voice burst out in contemplation as all of his court looked on.

"Well, let me begin by asking you something, sire," Doeg calmly replied. "You magnificently led over 200,000 men into battle and won a substantial victory over the Amalekites," he first acknowledged, setting up his question. "How is it that you gathered such a large force?"

The king explained the process, "After the many skirmishes that we have gotten into with the Amalekites throughout the years, it seemed that the declaration of all out war was the only option left to deal with their constant attacks upon our southern borders. On this vital issue, I sought the will of the people, the will of the elders, and of the priesthood. I sought the very will of God." Saul rose to his feet and ardently spoke to the entire room, "This was, after all, our first and oldest enemy, the swine that attacked our people after we left Egypt and traveled through the wilderness so many generations ago." Concurrence over the issue spread across the room in the form of utterances and nods from the king's advisors as he continued, "And yes, prophetic and priestly approval was given, but only on one condition. I was to completely see to it that our enemy was wiped off of the face of the earth. I subsequently approached the Council of Seventy. I directed them to issue orders to the lesser elders and judges from each of their respective tribes, so that I could be provided with enough men to successfully carry out such a campaign. And they greatly complied by providing me with more than enough soldiers to carry out a swift victory. They did of course keep a capable amount of forces back at home for their own militias in order to protect their lands and our distant borders."

"Therein lies the crux of your problem," Doeg explained in a judicious manner. "Because you have been made to rely so heavily upon others—the priests, the judges, and especially this Council of Seventy—all seem to be under the pretense that it is them who are still running the country." The newly appointed Supreme Advisor made this last comment in a tentative voice as Saul's court began to murmur in nervous apprehension over what the king's response would be.

"It is true," Saul surprisingly conceded after contemplating Doeg's assertion for a drawn out moment. "You have considered my personal concerns well, Doeg. I have let them retain much of their authority. This was an agreed upon stipulation when I assumed the throne and has been considered a temporary safeguard to ensure that I would not become a power-hungry despot. Besides, an echelon of governance has always been the tradition within the tribes, practiced from the time of Moses and throughout the leadership of the distinguished High-Judges."

Doeg quickly spoke up, "But you are not a priest or a High-Judge. You are the King of Israel." The court once again began its murmurs as the Supreme Advisor continued, "And it is fine to allow the elders to administer your will over the people. But their main tasks should be collecting your taxes and seeing that your decrees are carried out. Instead, the Council gathers together in their own court, which resides hardly a stone throws away from your very throne." Doeg said this as he looked out of the open alcove of the king's court and onto that of the adjacent edifices, which housed the Council of Seventy's courthouse and the prison-yard as well. "And what do they do? They vote on issues as if this was still a loose knit nation-state ran by them and the tribal elders. Did they not all declare you their king long ago? Can anyone here please tell me what was temporary concerning these outlandish sanctions of the Council's, which do nothing except suffocate our king's authority? After over twenty years they have still not been lifted."

This last comment both enraged and emboldened Saul who immediately grabbed his scepter and clanked it firmly on the ground as he sat back upon his throne. "That is right!" he proclaimed in a maniacal manner, "I am the king of all these lands, and no one should usurp my authority!"

"Well, you need to prove this power of yours in a manner that the people of Israel will deem worthy of a truly great leader," Doeg offered.

"Yes that is what I need," Saul agreed with a look of consternation. "But what can I do to prove such a thing?"

"How much of your 200,000 man force have returned to their homelands?" Doeg asked.

"None, as of yet," Saul confirmed. "They await my official proclamation of victory and their subsequent orders of release as we speak."

"Perfect," Doeg acknowledged. He continued on enthusiastically with his advice, "This last military campaign of yours against the Amalekites was a true display of Israel's potential. But what if you were to take this vast army that you have already gathered and defeat an even greater enemy than

Amalek?"

The king thought it over, and after realizing that there was potential in this plan, he uttered his thoughts, "Yes, take my armies and annihilate the Moabites, or even the Ammonites."

"I speak of the Philistines my king," Doeg slyly said.

These last words instantly alarmed those present in Saul's court. For, the king had already attempted such an exploit, long ago during the first few years of his reign. Unfortunately, his efforts to take on the Philistines had been unsuccessful. The memory of that failure had haunted him every since. Perhaps this is why Doeg's proposal was immediately appealing to Saul. "Would it even be possible for Israel to take on the armies of the Philistines?" the king asked his Supreme Advisor.

"Maybe not with the amount of forces that you commanded against the Amalekites," came Doeg's answer. "To take on the Philistines, you would have to rally an even greater army. And there are more than enough men to choose from amongst those tribal militias that you mentioned as having been held back from you. You will need all of their numbers as well. You will need each and every available sword throughout our lands."

But the king began to utter a contrary opinion on such a plan of attack, "The very thing you speak of, Doeg, would require even further dependence on the elders, what authority of mine would that possibly display? For, the allocation of troops from each tribe has always been decided by the consortium of elders, not by me. And besides, why should I possibly go to them and ask for more? I have been victorious with whom they have already sent to me. My recent campaign against the Amalekites proved my overwhelming power, despite the opinion of some." The king immediately took on a look of contempt after his own allusion to his reproach by Samuel.

"That is exactly my point," Doeg argued. "As King of Israel, you alone should hold authority over who is and is not required to fight. In all my years as an envoy to other nations the one thing that I have always found to be true is that whoever controls the army also controls the fate of his nation. Your victory over the Amalekites has temporarily rallied the country. Yet, partial credit goes to the elders of the tribes for providing you with 'their men' of war during such campaigns. Your soldiers should be more than just lent to you in time of need. Instead, you should command an army year round consisting of every available Israelite. Imagine your chances of success with such a force. Imagine the response of the people when you lead the country into battle and deliver victory over each and every one of their enemies, starting with the likes of the Philistines."

The king looked to his other advisors and asked for their counsel on the matter. As these advisor spoke amongst each other, it was apparent that the floor was generally opposed to the proposition. One of these subordinate advisors spoke up, "As Doeg has already explained, to go to war against Philistia with any hopes of victory would require the support of every warring aged man in Israel. Who would protect our other outlying boundaries while we concentrate all of our forces on our western borders?"

Another advisor added to the doubt, "This would be a foolish move. Surely Doeg is not suggesting that we instigate an all out war with these Philistines. Let me just speak bluntly. The king's past efforts to take on the Philistines were a debacle. In spite of this, we are still enjoying a tenuous yet long standing treaty with them. And besides, they are five kings strong, their armies are better equipped, better trained, and an attack on them would be as foolish as stirring up a hornet's nest."

Still another word of doubt followed from amongst the king's advisors, "Well said. Sure they make an occasional raid on one of our villages now and then, but for the most part, the Philistine's ultimate resolve to conquer our nation was halted with the leadership of Samuel and his—"

"—Do not ever utter that name in my presence again!" the king shouted. "Samuel is not to be credited with any accomplishments of my regime."

"Absolutely not," Doeg retorted. "And by rallying all the men of war and facing off with the Philistines, your Highness, you alone will be credited with remarkable braveness, the champion of Israel. You will be remembered for your greatness for all time." He then turned to the other advisors and rationalized with them, "With all of our forces combined, Israel could be victorious. Our recent victory over Amelek was accomplished with only a portion of our tribesman. Imagine what we could do if we substantially reinforced our standing army with all the remaining forces in the tribal militias."

Doeg's argument was slowly beginning to sway the court, and as a low murmur of assent broke out amongst some of them, Saul asked one final question to his advisor's, "Can this feat be accomplished or not?"

Once again the advisors spoke amongst themselves, and then a single representative stood to give the verdict, "There is some risk, but with the whole of Israel under the king's command, victory would indeed be plausible this time."

Saul thought about Doeg's suggestion for a bit longer. Encouraged by the response of his advisors, he then reacted with enthusiasm, "Yes, victory would mean the acknowledgment of my greatness, not only by the people of Israel but throughout all the inhabitants of the earth!"

"Nations would tremble before you," Doeg added, bolstering the kings resolve.

"I have decided then," Saul announced. "Our current forces will remain in service and every additional man of warring age throughout Israel shall immediately report to fight in this new campaign."

"And those who do not adhere to your decrees will suffer the consequences my king," Doeg interjected.

Realizing that this plan would undermine the authority of the elders and prove his legitimacy as a great leader once and for all, the king praised his Supreme Advisor, "You do have a brilliant mind, Doeg. I am very impressed with this first proposal of yours. So tell me then, what plans do you have for the High-Judge, Samuel, and his brazenness?"

"That might be a more delicate situation," Doeg said, pondering the options. He then spoke in an artful tone, "My suggestion is a simple one; prohibit Samuel from leaving Ramah. There, he will sit at his home in exile, unable to meddle in your imperial decisions."

The king once again mused over Doeg's advice and then agreed that the plan was excellent indeed. He realized that it would require minimal effort while rendering Samuel powerless. "That is two grand ideas," Saul once again commended. "Finally, tell me how I should deal with the priests and their dissident actions, my Supreme Advisor?"

Doeg looked around the room with a pompous air and assured Saul, "I know little of the issue concerning their reported habits of speaking ill against you, my king. But I assure you that I will look into this matter at once and will handle it personally. Trust me. There will be no more reasons to worry about the priesthood…"

The formal edicts were immediately drawn up and served. The first was delivered to the prophet at his home. The decree was simple and directly to the point stating that,

> 'By imperial order, Samuel, the High-Judge of
> Israel,will hereby be restricted exclusively to
> his homelands within Ramah until further
> notice from his majesty, Saul, King of Israel...'

Samuel was not surprised by the order but instead received it rather graciously. The prophet even invited the messengers who delivered it in to join him and Adino for supper.

Next came the posting throughout the lands of a new requirement for all the men of fighting age to immediately report and serve in the imperial army of Saul. This order also pronounced that anyone who did not abide would be subject to imprisonment along with the loss of all their family's lands and possessions. This second edict, however, was not received with such a well mannered response on the part of the tribes.

Simply put, the warring aged men of the tribes were accus-

tomed to receiving their military assignments from the tribal
elders who had in turn always received directives straight
from the Council of Seventy concerning the matter. To
suddenly change this arrangement for no apparent reason was
indeed nonsensical to them all. Making matters worse, at least
for the moment, was the fact that there was not a single
communication from the Council regarding the issue. Most
of the population thus disregarded the edict, and while some
of the tribesmen were willing to immediately comply, they
were hastily asked to stand-down by their tribal elders who
felt that the order directly undermined both their own authority and the Council of Seventy's as well. Hence, all the tribes
waited anxiously to hear from the Council on whether or not
they should adhere to the unorthodox edict of King Saul.

A number of arrests had inevitably taken place already as a
result of the tribes' slow response to send forth the remainder
of the men from their militias. These arrests were merely a
show of force on the part of the regime and most of the men
heretofore targeted were insignificant non-loyal affiliates of
their respective tribes. Still, the arrests caused uneasiness,
especially amongst the lower-ranking tribesmen who soon
began to question the reluctance of the Council of Seventy to
offer guidance.

In more than one village, confusion led to disorder, and
then rebellion. Minor confrontations between the tribal-elders
and their usually respectful countrymen began to break out
across Israel. For a while these unruly incidents were few,
only existing in the more rural areas. But soon a familiar ring
of discord could be heard throughout the entire land as all the
people began to complain over the inefficiency of the elders
and the inauspicious nature of the Council's silence. It was
evident that the arguments within the tribes could turn much
more serious if things continued in this manner.

Realizing the gravity of the issue, and not wanting to
become more divided over it, the Council of Seventy finally
agreed to assemble and discuss the meaning of such an edict

along with what actions they each should take. Thus, with tension mounting, the Council of elders assembled at Gibeah. In their grand courtyard, built directly adjacent to the king's palace, the small faction of Israel's seventy chief men gathered. This was this same Council of Seventy elders who twenty years prior had demanded of Samuel that he appoint a king over Israel.

Noteworthy to many, and perhaps the very reason the Council operated so overtly was the fact that despite the subsequent coronation of Saul and the establishment of the crown, the king and the Council usually did their best to steer clear of each other's agendas. Hence, Saul's absence on this day was not surprising to anyone. But what did seem strange to those who gathered for the meeting was the fact that the Council operated without the presence of Samuel, the customary head of the assembly.

"Where is Samuel?" the representative of Manasseh, a man by the name of Eliel, asked in a blaring manner. His was the first question to be uttered on the assembly floor. "Do we not have our head of discourse?"

"Don't be too concerned over the absence of Samuel," was the abrupt response delivered by Ribai, a Benjamite and staunch loyalist to Saul. "The king is the head of this assembly, not Samuel." His voice was stern and a bit confrontational as he spoke to the entire Council. "And despite his absence here today, King Saul will be informed about our proceedings." With this last statement, the assembly broke out in murmurings over the subject of the king's authority and his recent edict...

"Gentlemen, gentlemen please refrain from arguing," a recognized voice of diplomacy rang out through the square. "We already have dissent within our tribes. Let it not extend into these chambers." The voice of reason was that of Jesse, a prominent elder from the tribe of Judah.

"Jesse is right," his fellow elder-tribesman, Hachmon declared. "We must maintain civility towards one another."

And thus, at the behest of these two men, the court came to order...

Jesse continued, "I do have a personal announcement to make, but let us first get to the issue at hand. The king has posted an edict stating that all of Israel's men of warring age are to report to him immediately. To better understand the significance of such a notion, let us therefore hold the tribal roll-call starting with the tribe of Reuben and the issue of their battles with our common enemy, the sons of Hagar."

"Indeed, we have engaged in much fighting with the Hagites," the report came from one of the representatives of the Reubenites, "and despite the 40,000 men who we have sent to fight in the king's army for the protection of Israel, the rest of our warring aged men—numbering over 8,000—have remained at home and secured a perimeter around the entire area east of Gilead. My own sons have helped establish a stronghold there, which will be long-lasting..."

After this announcement from the Reubenites, a representative from each tribe then stood and sounded off in succession. They boastfully reported their strength, signified by their number of men ready for battle...

"The sons of Aaron stand before you with over 30,000 men of war, of which 18,000 remain in Saul's command after the battle with the Amalekites..."

"The sons of Zebulun stand before you over 50,000 strong, 30,000 still with the king..."

"The sons of Ephraim stand before you 20,000 strong..."

"The sons of Issachar 22,000..."

"The sons of Naphtali over 37,000 including 25,000 currently under Saul and his generals..."

"The sons of Dan 28,000..."

"...Of Asher over 40,000, half to Saul, half ready and capable of being deployed to the stretches of our lands and borders."

"Gad, 50,000..."

"Manasseh east of the Jordan, 32,000; and west of the river

18,000…"

"Benjamin stands 10,000 strong 6,000 with the king…"

"Simeon, 7,000 men…"

Jesse now stood and gave his report, "Judah stands before you this day equipped for war with shield and spear; in all we have over 26,000 men of warring age, and of those, 20,000 are dutifully serving in the army of King Saul." He then turned to allow the final census to be tallied and recorded.

Since Samuel was not present, a member of the tribe of Levi, and from the Shiloh priesthood, stood and reported the totals, "God has blessed our endeavors giving us increasing prosperity and strength in the midst of our enemies. The men of warring age trained to fight in Israel thus number over 380,000 men with nearly 180,000 currently serving in tribal militias and over 200,000 men still serving under the king's command. And with an even larger generation of prospective males on the rise, who will someday reach warring age and be capable of drawing swords themselves, may God forever continue his espousal to Israel."

The room gave their muttered approval and the floor was once again turned back to Jesse who cleared his throat and continued, "This brings me to the matter of my own personal announcement. Although it may be unexpected, it is time that I relinquish my position as a representative of Judah." There was a mild grumble as Jesse continued to explain his decision, "I am growing older and wish to spend my last years in the serenity of my home, with my family."

"We are saddened to see you relinquish your seat," Eliel responded in a concerned tone. "Will it be one of your sons who will take on your station and control your seat?"

"No, I will allow my sons to report to the king and serve under him as deemed in the Saul's recent decree. For, none of them are beyond warring age and they are likewise too young to join the Council at this time. It has instead been decided that Zabdiel, Hachmon's esteemed son, will take over my seat," Jesse explained all of this as he held out his hand toward Zabdiel who was currently sitting amongst the rest of Judah's elders. Meanwhile, Hachmon reached over and patted his son on the back as Zabdiel accepted still more congratulations from amongst the other elders who sat near him.

"What nonsense!" Eliel of Manasseh surprisingly replied. "I mean no disrespect to Zabdiel," he quickly said as he gave a nodding approval toward the man. "We all know that the son of Hachmon has earned his place amongst us. But my concern pertains to the main issue that we have all come here today in order to discuss. Jesse, you speak as though the decision of whether or not to follow this decree of the king's has already been decided. Really, out of all the elders gathered here today, how many intend to follow this decree and send all of their tribesmen, including their own sons, to serve in the king's army? You heard the report given concerning the struggles that the Reubenites recently had to contend with as they went up against the Hagites. Our homelands need to keep the benefit of maintaining a self-regulated militia. We further need our bloodlines at home in order to head up these militias and lead the next generation, thereby ensuring the survival of our individual tribes. Are there no better uses for them other than to send them to Saul? This last ploy of his is nothing more than an attempt to cause division within our tribes."

Eliel's comments were rejoined by one of Zebulun's tribal representatives, "That is right. Together we have provided Saul with more than enough soldiers to guarantee the nation's defense. These rolls show that he still controls over 200,000 of our men. What is his purpose for demanding jurisdiction over our personal militias?" Dissent once again filled the assembly as the elders griped over their concerns with the king's demands...

"...The question should indeed be why," one of the elders from the tribe of Dan commented, "why does he want us to send him another, what was it? Another 180,000 men? These are the sole protectors of our homes. Without them, we would be left completely vulnerable to our neighboring enemies."

"Tell that to our own tribesmen," a Councilman from Asher proclaimed. "They have begun to question our hesitation in sending our sons to Saul when they know good and well the vital role that these noble men play in the protection of our homelands."

"This is just a ploy to divide us," Eliel again suggested to the room. "King Saul is power hungry and has given us this edict to cause civil unrest throughout Israel."

"I happen to agree with the edict," Jesse responded. "This arguing over the matter is perhaps why we as a nation have not already defeated our enemies; the best trained men for war are the son's of those who sit in this very room. Yet they are missing from the nation's major battles." Again, debate flooded the square in pockets of murmurs and mumbling voices as Jesse continued, "And I am not arguing over whether or not your sons do their parts when it comes to local tribal interests and battles fought in defense of their own homelands. But if we are ever going to truly operate as a nation, we need to be willing to make sacrifices and take up measures, which will benefit all of Israel. My sons have remained home up until now, but I have encouraged them to make preparations so that they can adhere to this edict and to go fight in the army whenever they are called by their king. Surely Saul will continue to make provisions and send troops to protect our borders."

Once again, Eliel offered his rebuttal, "The majority of the men of Manasseh will remain with the king, but my sons will never serve under the leadership of a mad man. And by that, I am sure everyone in this assembly knows of what I speak."

"Why don't you enlighten us?" a voice unexpectedly boomed out as the abrasive sound of heavy gates opening at the far end of the quad interrupted the meeting. The hinges creaked and the wood clamored against the walls as the lone entrance to the square was flung open. In marched a troop of soldiers. After they had finished filing into the splendid court-yard, the king then made his appearance and repeated his question in a contesting manner, "Why don't you enlighten us, Eliel of Manasseh?"

The man that he was speaking to, along with everyone else in attendance, remained silent as Saul walked through the center of the assembly and towards his royal bench and platform. The king paused for a brief moment to take in the surprised expression on everyone's face before casually continuing, "I am here to clarify any misunderstanding about my recent edict. It seems that the Council did not understand it fully. Otherwise, I am sure that all of you would have already done more than your parts to comply."

As Saul sat down, Eliel finally spoke up in an attempt to explain his last statement, "I was merely trying to bring up the point that—"

"—Silence, you!" the king demanded in a loud voice as he leaned over his podium. Then with an arrogant voice, he spoke to the rest of the elders, "Just to let you know, Samuel will never again be in attendance during this assembly. Furthermore, it has been pointed out to me that this nation is filled with pompous minds. Judging from the poor response that I received after issuing my latest edict, it appears that this may be true. Thus, I have come here today to tell each of you personally that I expect full compliance from the tribes. As my decree has explained, you are to send me all of your men of warring age. And this edict does indeed apply to the sons of the elders as well as every other member of the tribal militias."

Low grumblings sprang up throughout the place but quickly dissipated as Eliel stood up to ask the king a series of questions, "And what is the purpose of this latest edict? I would like to know why you need control of all our men. And if we do send them to you, who then will protect our borders? Do you plan on simply hording them for your own personal objectives?"

The king sat silent for a short while twirling his scepter

between his fingers. It was all that he could do to hold back his outrage for being questioned. "I am your king!" he brusquely replied in an irate tone before taking another drawn out moment of silence. Then, after staring at the intricate carvings upon his scepter for a while, he looked at Eliel and spoke in a slow and controlled tone, "Furthermore, I do not answer to you. You answer to me." Saul paused one last time to completely gather his composure. He then at last continued, "Nonetheless, being a fair and upright king, I will let you know of my plan. I am gathering all the men of Israel to annihilate the forces of our greatest and most threatening enemy at the moment, the Philistines!" The king stated this in a fanatical tone as he stood to his feat and raised his scepter high into the air. But his actions did little in terms of rallying the elders or gaining any of their accolades.

Instead, his statement seemed to shock the entire assembly, and even the elders who had wholly supported the king up until this point began to doubt his judgment. Their pessimistic comments quietly ensued:

"He will lead us to our defeat!"

"The Philistines are too strong!"

"This plan is madness!"

Then Eliel again asked more questions, which did indeed infuriate the king, "What role will Samuel play in all this? And what do you mean that he will not be attending this assembly? Only with him could we be successful, for God has ordained that—."

"—I am tired of this foolishness!" the king responded in an uncontrolled yell. "I told you already, Samuel will not be a part of this assembly! He will no longer be a part of anything! He will live the rest of his days in exile, and I do not want to hear his name spoken again!" The king continued his rant as the elders astonishingly took in his words, "Israel will defy me no longer. I am the king and ruler of this nation! And to demonstrate my point, I have drawn up some additional edicts that all of you will comply with."

Saul sat back down. It appeared that he had become somewhat winded after this last tirade, and to the surprise of the Council, he waited for an unfamiliar woman to bring him a cloth, which he used to wipe his brow. She had emerged from the group of soldiers and then quickly returned. After another awkward moment of silence in which the members of the Council simply stared at the king in anticipation of his next statements, Saul spoke to them in a calm voice, "Forgive me for being so petulant, but I have not been feeling too well lately." He wiped the cold sweat from his brow again and repeated himself in a manner that seemed somewhat rehearsed, "I have not been feeling too well lately, so here to explain the rest of my directives to you is my newly appointed Supreme Advisor, Doeg." The king held out his hand introducing Doeg who likewise appeared from amongst the guards and made his way to Saul's side.

Doeg immediately picked up where the king had left off, "That is correct. The king has not been feeling his best and has called me in to serve as his Supreme Advisor. After discussing some needed policy changes with him, I believe that I can serve his majesty well by directly dealing with some of the unruliness that appears to have become contagious throughout this nation." With the king at his back, it was clear that Doeg had taken on an emboldened air of confidence rather easily. He looked over his shoulder at Saul and then out at the members of the Council before proceeding in a menacingly brash voice, "And there does seem to have been an outbreak of rebellion, which I believe derives from the influence of those who sit in this very assembly." The Syrian made this last statement as he extended his scrawny neck and raised a wiry eyebrow around the room. The hall broke into an insulted murmur, but still, no one dared to make a direct challenge to Doeg with the king in his present state.

Doeg made his way down the steps and to the center of the courtyard. There, in dramatic fashion, he continued his reprimanding speech, "It seems to have gone unnoticed, but this nation is now under the auspices of a monarchy. Yet, many of those present in particular have refused to give the required support needed for us to prosper as a nation. Many have refused to support the edicts of the king. You have not properly collected the taxes that are required from your tribes. You have continually second guessed the monarchy and—"

"—This is preposterous," a voice echoed loudly throughout the courtyard. "Who is this man that brings such unwarranted accusations against the noble elders of this assembly?" The tongue that could no longer remain fixed in silence was once again that of Eliel's. The assembly looked on intently as he continued, "This latest edict is completely absurd. The men that we keep at home not only work as tradesmen, farmers, and shopkeepers, which promotes the stability of our tribes, they are also given posts to protect our distant homelands. I for one will not sit here and listen to such nonsense over our loyalty to King Saul." Eliel then rose and began to leave along with his fellow tribesmen from Manasseh, but was quickly stopped in his tracks.

"Guards, arrest that man," Doeg ordered to the surprise of everyone in the room.

The assembly began to break into dissent but the gripes were quickly quelled when the king spoke up, "And arrest anyone else who refuses to give proper attendance to my Supreme Advisor."

The remonstrations slowly died down until the only sound that could be heard was the protesting voice of Eliel. "This is a big mistake," he said as he was escorted away from the assembly and in the direction of the adjoining prison-yard. "You haven't the authority. Manasseh will not stand for..." His words faded away leaving the square completely quiet.

Saul quickly spoke up in order to fill the uncomfortable silence, "That's right; I have given my Supreme Advisor all of the power that he needs to put my muddled administration in order. Part of that job requires him to reign in any rogue voices from amongst the tribes of Israel." Saul attempted to stand up, but it quickly became evident that he hadn't the strength. As he sat back down, murmurs within in the room over the king's sudden affliction rose to an audible roar. Once the assembly quieted back down, Saul cleared his throat and continued his earlier sentiments in an unremitting tone, "This assembly will not convene in the future unless either I or my new Supreme Advisor are present to keep order and to see that my interests are the first thing on the agenda." He looked around the room in a challenging stance. It appeared that despite his weakened condition, the king was nonetheless enjoying the benefit of his sovereignty at the moment. "Now then," his directives continued, "Doeg will finish by explaining the other changes that I have discussed with him. I must get some rest so that I will have the strength to lead my army into battle and on to victory. I expect that their will be no more unruly interruptions in my absence." With this last statement, the king motioned for Zephaniah, the same woman who had assisted him earlier, to come and help him to his feet. She then escorted Saul from the square as the assembly continued to look on and make hushed comments over the king's frailty.

Doeg waited for the king to completely exit the courtyard and the voices to die down once again before continuing, "I say that this day each of you will pledge your loyalty to the king by collecting two fold your previous taxes. These will be due to him by all the inhabitants of the tribal lands. I will take control of the rolls here and have the calculations made so that one fifth of every man's fields and one fifth of his vineyards shall be surrendered, starting immediately--"

"—Well you can have my answer right now you miserable, frog of a man." This time it was the voice of Dodai, the Benjamite and tribesman of Saul himself, which rang out. His contemporaries plead with him to sit down, but Dodai would not hear of it. "No, I have heard enough," he complained. "This is preposterous. We have given nothing but support to the king, and this is how he repays us? He talks of our loyalty to this nation as if we have something to prove. Yet, it is the families of those who sit in this very room who founded this nation under the direction of our God. I will therefore not be subjected to extortion by anyone, and my house will not give any additional taxes to support the greed of Saul."

"Guards arrest that man," Doeg shrieked.

The entire assembly then exploded into an upheaval as the elders all began to dispute the orders and authority of Doeg. Meanwhile, the king's soldiers attempted to do as they were told by making their way through the center of the square with the intention of arresting Dodai.

Once again the mammoth gates, which had dramatized the king's entrance earlier burst open and interrupted the pandemonium. Yet this time it was not the king who entered. It was instead a rowdy looking troop of men, led by a battle clad warrior with long red hair and the face of a regal lion, who now made their way into the assembly. "That might not be a good idea," the red headed warrior said, speaking to the soldiers who had apprehended Dodai. "Come father we are getting out of here," he then yelled out. This was Eleazar, the renowned son of the outspoken Benjamite. His opportune timing in the situation was a result of his vigilance—Eleazar had escorted his father into town earlier that day and was waiting warily outside of the courtyard with his men the entire time. Thus, when he saw the surprising exit of the king moments earlier and overheard Saul's departing commands to his soldiers, he knew something was awry.

"Return to the assembly," the king had gruffly ordered as Zephaniah led him away. "And arrest anyone else who attempts to start trouble."

After hearing this and the subsequent episode of muffled shouting coming from within the hall, Eleazar decided to look into the situation.

"Watch out Eleazar," Dodai yelled to his son who had come under attack by two soldiers. Fortunately Eleazar was more than ready and made short work of his foes. Without

even drawing his sword, he rushed forward and simultaneously pummeled the two of them with his massive forearms.
He then proceeded directly toward those who had hold of his
father. He was followed close behind by his able bodied
legion.

The soldiers, seeing that they were no match for Eleazar
and his warriors, instantly released Dodai.

But Doeg wasn't about to allow them to give up so easy.
"What are you doing, you fools? I said to arrest that man and
take the rest of these intruders away too," he commanded.

Doeg's orders were convincing enough to encourage the
soldiers to draw their swords, but it was a momentary notion
to continue with the arrest. Eleazar's men all drew out their
own swords, and their actions were followed by many of the
elders who likewise stood to their feet, ready to fight.

Doeg contemplated the predicament in his mind, not
forgetting that these Councilmen were more than capable of
defending themselves. Their gallant sons, after all, had
learned the art of war from the best. The king's Supreme
Advisor was thus at a momentarily loss on how to handle the
riotous situation and remained frozen in silence.

Then, in an act of capitulation, Saul's ranking soldier, the
scar faced captain, arrived on the scene and took control; he
immediately told his men to stand down. Doeg remained
incensed but recognized the captain's efforts as all that could
be done in order to avoid the outbreak of a deadly skirmish
between the king's soldiers and the elders.

The Councilmen stood quietly and stared back and forth at
each other in a perplexed manner as the captain of the guard
conspicuously rubbed the scar on his face. He then signaled
his men to hold open the gates and further showed his respect
by calling his men to attention. He allowed the elders, along
with Eleazar and his men, plenty of time to put away their
swords and gather all of their belongings before they filed out
of the courtyard in an orderly fashion.

Despite the absolute disaster the scene had almost become

and ignoring the fact that he had lost all efforts to reign in the authority of the elders, Doeg regained his dogged attitude as the last of the Council members mounted their horses and made their departure. Only then did he shout out to them, "This is only the beginning...the king will not stand for such disobedience!!!"

12

After the king's messengers finished with their supper and respectfully took leave of Samuel's home, the prophet glanced over King Saul's edict and its wording once more —"Samuel, the High-Judge of Israel, will hereby be restricted exclusively to his homelands within Ramah..." He thought about this for a while and also of the king's plans to assemble all of Israel in order to attack the Philistines. The latter was learned during the conversation that he had shared with the messengers while they ate. Samuel stood up and walked over to a low burning candle. He held the corner of the edict to the flame and let it slowly catch fire.

Adino, in the meantime, watched as the prophet waited for the entire contents to go up in smoke. Samuel then turned to the mighty man. "This is not the first time that the king has tried to prove his strength by taking on the likes of the Philistines," the prophet assured Adino. "I am sure you realize that his actions mimic what he decided to do after defeating the Ammonites during his first year as king. He won the support of Israel for a short while at that time, but do you remember what he did next?"

Adino thought for a while before responding. "That is

right," he recollected. "I believe that the following year King Saul led an unprovoked attack on a Philistine garrison."

Samuel nodded his head and corroborated the account, "He wanted to prove his strength to Israel. Yet, do you remember the outcome?"

"The Philistine kings rallied together with plans of an all out attack," Adino answered. "Next, Saul requested that the elders call together all the tribes to join him at the battlefront, but the Council remembered the last war that we had with the Philistines, which culminated at the battles of Ekron and Gath."

"Yes, they did not remember our victory," Samuel took over the narrative, "but instead thought only of the amount of bloodshed that was required to drive back the Philistines. Hence, they trembled in fear. And instead of obeying the king's summons, they refused, leaving Saul vulnerable as he stared into the face of certain defeat at the gates of Gilgal."

"I remember well," Adino offered. "I was disappointed in Israel on that day and willing to leave my work as a manager of the quarry outside Gibeah and ride into battle against the Philistines on my own if I had to. I may have done just that if you had not stopped me." Adino concluded his memory of the incident with solemn inflection, "You gave me the same instructions that I remember you giving to Saul. Wait, you said. Wait upon the Lord."

Samuel walked over and patted Adino's shoulder. "You were obedient," he said with a smile. "But Saul was not. He overstepped his boundaries with God on that day by usurping the authority of the High-Priest. The king rashly presented both the ceremonious burnt offering and the peace offering to God. I subsequently told him that his kingdom would not endure and because of his impetuousness the Lord sought for Himself a man after His own heart who would be the true commander of His people."

Adino looked astonished over this last revelation as Samuel continued, "Yes, the Lord had divined long ago that Saul was unworthy of his commission. In that precarious situation of his, Saul was only saved when Jonathan did something that his father had refused to do. He waited for a sign from the Lord before leading a defense against the Philistines. And God did indeed save Israel on that day."

"But why? Why was Saul chosen in the first place then?" Adino questioned, "If his kingdom was not to be established for very long?"

"Every man serves a purpose in life, Adino. The fortunate, such as Saul, get the opportunity to serve a divine purpose. And, if for no other reason, perhaps he became king in order that all of Israel would see their mistake in asking to be ruled by man. This brings me to our current agenda. Over the next few days, there are two important events, which will be taking place. You know that the time has come. Do you not?"

Adino responded with a nod as he answered, "The time of my Nazarite vow has come to an end."

"Yes," Samuel affirmed. "But we have something very important to tend to first. We leave in the morning for your homeland, Bethlehem."

That night Adino did not rest well at all. He continually tossed and turned as he faded in and out the same familiar dream of the lonesome valley. His rest was completely intermittent, prohibiting him from ever getting to experience the vivid eyewitness of any of the dream's usual characters. Instead, he saw only short flashes of it all, which in turn made his rest all the more sporadic.

As the two set out towards Bethlehem the next morning, Adino tried to disregard his own weariness and instead concentrated on the peculiar fact that Samuel carried with him a horn filled with oil and escorted, on their journey, a heifer for a sacrifice. This was a very bold move on the part of Samuel, considering the stipulations of the edict that had been served on him. To appear in public out of Ramah was a risky venture, but to do so with the tools traditionally used for the anointing of prophets was brash even for Samuel. To say the least, it was an act that could be considered treasonous by those loyal to the king. Nonetheless, Samuel appeared unflappable as he carried with him the implements of the priesthood and journeyed with Adino out past the boundaries of his homeland. "Our directives come from God," he assured the mighty man.

Almost out of Gibeah, they had managed to make it quite far without having drawn any attention to themselves. But as they drew nearer to the edge of town, they were stopped by a regiment of the king's guard. "Halt, stay where you are," the soldier in charge shouted to them. Adino turned towards the man as he approached. Samuel himself looked up to the sky and seemingly began to pray. The soldier walked directly past the mighty man who sat unassumingly upon his horse and spoke to the prophet in a suspicious manner, "We heard reports that you were sighted traveling south, prophet." The man inspected Samuel's belongings as Adino smiled casually over toward the rest of the soldiers; his hand meanwhile clung inconspicuously to his sword. The lead soldier looked over at Adino then back at Samuel before continuing, "You do realize that we have orders from the king concerning you. What purpose do you have for your journey?"

Samuel felt like revealing his entire plan, "I am carrying this oil to find and anoint a chosen man of God, a leader appointed by the Lord from the tribe of Judah." But Samuel did not reveal his full intentions to the king's men. Instead, he told them another story as he dismounted his horse and humbly stood before them, "I am taking this heifer to Bethlehem, my companion's homeland." He gave a nod over to the mighty man as he finished his explanation, "It is meant as a sacrifice and celebration unto the Lord."

The soldier thought for a brief moment and then walked back to confer with one of his men. From Samuel's distance, he was able to make out a few words from their conversation and was relieved to distinctly hear the words "king" and "paranoid" spoken in the same breath. The soldiers laughed

amongst themselves. The one that had been doing the inter-
rogating then returned. Grabbing a fist full Samuel's
garments, the soldier looked into the eyes of the prophet and
contemplated the propensity for him to act as a threat. Adino
began to slowly draw his sword. "Very well," the soldier
suddenly replied as he released Samuel with a slight shove
that likewise restored Adino's blade to its sheath. The soldier
then turned and looked at Adino who purposefully avoided
eye contact with him. He then turned back around and
addressed Samuel once more, "Be on your way old man."

Samuel did not intend to hang around for very long, he
quickly organized his belongings and signaled for Adino to
follow as he immediately took up the journey once more.
Passing into the borders of Judah, they eventually made their
way through fields of wheat before arriving into the city.
Many people came out to greet both of the well-recognized
men, and by the time they reached the steps of the city gate a
large crowd had gathered to usher the two of them into meet
with the town's elders.

As Samuel entered the assembly room of judges, he
immediately instructed them to prepare for a ceremonial
sacrifice to God, which would require the attendance of all the
elders of Bethlehem. Samuel then inquired about the man
whom he had taken great risks to travel and see, "Is Jesse, the
descendant of Nahson, not present?"

Favor of Jesse was announced by all of the elders as they
explained that after stepping down permanently from the
Council of Seventy he had also recently turned down a seat in
their local chambers. Still, they assured Samuel that it would
be easy enough to request Jesse's attendance at such an event.

Samuel was pleased to hear this and affirmed that Jesse's
presence would certainly be required along with the rest of the
men from his house. The prophet then instructed them to
prepare a feast. All the elders were then made glad over
Samuel's visit and relieved that it was one of good tidings.

The ceremony was later held in the presence of over forty

men: Samuel, the elders of the surrounding lands, Jesse, and his sons. Adino took a seat in the back of the sanctuary where the proceedings were taking place and acted as a reverent observer during the service.

As the ceremony drew to its conclusion, Samuel prepared the oil, and made an announcement, "I now ask for each of Jesse's sons to step forward one by one from oldest to youngest. Of these fine men, one is chosen of God to become an extraordinary leader." He waved his arm to begin the procession of young candidates from the house of Jesse. The first and eldest son, Eliab, made his way up to Samuel. He was tall and handsome with the stately appearance of regality. Yet, after looking into his eyes, Samuel let him pass and called for the next. The second eldest was Abinadab who was also markedly distinguished in his looks, but he too was passed over. The next four sons, all very notable in appearance and stature, passed before Samuel: Shimea passed, Nethanel passed, and Raddai passed, followed by Ozem, the last of Jesse's sons currently present. Samuel looked him over and then turned to the elder tribesman. "None of these are the Lord's chosen," he told Jesse. "Have you brought all of the men from your household?"

"Yes, I have indeed," Jesse responded. "The only person left out is my youngest, but he is much too young to be considered amongst those who stand before you here today."

Samuel's momentary perplexity subsided. "Bring him to me," the prophet ordered.

"He is out tending to the flocks of my lands. It will take some time to find him," Jesse explained as the elders of Israel whispered skeptically over Samuel's interest in the young shepherd.

"Bring him," Samuel insisted. "The ceremony will not end and we will not eat until he is brought before me."

Men were sent out to Jesse's lands in order to find the 'sheep herder' as everyone in attendance of the ceremony stood by. The elders of Bethlehem grew weary as the evening past and the youngest son of Jesse still did not arrive. Then, finally, the door of the great hall opened and in stepped a young man. He approached and was directed by his father to stand before the prophet. Samuel looked him over. He was ruddy, with bright eyes, and a handsome appearance. Samuel instantly made an announcement, "Today a boy stands before you, but he will soon be a man, and as a man he will one day lead this nation as the anointed of God." The prophet then turned and asked the sheep herder his name.

"My name is David," he confidently replied.

"David, listen to the words of your patriarch, Israel," Samuel told him, loud enough for everyone in attendance to hear. (*)- "Judah is a lion's whelp; from the prey, my son, thou art gone up: he stooped down, he couched as a lion, and as an old lion; who shall rouse him up? The scepter shall not depart from Judah, nor a lawgiver from between his feet, until Shiloh come; and unto him shall the gathering of the people be." Samuel then anointed the boys head with oil.

Immediately after the ceremony, the prophet quietly slipped away with Adino and returned to Ramah so that his brief absence from his home went completely unnoticed by the king.

Two days later, Samuel and Adino prepared for a ceremony of a different sort. After emerging from the natural spring which flowed directly behind the grounds of Samuel's home, Adino dressed in what had become his customary attire, the hooded robes of a cleric, for the last time. As he later stood before the prophet, Samuel commended him, "Today, you have fulfilled your pledge."

After being asked what he had learned over his time as a Nazarite, Adino readily acknowledged what his experience had revealed to him, "From my own perspective, the many years spent with you have past leisurely enough, prophet. And I learned many things from you during this time. But over the past several years I have grown the most by taking on my vows and consecrating myself fully unto God. I have at last obtained true knowledge, and only now do I feel complete."

"Ah yes," Samuel confirmed. "The road of the Nazarite is fruitful, revealing much to a man. Some travel it for only a short time while others like myself are fixed to such a saddle for life. The length of time required for this endeavor is different for all. You have chosen a good season for this delegation, and I am proud of you, Adino."

Offerings were then given, and afterwards, the mighty man's head and beard were completely shaven. Released from his vows, Adino then exchanged his attire for more contemporaneous clothing.

Next, Samuel summoned Adino and spoke to him of the future, "With your previous delegation complete the time has come for your new appointment. As I said before, the God of our nation has divined that the kingdom has been shaken. This David is the key to all of this. Saul selfishly dreams of greatness and the reverence of the people. But David will be the one to realize all of those dreams, because only he can successfully unite the country."

"You have chosen your replacement then?" Adino questioned in an assuming manner. "This young man, he will be the new High-Judge of our nation?"

"Did you not hear the words that I spoke to David yesterday?" the prophet asked. "Did you understand the words of Israel, the patriarch?"

"I heard the words but did not fully understand them," Adino admitted.

Samuel then boldly explained the meaning of the prophecy for Adino, "When Israel was on his death bed, he gave a word of revelation to each of his sons. Amongst the most important words that he spoke on that day are those that he forecasted to his son Judah. Israel told Judah that he would bear the scepter. And you see, it is a simple lesson." Samuel halted his story long enough to retrieve a long staff from the adjoining room, which he used to illustrate his point. "The answer lies with this instrument and what it represents," he said as he took a seat and held the staff out in front of him. "Just think of King Saul when he sits before his court. In his hand he holds the royal scepter. It is the symbol of the king's authority. And by revealing those words of the patriarch to David, I was informing him that he, a man of Judah, is the rightful owner of the scepter."

"What?" Adino suddenly asked. "Are you saying that he will indeed become—?"

"The man after God's own heart," Samuel made clear. "And he is indeed God's chosen king." The prophet then spoke in a solemn tone, "His true identity makes for a dangerous existence. For, although he will not assume his role as king for many years, David will soon become an unlikely hero in time of crisis for Israel. Saul will then despise him and attempt to kill him. This is where you come in, Adino."

"What role could I possibly play in all of this?" Adino asked.

"Yes, you are just one man, after all," Samuel answered in a reflective tone. "Isn't that what you told me when I gave you your first charge in the quarry those many years ago? Do you remember my answer?" Adino quickly reminisced over those past years as the prophet continued, "You would have made a great king, my friend." These last words came as somewhat of a surprise for the mighty man, but he nonetheless remained silent and allowed the prophet to finish what he had to say. "You are humble, yet mighty. These are two very noble attributes indeed, and from the first day that I met you, I knew that you possessed many additional qualities requisite of a king— discernment, leadership, and devotion to your cause. But there was one thing that you lacked back then that you now have, and that is direct knowledge of your God. You have gained this familiarity with Him over the years that you have spent with me, and you will need to lean on that faith in order to be successful in the future. For, I am now turning a very important designation over to you.

You are to organize a group of men, Adino. They will be mighty men of valor like yourself and must be willing to lay down their own lives, both for the future of the nation and also for this man David's protection. I reveal to you this day, your destiny.

You were never to be king, but instead, Adino, you were chosen to fill the privileged role of King-Maker. For, in order for God's anointed, this young David, to assume his own role, in order for him to one day be made king, you will need to gather a forum of supporters straight away that will help hold together our nation during the perilous days of our near future; these men must likewise agree to stand beside you in the protection of David with the knowledge that with one voice you will one day all declare him your king. God has created in you a leader, and this is your divine purpose, Adino.

So gather now men of intelligence and brawn. Gather now the sons of the elders, the battle-proven, and the brave. Gather now the mighty..."

13

Adino's first impulse after being instructed by Samuel to gather up a worthy group of Israel's mighty men for the refuge of the nation and the protection of Jesse's son was to return home. He anxiously wished to tell his father and grandfather all that had transpired. Their connection amongst the tribes would likewise make them valuable collaborators in his mission. Yet after arriving back to his family's lands, Adino realized that neither Zabdiel nor Hachmon were present.

He asked his mother where they had gone and disappointingly learned that the two of them had left earlier that same morning in order to attend the Council of Elders assembly in Gibeah. After waiting impatiently for two days, and with his body once again aching for action, the mighty man decided to act alone. His mother overheard Adino ordering his servants about and decided to look in on him...

"Prepare my horse and armor," Adino said giving final instructions to his footman, "and inquire for me where the army of Saul is. Specifically find out if General Abner is still camped at Carmel?" He then began searching amongst his father's collection of manuscripts and scrolls.

"Do you need help locating something?" his mother asked

in a curious voice after he had been at it for a while.

"No, it is just a simple document that I am looking for," Adino responded as he quickly poured through dozens of annotated writings. "It must be here somewhere, for I was present when it was delivered to father. And I've never know him to dispose of a single parchment entrusted to him in all his life."

His mother nodded her head and obligingly left him to his hunt. Soon he had abandoned any sort of methodical manner of probing through the volumes of records. Adino instead took on a frantic and coarse search. Until recently, he would have counted the particular report, which he anxiously looked for, as nothing more than another worthless article amongst the many hundreds of documents that his father had kept over the years, but suddenly its contents were of vital importance. Finally, after searching through countless parchments and reports, he found exactly what he was looking for.

As he perused the contents of the treasured document, Adino's mother returned to check on his progress. "Do you have to make such noise in—", she began to speak but stopped mid-sentence with a look of trepidation as she viewed the wreck that had been made of the place.

The mighty man comprehended the consequences of his reckless hunt seemingly for the first time as he looked at his mothers astonished expression and then around at the room. In his search, he had absent mindedly ransacked the place, leaving dozens of parchments, maps, and scrolls thrown haphazardly about the span of his father's once meticulously ordered archives. Adino looked remorsefully back at his mother as she forgivingly spoke to him, "I only hope that whatever it was that you were looking for was worth all this and that you have indeed found it." She then shook her head, picked up a few of the documents from an adjacent chair, and flopped herself down into it.

"A sentinel at the gate of Bethlehem has reported that Abner's forces have once again given chase to the Amalekites and are making final sweeps into their country," his servant anxiously interrupted, holding smartly onto a handful of Adino's battle-gear. "It is there, beneath the most southern region of Israel, that Abner and the army can be found."

The mighty man eagerly listened to the details of Abner's whereabouts from his loyal servant along with the convenient fact that his horse had been made ready for immediate departure. But his enthusiasm was soon subdued as he looked back at the pillaged room. It would be a time-consuming venture to return the contents of the archives to its former order.

Anticipating Adino's anxiousness, his mother came to his rescue. "Go ahead with your plans," she wearily told him, dreading the consequences of volunteering her assistance. "I have helped your father organize his records on many occasions. I will have the place back in order in no time."

Adino gave his mother a kiss on the forehead as she sat there amongst the strewn out documents and thanked her. He then immediately departed with the intention of paying a visit to General Abner's camp and retrieving his loyal troop of men, some of which had accompanied him and Samuel for well over ten years. With them, and the documents he now had in hand, Adino believed that he could properly begin his undertaking.

Anxious and battle ready, the mighty man rode from his family's home on the outskirts of Bethlehem and headed south towards the lands of Amalek. But after reaching the Wells of Moses, Adino began to feel that perhaps his servant had misunderstood the sentinel's report on the army's location. He searched the area all the day long, but there was no sign of anyone. The land was barren and desolate and soon a sandstorm approached, forcing Adino to camp out for the rest of the day with plans to continue his search the next morning.

That evening, he studied his father's reports carefully. Two more days passed in this manner giving Adino plenty of time to make mental notes of all the documents he had brought with him, but still there was no sign of the winds letting up. Instead, the land and climate became increasing harsh, and to make matters worse, Adino had eaten all of the food that he had brought with him. Ironically, there was plenty of water next to his campsite, but it was much too bitter to drink. He began to realize that in his zealous desire to start on his journey, he hadn't planned properly. Thus, feeling hungry and dispirited, Adino gathered his things and decided to fight through the sandstorm and return to civilization where he could hopefully find a place to re-supply.

Through the hot wind and sand of the desert, he could only see a short distance and was regrettably unable to distinguish any distant landmarks. The desert in his short range of view all looked the same, the brush looked the same, and the sand filled sky looked the same. Conditions were unrelenting as the tempestuous sand continually whipped at Adino, beating down on his tired body. He wandered through it for another day, stopping to rest only when it became unbearable. Finally, he came upon some water again. As he jumped from his exhausted and failing horse, he ran rejoicing toward the waters edge only to realize an awful site; Adino unexpectedly recognized the remains of his former camp and understood at once that he had been traveling the desert aimlessly in circles.

The mighty man fell to his knees, his throat burning from thirst, and pitifully crawled the rest of the distance to the well. With a craving for something to quench his dry throat and cracking lips, Adino cupped his hands, reached them into the tempting water of the pond, and poured some into his mouth. But after forcing himself to swallow the putrid liquid, he realized that it would be impossible to keep it down. Sure enough, his stomach convulsed causing him to expel the water back up and vomit it out. There was nothing left to do but dash his hand through the deceivingly pungent ripples of water in frustration.

As his horse whined and thudded to the ground, agitating the desert air with bits of sand, Adino rolled over onto his back and looked at the sand, which tauntingly whistled as it blew over him. It filled the entire sky above. He began to think of the failure of his journey thus far. He thought of his father and the rest of his family. Then he realized that his strength, along with all of the wealth that he had been promised as an inheritance was at this moment worthless. For, it could not placate the fierce thirst that now set his entire body ablaze.

Through a haze of delirium induced dehydration, he then thought of the prophetic instruction that Samuel had given to him, "You will need to hold together our nation and prepare for the angst of battle against our enemies... Your destiny is revealed... You now bear the burden of the King-Maker... Gather those who will stand strong together for Israel... Gather now the mighty..."

Adino drifted once more into that strange dream of his. It was vivid: The approaching tempest, the lengthy expanse of the valley, the bellow of the lion, and the men who had gathered in an attempt to vanquish the land of that sinister tree with its claw-like branches, which spread out over the plain in looming fashion once more. Then the storm-clouds finally arrived overhead and rain began to fall, instantly creating luscious pools of water upon the dry undulating earth below him.

Adino deliriously basked in the refreshing downpour of his subconscious interlude even as he lay in the heat of that harsh desert floor. But his redeeming flight of the imagination was suddenly halted as he felt something prodding him in the shoulder. He struggled to focus his blurred sight. In the foreground of the gusting sand, he saw the hazy image of a wild animal above him. But no, it was not an animal. It was a foreign looking man with a staff in his hand and a headdress adorned with a large feather. Behind him in the midst of the storm was a procession of other men who were carrying goods and leading many beasts, including a number of donkeys, horses, and camels, which were all packed with supplies.

"Come sir, let me lend you a hand," the man offered as he prodded at Adino with his staff whilst directing others from the caravan to assist him in helping Adino off the ground. He spoke in a loud cheerful manner over the howl of the wind, "You must be awfully tired my friend, but still, this is no place to be getting rest." The jovial man then pointed toward some distant trees, which Adino himself had never before noticed. "You see those palms over there. Let us go there and set up camp," the stranger instructed his men as they struggled over the mighty man's large frame.

While some of them half dragged Adino up the desert's sloping hills toward the small group of trees, others collected the supplies from his lifeless horse, including the parchments and his armor. Meanwhile, all the mighty man could do was watch them, for he was too weak and his mouth too dry for him to even speak. Nonetheless, the stranger kept talking, "My name is Bacchus, and you my friend, whatever your name is, are very lucky. The weather is much too brutal in these parts for any man to travel through for very long without proper supplies. I am likewise lucky enough to have an abundance of provisions. So come, and we will both sit. I see that you could indeed use a respite from this remorseless storm. Would you like something cool to quench your thirst?"

An ornate rug was laid down under the protection of a quickly staked tent and Adino was led to lie down on it. His possessions were likewise set beside him. He was then given a sweet drink, which immediately quenched his thirst and provided him with some much needed energy. "Nedjem, from the carob tree," his host informed Adino while he drank greedily. Bacchus continued, speaking in an excited manner after noticing the mighty man's dusty yet stately attire along with his large handsome sword and valuable armor, "Tell me, what is your name?"

"I am Adino the Eznite, son of Zabdiel, son of Hachmon." The proclamation was sputtered in a cracked voice as Adino felt the life coming back into him.

"A strong name for a strong individual," Bacchus said as he raised his glass and took a seat on the large rug.

Adino was revived by the sweet drink and thanked the stranger for his kindness as an elderly man came over and sat down upon a small rug of his own. It was apparent that the man was very interested in joining the conversation as he spoke some words to Bacchus in a different language and then gave an enthusiastic nod to Adino.

"He is interested in you. He says that he has heard, in his homeland, of a mighty man of war from the tribes of Israel by the same name," Bacchus explained.

"I am flattered," Adino responded. "And where exactly is your friend from?"

"We are both Assyrians and hence come from the east. I am of the royal interpreters, and this is my father, Nasir. He served for many years in Babylonia as a court counselor. Being part of the sacred order of the Magi, he too was once well known and celebrated as an interpreter of dreams, but he was deposed from his position and now travels with me instead. Currently, we are on our way to the land of Egypt after already making a short visit to Moab."

"I see, and what business do you have there?" Adino questioned.

"Our people have a long alliance with Egypt," Bacchus explained. "We will get to all of that, but you must first tell me, what is it that you are doing in this wilderness?"

"I am looking for someone," Adino briefly replied, preoccupied with rehydrating himself once again by taking a drawn out drink. He then inquired about the old man's presumed powers, "You say that your father can interpret dreams accurately?"

"Tell him any dream and within three days time he will likewise give you its meaning," Bacchus answered confidently. "It is an ancient art, practiced by only a small group of gifted individuals from our homeland. As I said before, they are known as Magi."

Adino was intrigued but appeared skeptical with his next question, "Why then was your father deposed from his position at Babylonia if he is so talented?"

"He was ousted only after the king became very angry over his forecasts. Although his interpretations of the royal family's dreams were always accurate, they were also often prognostic of unfortunate events. This did not make him popular at the palace in Babylonia for very long." The man's attitude remained positive despite this last unfortunate account concerning his father.

"I have a dream that I would like interpreted," Adino then stated hopefully.

"Impossible!" Bacchus confessed.

"What?" the mighty man asked in a puzzled state, "but you just said—"

"—My father must use the stars in order to accurately give an interpretation. And as you already know, because of the storm this is impossible."

Adino nodded his head, assuming his previously skeptical attitude. "Uh huh, I am sure," he said in a less than amused tone.

"As I spoke of before, my father has accompanied me ever since leaving Babylonia," Bacchus persisted with his earlier narrative, taking no apparent notice of Adino's skepticism. "We cross these deserts twice a year. My understanding of languages complements our enterprises very well and has allowed me and my family the ability to travel year in and year out in order to trade goods. I have seen many things in that time, and my endeavors have truly paid off very handsomely. We have little to complain about."

"I am impressed," the mighty man answered back as he took a look out at the throng of people who labored outside for Bacchus, smartly preparing tents and shelter for the night. "Do you always find such harsh weather in these parts?" he then asked.

Bacchus appeared indifferent to the sandstorm as he

responded, "I have seen my fair share of this. We never let it completely stop our advance. We must make at least a little headway each day, no matter the weather. And it's a good thing for you too, my friend," he said with a smile as he slapped Adino on the leg and wagged a half open-palmed finger at him."

"Yes, it was," Adino granted with an appreciative smile. "I thank you for the hospitality."

Then Bacchus said something peculiar as he leaned in closer to Adino, "You say that you are looking for someone in these parts? It seems that I too am always looking for someone. I have made my fortune in other ways besides just trading goods, you see." The mighty man leaned back with one eyebrow raised as Bacchus put forth a proposition, "I noticed that you have a large sword of sophisticated workmanship. And your stature is perhaps as impressive as any that I have seen in my many travels. In addition, it seems that your reputation as a warrior precedes you. I must ask again; what are you doing out in this wasteland and where are you headed? Perhaps you seek to add to your fine possessions? I can tell you how to accomplish such a thing."

"No," Adino replied as he shook his head, "fortune is not what I am seeking."

"Perhaps it is distinction and further notoriety then?" the strange man offered with a coaxing smile.

Once again Adino gave a shake of his head and solemnly replied, "No, but you have reminded me that I need to get going if I am ever to find what I am looking for." Adino rose to leave after thanking the stranger for his hospitality.

"But how will you get out of this wilderness?" Bacchus asked. "The storm has not yet let up and you no longer have a horse. Listen, just sit down for a little while longer, wont you? I haven't finished explaining my scheme to you."

Adino realized that the stranger had a good point. There really was nowhere else for him to go at the moment. He sat back down as his cup was refilled.

"I am indeed from a far off land that lies east of here," Bacchus reiterated. "I have traveled the world over, from the furthest corners of the east to the western lands that lie over the Great Sea. I am headed that way now. You see, I will merely be passing through Egypt where ships await me on the coast. Then I will sail to the Greek islands and finish my labors by visiting their mainland. When I get there I will trade off the goods, which I have collected along my journey. And for many years whenever I happen to travel to that region I make sure to take something very special with me or should I say someone.

You see, men with reputations such as yourself, warriors of renowned, are a great commodity in the land of the Greeks. This is because that once refined region has become a dark and haunted place of conflict as one warlord battles against another in the pursuit of self proclaimed kingship. Some have gained control of vast provinces, dubbing themselves emperor of the region, but such regimes are short lived. For competition is fierce. Lesser kings spend years planning their own rise to power. They not only rely on the strength of their own countrymen, but they have taken to the habit of recruiting mercenary armies to fight for them.

The greatest of these foreign warriors are very much rewarded for their service, given both tribute and their pick of the spoils, which there are always plenty of. This is where I come in. For a hefty price of my own, I have been known to provide such mercenaries for the Greeks. In the past I have taken back Egyptians, Assyrians, and many other men of various nationalities. Of late, there has been an increased interest in the recruitment of Philistine warriors, but an Israelite such as you would make a welcome addition to any number of the Greek warlords."

Adino found the former statements quite interesting. "Tell me something," he said in an intrigued manner. "This sounds like little more than being sold into slavery. Why would anyone volunteer to go with you to such a strange land?"

Bacchus began to laugh as he finished pouring the remainder of the Nedjem jug into Adino's cup. He then continued, making his point with a wide smirk and a sporadic chuckle, "I have already told you. Fortune, my friend, it is a powerful motivator. Besides, in Greece these men are treated no more like slaves than you and I. In fact, if they are good at what they do, many enjoy a better life than either of us could probably ever fathom."

The mighty man rubbed his chin as he asked his next question, "And why are the Philistines suddenly in such high demand?"

"That's right, you haven't met my personal guard," Bacchus exclaimed with delight as he called for his Philistine protector, Lahmi. "Traveling with such a wealth of goods can be a dangerous venture. Proper protection is a must," he confided to Adino as the man whom he had summoned made his way into their tent wielding a mammoth battle-axe. "Put your weapon away, Lahmi, I merely wanted you to meet someone. This is Adino Ben Hachmon," Bacchus said with delight as he waited for Adino's predictable response.

Adino was indeed taken off guard as he obliged Bacchus and turned around to meet the Philistine with an astounded reaction. And it wasn't only the impressive weapon, a mammoth battle axe, which Lahmi wielded that captivated Adino, but it was the man himself. The Philistine was of magnificent stature and a true giant in the order of the great tribe of Raphaim. This Philistine's proportions became all the more apparent as Adino stood up and gave him an awkward nod of assent. For, the mighty man was accustomed to looking down on others; stretching his neck in the extreme opposite direction in order to look up at this Philistine's face was quite out of the ordinary. Lahmi was nearly three feet taller than himself, Adino disturbingly realized; this was an authentic giant.

To add to the uneasiness of the situation was the fact that on another day, these two men might very well be meeting as enemies, but today, neither held a military rank. And despite Adino's past contempt for all Philistines, he acted on his best behavior out of respect for his mild mannered host. The two simply looked each other up and down before Bacchus dismissed the behemoth of a man in a rigid tone, "That is all, Lahmi. You can return to whatever it was that you were doing."

The giant turned and walked away without a word as Adino resumed his position back on the comfortable carpet. He contemplated what he had just witnessed before making any comments about Lahmi and his amazing size, "I've only recently heard that there were giants in Philistia, but I had no idea that these rumors could be true. Are there indeed others?"

Bacchus nodded his head in a fed up manner before answering, "Yes, there are many, but they are an unruly bunch. Traveling with Lahmi over the past few months has not been without its anguish. You see, I picked him up on my trip back home last year after paying a hefty price to his uncle, a giant of even greater proportions than Lahmi. At any rate, this nephew of his was supposed to travel back and forth with me as protection, and I must admit that he has been great at intimidating any would be raids and for amusing guests with his magnificent size, but he is also a terrible lout of a man. All he does is eat and sleep all day. I originally planned to keep him with me, but once we get to Greece, I will seek reimbursement for him by allowing him to leave my paid services early in order to join the efforts of one of the Greek's or to return to the services of his uncle. Either way I will get a good price for his transport. Lahmi too will be much happier with a cause or some sort of war to dedicate himself unto, and I will finally be done with him."

Adino could see that Bacchus was in no mood for answering any further questions concerning the giant, so he abruptly changed the subject, "Tell me then, how is it that Greece has come into such an unsteady age? Was it not once the greatest of nations?"

"To comprehend this, you merely need to look to the history of your neighbors," Bacchus explained. "You see the Philistines, as I have been taught from Lahmi himself in one of his very few intelligible conversations, are a warring people, which trace their ancestry to that of the Dorians from Greece. The Dorians were the sea-people who long ago mastered the skill of both sailing the seas and making iron weaponry to fight the people of their many lands of conquest. Eventually they migrated to Greece. They settled in just long enough to almost become civilized. But their barbaric nature could not be wholly refined. Their brashness and claims of being the returning heirs of Hercules only alienated them all the more from their Greek hosts.

In time, conflict arose in the Mediterranean, requiring the greatest men of Greece to head off to a decade long war with the Trojans, where most were killed. This was the perfect time for the Dorians to rise to power. Thus, they used their iron and might to crush the Greek empire, tearing apart its sophisticated culture. I have heard many stories from the current inhabitants of Greece who have reported that the Dorians dismantled complete cities during their barbaric take-over while also killing off the various aristocratic families throughout the land. Along with the latter, they executed any and all educated Greeks, and destroyed their religious writings along with most of their written history.

But over the years this sort of barbarism did not remain popular with all Dorian's and those desiring an alternative, more cultivated way of life, intermarried with the native Grecians. Many of them thus spread out from their subjugated homeland to all of the coastal regions of the Mediterranean where they would eventually have a great deal of influence. To this day, their ancestors continue to settle in pockets over their conquered areas, which they traditionally inhabit as nation-states. As you know, Philistia too is made up of not one but five great cities, each with its own king. Their bloodlines, they claim, can be traced straight to the Dorian Kings of old and to Hercules himself.

For the most part, Philistia has been more successful than its motherland in its respect to education and keeping peace between kings, but they have always trusted one another just barely enough to remain a moderate powerhouse in this region and nothing more. They are doomed by their divergent natures, which they arrogantly hold to. But make no mistake about it. Give them good reason, and they will join together, just like their Grecian progeny, which have likewise banded together at various times in the past."

"You seem to have become quite an expert on the subject," Adino responded after the extensive explanation of both the Greek and Philistine histories.

"Indeed, I am not only a pupil of languages," Bacchus said with pride. "I also like to learn about the history of those that I visit during my travels."

The two men continued their conversation over supper and into the late evening, discussing many topics along with the intricacies of their own cultures. As the wind noticeably began to die down, the men finally realized how late it had gotten after looking outside and seeing that most of the camp had already retired for the night. "You must promise to reconsider my suggestion for you to stay with us and join our travels to Greece," Bacchus said with a yawn as he grabbed a torch and prepared to head to his own tent. "My father would then have plenty of time to interpret that dream of yours."

Adino stretched out onto his carpet. He had already accepted an offer to spend the night in the comfort of his new environment and hoped the storm would relent enough for him to get an early start the next day. He reciprocated with a yawning voice of his own, "I'll tell you what Bacchus. Let me sleep on the idea."

14

The following day, Adino rose early and looked out at clear, peaceful skies. He had finally gotten a good night's sleep and appreciated the restful stay in the camp of Bacchus. Realizing that much work still lie ahead of him, the mighty man immediately gathered his things in preparation to leave.

Bacchus was sorry to part company with him. "I had hoped that you would accept my offer," the Assyrian said with a genuine look of remorse on his face. "But I understand. You have your own priorities to keep. I wish you well wherever destiny may lead you." Before leaving, Bacchus proposed a generous trade for Adino, "You will not get far without a horse. If you are willing, I know that the fine cloth of your garments will fetch a good price in the markets that I will be visiting. Choose any of my steeds and all the supplies that you can carry in exchange for them."

Adino happily accepted the offer. He thus cast off his fine articles of clothing and donned his battle gear. As the mighty man departed from the camp, Bacchus contentedly bid him an encouraging farewell.

Having traveled east for just a short while, Adino soon came to the top of a hill and was quite surprised as he looked out at the basin below. There in front of him was the camp of the Israelite army. He had been looking for them for days, and all the time, they were just a short distance away. As he came up to a sentry post, Adino had the good fortune of being met by one of his own men, who recognized him from the distance and immediately rode out to give his greetings. The loyal man, Micah, caught Adino up on all the latest news concerning what had happened in Gibeah and the arrest of Eliel of Manasseh. "Word around camp is that the Council remains at odds with the king," Micah worriedly explained to Adino. "And the elders still refuse to issue an order for the tribes to comply with Saul's edict. Worst of all, after hearing of the king's plans, Abner has informed us that he expects us to comply with the directive by permanently taking our place amongst the rest of the king's soldiers."

"We will see what can be done," Adino said consoling the man. "Take me to the general."

Abner sat quietly. He seemed to be in deep concentration as one of his men interrupted him, "General, there is a man here to see you. He says that his name is Adino."

"Well, send him in immediately," Abner responded looking pleasantly surprised to hear about Adino's arrival. The mighty man entered the general's tent and stood in grand fashion. His splendid battle gear and recently shaven head was a dramatic change from his appearance when the two had first met. Abner contentedly addressed him, "Good morning, Adino. I was just thinking that we could use some more strong men to stand with us as we begin the preparations for the king's bold and daring charge against the Philistines. Your men are quite skilled on the battlefield and have already been a tremendous asset."

"It is good to see you too, general," Adino said with a smirk on his face. "But I have actually just come to take my men and leave."

Abner continued in a lively mood, "My friend, I am sure

that you have heard by now. We are preparing for a great campaign against a great enemy. Warring against the Amalekites was one thing, but this is going to be a far larger undertaking. All Israelite men of warring age are now considered part of the king's army. Surely that is the reason you are here, to answer that call along with the rest of your troop."

The mighty man disregarded Abner's blithe attitude and spoke only of his own requirements, "I am glad that you call me friend, because I have also come to ask a favor of you."

Abner's jovial mood quickly changed as he realized that Adino was genuinely in need of assistance. The general sat up in his chair and spoke in a staid tone, "Yes of course. What is it that I can help you with?"

"Besides leaving here with my men," Adino stated in a hesitant tone, "I would also appreciate it if you could possibly lend me some of your own men."

Abner thought for a moment, considering Adino's request. He then began to shake his head in critical fashion as he inquisitively spoke, "Adino, you are an extraordinary character. Do you have a rebellious mind? This is something that I find myself wondering all of a sudden." Abner tilted his head back and stared aloof for a moment, deciding the matter. He appeared remote, thinking the issue over intently before suddenly answering his own question, "No, I don't think that you do have a rebellious nature. Tell me then, what is it that you need these men for?"

"I am..." Adino hesitated once again. "...I am gathering a group of men at the request of Samuel."

"Ha!" Abner blurted out, genuinely amused by Adino's audacity. "Come now, don't make me laugh. I haven't even agreed to release your men back to you, or to let you shirk your duty by leaving us for that matter, and you are asking me for additional troops to carry out the directives of Samuel?" The general gave an obliging snicker before commencing, "Maybe I was wrong about you. Are you indeed a defiant soul?" Abner stood up and walked towards Adino. This time the general looked him in the eyes and spoke in a forthcoming manner as though the two were old friends and could thus easily confide in one another, "What are you and Samuel up too, eh? You can tell me. Are you planning some sort of retaliation on the king to get back at him for the prophet's exile? Could it be possible that you are gathering some loyalists to join up with you and help overthrow Saul?"

"Ha, ha, ha," Adino chuckled as he shook his head. "Now you are making me laugh. Don't be ridiculous."

"Then what is it that you want with these men?" Abner continued in his sporting, yet leery manner. "And did you have anyone in particular in mind or will just any old run of the mill soldier serve your purpose?"

Adino produced the documents that he had taken from his father's library and handed them off for Abner to look over. He waited for a moment before questioning the general, "Recognize any of those names? Perhaps some of them are in this camp?"

Abner examined the manuscripts. "I knew it!" he cried in a pleased manner.

"Knew what?" Adino questioned.

"Let me just start off by saying that I do not deal easily with conspirators, Adino. Ask any of my men. They can attest to my severe methods of punishment for such individuals. That being said, what you are requesting only proves what I was suggesting earlier. If you had taken me up on the offer of allowing just any average soldier accompany you, I might have had no reason to suspect any sort of treasonous plot on your part. I can stretch my imagination to the point that maybe you do have some sort of extra work to accomplish and could thus use the extra manpower. The latter, while suspicious enough, would have been somewhat plausible, but this! This is altogether different," the shrewd general surmised all of this as he looked over the manuscripts again. "I know exactly what these are. These are the old listings of the men who once proved themselves in battle, who could be counted on as improvised captains of men before Israel had a king or any organized forces. Our modern army has all but done away with having to depend on such lists. Maybe that is why you thought that I would not recognize what these were. But I know good and well the purpose of these documents. Why your name is listed here over a dozen times, along with other names of renowned men, the battles which they fought in, and... hey!" Abner stopped himself mid-sentence as he arrived at another conjecture. "How did you come upon such a list?" he asked as he looked up at Adino. "Of course! Your father must be in on this too? How about your grandfather? And how many more of the elders?" Now the general was engrossed in his own thoughts and merely thinking out loud over his grandiose conspiracy theories.

Adino finally decided to put an end to it. "Alright, listen to me," he said as he took a seat on the bench opposite of the one Abner had recently planted himself on during all of his theorizing. "I am going to try and level with you, but you have to hear me out."

"Go ahead. I am listening," Abner coolly replied.

Adino began, "I can not tell you all that I know or my exact plans for that matter. That would require me to betray my own loyalties, which I admit to lie with Samuel. But I can give you my word; I am attempting to gather a group of men who will help me in the protection of a certain individual. And although I can not tell you this man's identity, know this, I am only interested in bolstering our nation, not weakening it, and I am asking you to trust me." Before saying anymore regarding the matter, Adino began a feeling out process of Abner's true dependability, "You are indeed loyal to King Saul, but it seems that you don't always see eye to eye with him? That was evident the day that you distraughtly confided in Samuel over Saul's actions against the Amalekites and also told him that the king was having a statue constructed in his own image. You were obviously bothered."

"Yes, of course. I don't always see eye to eye with the king, but we openly discuss our different views," Abner said defensively.

"Is that right?" Adino asked, knowing that Abner wasn't being completely honest. "That is not the way I see it. Sure you disagree with Saul, probably on many things. This is understandable, but I truly doubt that you would ever confront him. Instead, I imagine that you always hold your tongue and remain loyal, partly because you feel that you owe him. He has appointed you as a general in his army because of your relation to him, has he not?"

"He is my cousin," Abner blurted out in an obstinate manner, "But I have certainly earned my rank. Besides, it is no secret that as far as my own loyalty goes, my blood relationship is the one thing that I likewise admit will always keep me on the side of King Saul. Secondary to that fact is the obvious point that Saul is the king of this nation, chosen by the people and recognized by the elders, including your own father and grandfather. He was crowned by the prophet Samuel himself."

"Aha! So you do heed the justice of Samuel, and recognize him as High-Judge and prophet," Adino stated.

"Of course I recognize Samuel's position and also his past role in this nation's triumphs," Abner confirmed with an agitated look on his face. "But Samuel is no longer a part of the equation. He has been stationed in Ramah and his voice has been quelled."

"Well, you are so close to the king, surely you know as much or more than I do on the details of the recent falling out between the two men," Adino yielded, before changing the subject. "And I am quite positive that you know much more than I concerning the details of the kings plan to attack Philistia. But surely you can't be in agreement with Saul and his brash tactics. It is just not an opportune time to engage in such a substantial undertaking. You said it yourself, our prophet, the man responsible for our victories in the past, is currently exiled in Ramah, meanwhile there seems to be a power struggle going on between the elders and the king. Don't you understand the significance of all this?"

"Yes, I understand," Abner answered with confidence.

"I see," Adino said as he nodded his head in patronizing fashion, which seemed to perturb Abner all the more. The mighty man understood that his questions were beginning to get to the general and continued, "We can not just stand by and watch our nation fall apart around us. Are you willing to act on behalf of your country and help me out or not?"

"No doubt Samuel has put you up to something," Abner responded while trying to remain composed. After a few brief moments he was able to shake off his slight irritation, and return to an amiable mood as he conceded the issue, "Listen Adino, I like you. I think that you are a somewhat peculiar man, but nonetheless I see strength and honesty in you. Plus, what you have said is true. This nation is once again becoming divided, and I can't honestly say whether or not this new plan of the king's will bring us closer together or tear us apart. That is not my job. I am a soldier. Nonetheless, if things are to turn for the worst, you and I should not become enemies. Let us work things out. I want to see Israel prosper as much as you do."

"Great, so you will grant my request," Adino said in anticipation.

"I trust the motives of Samuel. That is the only reason that I will not completely stand in your way. I will therefore allow you to take your men and leave for now," Abner offered. "Nobody really knows that your small entourage has been with me over this short period of time, so I don't see any harm in them leaving. And you have probably already realized that I was never really serious about stopping their departure or yours for that matter. I figure that unless you and your men follow the king's edict and report into duty, the lot of you will eventually be considered seditious rebels and end up warranted for arrest. Well, I say let the king's henchmen worry about all that. I have enough to agonize over. But as far as releasing other men who are already accounted for, not even the elders have that authority anymore. And besides, no one from that list is in this camp."

This last statement of Abner's was uttered with a suspicious tone, which caused Adino to push the issue, "Are you sure? There are a lot of men here. You couldn't possibly know them all."

"There may very well be some," Abner allowed, again in an annoyed voice. "But I could hardly account for the names of every soldier under my command. You asked me if I recognized anyone from your lists currently in this camp. My answer is no." As Adino stood up to leave, Abner continued to express his remorse over the issue, "I wish that I could do more to help you, but considering the circumstances, I don't know how I could possibly offer more assistance without breaking my allegiance to Saul. I mean what can I possibly do? I am stuck in the middle."

Just as Abner finished, one of the palace scribes arrived with a message from the king. The general read it and enthusiastically let Adino know of its contents, "The king has ordered us to begin preparations. The army is to march directly from here to Azekah and Sochoh where we will wait for the rest of Israel's men from the tribal militias to meet up with us as directed by Saul's edict. Once that plan is in place, we will mount an offensive against the Philistines. Maybe you should reconsider staying with us, Adino? There will be much valor to claim in such a campaign."

"I see that you do indeed see Israel becoming victorious in this war against Philistia then?" Adino responded. "You seem bent on war."

"I can't help it," the general admitted. "Like I said, I am a soldier at heart. I believe in fighting to win."

But then Adino told the general something that thwarted his momentary reverie, "I haven't mentioned it yet, but I am afraid that your men's worst fears about facing off with the

Philistines are justifiable."

Abner gave Adino a perplexed look as he questioned him, "What are you talking about?"

"Back in Carmel, when we first met," Adino explained.

"Yes, what about it?" the general asked. He now wore a smirk and was very intrigued over any further undisclosed information that Adino could offer.

"Your men were afraid of the Philistines, and claimed that they had giants, which fight for them," Adino told him in a foreboding tone. "Well, it is true. I have seen one with my own eyes,"

The general immediately chuckled nervously over Adino's assertion as he had previously done after mentioning the prospect himself back at Carmel. Though, his delight was short lived. After recognizing the solemn expression Adino wore and realizing that he was actually serious, Abner's countenance likewise became somber. "Why didn't you tell me this before," he questioned with a severe look. "And how many giants could they possibly have in their armies?"

Adino quickly recounted the story of how he had met up with Bacchus and his Philistine minder, Lahmi. He told the general all he knew about the true existence of the giants and their current role of making war in the lands over the Great Sea. "...So you see," Adino finished with his recap, "I have learned some interesting details about these giants and am personally able to substantiate their existence. I have also learned that declaring war on their homeland could be a terrible mistake on the part of Israel."

"But you told me before that these giants are mere men. You of all people could go up against one of them, could you not?" Abner worriedly asked.

"Perhaps, but bringing down a giant would be no easy task, and if there are numerous such beings that would be all the more difficult," Adino admitted. "That is why I have already told you that in serious times such as these it is important to take directions from the likes of Samuel, a pious man who is directed by God."

After contemplating all that Adino had to say concerning their formidable enemy, Abner reconsidered his offer to help. He sized up the mighty man by audibly discerning his intentions one last time, "You say that you are gathering these men for a noble purpose?" The general then pondered the issue over for a moment longer before calling for his courier who was waiting outside of the tent. "Against my better judgment, I am going to trust you," he told Adino. "And despite your unwillingness to completely confide your plans to me, I will have some of the men off of your list called up for you. This should prove to you my propensity for confrontation with the king."

"But I thought you said that you did not recognize anyone from the lists?" Adino asked.

"I said that there was no one currently in the camp, which I recognized. The fact is, there are presently three men whose names are likewise mentioned on those rolls that are out leading the last of the raids into Amalek; they are the brothers Abishai, Azahel, and Joab. The problem is that these are the renowned sons of Zeruiah, three of the best men in all of our ranks. If the king finds out that I let them accompany you on an errand for Samuel, he will probably be more than a little irate."

Adino began to think of the king's recent edict along with Abner's concerns. "Yes, it does seem that the king and I are interested in procuring the best possible support for our individual agendas," he said, uttering his sudden realization aloud. "Trust me. Don't worry about the king," Adino then declared with a glimmer in his eye.

"What are you up to now?" Abner asked. "No, don't tell me. I think that you have the right idea. The less I know the better."

"After these three brothers return, just have them meet me at the king's palace in Gibeah. I will take care of the rest," Adino said with a smile. "And don't be surprised if the next time the two of you meet the king commends you for your decision to help me out in such a manner."

The mighty man and his troop left the camp of Abner that very night. As they rode away, Abner shook his head in contemplation over what it was that Adino intended to do. "Ride, my friend," the general said under his breath with a look of concern, "and may God save us all…"

15

After hearing of the debacle that Doeg had caused at the assembly, the king immediately summoned the Syrian to appear before his court. It was evident that a reprimand was in order.

"Are you my Supreme Advisor or not?" Saul barked. "You come to me with all these plans for change, but when I entrust you to impart my new decrees to the Council of elders, you botch the entire affair. I will not be made a fool. Do you understand me, Doeg? Maybe you are unprepared to assume the authority, which I have granted you? Do you know what other advisor of mine was unprepared to assume authority?"

Doeg knew all too well of whom the king was referring to and began to utter his name, "Jepth—"

"—That's right," the king cut him off and continued in his incensed tone, "Jephthah, and if you can recall, your predecessor did not meet with a very enviable fate after you took over his position. Do I need to start looking for your replacement already?"

"No! No your Highness," Doeg plead. "I have already made plans to reassemble the Council. Then I will reiterate your orders and see that the proper changes are being made, my king."

Saul looked over to his advisors deciding which one of them to seek advice from over the current matter. He then suddenly fixed his gaze upon Zephaniah, who had taken a seat amongst the rest of the court, and addressed her in a probing manner, "Tell me. What do you think of Doeg's inability to keep order amongst the Council of Elders, and what exactly should we do about his apparent incompetence?"

Everyone knew that the fate of the Supreme Advisor was being placed into the hands of Zephaniah who now stood up and then looked directly over at Doeg as she thought about the situation for a moment. "What do I think of Doeg?" she repeated as she gazed ambivalently at the man in question and then back at Saul. Meanwhile, Doeg lowered his head and walked up the steps of Samuel's platform. It seemed his only place of refuge at the moment.

Although no known offense had been committed on the part of either party, many of those present believed that Zephaniah and Doeg were enviable of each other's authority and ranking. The rest of the king's advisors therefore waited anxiously for her response. But then, to the surprise of everyone in the room, she exonerated Doeg. "Nothing my king," Zephaniah said as she turned back to face Saul. "Do nothing to him for the time being. Perhaps he will be more successful at the next Council meeting."

Doeg seemed to breathe a big sigh of relief before lifting his head up in a composed manner. Meanwhile, King Saul appeared rather astounded with the woman's sympathy for the Supreme Advisor. Saul had sensed animosity amongst the two from the beginning of their appointments and was somewhat displeased that he was unable to use this occasion to draw it out into the open.

"Very well," Saul replied rather drearily, announcing his acceptance of Zephaniah's verdict. "I will give you one more chance to prove yourself, Doeg. But you had better not let me down again." The king then began to massage the sides of his temples with his palms and to grab handfuls of his hair between his fingers.

The Supreme Advisor took notice of this tell-tale display of agitation. He immediately gave a look in the direction of Zephaniah who likewise stared back at Doeg with an understanding expression on her face.

"It appears that you are showing signs of fatigue, my king. Perhaps you need something to ease your troubled mind," Doeg said, offering his condolence. "I am afraid that you have become much too worried over my ability to handle Israel's current affairs, and I only wish to ensure you and your entire court that I will not let your Highness down." The Supreme Advisor then called for Saul's instrumentalists who immediately entered the king's courtroom and began playing some soothing music.

Meanwhile, Zephaniah did her part to aid the king. She quickly went to Saul's side. "I believe some medicinal herbs will likewise help ease your troubled mind," she offered. The woman then made a declaration to the court as she administered the king his tonic, "I believe that Doeg is correct. King Saul's recent afflictions are more than likely a result of the agony that has been caused him by the likes of the uncooperative Council members. At times such as this, he needs to be able to count on all of us as his advisors."

Saul patted Zephaniah's arm and thanked her for the empathetic avowal, "...I am pleased to see that you and Doeg are starting to work well together while promoting my concerns and wellbeing." The king spoke in a contented yet agonized tone as he continued to massage his right temple and exercise the hinge of his jaw by rotating it about. "Tell me then, Doeg," he said with a calm voice, "how exactly will you remedy all this trouble that you imprudently stirred up at the assembly with those miserable Council members?"

Doeg then explained to Saul and the entire court of imperial advisors what his new plans entailed, "The next time we meet, the elders will learn their place. As I previously mentioned, I have already arranged for a future meeting between the Council of Seventy and myself. As part of the summons that I sent out to them, each of the senior Council members have been informed that this meeting will not take place in the customary grand courtyard, adjacent to the palace here, and which they hardly deserve to call their own. It will instead be held at the opposite end of Gibeah, in the modest setting of the soldier's headquarters. I want the elders out of their own element, and besides should events become riotous I want their actions quelled immediately, with overwhelming force. I have likewise had messengers inform the Councilmen that no one else is to accompany them into the city and that no weapons will be allowed at the meeting. So, please believe me when I say that the matter is settled. The Council will reassemble in a fortnight with me as the head of discourse, and all of the new decrees will be heard without interruption and obeyed without question."

The king seemed to approve of the plan, only inquiring what Doeg's motives could have been for delaying the meeting for such a long period. Doeg bowed graciously before continuing, "Two weeks gives me plenty of time to tend to the other matter that you appear so anxious about, my king." At this point the Supreme Advisor had regained his poise and spoke boastfully. "I intend to look into the situation concerning the priesthood and finally wrap up the loose ends that my predecessor has left for me," he maintained. "I had hopes of surprising you with a remedy to it all only after my plans were completely carried out."

Suddenly the king slumped forward on his throne. Zephaniah and a number of other persons in the room immediately rushed over to help him. But Saul quickly recovered and repelled the lot of them, save Zephaniah. "My headaches grow worse every day, and I become exhausted so easily," he said quietly as he began to stare remotely at Doeg, who still stood atop Samuel's platform. He attempted to gather his thoughts while closing his eyes and beginning to rub his temples once more. Then the king's vision suddenly became blurred.

Saul opened and closed his eyes several times to try and focus on the person now situated on top of Samuel's stage. As his eyesight converged upon the face of the individual, Saul saw not Doeg but the image of Samuel standing there instead. He began to shout in a loud voice, "No, you will not take away my kingdom! You will not have my kingdom!" Then, while King Saul continued with his words of rebuke, the face slowly morphed from that of Samuel's to the form of a hideous specter. With ghostly white skin and hair, along with a contorted face, the creature deliberately began to float in the direction of the king.

Saul's sudden yells had already halted the music as Doeg and the rest of the room looked on with bewilderment over his nonsensical behavior. "What is the matter, my king? I am not after your kingdom. It is me, Doeg," the Supreme Advisor said as he began to walk down from the platform and make his way towards the king.

The phantom, in the intervening moment, hovered over the room and then began to speak to the king with a weeping voice, "Saul, we are coming for you." Then the courtyard's doors flew open and an uncanny wind rushed into the room. "We are coming for your soul!" the voice screeched as the phantom gradually began to pick up speed and descend in the direction of the throne.

On hearing the voice of the evil spirit, the king yelled out once more, "I know who you are, I know what you want!" All the members of the court watched—unaware of the apparition's presence—while the king then threw his arms up and covered his face as if he was bracing himself for a fall.

Saul then heard nothing but silence. He lowered his guard and was finally able to hear the feigning voice of Doeg, "...your soul. And peace to your mind."

"What? What did you say?" the king demanded in nervous

apprehension. The treacherous figure was no longer there only Doeg and next to him was Zephaniah. The two were crouching near Saul and attempting to calm him.

Doeg repeated himself with a touch of artifice in his voice, "I was asking that the Almighty have mercy upon your soul, my lord, and bring peace to you. That is all. You seemed to have gotten yourself so stirred up. An appeal to the heavens seemed in order."

Saul examined Doeg with a scrutinizing eye and then looked up at the ceiling to reassure himself that the apparition was no longer there. "I did not know you to be a man of such admirable faith," the king said. "Nonetheless, I seemed to have recovered in a timely manner."

Doeg then stood up and sermonized to the king's court with an officious yet pretentious air, "We must use wisdom in times of trouble, and a plea to our God is often our best option. For, what better wisdom is there than that of our Lords?"

The king then complained, "It is this place. I tell you that it haunts me. I must get away from here and join my army as they trek to Elah and ready themselves for battle."

This last statement of Saul's seemed to trouble Doeg greatly. He hastily tendered his advice, "You must first rest, my king. We will send word that you will join your officers at Sochoh and Azekah within the coming weeks. And once you are feeling completely up to it, you will indeed join them. But to rush off at a time like this, when you are feeling so poorly, would not be a good idea at all."

"Perhaps you are right, Doeg," Saul conceded, apparently either forgiving or forgetting any and all of his earlier annoyance with the man. "A king who lacks confidence and poise does not instill the same in his soldiers." He then clanked his scepter on the ground and stood up as Zephaniah rushed to his side. "I am entrusting you to watch over my affairs and deliver what you have promised, my Supreme Advisor. In the meantime, I will continue to rest in hopes of a better morrow."

After Zephaniah ushered the king away and hastened him unto his chambers, Doeg addressed Saul's court in the same sanctimonious manner that he had assumed earlier, "I assure you that King Saul is smart to follow my advice. For, in truth, it is my greatest fear that his condition may yet worsen." The court muttered their agreement while Doeg continued with his discourse, "We will keep a watchful eye on him in the meantime..."

Upon her return, Zephaniah was surprised to find Doeg still speaking to the king's advisors concerning his future plans for Israel. She stood and listened at length noticing that the Syrian's demeanor was authoritative and self-assured. And as he spoke, it was becoming evident to her and all those present that Doeg was starting to live up to his sanction; he was without a doubt becoming the king's Advisor Supreme in uncontested form.

16

Feeling rather confident about himself, Doeg left the king's court late that day in high-spirits. He was accompanied by Zephaniah who likewise appeared pleased with Doeg's influence over both Saul and the members of the royal court. As they strolled through one of the remote corridors of the palace, Zephaniah gave him report, "I have given the king another tonic, his last of the day. It will soothe his mind."

The self-possessed Doeg stood, contented. "The king is becoming quite the mad man!" he commented in a calm voice.

"Careful what you say," Zephaniah warned him.

"I have to tell you; I am getting a little concerned with his mood swings and peculiar behavior, which I fear may one day occur at my expense," Doeg professed. "When he loses his temper, it makes me a little uneasy." Doeg then began to talk in a whispered voice as he looked around to make sure that there were no bystanders in the vicinity, "I thought that we had him under control, but it appears that more drastic measures may be needed. I want you to head back up to his chambers and administer him another dose of his medicine. I will be up in just a short while."

"Yes, it seems that Saul's paranoia is more difficult to manage than I originally realized. I should perhaps adjust the medicinal tonics that I have been giving to him," Zephaniah suggested.

The conversation was then interrupted as Zephaniah's gaze was drawn over the shoulder of Doeg and to the captain of the guard who had suddenly appeared standing behind the scrawny framed Syrian. Noticing the distracted stare of Zephaniah and guessing at the cause, the supreme advisor reeled around and instantly began complaining, "I told you never to lurk up behind me like that. What is wrong with you?"

"I am sorry to interrupt," the captain said in an acquiescent tone, "but I have been told by the entrance hall guards that there is a visitor here with a request to see the king."

"Well get rid of him!" Doeg ordered. "The king is not feeling well and is in no position to accept guests. And after you are finished with that task," Doeg then told the captain, "I want to see you in my quarters. I have some important plans that I need to go over with you concerning my upcoming dealings with the priesthood."

"Very well," the captain replied. "I will relay your orders to the guards."

"What an imbecile" Doeg remarked in reference to the captain as the man walked away.

Zephaniah just shook her head. "I will speak with you later then," she interposed as she turned and headed off in order to pay a visit to the king.

A short time later, Doeg made it to his private dwellings, which were located in one of the far corners of a forgotten palace wing. The Supreme Advisor had purposefully chosen the locale, because it was away from the bustling activity of the king's court. Here, in a room adjacent to his bedchambers Doeg had set up a headquarters of sorts, complete with many luxuriant articles and modern contrivances. This is also where he would receive his meals, at a large table with several mundane chairs on each side. These were all offset by the ornate quality of one grand seat at the end, which resembled a modest yet discriminative throne.

It was in this same garish seat that Doeg now sat, as he had on many other afternoons, planning his next course of action while awaiting the captain. After hearing a heavy knock on the door, Doeg impatiently answered it. "What took you so long—" he began to say but then cut himself short. Instead of the captain, whom Doeg considered a craven being, the man who now stood before him had a very commanding presence. He was a specimen of strength, face aglow with confidence. "Yes what is it?" Doeg said in an exasperated voice. "Why, for all good reasons, could you possibly be banging on my door?"

"My name is Adino Ben Hachmon, and I am here to see the king," the stranger said to the surprise of Doeg.

"That inept, pitiful man. He never gets his orders right," the Supreme Advisor lowly whispered, referring to the captain of the guard. "Well, you were supposed to have been told that the king is unavailable. Now go away. I am very busy at the moment."

But as Doeg attempted to shut the door, Adino reached out and stopped it. "Listen, I said that I have come to see the king," he assertively announced. "And I am not leaving here until I do."

Doeg's first reaction was to call the guards and have Adino escorted away. He looked down the hallways in both directions, but strangely there were no such guards in the vicinity at the moment. The Supreme Advisor then perused the determination on the mighty man's face and the handle of the large sword that he now rested one of his hands upon in an intimidating manner. Doeg decided that it would be better to hear him out. "Very well," he said as he turned and allowed Adino to follow him into the room. "I know who you are, Josheb-Basshebeth. Being related to two of our prominent Council elders and a mighty man of war, your reputation precedes you," Doeg stated as he confidently took a seat on his grand throne. "As for my name and rank, I am Doeg the king's Supreme Advisor."

Adino immediately took notice of some of the ostentatious articles within the room. "Nice place you have fashioned for yourself here," he commented as he took a seat at the far end of the table, opposite Doeg. "And yes, I already know who you are as well. The guards at the front entrance informed me of your status and relayed the message that the king was resting but that you could see me in his stead?"

"Yes, well sometimes messages get misconstrued, but that hardly seems relevant at the moment," Doeg said with contempt for the captain in his voice once again. "Since you are here now, tell me, why do you appear so adamant in wanting to see King Saul?"

"I am concerned about the lack of support that the king has received in his attempts to take the fight to the Philistines," Adino said as he began to explain his personal wishes to join up with Saul on a mission to recruit the thus far reluctant tribal militias. Having thoroughly prepared himself to argue his case before Saul, Adino went into vast detail over his thoughts on the matter, telling of his past service to the country, his history with the Philistines, and his loyalty to both the king and Samuel over the prior years. "...I am ready to serve Israel again in any way that may be necessary," he concluded as Doeg sat in the same taciturn position that he had maintained the entire time Adino had been speaking.

It was not immediately apparent if the Supreme Advisor was in favor of such a proposition. The man simply remained silent for quite some time as his expression changed from that of perplexity to nervousness and then to intrigue. After pondering the prospects of the situation in this manner for quite some time, Doeg looked musingly at the mighty man. "And what would you do if you fail to coerce the elders and their tribesmen to obey the king's edict?" he asked curiously.

"Is not the punishment for this imprisonment?" Adino replied. "Any man who refuses me by disregarding Saul's royal order would simply be subject to arrest on the spot."

"And you would be willing to go that far?" Doeg asked, testing Adino's devotion to the task.

"I would indeed," the mighty man replied. "But I would also need a small force of men to back me, of course."

"But of course," the Supreme Advisor unexpectedly assented. "And how many men might that require?"

Never guessing that his case would actually be considered so readily, Adino pondered the question for a moment, "In addition to my current troop of men?" He then gave his answer in a hesitant voice, "If I am going to be successful in an important task such as this, I would like to have at least an additional thirty or forty loyal men to serve directly under me."

Doeg appeared pleasantly surprised at the trifling amount of men that Adino was requesting for what he himself understood to be an impossible undertaking without the support of the elders. "That is all that you need to enlist thousands of possibly uncooperative men for war?" he asked with an uneasy look about him. "And I suppose that you will want to hand pick the best in all the land to accompany you?"

For a moment, Adino thought that Doeg was beginning to suspect ulterior motives in the same manner that Abner had. The mighty man immediately referenced the general hoping that Doeg would accept the high ranking man's espousal as proof of his own integrity, "General Abner has told me that it would be possible to spare a few soldiers in order to help me out on a full time basis." Adino then spoke very quickly as he continued to take his previous conversation with Abner somewhat out of context, "Furthermore, the general has volunteered to help me out in any way that he possibly can. Should I therefore ever need a larger force to implement the king's edict, Abner could easily supply me with a compelling group of henchmen from his large battalion. I am sure that he wouldn't mind at all."

Adino prepared himself to argue his case further, to

additionally stretch truths if he had to, but before he could say another word, Doeg spoke up once more, "I think it would be fair to call it providence which has brought you to my table today. For, I believe that your efforts could possibly breathe new life into the king's seemingly failed edict. And I do not believe that the king could have asked for a more inspiring person to step forward at the moment. This will certainly bolster his mood. To be sure, after hearing your sincerity, I am prepared to present your case to King Saul even as he lay sick in his chambers. I want you to wait here, Adino. I should be able to give you the king's response directly.

Doeg did as he had promised and made his way straight to the king's quarters. As he arrived, he met Zephaniah who was just stepping out of Saul's chambers.

"Quiet, he is sleeping, but not very soundly," she quickly informed him.

With a look of dismay on his face, Doeg confided to her the arrival of Adino and told her what he was offering. "...I do not however trust a word that this man is saying," he said at the end of his summary concerning the impromptu meeting. "I believe that he may instead be here as an agent of Samuel, to spy on us and bring ruin to you and I both."

"I don't understand," Zephaniah stated. "You just said that he has volunteered to gather the militias. Is this just a ploy?"

"It very well could be. Anyways, the last thing that I need is this meddlesome man interfering with my plans around here," Doeg divulged. "He sounds like more of a hindrance than a help."

"What possible trouble could this man be if we grant him his wish then?" Zephaniah questioned. "Unless of course you are afraid that he will show you up by successfully enforcing the king's edict?"

"That is the last of my worries," Doeg grumbled in a low voice. "He will not get anywhere without the backing of the Council elders. That is what makes me so suspicious of him. Showing up here with an offer to help gets him conveniently involved in the middle of my plans. He works for the prophet I tell you. And just suppose what will happen if Samuel gets back into the good graces of King Saul."

Zephaniah calmly spoke back to Doeg, "Then you have your answer on what you should do. Call his bluff and let this Adino attempt to raise support for the king. If he is sincere, it will keep him distracted and far away from Gibeah. Besides, if and when he fails, it will only make you look all the better for effectively convincing the Council members to adhere to the edict."

"Yes, you are right," the Supreme Advisor consented. "I believe that the king should grant this request of Adino's. He will be deputized immediately." Doeg then gave Zephaniah a sly smile. "I trust that you can attain the king's seal and make the act all the more official."

"I don't think that will be a problem," Zephaniah answered back as she bore a cunning smile of her own.

"And how exactly is our beloved monarch faring?" Doeg inquired as he peaked in on Saul who was by now sound asleep. As he closed the door once more and turned around to face Zephaniah, he began to laugh. "Did you see their faces earlier today when the king asked you how to deal with me? Ha! Can you imagine? Of all the people to ask, he chose my most unwavering ally. They are all fools."

"I believe that I have proven my loyalty to you then?" Zephaniah asked rather brashly.

"Indeed you have, my sweet. Indeed you have," the Supreme Advisor affirmed in a pleased tone. As the two walked away from the king's chambers, Doeg continued speaking in a loud and boastful voice, "And did you see the response that I got when I offered my prayer for the king. Ha-ha, I know the power that piety carries. I know very well the importance of appearing just a little righteous for the comfort of one's underlings..."

PART III

LION'S SNARE

17

According to Saul, the priests were guilty of continually undermining him and his authority while constantly speaking poorly of his administration. This incensed the king, and as explained by his personal physician, Zephaniah, as she addressed the king's court the day following his majesty's partial breakdown, was also a major cause for Saul's increasingly ill health. "It is the very reason that he lies in bed today, absent from his throne," the woman of Endor explained. "Doeg's expertise on resolving the issue is at the moment of the utmost importance to our nation..."

Thus, in order to prove that he had the ability to deliver in time of need, Doeg, his majesty's Supreme Advisor, made a scrupulous effort to handle the matter with the priesthood. By accomplishing what others had not been able to, he hoped to further his status as a superior amongst his contemporaries, an ambition the piteous man found to be worthy of all his efforts.

And with the knowledge that he had attained over the years, the Supreme Advisor honestly believed that this would undoubtedly be a simple problem to address. For, he had learned from his time spent as an ambassador that the easiest method of dealing with a well respected group, such as the priests, was to designate a scapegoat from amongst the lot of them, one who would bear the sins of all and stand as an exemplar for punishment.

But after a week of attempting to corroborate the claims of the king concerning the disparaging priests, the Supreme Advisor was not able to find one single case that was worthy of prosecution. Doeg began to consider the fact that the king truly was a paranoid mad man and that as the Supreme Advisor he would simply have to let Saul know that all accusations against the priesthood truly were unfounded. But then Doeg remembered what had happened to Jephthah and considered the king's inclination to act illogically. Regardless of how beneficial Zephaniah's tonics had been for Saul, his outbursts were unpredictable and dangerous.

With all of this in mind, Doeg continued his pursuit of an offender with the persistent aid of the captain of the guard. On the eighth day of his investigation, after looking into the proceedings taking place at the sanctuary in Gibeah and dejectedly returning to the palace, Doeg finally caught his break. The palace priest of all people was busily engaged in conversation with one of his cohorts and uttered the name of Saul while pointing out that going to war with the Philistines could be a costly mistake on the part of Israel. Doeg motioned for the captain of the guard to take notice. "Bring this man to my quarters," the Supreme Advisor ordered. "I would like to have a word with him."

An interrogation ensued, but at the end of it all the palace priest appeared less of a threat than originally anticipated. Yet, all hope was not lost for Doeg. During the course of the palace priest's examination a name was elicited that did indeed seem promising as one that would merit castigation. Doeg subsequently made immediate arrangements for a visit to the Chief Priest of Beersheba. He then called in the captain of the guard once more. "I have declared that I will personally reign in the priests," he explained to the scar faced man.

"And with your help I will accomplish just that."

"I don't understand," the captain said in a hesitant tone. "What wrong have these men done? To me, it doesn't seem like they should be scrutinized for such trivial practices."

Doeg immediately became enraged, "How dare you question my authority. You aren't here to ask questions or offer your opinion. You are here to take orders." And then, using the same similarly threatening methods of the king, he yelled at the man, "Is it possible that I need to find someone else to do your job? You know that's what we do with the incompetent! We replace them with someone who knows how to get things done properly. And I don't have to remind you of the fate that befalls the pitiful soul who needs replacing."

Although the captain was mammoth compared to other men, and especially in contrast to the puny Doeg, he had learned not to challenge authority. Thus he asked no more questions and instead responded in a down trodden manner, "That sort of talk isn't necessary. Just tell me the plan."

"Good, you understand your place then," Doeg said, now in a more composed tone. "Listen up carefully. We are going to pay a little visit to someone who holds a very powerful position, and when we are done with him, he will forever remain an example of what happens to those who disregard the authority of the king..."

The man whom Doeg spoke of did truly hold a highly esteemed position. Appointed by Samuel personally, he was well admired by the other members of the priesthood and loved by all those who were acquainted with him throughout the southern lands of Israel. He was both honest and sincere in his duties as a priest. His name, Jehoiada, meant "The one God knows", and it was certainly a very fitting name; his entire life was dedicated to serving God. Second only to this sublime commitment came an undying devotion to his son, Benaiah. This was his only child, and because of very sad circumstances, Jehoiada had raised him alone as a widower since the boy was a mere five years of age.

Fourteen years had elapsed since the tragic incident, fourteen long years since he had received his first major appointment as the regional priest of Beersheba. The occasion had been a joyous one as he led his household from their previous home, in Bethel, and south to Beersheba...

In all, there were twenty eight men and twelve women including servants and hired hands who helped Jehoiada and his family relocate to their new home. With a large flock of sheep and many head of oxen to travel with, the journey was often slow and arduous, but Jehoiada encouraged his family to enjoy the trip and did his best not to rush the expedition. They would often stop and take long rests, which would include a hearty meal where Jehoiada would visit with his family and point out the natural beauty of the countryside.

At night, he would walk out to the fields and check on his flocks and his trusty group of shepherds. On many occasions, he would even have the men get rest while he himself would stay awake with the animals. The contented priest found tranquility and peace on those nights and would often tell his wife, Moriah, how close it made him feel to God. His sanguine attitude often rubbed off on her and it wasn't too long before she was joining her husband for evening walks out to the fields where the animals were peacefully grazing.

"The moon is exceptionally beautiful, more so than I could have ever described it to you. I am glad that you came out," Jehoiada told his wife one particularly wondrous night as they sat on a large boulder overlooking the grazing sheep.

"Yes and the crisp night air is very inspirational," Moriah added as she took in a deep breath and stood up looking out at the sky. "I have never seen so many stars; they stretch from one end of the heavens to the next. And to think, our God has created it all."

Jehoiada looked at his beautiful wife in appreciation. He knew that he had married the perfect woman for him, and as he glanced up at the star filled sky, he whispered thanks to God for his blessings.

"What did you say?" Moriah asked as she turned to her husband.

"I didn't say anything to you," he responded.

"Yes, I heard you say something under your breath," Moriah persisted in a playful manner.

"Oh no, it wasn't me. Perhaps it was one of the sheep," Jehoiada jested as his smile grew bigger and his teeth shown brilliantly in the moonlight.

Moriah giggled. "I feel so youthful out here tonight," she commented, truly feeling nostalgic. "Remember when we were young and we used to go out and gaze at the stars all night and talk?"

"Come back and sit by me. I have a surprise for you," Jehoiada told her as he reached over to his satchel and pulled out a small khalil. He put the small reed instrument to his lips and played a delicate song for his wife.

Moriah sat and listened intently as she continued to enjoy the beautiful night sky. "That was nice," she said softly and kissed her husband on the cheek as his serenade came to an end. "You haven't played for me in quite some time."

"I know," Jehoiada said as he took off his fleece and wrapped it around his wife's shoulders. "I promise that I will more often after we get to Beersheba."

They sat quietly for a little while longer enjoying the serenity until Moriah began to shiver. "It seems that your sweet song has summoned the cold," she regretfully told him. "And unfortunately, my dear husband, I must get out of this chilly air and head back to camp. Are you coming with me?"

"I want to stay a bit longer," the contented priest explained before promising to shortly join her. He then called for one of the shepherds to escort her back to their camp.

Moriah carefully climbed down from the boulder and reminded Jehoiada, "You know, Benaiah has been asking, for several days now, when he can come out with you to watch the animals."

"I know. That is all he has been talking about lately," Jehoiada responded.

"Will you let him come out soon then?" she asked.

"I realize that he won't let either of us alone until he gets the chance to be a shepherd," Jehoiada conceded. "I suppose that I can plan a night for us to camp out amongst the sheep. As long as there is a warm fire and plenty of blankets, I don't see any harm in it."

Moriah smiled. "That would please him very much. Don't stay much longer. It is too cold out here," she said turning to go. "You could get ill with what little clothes you have on." Jehoiada took heed of his wife's advice and played only one more short song for the night before returning back to camp.

As they set out the next morning, young Benaiah walked beside his father, whom had assumed his customary position at the front of the expedition. Once again, he asked when he could spend the night out watching the animals, "I would be a good shepherd, papa. I would watch the sheep and make sure that they did not wander off too far."

"Yes, with all your energy, you would make a fine shepherd," his father agreed. "I'll tell you what. The next time that I camp out, I will take you with me."

After hearing this, Benaiah went wild. He yelled out with glee and ran a circle around his father. He then proceeded to run back to where his mother and the rest of the women were to make his announcement, "Mother, papa has said that I can camp out with the flocks and be a shepherd with him."

"That's wonderful, sweetheart," she said as she smiled at Jehoiada who was now walking backwards up ahead, watching them.

"And will you stay awake, or will you fall asleep?" Moriah's hand maiden asked Benaiah.

"A good shepherd sleeps with one eye open and one closed," he explained proudly.

Moriah laughed. "It sounds like you have been listening to

your father's stories again," she said as she looked up toward Jehoiada with plans to give him a scolding finger, but he wasn't there.

"I tell you, my stories are all true," Jehoiada exclaimed, now standing next to her. He had relinquished his position at the head of the procession and had come back to visit with them.

Benaiah ran over and grabbed his father's hand. "Yes, papa. Tell me another story," he pleaded in excitement.

"Please do," Moriah said as she took hold of his other hand. "Tell us a wonderful story."

"Alright, if I must," Jehoiada pleasantly consented. "Which story would you like to hear?"

"Tell us about Samson again, wont you, papa?" Benaiah asked as the three of them walked hand in hand on their journey.

"Ok, Samson it is," Jehoiada obligingly agreed as he launched into one of his familiar narratives on the life of Samson...

* * *

"...It had been seventy years since the death of the High-Judge Abdon the son of Hillel the Pirathonite, and all twelve tribes had since fallen into subjugation under the rule of the Philistines and the might of their iron weaponry. It was well known and accepted that, as prophesied, the son of Manoah and Lydia was to be the next High-Judge of the twelve tribes of Israel and that their son, Samson, would likewise be the one who would bring deliverance from their enemies. He was raised accordingly and would keep the vow of a Nazarite for his entire life.

That meant that starting from the time that he was in his mother's womb unto the day of his death, Samson was to commit himself to God while denying himself three specific things: He was not to drink wine or other strong drink; he was not to be exposed to the contamination of anything dead or unclean; and he was not to cut his hair. Yet despite his strict rearing, three weeks after his twentieth birthday, he was beginning to show signs of a disconcerting nature.

The first of his actions that brought scrutiny from his tribesmen was the fact that Samson had asked for his father to make arrangements for him to marry Alenia, a Philistine woman. He said that he had met her on a visit to the Philistine city of Ashkelon and that they were in love. Although this act was not explicitly forbidden, it was looked upon by everyone from his homeland, including Samson's mother and father, as a questionable decision, mainly because the Philistines worshipped strange gods. Nevertheless, his father, who never denied anything to his son, made arrangements for the two to get married.

Considering the circumstances, Manoah did try his best to make it a quiet event in order to avoid drawing too much attention to this controversial decision. After all, Manoah reasoned, there were plenty of eligible women throughout Israel, which Samson could have chosen as his bride. And indeed on the day that the young man made his wedding announcement, there was much for the women to bemoan. For, he was both handsome and strong with long curly locks, which draped his astounding physique. It was also well known that Samson possessed magnificent strength to match his build as the result of God's bestowment.

"Alright, Samson my son, the ceremony will take place in one year," his father told him after making arrangements for the wedding.

Samson sat talking with his mother about his plans after the wedding. "Thank you father," he said with excitement. "I was just telling mother about my future. After the festivities of the wedding feast, I shall return here with Alenia and dwell in my homeland as I seek a seat amongst the men of the city."

"You do have much to look forward to," Manoah exclaimed with a smile on his face. "But tell me something. Surely you don't intend to celebrate your wedding with the same revelries that take place as part of today's traditional marriage?"

"Oh Manoah," Lydia interjected. "Let our son live his life like an ordinary young man."

Manoah gave both his wife and his son a stern look before scolding the two of them, "But he is not just an ordinary young man, Lydia. And you Samson, have you forgotten your vows? You can not take part in such revelry, getting drunk on wine for an entire week and acting like a fool."

"No, father. Of course I will not be acting in such a manner, but still, I would like to have a traditional celebration like others have, an entire week when our families and friends come together in merriment for me and my beautiful wife. Let them drink their wine and toast to our success in matrimony, father. It will bring no reprieve on you."

"Well said, my son," Lydia rejoined.

His father thought over the prospect for a while and then nodded his head in agreement. "Very well, then. Let us plan the festivities."

Samson, accompanied by his mother and father, soon traveled to Timnoah, the village of his lovely bride-to-be, which was located on the outskirts of Ashkelon. There, his father happily gave into the whims of his son and used his wealth to organize a grand feast. At this feast there would be hundreds of friends and family belonging to both the bride and groom. Manoah began to get into the spirit of things as he bragged that it would be the most splendid celebration that the village had ever seen.

Samson left all the remaining wedding plans to his father and mother after telling them that he would like to get away for a while and think things out by taking a walk through the countryside. This was a usual habit of Samson and one that he had engaged in quite often. Both of his parents rather admired the young man's pensive tradition, and whether he was enjoying the countryside on foot or horseback it always seemed to help him unwind. "Yes son, that is a good idea," his mother told him. "But don't be gone for too long. We are leaving early tomorrow morning."

"I won't, mother," Samson assured her. What he didn't tell his parents was that his real motive for getting away on his own was to hopefully get another chance to visit with Alenia. He quickly made his way out of town and took a shortcut to the lands of her family, crossing over the hills and vineyards of the region. But soon the long walk and hot sun began to intensify the thirst of Samson, and as he meandered through the vineyards, he was reluctantly drawn to the richness of the grapes. They hung on the vines in an insidious fashion and the more he tried to ignore their plump skins, which shimmered with opaque ripeness, the more he was attracted to the fruit. Moreover, even though he knew that it was against his vows to partake of any type of grape, or drink made from the grape, his temptation grew by the moment.

Samson quickened his pace in an effort to keep his mind off of the lure of the vines, but this only enhanced his thirst all the more. Fully parched, he finally came to a stop. Standing within arms reach of the bundles of grapes, he leaned over in an effort to pluck the delicious looking lot from its vine, but then he froze as his ears picked up the faint sound of an animals growl. Samson stood up and perused the surrounding topography, but he saw nothing. After studying the many rows of grapevines for a little while longer, he temporarily forgot his thirst and once again set out.

As he navigated his way through the field this time, the Nazarite was no longer distracted by the sweetness of the forbidden fruit that surrounded him. Samson instead concentrated as he looked and listened for any evidence of what he suspected to be an unwelcomed follower. The vigilant young man stepped softly over the brush, turning his head slightly to listen behind him. He then froze as the hairs on the back of his neck stood up.

Samson was suddenly sure that he heard the ravenous deep purr of something wild and dangerous. He spun around in a flash while the source of his suspicions revealed itself with a deafening roar. It was a lion of enormous proportions and it was running fiendishly towards him with every intention to pounce on him and devour his flesh.

But Samson was not afraid. On the contrary, just as an unassuming bear can be transformed into a fury when startled, the wrath of the mighty man was awakened. As he braced himself for the beast's tackle, the power of God came upon him and he caught the lion by the jaws just as it lunged toward him. The lion's eyes widened with instant regret over its choice in prey, and it tried in vane to immediately retreat from its attack, but it was too late. For, Samson already had a crushing grip on the beast and was relentlessly beginning to pull the lion's jaws from its sockets. Then with a loud cracking sound, the will of the vicious lion gave way. It soon lay lifeless in the grip of Samson who lifted it over his head with ease and hurled it out and over several rows of grapevines. Without any further distractions, Samson was soon able to make it to the home of Alenia's family.

After returning to see his own parents later, he told them how happy he was with his decision to get married. Yet, he had told neither his betrothed nor his parents of the incident with the lion that day.

In the spring of the following year, Samson and his parents returned to Timnoah. There was still much to accomplish before the wedding and once again while Manoah busied himself with the planning, Samson was off on another adventure. He had again decided to pay a visit to the lovely woman that he would soon be marrying, and for a second time, his planned visit led him through the vineyards of Timnoah's countryside. But this time there was no luscious fruits waiting to tempt him nor was there any wild beast lying in wait as Samson hurried to see his beloved. He was therefore able to make it to his destination without an incident, but he was soon to realize disappointment.

After a long afternoon of walking, Samson became very annoyed with the fact that neither Alenia nor her family was at home to greet him. He waited on their return, but after a short while, he began to feel hungry and rather put out. Hence, he decided to head back to the village. As Samson walked back through the vineyards, he began to think of the sweet grapes that he'd missed the previous summer. "If it hadn't of been for that menacing lion, I may very well have had the very first taste of the forbidden fruit of my vow," he thought to himself as he began to feel more and more irritated over the situation. His increasing hunger did little more than fuel the situation.

Samson walked for a while longer thinking about his disappointment until he suddenly realized that he was approaching the exact spot where the lion had made its hasty attack. He slowed his pace and began to scan the area. Sure enough, behind some blossoming vines next to an old tree stump, he spied the dried up carcass of the beast. Samson's soreness toward the animal peaked as he spied its remains in passing. But then he noticed something fascinating indeed. In the hollow of the animal's skeleton was a large beehive. He couldn't believe his luck and in an instant Samson had kicked, swatted, and scooped his way to a delicious golden harvest of sweet honey. His anger then turned to amusement as he walked along enjoying the treat, all the while thinking over the entire scenario.

By the time Samson joined up with his parents he was in such high spirits that he shared the honey with them. They appreciated the rich delight so much that they didn't even think to ask where he had gotten it from. Little did they suspect that their son had retrieved it from the remains of a dead lion.

* * *

...And that is all the time we have for storytelling right now," Jehoiada explained to the disappointment of Benaiah."

"But papa you didn't finish the story," the youngster complained.

"I know son," Jehoiada answered back, "but maybe after we have supper, I will tell you some more..."

18

Benaiah didn't let his father forget about the story. After they ate, he squeezed in between Moriah and Jehoiada. "Ok I am ready," he declared.

"Ready for what?" his mother asked inquisitively.

"I'm ready to hear more about Samson," Benaiah answered as he looked at his father impatiently.

Jehoiada rubbed his brow and then his eye with the palm of his hand displaying his weariness. Seeing her husband's dilemma, Moriah answered for him, "Benaiah, aren't you tired of your father's tales? He has already told you all about Samson many times before."

"No, I will never get tired of Samson. I am going to grow up to be strong just like him. And I will fight the Philistines and beat every last one of them," the boy adamantly declared.

"Benaiah, maybe another night. Now get yourself washed up and ready for bed." his mother told him firmly.

"Aw but papa promised me."

"I don't think he promised you. He merely said maybe—"

"—He did too," Benaiah demanded. "He told me that after we ate supper that he promised to tell me more about Samson. Didn't you Papa? Didn't you promise?"

"Benaiah!" his mother said in a scolding tone.

"I'll tell you what," Jehoiada said, finally speaking up. "I have a better idea. Why don't we take that trip out with the shepherds tonight, and I will tell you all about the adventures of Samson?"

Benaiah shouted with glee once more, "Alright, I will get my things papa just wait for me. I will be right back."

Moriah spoke to her husband in a sympathetic manner, "Aren't you too tired to go out for another night? Maybe you should do it another time."

"I did tell Benaiah that I would take him out, and in two days we will have reached our destination," Jehoiada explained looking up at the cloud filled sky. "There seems to be a storm coming in. I imagine that tomorrow the weather may be too bad. So I might as well take him tonight. If he misses out, he will never let me live it down."

"Ok, it's up to you," Moriah said in a resigned manner. "Granted, I have to admit that you have a lot more energy than your wife does."

By nightfall, with the help of the shepherds, Benaiah and his father had gathered plenty of firewood and built a large fire out at the far end of a field with lush grass where the sheep had chosen to graze. In addition, Jehoiada had the men put up a tent to provide some warmth in order to fend off the coldness of the early morning.

"I thought that you said that you don't build a fire or a tent when you are out with the animals?" Benaiah questioned with a suspicious look on his face.

Jehoiada sat down on one of the nearby logs and explained as he fed the flames some branches, "A shepherd is usually out here by himself, my son. But since there are many of us tonight, we will take advantage of the situation. Some will stay awake while others will sleep. That way, when morning comes, we will all be well rested. What do you say?"

"Ah, well I guess that will be alright. Except, I am not going to sleep. I am going to stay awake all night," Benaiah insisted.

Jehoiada chuckled and patted his son on the head. "That sounds good, son. I bet you will stay awake. Now then, are you ready for the rest of that story?"

"Am I ever!" Benaiah said as he picked up a piece of wood and tossed it into the fire, mimicking the actions of his father. "Now remember to start where you left off, papa. Samson had just shared the honey, and he was waiting to get married."

"That's right. You have quite the memory, Benaiah," Jehoiada praised his son's recollection then made himself more comfortable by sitting down on the ground close to the fire. He then launched into the story...

* * *

"...Just as Manoah had promised, the wedding feast, which had been meticulously arranged for his son was the largest celebration that anyone in attendance had ever witnessed. Because the bride came from a somewhat influential family, the guest list, which already included the entire village of Timnoah, also contained the names of various local Philistine lords and their households.

The first day of the planned seven day celebration went off with spectacular appreciation on the part of the invited guests. And by the third day, word of mouth, coupled with the fact that the feast was held in the village square, assured that the event resembled more of a public celebration than a wedding.

Among the more rowdy guests who had arrived to engage in the revelries were a rough band of men, led there by a distant cousin of the bride. In all, there were well over twenty thugs belonging to this unsavory bunch. At their behest, Manoah sat with these men for a short while witnessing their heavy drinking and cursing. On his first opportunity, he immediately sought out his son. "These are bad men. Their purpose here is more than just to enjoy the festivities," he told Samson as they talked in private.

"What is it that they told you?" Samson inquired.

"Their leader, his name is Yamir, says that they are all here at the behest of the noblemen of Ashkelon to monitor our activities. He also said that his men expect to be treated as honored guests and to be given preferential treatment while they enjoy the remainder of the festivities. Their first request is to be served first during the evening banquet and to be given the choice wine throughout the remainder of their stay."

Samson remained calm as he consoled Manoah, "Don't worry father we'll deal with them accordingly. But first, let us find out some more information about this group." Samson summoned Alenia's father, Caphi, to verify who these brash men were.

"They are low-level thugs for sure," he reported, "but they are nonetheless backed by the nobles of Ashkelon who use them as henchmen to impose their usual practice of extortion and intimidation throughout the outlying villages."

"I see," Samson responded. "I'll have a talk with them." As he began to walk toward the bunch, both Manoah and Caphi implored him not to make any challenges to them, which they feared would surely ruin the wedding. In return, Samson assured the both of them that there would not be any trouble. He then set out to join this Yamir's table. As Samson approached, Yamir began to stand up, but he was quickly forced back into his seat by the coaxing hand of Samson upon his shoulder. "Sit down, my friend," Samson instructed in a non-threatening manner. "Now what's this that I hear about your men requiring special treatment while you attend my wedding feast?"

All of the men in the immediate presence of their leader's table looked at Yamir and waited for him to answer Samson's question. But the truth was that Yamir had currently begun to rethink his former demands. Once in the presence of Samson, this would be thug saw himself for what he actually was, nothing more than an unruly child trying to act like a callous adult. He cleared his throat to speak, and for an awkward moment the entire assembly of what Samson's father had referred to as bad men felt foolish as they realized that this one man, Samson, might very well wipe the floor with the lot of them.

"That's right," Yamir said after finally mustering enough courage to once again play the part of the brute. "All of the men that you see here are backed by a much higher authority."

"Uh huh, I see. A higher authority you say?" Samson responded. "And who might that be?"

"Ashkelon, like the other great cities of Philistia, is run by many wealthy and powerful men," Yamir smartly replied. "Throughout this region they are known as the Ceren, and when the Ceren want something done they largely rely on me and my men to do it for them."

"I understand," Samson said. "And what exactly was your purpose for coming out here to my wedding?"

"Well," Yamir hesitated and then spoke up timidly, "we were instructed to attend the celebration and check things out. You know, keep an eye on things. And we figured we might as well have some fun while we were at it."

Samson nodded his head in an understanding gesture. Then, to the relief of this group of 'bad men', he announced that there was no reason for them not to have a good time while they attended the wedding feast. "Listen, I want everyone to remain here as my personal guests. Enjoy yourselves," he announced to the delight of the group. "Drink your wine and let me know if you need anything else."

As Samson left the crowd, it was evident to Yamir and the rest of his group that Samson was not giving into their demands out of fear. They realized that he had sincerely accepted them for his guests. Later that evening, Samson once again joined them. He was happy to see that they were all having a good time and blending in well with the rest of the guests by telling riddles, a favorite party game for the Philistines. Yamir currently had everyone guessing at a riddle that Samson had heard many times before. The groom was thus quite surprised when no one else was able to offer the answer. He waited for a little while to allow some guesses from the other guests and then decided to answer, "What animal goes about on four legs in the morning, on two legs at noon, and on three in the evening? The answer to that is simple. It is a man who crawls as a baby, walks upright as an adult, and ambulates with the help of a walking stick when his is old." Everyone was impressed with Samson's wisdom and soon the guests were beseeching him to pose a riddle of his own. After thinking it over for a while, Samson put forth a shrewd proposition, "I have a riddle that I would like to pose as a challenge to my esteemed guests, Yamir and his friends. But before I offer it, perhaps he would like to accept a wager over whether or not they can solve it?"

With the proposition put forth in such a public manner, Yamir and his group of ruffians had no choice but to accept the offer, and with cheers from his cohorts, Yamir responded in a confident manner, "I accept your proposal. What are the terms?"

"If you solve the riddle I will give each and every one of you new garments," Samson declared with a smirk on his face. "But on the other hand, if you can not solve the puzzle in lets say three days—the end of the wedding feast—then each of you shall provide me with a new garment."

"Very well then," Yamir said as he looked around at his nodding friends. "Let's hear it."

Samson cleared his throat as everyone present waited eagerly in anticipation of his riddle. Then in a boisterous voice Samson began, (*)- "Out of the eater came forth meat, and out of the strong came forth sweetness."

Chatter quickly broke out through the crowd over what Samson's riddle could possibly mean. It was apparent that everyone was amused with the riddle, everyone that is, except for Yamir and his men.

On the contrary, Yamir had taken on a rather serious frown. And after the first night of contemplating the riddle, he and his men began to grow more and more agitated over the plausibility of any of them figuring it out. Then an idea came to Yamir. There was a way that they could beat Samson at his own game. There was surely one person who could find out the answer for them, his beautiful wife Alenia. If they could get to the bride, they could win the bet.

It was with this idea in mind that Yamir and the other henchmen approached Alenia as she enjoyed a mid-morning walk with the accompaniment of her father. It was the beginning of the seventh and last day of the wedding feast, and the two of them strolled down by the river enjoying the cool breeze and talking over Alenia's plans to travel back to the home of Samson while he worked to gain a political position amongst his tribesmen. "He says that he wants to help attain Israel's sovereignty and realize freedom from the injustice of Philistine rule," she admiringly explained.

"Now be careful what you say, daughter," Caphi said as he browsed over his shoulder. "That kind of talk could be construed as treason."

Alenia nonchalantly responded, "Oh father, what did you ever care about disloyalty to Philistia? You know how unfair that they have been in the past by taking advantage of our neighbor, Israel, and how we have moved in on their territory during times of drought and famine."

"Is that what you think of your own countrymen?" a crafty voice materialized from the path directly in front of them. It was the voice of Yamir. As Alenia and Caphi approached, the two could see that he, as usual, had the backing of his group of henchmen. The lot of them were doing all that they could to appear threatening. Yamir twirled a stick in his hand while the others sat around sharpening knives and swords, trying to appear nonchalant enough. As comical as this bunch may have seemed to able bodied men, for the likes of a dainty woman and an old man, they were indeed threatening enough..."

* * *

"...What was that papa," Benaiah asked, suddenly interrupting his father's story about Samson.

"What was what?" Jehoiada questioned back.

"There is something out there in the dark," Benaiah answered to the surprise of his father. At first Jehoiada thought that maybe the story had riled the young boy's imagination, but then he too heard something rustling out in the woods. Jehoiada stood up and grabbed a nearby torch, which he quickly lit on fire and held out towards the outlying trees. Then a gust of wind came out of nowhere, nearly extinguishing both the torch and the camp fire. Jehoiada waited for the wind to die down a bit before heading out to investigate further. "Stay here," he told Benaiah, "and be sure to keep that fire going by adding wood if it gets low." He then headed out into the darkness. His actions were noticed by Achan, one of his trusty shepherds, who quickly followed suit and grabbed a torch for himself before walking towards the brush. Meanwhile, Benaiah did as he was told by staying behind and tending to the fire. All the while he anxiously watched his father from the distance.

The sound of rustling tree limbs became more audible as Jehoiada and Achan neared the foliage. They both held their flames out in front of them, purposefully disturbing the darkness as they exposed its remoteness. Suddenly, the temperature seemed to drop and another strong gust of wind whipped at the torches along with the long grass of the meadow, which the sheep now nervously picked at. From his position near the camp fire, Benaiah glimpsed the reflective beam of two fiendish eyes amongst the backdrop of the woods. He called out, "There is something out there, papa!" His shouts were followed by a loud shriek, which startled the sheep and sent them running away. Then the source of the commotion revealed itself.

It was a portly and panicked wild boar, which charged out of the bushes and rushed toward Jehoiada. It startled him and Achan both. Jehoiada dodged out of the way of the beast as it ran past him and headed towards the sheep before disappearing into the darkness. This last incident alarmed the flock and sent them scurrying in all directions.

It took some time for things to come back to order, but soon with the help of Achan and the rest of the shepherds, the sheep were all rounded back up and accounted for. "Is it always this fun?" Benaiah asked his father as they walked back to the now low burning fire. At some point he had left his station and went out to help his dad and the rest of the shepherds. The fire would have gone out completely had it not been for Achan who had kept it fed in between his efforts of rounding up the scattered sheep. Jehoiada and Benaiah were both very thankful for his efforts. For, the gusts of wind had given way to a steady airstream and the temperature had dropped significantly.

"Maybe, we should head into the tent," Jehoiada suggested. "It is getting awfully cold out here."

"I'm not cold," Benaiah insisted as he wrapped himself in a blanket and situated himself on a log close to the fire. "And besides, you were just getting to the good part, papa."

"You're not tired?" his father asked as he sat down next to Benaiah and mussed his son's hair with an amused shake of his hand. He gave a transitory laugh as Benaiah shook his head and smiled back at his father who now happily continued, "Alright I guess I'll tell you more about Samson then…"

19

As Jehoiada picked up where he had left off, Achan made his way closer to the fire where he stood silently watching over the sheep while he listened contentedly to the story...

* * *

"...Appreciating his current position of having Alenia and her father right where he wanted them, Yamir made his demands immediately by telling her and Caphi to give him the answer.

"What answer? You lowly scoundrels!" Caphi yelled in an attempt to appear strong, but his efforts to take up for himself and his daughter were useless. He had no more strength than a newborn calf, and Yamir knew it.

"Why don't you take a seat?" the slithery young man said as he used his walking stick to pull at the ankle of Caphi thereby planting the pitiful man firmly to the dirt on his rear end. "And you," he continued as he circled around Alenia with slow methodical steps and poked at her with his stick. "You will tell me the answer to the riddle or you will pay."

"What will you do to me? I will tell my husband. Samson won't put up with this," she said trying to convince herself that everything would be alright.

"Do you think that is an appropriate response to a man who holds your fate in his hands?" Yamir asked as he placed his foot on her father's chest and pushed him back to the ground relieving the chivalrous attempt that Caphi was making to raise himself off of the dirt in order to act the hero.

"And what if I don't tell you?" she said in a last attempt to play her bluff.

"If you don't tell me, then your father, mother, and entire family will lose all that they own and be thrown into prison for the rest of their miserable lives."

"What is so important about winning this bet?" Caphi questioned. "Are our lives worth so little?"

Yamir responded with derision, "Listen old man, this new son-in-law of yours is in for a rude awakening. He thinks that he can act like he is our friend one instant and then make us out to be fools the next? Ha, his conceit has already been reported to the Ceren." With this last announcement, both Alenia and her father were convinced that Yamir's threats were serious.

"Very well, then. You win," Alenia announced in an abrupt tone. "I will find out the answer for you, but you must first promise not to bring the wrath of the Ceren down upon my family."

Yamir chuckled at Alenia's demands before answering her in a threatening voice, "First you get me the answer, and then I will decide what further actions that I will take."

As the last evening of the wedding feast drew near a close, Yamir and his men played their parts well. Throughout the night, they acted as though they were already agonizing over their loss. Hence, when Samson once again stood atop a table at the center of the festivities in order to recite his riddle, he had every reason to believe that he had won the wager. "Out of the eater came forth meat, and out of the strong came forth sweetness..." he repeated one more time for the guests.

But then, just as he was about to reveal the answer, the voice of Yamir took over for him, "—The answer to the riddle is simple. The eater and the strong that you speak of are one in the same, none other than the ferocious lion and the ferocious eater of many a prey." He paused a short while for effect before finishing, "And what came out of him, which was so sweet, was likewise none other than the sweetest of delights, the taste of honey? So there you have it; the answer to your riddle. The riddle speaks of the carcass of a lion that has become host to a busy beehive."

Samson could not believe his ears. "How could Yamir have possibly figured it out?" he wondered to himself.

And then Yamir started to brag, "It was really a simple task to solve this riddle of yours. I merely began to imagine that it stemmed from a personal account. I thought to myself, yes, Samson probably experienced the adventure one fine day as he walked to visit his beloved Alenia." This last comment immediately gained the full attention of Samson who now listened in disbelief as Yamir went into detail about the entire incident saying things that no one could have known unless they were privy to the information. The re-telling of the story from Yamir was indeed enough to wow the audience, but Samson was not so pleased with Yamir's apparent brilliance. A stern look of bewilderment towards Yamir, followed by an angry glance at Alenia, clued his father and mother into the fact that it wasn't mere deduction that allowed Yamir to detail the story.

Remembering the honey that his son had eagerly shared the year before, Manoah quickly approached Samson. "Is this true my son? Did you really overcome a lion in the wild with your bare hands?" he asked aloud as the party members sat, all ears, waiting for an answer.

Samson then confessed that the story was without a doubt more than a mere riddle as he gave a hostile stare in Alenia's direction once more. A loud murmur spread through the crowd, both at the astonishment of the story being true and because of the fact that they all knew that it must have been Alenia who had revealed the secret to Yamir. For a brief moment, Samson stood speechless, never feeling more humiliated in his life. He then cleared his throat and spoke to Yamir, "Very well, it looks as though you were successful in finding the answer to the riddle, but I know that had you not conspired with Alenia, you would not have solved the riddle on your own. Nonetheless, you will have your payment."

Then Samson stormed off as Alenia, who up until this point had remained silent with her eyes diverted towards the ground in shame, now stood and called out to him, "I had to let them know, Samson. They were threatening us with ruin."

Unwilling to face the dishonor that his bride had dealt him, Samson mounted his horse and rode off without one word to her. Alenia started after him but Manoah stopped her and told the distraught girl that Samson just needed some time alone. "He probably just wants to take a ride and clear his head. After wandering aimlessly for a while, he will return," Manoah assured her.

But it wasn't Samson's intention to ride around aimlessly as was his customary habit. When he rode away that late afternoon, he knew exactly where he was headed. There was a root cause to how all of this had been played out and a reckoning that had to be dealt, he figured. And he was not about to start setting things straight at the bottom with Yamir and his men. Hence, directly to the heart of Ashkelon he rode, to deal out some punishment to the men who had instigated this entire mess. And the spirit and the strength of the Lord came upon Samson as he called upon his God to deliver justice unto him…"

* * *

…Jehoiada stopped his recital as he looked over to his son who was by now curled up next to the fire fast asleep. He then glanced over to Achan who to his surprise had stuck around to hear the story. Achan gave an embarrassed look of disappointment at the abrupt end of the narrative. "Eh hem," he cleared his throat. "I am going to go and grab some more firewood. The flames are getting low, and it is only getting colder out here."

"I thought that you were going to get some sleep and take the second watch?" Jehoiada commented.

The shepherd acquiesced, "I know it, but it was nice not to be out here all alone, and besides that story you were telling was a lot more entertaining than sleep ever was."

Jehoiada smiled as he answered back, "I guess you are right. Here, give me a hand. I am going to take Benaiah back to the tent and get him out of this cold." Jehoiada attempted to pick up his son who immediately woke up as if he'd been awake the entire time.

"What's going on? Are you going to bed already, papa?" Benaiah said, fighting to keep his eyes open.

Jehoiada carried Benaiah back to the tent as he softly spoke to him, "Yes, my boy. I am just too tired. You better come with me and get a little rest yourself. It will be daylight soon enough." As Jehoiada looked at his son he realized that the attempt he was making to indulge Benaiah was unnecessary, for the child had fallen back asleep almost immediately.

The early morning was calm. It was still dark and everyone was asleep except Achan and a few of the outlying posted shepherds. Achan stood and watched the mist pour out of his mouth as he breathed. It had gotten even colder since Jehoiada and Benaiah retired to their tent. He pulled his hood over his head and walked over to a group of trees in order to avoid the cold breeze. The shepherd then looked out at the perimeter of the camp enjoying the solitude of nature. Like the priest, he too could enjoy the outdoors. It was so peaceful and serene, but the scene was soon to change.

Achan suddenly heard a strange disturbance in the woods off in the distance. He listened intently to what he recognized as the sharp sound of twigs breaking. At first, Achan thought that the panicked little boar from earlier had returned, but then he ruled out that possibility. For, there was certainly something moving out in the darkness of the brush, yet whatever it was, it was much stealthier than any pig as it lurked behind the cover of darkness and shrubbery. Another thing that Achan ascertained as he listened to the creature moving through the trees was that it must be big, because there was a deep resonance that emanated from the stems that it broke as it prowled.

Achan pulse quickened as he realized that it was moving closer to him, both quietly and methodically. This could be no type of grazing animal. This was a stalker. Perhaps, it was the same thing that had scared the boar out of the shrubs earlier. His suspicions were validated all at once as the stalker suddenly made its move. It abandoned all caution and sped up its pace, breaking a number of large branches as it made its way closer to the clearing of the field and towards the flock. What happened next was pure pandemonium.

Suddenly the sheep also became aware of something coming for them and began to run in a panic. But this time they were not running out of an anxious impulse; this time they were running for their lives. Thus the sheep startled the oxen which occupied the adjacent hillside and initiated a stampede amongst them. Next there were shouts from one of the other shepherds and then a loud and frightening roar. Everyone in the distant camp was awake at once.

Moriah opened her eyes in horror. She had been dreaming about Benaiah. He was hurt and calling for her. She listened for a moment to the commotion coming from outside and became frantic after realizing that this was no dream. A loud roar enveloped the camp for a second time. It was a lion, and it was close. Far away, she continued to hear the shouting voices of the shepherds. "Benaiah," she said under her breath and impulsively ran out of her tent toward the direction of the shouting. Her motherly instinct took over as she realized that she had to make sure that her boy was alright. She began to scream at the top of her lungs as she sprinted forward, "Benaiah! Jehoiada! Where are you?" She ran and ran until she was nearly out of breath, but still she continued her calls,

"Benaiah! Benaiah!" Tears began rolling down her face as she made her way frantically through the darkness. Then, all of a sudden, something strange happened. Something tingly and white fell on her nose. It made her stop in her tracks.

She held out her hand and it landed there too. So pure and cold, it gradually filled the entire sky around her. She couldn't believe her eyes and stood in awe for a moment. Her bewilderment was halted as she noticed a figure out in the distance. There in the midst of thousands of white flakes was her husband.

He waved his hand up in the air motioning for her as he called out, "Snow! It is snow."

She began to giggle as she held her hands open and looked up into the sky. Completely caught up in the moment, Moriah felt like she was back in her tent dreaming again. She had never seen snow before. Then she remembered the dilemma and quickly yelled out to Jehoiada, "Benaiah? Is he alright?"

Jehoiada nodded his head and made his way toward her as he tried to yell over the now gusting wind and snow. It had picked up dramatically in just a few moments. "He is fine. They have killed the beast," he hollered.

"What? What did you say?" Moriah yelled back.

Jehoiada cupped his hands over his mouth and repeated himself, "They have killed the lion!" Moriah finally heard him and was relieved. She ran toward Jehoiada until she could clearly see the reassuring look on his face. She smiled from the distance and Jehoiada smiled back. But the moment did not last. Suddenly, Jehoiada's look of joy became a look of horror as his worst fears were realized. "Stop! Stop running!" he screamed out to her. But with the gusting wind, the falling of the snow, and the excitement of the moment she didn't comprehend his warning until it was too late.

All at once, she felt a crushing blow on her back that sent shockwaves of pain throughout her entire body. She saw the ground coming closer as she tumbled head over heals into the wild grass, and then she lost consciousness.

20

Benaiah wouldn't learn until months later what exactly had happened that tragic morning. There were indeed two lions in their camp. And while he slept, the shepherds had successfully killed one but the second more elusive lion had stayed under cover of the bush and had instinctively chased after Moriah as she ran unassumingly toward her husband. Jehoiada was able to scare off the beast with shouts as he ran to help his wife, but it was too late for her; the damage had already been inflicted. She never regained consciousness and died in her husband's arms in the middle of that white covered field.

That is the one thing that Benaiah would always remember, his excitement at waking up to the beautiful snow. It was a confusing day for the young child. With all of that cold, white powder to play with he couldn't imagine why his father did not want to join in and have some fun. And when he asked Jehoiada where his mother was, his father merely replied that she had gone on ahead of them. The innocence of childhood allowed Benaiah to trust the many excuses that Jehoiada would give concerning what had happened to his mother. And for several months that is how it went. His mother had "taken a long journey" or "she was waiting for them to finish up what they had to do in Beersheba so they could join her." No matter what the new excuse was, she was always waiting. And for some reason that offered just enough comfort for the boy, so that he would be fine without her for the moment.

Remembering back, Benaiah hadn't ever blamed his father for the excuses. It allowed him a cushion of time, to get used to living without Moriah, before he learned the sad truth. And that day did come eventually. Jehoiada sat Benaiah down and explained the idea of death to him. Once again the innocence of childhood allowed the boy to accept the rawness of the concept without many questions. He was sad of course, but it was a holistic sadness that he shared with his father. He knew that his father loved his mother as much as he did, and that made him have sympathy for Jehoiada. He even tried to offer comforting words to lessen the pain for the both of them as they shared tears, "Don't worry papa, she is watching out for us from where she is."

As the years past, they would grow ever closer. Jehoiada offered both the strength of a father and the compassion of a mother as he raised his son. Benaiah reciprocated the love and held his father in the highest esteem. Courage was instilled in him as a result of that past experience, and along with his father's continuous recounting of the stories of his favorite hero, Samson, he grew into a bold young man. He was constantly pushing limits and testing his own brawn while comparing it to that of Samson's. And to everyone's astonishment, Benaiah did seem to possess supernatural strength at times.

While out hunting, he would often leave weapons behind and stalk an animal with the menacing intention of subduing his prey with his bare hands. This was especially the case whenever he came upon any large beast, which was immediately deemed a worthy adversary to test his strength out on. In this manner, he had been successful on several occasions, fighting barehanded against the likes of wolves and even leopards. Benaiah would make odd claims to the source of his strength, claim's that even astonished his father. When anyone would ask him how it was that he was so strong, Benaiah would simply reply, "God was not pleased with the beast who took my mother's innocent life. He thus stole away the strength of that creature and bestowed it upon me."

As he continued to grow up, Benaiah became a renowned hunter. He traveled far and wide in search of prey and supplied the entire village with animal hides throughout the year. His gifts were greatly appreciated by the people who used them for coats in the winter and for trade with neighboring villages and traveling merchants throughout the rest of the year. All the while, Benaiah asked for no payment from them but merely seemed to do it for the enjoyment.

For the most part, Benaiah lived a contented life with his father. Still, there was a restlessness about him. It stemmed from the fact the there was one elusive animal which he had never came across, and that was the lion. The thought therefore burdened his mind. For years, he longed for nothing more than the occasion to come up against one. So he waited, knowing that some day he would cross paths with the beast.

His story was widely known throughout the surrounding villages. There was even a wager made between him and many of the men throughout the land, who did not believe that he would dare attempt what he had been claiming for years. "When I finally do get the chance to meet the lion," he would say in dramatic fashion acting out the scenario with an invisible contender, "I will wrestle it with my bare hands, my strength pitted against its own. And on that day we will see who the true king of beasts is." Fourteen years after his mother's untimely death, almost to the day, that moment would finally come...

Benaiah rode home on his horse followed by a group of his hunting companions. They entered the village just as dark storm clouds rolled in from the opposite direction. The temperature dropped and night fell as they each went their separate ways. Benaiah burst open the door, happy to be home. "I have something for you papa," he yelled as he entered the house and threw off his coat. But he didn't say much else. It seemed that his entrance had interrupted a recitation of his father's. A crowd of children from the village sat on the floor encapsulated as Jehoiada recited one of his familiar tales. Benaiah smiled at his father and gave him a slow nod, signaling him not to stop. As Jehoiada finished up with the story his son stood at the back of the room listening with a nostalgic ear...

* * *

"...The streets of Ashkelon were strangely empty as Samson rode into town with the intention of settling the score with the Ceren, whom he had held personally responsible for ruining his wedding and turning his wife against him. Although the streets should have been bustling with people visiting the markets and bargaining with merchants, the place was relatively empty. Samson didn't dwell on the anomaly and instead thought it better that he didn't have to waste any time maneuvering through the crowds. He inquired from the few people that he did come across, asking them if they knew anything of the Cerens' activities or whereabouts. Before long, he was speaking with an elderly local who offered the information that he was looking for. The man was grimy with a patch over one eye; he appeared to be nothing more than a hapless beggar. But when Samson offered to pay him for information about the Ceren, the old man refused, asking only what kind of business Samson had with them.

"I am here to settle a score," was the cold answer that Samson offered through his clenched teeth.

The response satisfied the one eyed man's curiosity and started him talking, "You are in luck. The Ceren frequent a small tavern just around the corner from here. On any given day, you can find at least a dozen or so of them there. But today you will be exceptionally fortunate to find at least twice that many. They have come together to spearhead a raid on some of the shops in town. It is common knowledge that the streets are a dangerous place whenever this sort of thing happens and also the reason why the place is empty."

"What sort of raid?" Samson inquired.

"They are going to pillage some of the merchant's shops and destroy their goods," the man grumbled. "This is because these same shopkeepers have either gotten behind on payments or simply refused to give them the exorbitant amounts of protection money and other fees that the Ceren are demanding."

"Does this sort of activity take place often?" Samson asked.

"Often enough," came the outraged reply. "It was only a few months ago that they burnt me out of my shop and left me with this." The old man lifted his patch to reveal an empty and sunken socket where his eye was missing. As Samson rode off, he could hear the man's anguished shouts, "I was one of the richest merchants in this city. Now I have nothing!"

Flowing locks and muscle made its way through a small crowd of local henchmen gathered outside the bustling tavern. The rough and dirty crowd parted in order to clear a path for the malicious looking Israelite. Before entering, Samson made an announcement to the group, "My fight is with the men inside. If you don't want a part of it, leave now."

As he turned in the direction of the door, a menacing man with shaggy hair, the biggest of the group by far, stepped in Samson's way. "I can't let you go in there," the robust man announced as he extended his fingers out in an attempt to stop Samson's advance. His hand was immediately captured in a potent grip, and he was subsequently tossed aside into a stack of empty barrels. Samson didn't waste time finishing the man off but instead immediately entered the tavern. The Ceren, all dressed in splendid attire, stared in astonishment as Samson loomed at the door in ominous silence rubbing his fist in his palm.

"What is the meaning of this?" one of the men arrogantly yelled out to him. "This is a private meeting. Get out!" But Samson stood his ground in eerie silence.

"What, are you deaf?" a second man added as he gave a whistle which should have signaled the henchmen outside, but the summons went unanswered.

"I'll take care of him," a third member of the Ceren announced after an awkward pause. Meanwhile, everyone else in the room still waited nervously for their men outside to answer the summons. The man took out a sword and approached Samson with a threatening voice, "I'll teach you to not show your respects to the lords of Ashkelon."

As he came closer, his weapon was kicked away by Samson who then proceeded to grab the shoulders of the man, wriggle him out of his fine garb, and give him a swift kick to his backside, which sent him flying across the room in pain. Adding insult to injury, Samson then demanded that all of the men give up the clothes from their backs if they planned on getting out of the room unharmed, "You swine have sent your henchmen out to spy and bring ruin for the last time. Now consider your garments a small price to buy your ticket out of here tonight." He then offered one last chance for redemption, "Give them up, leave this room peaceably, and do not let me hear of your conspiracies again."

Needless to say, these arrogant aristocrats had no intention of giving in to the demands of Samson, and as some drew their swords in preparation for a fight, others still waited haughtily and in vain for their henchmen to come to their rescue. What took place next was a one sided beating, as Samson forcefully took what he came for. In the course of the scuffle, tables were smashed and bones were broken as the complete demolition of the tavern ensued.

At one point, the candles atop one of the tables were knocked over, instantly igniting spilled liquor on the floor. In just moments, it had set the entire place ablaze. Samson himself was lucky to escape with his life and the thirty garments he needed in order to pay his debt to Yamir and his gang. But the Ceren who were present that night were not as fortunate. Only a few of them made it out of the massive inferno that resulted from the liquor fueled conflagration.

Samson immediately returned to Timnoah, wasting no time paying off his wager and retrieving his parents. They left at once back to their home. After receiving the garments of the Ceren as payment, Yamir and his men either decided to leave that very night themselves and go into hiding or were dealt with by the remaining vengeful lords of Philistia. Either way, they were never seen or heard from again.

Soon, Samson calmed down enough to return for his bride, but when he got back to Timnoah he found that Alenia had been married to someone else in his absence. "I didn't think that you would return for her," Caphi explained. "And I gave her to another. But don't be angry with me, Samson. Let me make better on the situation by giving you the hand of my other daughter for marriage. After all, she is even more beautiful than Alenia."

Samson could hardly believe it. He knew that Caphi was actually being sincere in his attempt to remedy the situation, but he couldn't understand the callous logic of Alenia's father. He figured that he had enough of the peculiar ways of the Philistines and decided that it was time to cut his losses and return home. But news of his arrival had already reached the ears of the officials down in Ashkelon and the remaining members of the Ceren immediately sent another mob to try and subdue him. This was a big mistake.

By the time that Samson had made his way out of the town, he was already perturbed over how the entire scenario with Alenia and her father had played itself out. As he looked back at the distant valley of Timnoah along with the surrounding farmland, he realized that he was being pursued by the Philistines. This made him all the more annoyed, and he consequently decided that it was time to let these people know that he should not be trifled with.

Just as he was thinking of how he could accomplish this objective, he heard men approaching over a distant hill. Samson rushed over the glen, determined to battle against his rivals, but instead of finding warriors, he found a group of horse-driven farm wagons coming his way. The brash approach of Samson sent most of their operators scurrying off in the opposite direction leaving behind all of their wagons along with a crippled man who despite being relatively young was in no shape to run. Samson took a seat by the man and assured him that he meant no harm. "Where are you headed?" Samson questioned.

"Out toward the wilderness," he replied.

"What do you have in the wagons?" Samson then asked after hearing a peculiar noise coming from one of them.

"Have a look for yourself," the young man said with a hint of intrigue. "You won't believe it."

Samson walked back and took the cover off of the top of the wagon that they were sitting on. It was stocked high with newly fashioned torches. "Torches?" he questioned. "What's so amazing about torches?"

"Not those. Those we are taking to the Philistine guard in Gath. Try the other wagons," the enthusiastic man instructed with an eager grin as he grabbed a walking-crutch and eased himself down from his position. To Samson's surprise, many of the carts were filled with caged foxes. The crippled man explained that they had all been caught by local farmers, and that for over a year, he and the other men were likewise given the task of exterminating them. "None of us had the heart to kill the little creatures," he said as he followed close behind Samson who was inspecting the other wagons. "We kept them caged and fed for as long as we could but now there are just too many of them. We were going to take them out to a remote area and let them go free."

"That's not a bad idea, but I think that I have a better purpose for them," Samson announced as he looked back down at the valley and its vast vineyards, olive groves, and newly harvested grain. "Now be gone with you," he ordered. "Consider your good deed complete."

The young man made no argument after Samson emptied the entire contents of torches onto the ground by tilting the heavy wagon onto its side with one hand. "Their all yours" he said after climbing back onto his bench and subsequently riding off without looking back. Next, Samson proceeded to tie each of the foxes together in pairs by their tails and attach a lit torch to each duo before sending them scurrying towards the valley and its fertile crops. Before long, the surrounding fields were up in flames as the foxes scurried along dragging the torches behind them. In their efforts to untangle themselves from the knots that linked them together, the little red creatures had inadvertently carried out Samson's capricious plan to bring destruction to his enemy's lands.

Prior to the last of the flames being be put out and even before the immense damages could be calculated, word had already reached the king of Ashkelon that Samson was responsible for the devastation. Troops were immediately alerted with the details, and they were ordered to send out patrols in order to capture Samson. It wasn't long before an unfortunate troop of men tracked him down. They found him not in hiding but instead making his way back home on the main road toward Zorah.

"Stop there," the captain of a large contingent of soldiers yelled out to Samson as they proceeded to overtake him with their horses.

Samson turned around with a smirk on his face as he answered back boldly, "Don't you people ever know when to quit?"

"Look Samson, we don't want any trouble," the captain earnestly claimed. "We were instructed to bring you back alive, but if we have to we will—"

"—You will turn around and make as though we didn't cross paths if you know what is good for you," Samson warned them in a conceited tone.

"Come now, Samson," the captain reasoned. "What are you going to do? There are many of us and only one of you. Don't opt for the same fate that has befallen your would-be-wife and her father."

This last statement changed Samson's indifferent countenance from a cavalier smirk to a solemn grimace. "What did you say?" he immediately questioned.

"Don't tell me that you haven't heard about what happened to them as a result of your exploits," the captain naively replied in a pitiless tone.

"What has happened to them?" Samson questioned impatiently.

"Both of them were burnt alive for their impudence and—" The man was instantly snatched off of his horse by Samson and given a thrashing along with all the other men who tried to come to his rescue. At the end of the skirmish all the Philistines lay scattered along the road, injured but alive. Samson set their horses free, save one, which he used to quicken his journey home..."

* * *

... As Jehoiada finished his tale, Benaiah started the applause followed by the children who begged to hear more.

"That will have to wait for some other time. Now you'd better all get home. I'm sure you're parents are missing you by now," Jehoiada said to the children with a kind smile on his face.

As they filed out, they exchanged banter over their hero, "When I grow up, I am going to be just like Samson. I'll show the Philistines not to mess with us," one of the children claimed.

"No you're not. I am. I am going to be just like Samson," another argued.

Benaiah closed the door behind them and smiled as he spoke to his father, "I see you are still telling the same old stories."

"I remember, not too long ago, hearing the claims of another child who said he would grow up to be just as strong as his hero, Samson," Jehoiada said with a chuckle.

"Yeah, well you know, the thing that I found so strange later on was the fact that for the longest time, you never did get to the most famous part of the story," Benaiah commented.

"Oh, you mean that whole thing where he falls for Delilah and ends up a laughing stock in Philistia. You know, children shouldn't hear such horrible stories. A true hero doesn't go out that way," Jehoiada said in kidding fashion.

Now Benaiah chuckled. "I suppose you may be right. That would be bad for their young minds. Fighting and carnage is fine, but don't let them hear about the cruelty of love," he teased back.

Jehoiada put an arm on his son's shoulder. "Let's have something to eat," he said as he led Benaiah over to the table. He then walked over to a kettle and dished out some mutton stew for each of them. "It's cold out there. This will warm us up."

They sat down and ate supper as Benaiah told his father about his last adventure out in the wilderness. His father listened intently as Benaiah explained the thrill of the hunt and how a pack of wolves had nearly stolen away his team's quarry in the middle of the night as they slept.

"It's truly amusing, son," Jehoiada remarked as the story came to an end. "Now you are the one who seems to always be entertaining me with tales of action and adventure."

21

Benaiah and his father sat and finished their meal reminiscing about the years gone by and how they both missed Moriah. It was customary for them to spend the entire evening chatting over such things, but on this particularly night their visit was abruptly interrupted.

First, there was a loud knock on the door, followed by the familiar voice of one of Benaiah's oldest friends and long time hunting companion. "Benaiah, Benaiah are you in there?" he called out in excitement. Jehoiada and his son looked at each other in a perplexed manner.

"What is it, Gabriel?" Jehoiada asked as he opened the door. "Don't you know that it is getting late?" Gabriel and Benaiah had grown up together, and from the time that they were just children Jehoiada had often answered the door in similar fashion before sending Gabriel back to his own house. "Your parent's are probably worried about you. Come back tomorrow and you boys can play then," the priest had so often scolded. But now, neither Gabriel nor Benaiah were children. They had both grown up to be fine young men, depended on by all the local villages for their skill at hunting. So, when Jehoiada saw Gabriel standing in front of him on that exceptionally cold night, he knew it meant that there was perhaps some type of problem with one of the shepherds whose flock or herd had gone missing.

But, what Gabriel had to say next came as a surprise for both Jehoiada and Benaiah. "We've caught a lion!" the excited young man said with enthusiasm as he rubbed his hands together trying to keep warm.

"What? Come out of that cold," Jehoiada told him in astonishment.

"The traps we set?" Benaiah asked as he donned his coat and threw a fleece to his father.

"Traps?" Jehoiada asked inquisitively.

Gabriel walked over to the stove to get some momentary warmth as he answered, "Yeah, we constructed them last summer when a number of Oneg's oxen had fallen prey to something that we knew just had to be big." Gabriel and Benaiah now looked at each other in elation.

"It was in the hills above his pastures," Benaiah added. "We dug some trenches along the natural valleys and then covered them with palm leaves. We let Oneg know that if anything came walking through there it would definitely be caught in one of those pits. We hoped that we would catch something, but we had no idea."

"Yeah I had almost forgotten about the traps until Oneg's son came running to tell me that there was something snarling angrily up in those hills," Gabriel said grinning from ear to ear. "So I guess we will finally get to settle that wager after all."

Benaiah lifted his hands up in the air and twisted his torso back and forth as he stretched out his muscular frame. "I guess you are right. Let's go, you two," he directed. "There's not a moment to lose." The three men quickly mounted their horses and began to ride out toward the lion as news of its capture went out through the entire village. Word of what was to happen next spread fast...

"Benaiah is going to fight the beast."

"He is so brave."

"He is so foolish."

"He will surely be maimed."

"He will surely die."

"He will prevail like Samson prevailed."

The villagers all argued over the scenario as they ignored the cold and made every attempt possible to get themselves out to the site where they could witness such a marvelous attraction, a true man against beast battle. Besides those who rode out on horses, there were hordes of people who made their way out on foot to brave the cold and witness the match. Benaiah, accompanied by Jehoiada and Gabriel, made their way to the edge of town amongst the bustle and excitement. Then the most auspicious of things happened, which stopped Jehoiada in his tracks and prevented him from going any further. It began to snow.

Benaiah halted his horse and turned around towards his father who sat still on his horse and closed his eyes in silent reverence as the snow came down.

"You go on ahead. I can do nothing to aid you at this point," Jehoiada said in an encouraging voice.

Benaiah rode up alongside his father and spoke to him in a whisper, "You know that I have to do this, papa."

"I know," Jehoiada reassured his son as he opened his eyes. "You have waited all your life for this moment and God is surely with you. It's just that I am getting too old to be out in such weather, and besides the suspense of the whole thing is too much."

Benaiah looked as his father and then around at the falling snow thinking of that horrible snow filled morning so many years prior. "I understand, Papa," he said as he reached out and squeezed his father's hand. "Go home and get yourself warm. I will return victorious."

His father nodded his head and gave him some departing words of encouragement, "I have seen your strength, Benaiah. God has made you mighty, and you will prevail on this day. Wear your gear and don't get careless. Now go and realize your destiny."

By the time Benaiah arrived at the site, there was a huge crowd gathered there and a large bon-fire, which could be seen for miles around. The crowd cheered Benaiah as he dismounted his horse and walked to the edge of the pit to get a glimpse of his foe.

The beast roared at the faces up above. It was angry and out of its element. But what was going to be most dangerous for Benaiah as he went up against the animal, Gabriel reminded him, was the fact that it had been trapped in that pit for some time, and it was no doubt hungry. "You would make a small meal for such a creature, but nonetheless, I suppose that you'd be better than nothing," Gabriel kidded to the annoyance of his friend. Benaiah gave him a solemn look as he returned to his horse and put on a bronze breastplate along with a spiked collar. Gabriel continued, "Hey don't mind me. I have seen you take on some powerful predators over the years. I don't think that this one will be too much for you to handle, and besides look around you. I am the only one who has actually placed my wagers on you. The stakes are high, and everyone else is rooting for your opponent."

Benaiah knew that his friend's words were true. It had been years since he had been making the claims of taking on a lion, and the wagers had grown to huge proportions. "I'll give them something to cheer for," Benaiah thought to himself as he removed his breastplate along with the rest of his protective gear. It was understood that he would wear such equipment as he fought the lion in order to protect himself from its vicious teeth and claws.

After all, one swipe of the lion's powerful paw could mean death for the young man, and that was the last thing the villagers came to see, for, he was endeared to them for his bravery and strength. The spectators had gathered that day thinking they'd see Benaiah knocked around a bit before having to be pulled from the pit. The lion would then be put down with the help of some spearmen, and everyone would go away happy, but this was a different development altogether. As Benaiah finished removing his last piece of gear, the crowd, which had taken to high ground above the pit yelled out with confused complaints…

"What are you doing?"

"Put your armor back on…"

"I knew he wouldn't go through with it…"

"We came out in the snow for nothing!"

Then they briefly fell silent as Benaiah leaped into the pit without his protective wear.

"He's crazy!"

"He wishes to die…"

"Get out of there you imbecile…"

"Your father will be left alone, with no family of his own…"

The crowd continued to yell as Benaiah landed on the soft snow at the bottom of the pit. He instantly looked up in front of him. The beast was enormous. Much bigger than it had looked from up above. Its mane outlined its menacing pelt covered skull, and its body flexed with power as it seemed to yell out angrily at Benaiah with a deafening roar that instantly hushed the audience.

The lion charged. Benaiah rose from his crouched position and met it head on as it attempted to overwhelm him within its grasp. Its claws dug into his skin and its powerful jaws opened to consume him. But Benaiah stood his ground as he reached up and grabbed the bottom jaw of the lion from underneath while stretching out its neck so that it could not bring its teeth down onto him. Benaiah considered the situation for a quick moment realizing that he was up against pure power, the likes he had never witnessed before. "What have I gotten myself into?" he thought. The creature was astounding. Then he remembered the story of Samson and told himself how to proceed, "Must grab its jaw and rip it apart." The young man coached himself on as he rolled around the pit with lion.

But as much as Benaiah tried, he just couldn't get a grip on the beast's snout. Each time he would grab for it, the lion would wriggle its powerful head away from him before coming back with its teeth flashing in a dangerous assault of its own. The energy that the rivals had expended at this point was staggering.

Meanwhile the crowd looked on in anticipation and awe over Benaiah's capacity to wrestle with the beast. At this point they had completely disregarded any interest in their wagers, and starting with the voice of Gabriel they began to root Benaiah on until they were all yelling for him to defeat the lion.

As Benaiah thought of the situation and the cheers of the crowd, his emotions were roused. He had spent so long waiting for this opportunity and now that he had the object of his reprisal in his grip, there was no way he would give up. With this last bit of determination and encouragement from the crowd, he gained his second wind. He grabbed the animal by its mane and sent it hurling backwards. It subsequently bounced off of the icy wall and back onto the floor. As the animal shook off the blow it looked around in a perturbed manner for somewhere to escape. "There is no where to run!" Benaiah yelled out at the beast as every muscle in his own body flexed and his veins and arteries pumped him full of adrenaline. "Come on you, let's end this!" he sneered through his teeth.

The lion answered back with yet another violent roar and then charged once more. This time Benaiah waited for it to come into close proximity. He then dodged to the side and with one arm tossed it to the ground. He immediately jumped on its back, wrapped his massive arms around its neck, and squeezed with all his might. The animal rolled and bucked trying its best to break free, but it was no use. The death grip that Benaiah held on with was unbreakable, and the beast could do nothing besides stubbornly accept its fate. The next roar to be heard came not from the lion but instead from the cheerful crowd. Benaiah eased his grip and stood up leaving the lion motionless on that cold icy floor. He climbed out of the pit wearily as the people gathered around and congratulated him...

"I knew that you would prevail the entire time..."

"I never doubted you for a moment..."

"You were so brave..."

The people continued with their praise as a few of the men hoisted the huge lion out of the pit. It would usually be displayed in the village as a trophy for the night, but with the snowfall it would instead be immediately taken to the village tanner who would cure the skin and present it as a prize to commemorate Benaiah's victory.

As he mounted his horse and prepared to ride home in triumph, Benaiah was joined by Gabriel, who continued to gloat over his friend's success, "We are rich. After I collect from our village alone, I will be a wealthy man." He continued his bragging as he patted Benaiah on his back, "And just wait until I collect from all of the others. You know, maybe we can take this type of spectacle on the road. It would be great. People would come from miles around." Benaiah glanced over at Gabriel with a stern look on his face, which immediately changed his friend's proposition, "Well, I mean you don't have to fight a wild lion every time. Maybe we could get a tame one or one that is kind of getting on in age."

"I already told everyone to keep what they owe me," Benaiah announced as he rode off towards the village.

"No, surely he wasn't serious," Gabriel said to himself aloud. He then yelled out after Benaiah as he rode to catch up with him. "You don't think that they'll want me to be so lenient with my winnings do you?"

Jehoiada had returned home after giving his blessings to his son, and there he waited, confident of Benaiah's successful return. So when he heard the door rattling later that night, the old priest quickly made his way to open it. "Son, tell me of your conquest..." he said with excitement in his voice. But as he flung the door opened, Jehoiada was surprised not to see his son standing before him but instead the cruel bony face of Doeg staring back at him. "Can I help you stranger?" Jehoiada asked in his usual polite manner as he smiled.

"Is your name Jehoiada?" Doeg inquired.

"Yes, I am," the priest responded. "Please come in. You must be very cold out there in that horrible weather."

Evidence of what had happened next was quite apparent as Benaiah arrived home later that evening. The front door was left wide open and the inside of the house was torn apart. A struggle had ensued there. As Benaiah entered the cold muddled house he realized this and immediately called out to his father, but there was no answer. Not being able to imagine what had taken place, Benaiah feared the worst for Jehoiada. It made him feel sick with worry.

Because practically everyone in the village had attended the pit-fight, it was very hard to get any answers, but after some time Gabriel rounded up an eyewitness, an elderly gentleman with hair as white as the snow. "I only stayed back here because I am too old and crippled to travel very far," the white haired man explained.

"Yes, I understand, but it is a good thing that you stayed, because you can tell me what has happened to my father," Benaiah coaxed him on.

"Oh, yes I heard the commotion as I sat at home in my chair," the old man said before pausing and giving a fretful look at Benaiah and his friend. "I immediately rushed over and cracked open my door just in time to see the worst thing,"

"Go on," Gabriel instructed.

"Poor Jehoiada was being pulled out of his house by two soldiers. And there was a man there who was very cruel. He kept referring to himself as the Supreme Advisor to the king. He wanted to know why your father, Jehoiada, had betrayed King Saul. And he told him that he would pay for his insolence."

"Betray the king? This is ridiculous," Benaiah responded, trying to control his anger. "Have you told me everything?" he frantically asked. "I need to know what happened next."

"They took your father off with them," the man mumbled in a sympathetic voice.

"They more than likely have taken him either to the jailhouse at Gilgal or the main prison in Gibeah," Gabriel declared. "All those accused of treason eventually end up at one or the other."

"Then that's where I must go," Benaiah immediately declared. "To Gilgal, and if my father is not there, I will continue onto the city of Saul."

"And I am going with you," Gabriel added.

But seeing the seriousness of the situation and wanting to keep his friend out of trouble, Benaiah convinced Gabriel to remain behind in case his father was somehow to return home. Then, after quickly cleaning up and grabbing some hasty supplies, Benaiah left that very night for the jailhouse at Gilgal.

22

On his way to Gilgal, Benaiah recalled the first time that his father had reluctantly told him about the fall of his hero, Samson...

"Come on, Papa," young Benaiah begged. "The other priests have already told me that you always leave out the story of when Samson met Delilah. You promised that you would tell me, Papa. I know all of the other tales."

"Okay, okay. I will tell you, but I must warn you that it has a very sad ending, Benaiah. Are you sure that you want to hear it?"

"Yes papa. I want to hear it."

"Okay, Benaiah. Here it goes...

* * *

...The years past, and the bad blood between Samson and the Philistines continued. Legends of his strength as he fought against the Philistines on various occasions abounded. It was widely rumored that he once defeated a thousand of their men at once with nothing more than the jawbone of a donkey. The Philistines had thus become sore afraid of coming up against this man from Israel.

Understanding that his strength was an attribute of God,

the Israelites correspondingly hailed Samson as their champion and hoped that he would one day bring about the end of their long time suppression by the Philistines. Yet, if there was one weakness of Samson it had been said that it was his desire for the wrong type of woman, and after Alenia, his want led him to bounce from one to the other.

For quite some time, the threat of his relationships upon his personal success was benign, but he could only go for so long before he met the one person who had the power to devastate his existence and leave him with nothing.

Delilah. She was a beautiful woman with long black hair and deep blue eyes that mesmerized all those who gazed upon her. Men pined for her insidious affection, and women likewise envied her for her beauty and blithe attitude.

By the spring of the following year, Samson was once again courting a woman from Gaza of Philistia. It was on his way to visit this woman in the valley of Sorek that he happened to see the beautiful Delilah for the first time. She was carefree and happy at that particular moment, enjoying the presence of a group of men who were vying for her affection. Two of the men were engaged in a primeval wrestling match to the delight of Delilah. She looked on and laughed with amusement as she watched them, occasionally pausing to pay attention to one of the other men on hand.

Samson hadn't any regard for the two men who were grappling nor did he say one word to the other suitors. He instead made his way through the crowd, and while standing head and shoulders above the rest of the men—who readily recognized who he was—spoke to her with an arrogance that was immediately appealing to Delilah. If a cold blooded creature can be warmed by the feelings of love and passion then such was the case for Delilah. And ever since that very first meeting, she was immediately enamored with this mighty man from Israel. Samson too forgot the original purpose for his visit to Sorek that day, and the pair were inseparable from that time forward.

It must be pointed out that the manner in which Samson carried himself around the local villages with Delilah by his side did not sit well with the Philistines. Yet the men were likewise powerless to the whims of Samson, and remembering the devastation that he had delivered to Philistia's best men of war, they dared not come against him. All that could be done was to wait for the day that he left himself vulnerable. In the meantime, they did bide their time.

Delilah was herself a tiresome spirit, and the fact that her own countrymen readily showed such a great deal of respect to Samson made her curious all the more. She often thought back to the first day that they had met and how no one had even challenged this foreigner when he sauntered into town and walked off with her. At first this was flattering to Delilah and she felt herself lucky to be on the arm of a man who was fearsome to so many others, yet gentle with her. Though as time past, there were no more exciting occasions with men competing for her as long as Samson was around. Thus, after he had left for home to visit his parents and Delilah was approached with the suggestion to deal Samson a blow, she was more than eager to listen to the proposition.

"Just find out for us what it is that gives this man such great strength," Marmack, the leather-faced leader of the Philistine guard suggested.

"It won't really matter either way though will it?" Delilah said in a haughty tone. "None of the men around here would be brave enough to test the answer to that question. They have all lost their nerve. Or perhaps I have lost my beauty," she concluded as she turned to leave in a huff.

"I promise you this," Marmack spoke up quickly. "If you let me in on that secret, I will personally be the first in line to test the theory. That is if it gives me another chance at cozying up with you."

Delilah stopped in her tracks and paused for a moment.

"You never had a chance, you big oaf," she said in a sulky manner. She then turned and faced Marmack with her interest sparked again. "Would there be others, do you think?"

"An army would line up to challenge the man who has kept you to himself for all this time," Marmack answered her with a widening smirk of confidence as he began to feel more and more sure of himself.

Delilah studied the conniving expression on the soldier's face before she gave her curt reply, "Then why hasn't anyone ever challenged Samson thus far?" With this she again spun away from Marmack and stomped off in a smug manner.

Seeing Samson's approach on horseback from the distance, Manoah ran out to greet his son as he arrived down the dusty road that led to their home. He stopped in the high grass and waited excitedly.

With a smile on her face, Lydia too came out to meet her son. "Finally", she said to Manoah, "you will be able to ease your anxious mind and tell Samson the good news."

"Yes woman, I will indeed," Manoah replied as he squeezed his wife with one arm and jovially kissed her on the cheek.

As Samson rode up, he bounced from his horse in acrobatic form and landed squarely in front of his parents. "It's always nice to have a friendly welcoming party," he announced as he embraced his mother and then his father. It had been several months since he had seen them, and the reunion, as always, was filled with joy on all of their parts.

Manoah called for one of the servants to take care of Samson's horse as he quickly ushered his son toward the house and spoke to him with enthusiasm, "I have some great news, great news indeed. Let's go inside, and I will tell you what has taken place since last I saw you."

"Let him catch his breath, Manoah. He hasn't been home long enough to even relax," Lydia said as she followed the two men inside the house.

As they sat down at the table, Manoah told his son the details of how the Philistines had offered terms of a treaty with Israel and had allowed the Council of Elders to reconvene. "The first thing that the Council recognized," he explained, "was how much they owed to Samson, son of Manoah, who has single handedly turned the tables on the Philistines by causing an uncomfortable intimidation throughout their land. The elders want to offer you a seat in the Council as the new recognized High-Judge of all the tribes, son."

Samson was very pleased with what his father told him. Despite his tendency to lack restraint in certain areas, his one true desire was to see the end of his countrymen's subjugation to the Philistines. "It is all that I could hope for. This is truly great news," he responded.

"There is one stipulation to the treaty that may not sit well with you at first though," Manoah said as he looked at Lydia and then back at Samson. "As part of the treaty, the Philistine's require that you do not return to their lands."

Samson sat for a while pondering the provision of the treaty as his parents waited quietly in anticipation of his response. He thought of Delilah and the fact that he may never see her again. But he also realized that this proposition was more important than his own feelings and after thinking it over for a bit longer, he had his answer, "Very well then. If that is what is required for the complete withdrawal of the Philistines then so be it."

Manoah breathed a sigh of relief. "You make me so proud, son," he exclaimed. Looking at his wife, and with tears in his eyes, he then spoke of the past forecast of Samson's life, "It is just as the Lord promised. Our son will see to our deliverance."

Over the next few days, as Samson half-heartily prepared to make the trip to the northern region where the elders had begun to once again convene, he realized something. He was missing Delilah. Seeing his son's solemn spirit, Manoah spoke to him, "What is the matter? Is this not more than you could ever hope for? You have not had to spend years working your way up to a respected tribal position. Instead, in one day, you have ascended to the most powerful seat in the land."

"I know, father," Samson responded in a somber voice. "It is just that there is one thing missing."

"You speak of the Philistine woman? How much do you care about one another?" Manoah countered in a frustrated tone. "Son, you have been down this road before. Can she not wait?"

"That is a good question," Samson said, wondering to himself the true answer.

As time past and the spring of another year was upon him, Samson grew interested in what had become of his Delilah. As agreed, he had never returned to Philistia and instead devoted himself to her in memory only. Hence, weeks had turned into months, months into years, and he was left only with thoughts of his brief yet passionate tryst with that most beautiful woman from Sorek.

He still thought of her quite often; while he worked to solve tribal issues, or when he visited his parents and they asked if he had any prospects of marriage, he thought only of her. But most of all, he thought of her when he saw other couples in love. Never before had Samson experienced such strong emotions over a woman. It pained him to think of her with someone else and it pained him to think of himself with another. With sentiments of this nature on his mind, Samson met with Marmack one day.

Marmack had risen to an authoritative position over the years in his own right. He was now the newly appointed diplomatic officer representing the interests of Philistia to Israel. On this first meeting of theirs, he immediately proclaimed to Samson that he had become a changed man over the past few years, "Despite having once acted unscrupulously, I have since denounced such unbecoming behavior. I believe that every man deserves a second chance in life, don't you?" He spoke with seemingly sincere hopes to work peaceably with Samson as they began discussions over their country's relations with one another.

"I do indeed believe in offering second chances," Samson naively responded. He didn't after all have any recollection of Marmack's connection with Delilah. Next, Samson brought up the current issue of Israel's desire to once again take up arms and form militias without any future Philistine harassment. He made no effort to hide the fact that he was preoccupied and distant at the moment.

Sitting across from him, Marmack delivered the news that his people were willing to agree to the terms. He then changed the subject abruptly by alluding to Samson's apparent preoccupation, "She did not take-up with anyone else."

Samson looked up suddenly. After taking a short pause to read the man's face across from him, he responded in a puzzled voice, "Who didn't?"

"Delilah of course, who else?" Marmack offered in a discerning voice. "Look here, I know that before this meeting we were never formally introduced, yet I know of your circumstances and feel as though I already know you. More importantly, I am acquainted with Delilah very well and understand how much that you must have meant to her."

Samson sat quietly feeling a little uncomfortable before responding, "What do you mean?"

"When you left Philistia, she wasn't the only one who anticipated your eventual return. In fact, there were a number of your enemies, very powerful men, who were sure that you would defy the covenants of the treaty by eventually returning for Delilah. They hence tried to set up an ambush for you by getting to her before you came back."

"And what part did you play in all of this?" Samson questioned.

"I'll admit that I was ordered to find out how loyal Delilah was to you," Marmack tentatively explained. "But I soon found that she was not so very fickle. I couldn't believe it. No one could. After I let the lords of Ashkelon know of her undying loyalty, they personally summoned her and offered her eleven hundred pieces of silver from each of them if she would agree to inform on you. But Delilah straight out turned them down claiming she would never betray her one true love. And those were the very words that she used both on that day and when she came to talk to me just a few short weeks ago. She had somehow found out that I would soon be meeting with you."

Samson's heart began to pound with the news of Delilah's devotion. "Do you mean she wanted you to speak to me on her behalf?" he asked.

"No, she has too much pride for that," Marmack said as he began to rise and leave. But then he sat back down and pondered aloud, "Even though, she did admit that since the day you left she has not thought of any other person. You know, she is a perplexing woman. I personally think that it was that same pride of hers that kept her from loving anyone else after you left. It also kept her from denying that bribe. As a matter of fact it is probably the one thing that has convinced her to stubbornly wait for your return. Maybe she feels that she can prove her loyalty to you, and retain her pride all at once." Marmack finished his thoughts whilst feeling a little awkward for having become so involved in the situation, "But you would know her better than I. Anyways, I have talked too much, and I must be getting back to Philistia."

"You will provide the documents with your monarch's seal in regards to our agreed upon terms then.., with the issue of Israel's militia that is?" Samson concluded in an attempt to appear composed as the meeting was wrapped up. He was trying his best to hide his joy over the news about Delilah, but it was no use. Before Marmack had even departed, Samson was eagerly giving orders for his chariot to be brought around. He would leave to see Delilah that very day.

It was the first time that Samson had entered the land of

the Philistine's in nearly ten years, and as he finally met with his one true love in secret, it was just as Marmack had explained; Delilah assured Samson that she had waited faithfully for his return. During that brief encounter, he asked Delilah to leave with him immediately and join him in Israel as his wife.

"What you say sounds wonderful," Delilah answered with enthusiasm. But then her voice changed to a melancholy tone, "Although, I don't know if I can just leave my family, not knowing if or when I will see them again. I have to be given time to at least say goodbye." Her words were very disheartening for Samson. Seeing his disappointment, she then made a proposal of her own, "You can come and live here. That would solve the whole matter." But as she looked at Samson, she knew that her suggestion was impossible. Samson could not leave his country and his position. This realization pained her as well. "I suppose that we were never meant to be," she concluded.

Samson merely held her close and kissed Delilah before speaking softly to her, "Don't say such things. We will figure it out in time."

They spent the rest of the afternoon together, and as the sun began to set, Samson prepared to leave. Delilah then asked a peculiar question of Samson, "Tell me something. How is that you are so strong? And what is the source of that strength?"

Samson looked at her in amusement. "Why do you want to know the answer to this? So you can manipulate my might?" he said in an amused voice. But his antics were not pleasing to Delilah.

"Don't mock me," she told him. "Please, just tell me."

"Alright, alright," Samson gave in. "If you want to know the source of my strength, I will let you in on the secret. If you were to take seven fresh bowstrings and tie me up with them, I would become afflicted and powerless." After this Samson walked Delilah back to her home and said his temporary goodbyes, "I have to return to Israel, but I promise to visit you soon. I must never again go so long without seeing you."

"When will you come back?" Delilah questioned.

"The first chance that I get, and then we can talk more about our future," Samson promised.

With this last pledge, the two parted in hopeful merriment. But soon after Samson had left, the Lords of Ashkelon accompanied by Marmack and the King of Gaza himself summoned Delilah to appear before them. "Ah, it seems that Samson has paid you a visit," Marmack pointed out straight away. "But he didn't stay long, did he? I don't mean to pry, but I don't know if this Samson has proper intentions."

"And what concern of yours is that, Marmack?" Delilah replied disdainfully.

"Come now," he responded. "I am only trying to look out for your best interest. As a matter of fact that is why you were called here today. The Lords of Ashkelon are concerned about the objectives of this foreigner. You know that he already holds the most powerful position in Israel. Perhaps he schemes to extend his authority into our lands. Why else did he only come for such a short time? Was he not conducting some sort of reconnaissance of Philistia?"

Delilah thought of this possibility and from her worried expression, it was evident that Marmack's words disturbed her.

Then the king of Gaza spoke up, "If what these men have told me is true and Samson is out to infiltrate us, then you owe it to your countrymen to find out the answer of how he can be stopped."

The high-lords of Ashkelon likewise attempted to sweeten their previous offer, "We are each prepared to give you 2200 pieces of silver if you find out for us the secret of this man's strength," their representative said in a cunning voice. "That is twice what we offered before."

This was a vast amount of money, and in truth, this was not the first time that Delilah had actually considered taking the bribe. It had lain heavily upon her thoughts after seeing Samson; she was then forced to realize that perhaps they did not have a future together. This amount of silver would provide well for her, and the prospect of such wealth was the very reason why she had already asked Samson the source of his strength. But still she decided not to betray her love. "I will not be disloyal to him," she declared. "You want to know Samson's intentions? He has asked me to marry him. And when he returns, I will tell him yes. For, he is not like any of you. He is faithful and a man of his word."

This last announcement disturbed the Lords of Ashkelon. But thinking quickly, Marmack spoke up and convinced Delilah that if Samson did not return for her within the year, she should reconsider her stance. Delilah acquiesced, agreeing with Marmack's reasoning before anxiously returning to her father's house to wait for her love. But her anticipation of Samson's quick return was in vain. Months past, and there was no sign of him, and Marmack was constantly there to remind her of this sad reality.

"I have not heard from the Israelite, but perhaps he will come tomorrow," he would say in a scoffing manner. All the while Marmack knew very well that Samson would not return anytime soon. For along with all of the Lords of Ashkelon and the King of Gaza, the Philistines were busy behind the scenes making sure that the year was full of political hardships for Samson. Playing the role of friend, Marmack was able to stay one step ahead of Samson. Whenever he prepared to visit Delilah, Marmack would create a supposed dilemma for Samson to have to deal with. One month he would spread rumors of a Philistine assault upon the lands of the Israelites, another month it would be unreasonable demands of the Philistine government upon that of the tribes. All the while, Marmack would play the part of diplomat and supposedly do all he could to smooth things over with the officials of Philistia in order to avoid any actual aggressions between the two countries. Thus, the entire year passed with Marmack keeping Samson entirely too busy to return for his love. And on the anniversary of the day that Marmack had coerced Delilah into giving up her loyalty for Samson if he did not return for her in due time, she was once again called before the king and his high-lords.

"Are you ready to comply with our requests?" Marmack questioned. "Before you answer, let me tell you what we are prepared to offer you. Our king and his most esteemed high-lords are each offering a purse of 2,200 pieces of silver if you will give us the secret of how to defeat Samson. This would in turn make you the richest woman in all the land."

But their exorbitant offer was hardly an issue, because Delilah had already proclaimed in her heart that if Samson did not return for her within the year, then his love was not what she had believed it to be. And with each day that passed during that time, her feelings for him became more and more contaminated until she was left with nothing but embarrassment and contempt over the issue of Samson. On this day, she stood before them a scorned woman. "Give me the coins, and I will tell you the answer to Samson's weakness," she told them. "It is true; I already know what it is."

"You will get the silver when our enemy is delivered to us," came the response from the king.

The strange proclamation of Samson's only weakness was thus soon tested. When he attempted to pay a visit to Delilah the next time, Marmack made sure that he was able to easily do so, and coincidentally, for the first time in over a year, the relationship between Israel and Philistia was in good standing. Sure enough, when Samson arrived in the valley of Sorek, Delilah was waiting with the bowstrings just as he had described them. She immediately had him take a seat, and then she tied him up. "We will now see if your confession was true," she proclaimed and then clapped her hands.

It was no surprise to Samson when a group of Philistines waiting in the next room burst in to take him away. He had heard their whispering shortly after he had arrived and chuckled slightly over the situation. Hence, their threat was short lived. As they entered the room, Samson flexed his massive muscles and snapped the bowstrings. He then stood up, grabbed two of the men off of the ground and shook them violently until they begged to be turned loose. Tossing them aside, he stared at the others who could do nothing except immediately apologize and make a clumsy exit. Samson then turned to Delilah. "Why would you do this to me?" he asked with a smirk. "Are you that angry?"

"I am more than just angry," she admitted in a feisty manner. "You promised to return to me as soon as possible. Well that was over a year ago. I have become a laughing stock throughout the entire land."

Samson sincerely apologized and tried to make amends with Delilah, but he didn't know that the Philistines had already turned her. He didn't know that her hurt was beyond healing. And worst of all, he didn't know that her tests would one day lead to his demise.

Thus, the years past, and the circumstances remained the same. Samson would vie for the love of Delilah and she would not reciprocate. He would return to see her whenever he had the opportunity, but Marmack continued his manipulation of both parties. "Samson must have found another," he would tell Delilah while making sure that Samson was wrapped up with his duties as Judge of Israel and its incessant discord with Philistia. "Delilah only needs you to prove yourself to her," was the line that he would give to Samson. "She doesn't know if she can trust your word."

Samson did try to prove his loyalty to Delilah, but it was impossible to completely devote himself to her with his busy life as Israel's High-Judge, especially because his schedule was so influenced by his underhanded friend, Marmack. They therefore grew older with Samson never losing interest in trying to win the heart of Delilah, and she likewise never ceased stringing him along as she tried to learn the source of his strength. It had become an obsession of hers, and this amused Samson to no end. His playful nature and enduring interest in her attention allowed him to go along with the game.

On three specific occasions throughout the years, she had demanded to know the secrets of his strength, and each time Samson would answer her with a more ridiculous reply while knowing full well that for whatever reason Delilah would be waiting to test the theory on his next visit to Philistia. He would then overcome the supposed affliction, thrash the Philistines—who of course would suddenly appear to take him away—and then laugh with amusement as the men would flee from him. Afterwards, Delilah would complain over his deceit and declare that she would never marry such a man.

Then one day, Delilah made an unexpected visit to Samson in Israel and made an interesting declaration, "When I first met you, I was at the pinnacle of my youth. I fell for you then, and in my own way, I have been devoted to you ever since. Yet, I am no longer a young woman. My youth is fleeting along with the prospect of my ability to captivate a new generation of suitors. If you love me and the offer still stands, I will marry you."

This announcement almost floored Samson. He had tried so often to win her over and now she was there. Now she was his. He reassured Delilah that he wanted more than ever to marry her if she was willing to come and live in Israel. She agreed on one condition, "I will not marry a man who is unable to share everything with me. You have mocked me many times in the past years by telling me lies about the secret of your strength. Give me the truth now and I will be yours forever more."

But Samson was unwilling to answer her at first, and she soon returned to her home in Philistia. It was then that Manoah paid a visit to his son and spoke to him concerning the issue, "You have judged Israel in wisdom, but what is it that draws you to this Philistine woman? I hear that she pesters you constantly about the source of your strength. Surely she only means to bring ruin to you."

"Oh father, she is harmless," Samson said, taking up for Delilah. "She merely sees it as a way for me to prove myself to her. The truth is that if I knew of anything that could afflict me, perhaps I would have revealed it to her long ago, but I know of nothing."

"Do not say such things, my son," Manoah warned. "God is the source of your strength, and thankfully, He has honored the vow that He made with you before you were even born. Still, you have done your part to test him. Understand that this is a very dangerous practice. A man can truly give away his birthright. Think of the brother who gave away his over a trivial reward. Did he not unknowingly give up everything in a moment of vulnerability? Do not make yourself vulnerable."

But Samson did not heed the warning of his father and instead returned to Philistia to see Delilah. "This is the last time that I will come to this land and ask for you to return with me," he demanded. "If you love me, Delilah, come away with me and be my wife."

"Tell me the source of your strength then, and prove to me that you love me," she replied.

This last statement irritated Samson beyond control and seeing no end to this struggle with the woman that he loved, Samson tried to explain everything to her, "I have made a pledge to God. From my birth I have lived the vow of a Nazarite, and He has endowed me with magnificent strength to fight against my enemies. If I forsake this vow, then God will depart from me. Then I will be no stronger than the average man."

"I don't understand. How can you forsake your vow?" Delilah questioned.

"My hair," Samson suddenly explained. "It is one of the signs of my Nazarite vow and it is never to be shaven."

Seeing his sincerity, Delilah immediately embraced him and accepted his offer of marriage. She then told him to rest while she went into town to let her father know of her intention to return with him to Israel for good. But while in town, she ran into Marmack who demanded to know what had transpired between the two of them.

After Delilah told him what Samson had declared to her, Marmack made arrangements for a man to return with her and cut the hair of Samson while he slept. Shortly after this terrible deed was complete, soldiers arrived to take Samson away. Afraid of the part she had played in the scenario, Delilah cautiously woke Samson. "There are Philistines at the door, Samson. They are here to arrest you," she sorely reported as she agonized over the possibility that this time his strength would truly be gone.

But Samson awoke and was not afraid. Realizing that his hair was cut, he merely shook his head and told Delilah that her tests for him must come to an end. He then prepared to go out and confront the Philistines once more, but as he walked out into the sunlight, he was instantly overtaken. For the first time in his life, God was not with Samson. His immortal strength was gone. Just as his father had warned, he had unknowingly relinquished his birthright in an act of imprudence. What came next for Samson, the mighty judge of Israel, was unbearable for all those who knew and loved him. His eyes were put out with hot pokers, and he was thrown into prison where he was given the job of a mill grinder, a task usually reserved for the beasts of the fields.

Despite their age, his mother and father traveled to Philistia on many occasions to try and visit their son, but they were never allowed to speak with him. Instead they could only watch from afar as he walked around and around the mill, all the while being whipped and treated worse than an animal.

The people of the town likewise looked on at Samson and laughed as they mocked him. "Is that the mighty man? It looks as though our gods have dealt with him justly in our stead," they would claim while delighting in the fate of Israel's High-Judge.

Delilah was given her silver as promised, but the betrayal of the one she loved was too much for her to bear. It is said that she went insane and lived the rest of her life haunted by the memory of her unfaithfulness. It was reported that she often spoke to an imaginary companion, referring to him by name as Samson.

As far as the fate of the Israelite, Samson did in fact eventually realize his revenge upon his enemy. After many months of holding him in prison, the lords of Philistia organized a day of merriment to offer sacrifices to their god, Dagon, for delivering their enemy unto them. On this day, over three thousand officials and lords of Philistia gathered in the grand palace in Gaza with their king. There, they held a ceremony to celebrate their men of renowned. The lords of Philistia then ordered that Marmack go to the prison and bring back Samson so that his strength could be tested against that of their own great men.

Because of his blindness, Samson was unable to manage even the simplest of tasks that he was instructed to carry out before the crowd. He did however prove to be a good source of entertainment as the Philistines laughed at him and watched him try and maneuver his way amongst their renowned men, who cruelly knocked him over and kicked him from behind. They then acted as though they intended to help him up and caused him instead to fall on his face over and over again. When the crowd grew tired of this spectacle, it was instructed that the Israelite be led away.

But as he waited to be taken back to the prison, Samson realized that he had been left alone in an opportune location. He asked a young man who was walking by to lead his hands to the great pillars of the temple so that he could lean against them. There, he called out to the God of Israel, (*)- "O Lord God, remember me, I pray thee, and strengthen me, I pray thee, Only this once, O God, that I may be at once avenged of the Philistines for my two eyes!" And then Samson pushed against those great pillars, one with each hand. And as Philis-

247

tia's men of renowned continued to entertain the crowds, Samson declared to the Lord, "Let me die with my enemy!"

The spirit and strength of God came upon Samson one last time, and with all his might, he toppled the pillars and completely destroyed the integrity of that grand temple of Dagon. It crumbled and fell violently to the ground, abruptly falling on all the Philistines gathered there that day. Samson tragically perished as well.

His family came to Philistia one last time and was allowed to retrieve Samson's body. He was buried back in the land of Israel, which he had judged prudently for twenty years...

* * *

PART IV

VALLEY OF THE SHADOW

23

Within days of arriving at Sochoh near the Philistine border, as ordered by the king, Abner had good reason to be thankful for his newly established friendship with Adino. The general had come through with his promise to remit the three brothers from Zabdiel's list and soon learned that Adino had indeed reciprocated the favor by volunteering himself to begin enforcement of the king's edict. Hence, additional men of war began to arrive to the front lines immediately where they were divided amongst the army divisions of both Abner and the king's son, Jonathan. For the next week, these needed warriors trickled into Israel's camps by the thousands, and it appeared that if the circumstances continued, the army of Israel would readily meet its required troop levels. They could then commence with their next objective, the sacking of Philistia.

But just as things were beginning to look promising, there were a number of serious problems which arose and began to amend the positive outlook of the Israelites. The first issue was the waning amounts of troops that arrived each day starting with the second week of the buildup, because although there had thus far been an impressive response by the men of

Judah, the tribes from the north had not yet responded to the king's edict in kind. The second problem that neither Abner nor Jonathan had foreseen was the fact that they would not readily hold the advantage in numbers for very long; the latest word from Abner's scouts revealed that the Philistine forces would soon match that of Israel's. Furthermore, Philistia's build up, unlike that of Israel's, showed no signs of slowing. This was all the more reason for Abner to continue his hope in Adino to successfully coax the rest of the men from the powerful tribes of the north to join up with him and Jonathan.

Besides these obvious setbacks, Israel was additionally faced with a tertiary problem, and this was perhaps the most serious problem of all. It was apparent to the leaders of Philistia that King Saul's decision to attack them had awakened a spirit throughout their lands, a spirit that had not existed in many years. His affront had ignited the flames of war in all five capitals and brought together the resolve of the Philistine people. The kings of the Pentapolis had likewise adopted the prospect of not only defending themselves, but they had decided to muster a strong enough force to act with a vengeance and completely crush the Israelites. Analogous to the edict of Saul, a similar pronouncement was therefore issued throughout the lands of the Philistines calling for the aid of each and every one of their men of war.

The advantage that Philistia held in the current situation was the fact that not only were they a more populous nation, but their attempts were also immediately and wholly supported by their citizens, who viewed Israel's intention to bring war upon them as an unprovoked act of malice.

A retaliatory plan of all out war was hence swiftly declared throughout the lands of Philistia. Word then spread out across the Great Sea and into the expanses of Greece. There, those men whose very existence had struck fear into the heart of Abner, those whose likeness had humbled the might of Adino, the warring giants of Philistia heard report of the situation.

One of these giants in particular would play a significant

role in rousing the spirit of his contemporaries. His name, Goliath, had already struck fear in the hearts of many throughout the Aegean, for he was indeed a sight to behold. Standing at over ten feet tall, he was a behemoth. As he strode into past battles, he was recognized both by his unparalleled stature and also his heavy bronze scaled armor. Upon this armor was the image of the Philistine's chief god, Dagon, and the thickness of his bronze scales were such that they appeared to be impenetrable by sword or arrow. He was also known to carry with him an enormous spear with a handle of great length and an iron tip that was so lofty a typical soldier could perhaps throw it but a foot. Because his countrymen's call to arms currently led him on a course across the Archipelago, the Israelites would soon understand why no man had ever faced this fearsome Goliath in battle and lived.

Still, it was better that Israel remained ignorant of the lingering threat of giants. They had enough to contend with for the time being. This became very evident as General Abner was awakened one morning during his third week in Sochoh to the sound of heavy armor clanking together in unison. It was the familiar caveat of the Philistines, and it alerted him to the fact that they were marching upon his camp amidst the lofty heights of the Elah Valley. He grabbed what he could of his armor and ran out of his tent, yelling at the guards outside to wake everyone. "Why weren't we alerted by our scouts?" he questioned as he looked out at the wall of Philistine soldiers advancing rapidly up the hill towards his headquarters. The general quickly realized that because of the Philistines' swift speed, his lookouts must have been literally taken off guard. "Muster the ranks immediately we must establish our lines," the general ordered as his horse was brought to him.

The entire camp was now running to and fro, confused and panicked as they attempted to establish a proper defense, but it was too late. As the dawning of the daylight would soon enough reveal, the Philistines had already pushed their way far up the hills of Sochoh.

"Get every archer on line now!" Abner ordered as he looked down the tor, witnessing the devastation that had been wrought upon the lower encampments of Israel.

What was not destroyed with Philistine swords or spears had been immediately burned so there would be nothing left to recover even if Abner could somehow rally his men. In this ruinous manner, Philistia's troops marched ever forward toward Abner in full battle array.

The general knew that his enemy's phalanx formation would become unstoppable if they could reach the summit of Sochoh. Yet, there was no way to defend against the impetus of Philistia's forces, and as Abner aptly ordered his men over the opposite hill in an attempt to try and establish a defensible line, the Philistines were given the high ground. They were then able to launch a fearsome attack as they ran full speed ahead in ranks, cutting down the Israelite camp in a tide of consummate destruction. "We will have to defend with our cavalry!" Abner shouted as he watched his lines of hastily formed infantry fall before their enemy. He rode forward but as his cavalry came upon the philistine line in a frightful clash, Abner quickly realized that the enemy's phalanx could not be broken. The lengthy spears of the philistine's infantry were more than enough to rebuff the cavalcade of horses that ruefully met them as they charged forward.

Fearing the loss of too many in this manner, the general called for an immediate retreat. Then, before he could himself turn around, Abner realized that he was somersaulting down the hill. His horse had not been able to maintain its footing, and the general had likewise been thrown down the steep incline. This left him tumbling down over rocks and roots for quite some time before coming to a stop on a rough embankment.

With his vision blurred and his hearing intermittent, Abner rose to his feet and tried to make sense of the chaos of close combat fighting, which was now taking place all around him.

The pandemonium escalated with each passing moment, contributing all the more to the general's difficulty to gather his bearings. Instinct told the battle-proven man to grab for his sword and fight, but after clumsily grabbing for his weapon and taking only a few small steps forward, he found it harder to focus. He fell back to the ground, fighting loss of consciousness. Then unexpectedly, he heard one of the Philistines yelling orders, "Grab that one. He is a high ranking officer."

Abner awoke some time later not knowing where he was. After a short while he surmised that he must have been in the camp of his enemy. If he had been recognized as an officer, he would have definitely been spared. A captive general does after all make for a great bargaining tool in time of war.

With his head and body aching from the tumble, Abner studied his surroundings. He noticed from a crack in the tent, which he was now in, that it was getting dark outside. He thought of the men from his own camp and hoped that they had somehow rallied to fend off the attack of the Philistines. It made him feel angry knowing now that if they had been given some type of warning they would have put up a much better fight. Still, the Philistines had delivered an astonishingly strong attack. They were without a doubt a well trained army, and the element of surprise had only added to their advantage that morning. Abner wished that he had been the one to use such a brilliant tactic against the Philistines.

Nonetheless, Abner also knew that this was going to be the last time that either force would be able to use such a maneuver. Both sides would no doubt be on their proper guard from this time forth. The way Abner reckoned it, the advantage of this war would now go to whoever could gather the larger force, and he was now more certain then ever that Israel could only stand a chance if they had more numbers. This last realization gave the general a deeper feeling of remorse over his current situation. He needed some way to get word back to King Saul over the urgency of the successful enforcement of his edict.

Abner sat up. He must someway find a way to escape. As he looked around the tent, he could hear voices outside near the entrance, but whoever it was and whatever they were saying, they were speaking in too low a tone for him to understand. Abner decided to act immediately, while he wasn't being watched too closely. He stood up but almost lost his balance. It must have been a pretty bad fall, he realized, since he was still feeling the effects. As he reached up to rub his aching head, he felt a large knot and a bit of dried blood, but even though the pain was excruciating, the general knew that it had to be ignored. Starting to plan his escape, he also began to think that it was very strange that he had been left alone for so long. He could not hear the voices outside anymore and thought of taking a look out the front of the tent, but then he changed his mind. Surely there were guards out there, he surmised. If they knew that he was awake, they would come to investigate. He looked around again. This time he thought of the fact that this was an odd place to hold a captive. It was not very secure at all. There must be some sort of explanation. Then Abner realized that the Philistines must have thought that he was more injured than he actually was.

"Ha," he uttered quietly but then quickly fell silent once more. The voices were back and as they grew louder Abner realized that they were coming his way. It was time to act. The general made a swift dive to the ground. He would simply escape under the tent wall and make a run for it. But as Abner pulled on the heavy woven material of the tent, he was surprised that it was staked down in such a manner that he could not easily lift it. He struggled with it, frantically pulling with all of his might. And then he heard a voice that instantly made him feel a bit silly, "General, what exactly are you doing?" The voice was that of Jonathan. Abner turned and looked around at his surroundings once more. Of course this was not his enemy's camp after all, he realized. This was

Azekah, the neighboring camp of the king's son, Jonathan, who now stood in front of him with a group of soldiers. From the expression on all of their faces, they had somewhat guessed that Abner hadn't yet realized that he was safe in the camp of his own countrymen.

Seeing Abner's bewildered face and not wishing to make a spectacle of the situation, Jonathan dismissed his soldiers and quickly explained things, "Most of your men were able to make a successful retreat back to my camp. After fighting off the Philistines long enough to rescue you from our enemy's clutches, they brought you here to recover. Together, we were likewise able to make a stand and stop the Philistine advance, but sadly enough, we have lost Sochoh. The Philistine's now occupy that land."

Abner hung his head low. "I have disappointed your father and you both," he said to Jonathan in a remorseful voice. "To be taken captive would have been one thing, but this is altogether something else. My conduct as a leader is disgraceful."

Jonathan replied to Abner in a consoling tone, "This was not your fault, general. You have conducted yourself—"

"—My men were relying on me!" Abner loudly demanded, interrupting his contemporary. "As a general yourself, you must know just how such a defeat reflects upon me. I was unable to rally my men. I was unable to lead them, to get them in their respective defensive positions."

"General," Jonathan reproved.

"I must go to your father and apologize for my actions..," Abner continued, ignoring Jonathan once more as he now rubbed his sore scalp in tumult.

"General..," Jonathan said once more. "You need to listen..."

"...I must resign my commission and beg pardon for losing our lands so readily. I am not worthy of this command, of being looked upon as a leader of men. I did not fight a good fight. I did not—"

"—General Abner!" Jonathan now snapped in a loud voice, finally rousing the prattling officer from his remorseful monologue. "None of this is your fault. You were betrayed by your own men!"

Abner's momentary rant stopped, and he fell silent as he looked into the eyes of Jonathan. "But how?" he asked in bewilderment. And then, after another brief pause to think over the matter, Abner continued in an uneasy manner, "How could I have been betrayed? And how did you find this out?"

"It was your entire forward guard," Jonathan explained. "They simply left their posts in the darkness of the early morning, letting the Philistines enter your camp completely without warning. That is why you were overrun in such a manner." With this, Jonathan turned and walked over to the tent entrance where he gave the order for the deserter to be brought forth.

"You have one of the traitors here?" Abner questioned. "How is that possible?"

"I will let him explain the details to you," Jonathan responded. "I figured that it would be best to allow you to deal with this man. He does after all still fall under your command."

A man of small stature, with dark sunken eyes, and stringy, frazzled hair was brought in. His arms had been tied behind him, and it appeared as though he had been weeping.

"What is this that I hear of betrayal, Ephai?" Abner began the interrogation. He recognized the man. Only a week prior, the general had personally granted his heartfelt request to serve as a scout. "You came to me and asked to serve your country by being stationed as a forward lookout, a dangerous post indeed. The man that you replaced at the time was gracious enough. Tell me, did you have plans of treachery even then?" Abner's question was spoken in a calm voice and it appeared as though he was very sincere in his concerns over Ephai's intentions.

The man replied in a remorseful tone as sobs began to

contort his voice and body, "Yes, general. I was propositioned by a friend who already held a post as one of your watchmen. He told me that everything was arranged, but that they did not trust Shaphan enough. You see, Shaphan was the man whose position was surrendered to me, and my friend had already told me that if I could replace him then I could get in on the bounty."

"And what was that bounty?" Abner now asked in a confiding voice. "You were promised riches?"

"The Philistines promised us treasure enough to last a lifetime," Ephai confessed, as the tears and sobs continued and all the men within the tent looked on in silence. After a while he regained his composure enough to speak once more, "They offered us sanctuary in their lands also, and not just for ourselves but our families as well."

"And is this what appealed to you," Abner inquired. "You wanted riches for your wife and children?"

Ephai just shook his head as he looked down at the ground. "No," he said in a timid manner. "That was the biggest concern for some of the men, but I don't have a wife or children. All that I have is an old crippled father." Ephai had once again returned to his sob filled discourse. "And yet, he himself didn't approve of the plan. When I told my father of it, he refused to join me and the others. He even threatened to report us. So, you see, when everyone else left their posts before daybreak and headed merrily on their way towards Gath, I followed. But as I have said, I did not have anyone to meet up with. I would be alone in Philistia with no real prospect for happiness. I was not quite as pleased with the decision that I had made like the others were."

"And so you came back, to confess your sins," Abner finished the man's sentiments.

"No, that is not entirely the reason that I returned either, general," Ephai countered in a penitent voice once more as he hung his head so that his face could not be seen. Then, after appearing to begin his usual routine of sobbing, he looked up to the surprise of everyone to reveal that he was now laughing in a maniacal gesticulation as tears rolled down his face. "We were all lied to!" he said with a smirking cackle. "You weren't the only one betrayed this morning, General Abner. For, the Philistines killed them all and their families too. All their pretty wives and children, even small babies, all dead I tell you! It was the very reason that I escaped. I had no one to try and protect, and I ran. Protect, ha! Can you imagine, trying to be chivalrous after already selling your soul? No, I did not come back only because I am repentant. I came back because there is no where else for me to go. You should have seen my father's face when I last spoke to him. Even he, my only family, will never be able to accept what I have done. I have heard of the defeat that was brought upon Israel this day, of the many men who died because of what I have taken part in. I know that I am to blame."

Abner let the senseless laughter and sobs of Ephai die down before responding. "Untie this mans hands," the general ordered to the surprise of Jonathan and the rest of those present. He then walked up to the defector and spoke to him in a soothing voice once more, "You have done a bad thing, Ephai. You have betrayed your blood, your fellow tribesmen, and your entire country. But I am going to go easy on you." With this last statement Ephai looked up in apprehension. A glimmer of hope showed on his face and remained there as Abner continued, "I am going to set you free Ephai, free from any scorn or derision. I am not going to allow you to torture anymore. At this point a trial would only be one more thing to add to your misery, and your father's as well. He sounds like a decent enough man."

"A decent man indeed, sir, with a kind heart and soul," Ephai responded.

"Yes, and how old is your father?" the general disquietly asked.

"He is getting on in age and has led a rough life since he became a cripple..."

Abner shook his head with concern as he looked at the pitiful man in front of him. He answered in kind, "Let him at least die in peace then, with the hopeful knowledge that you, although a traitor, lived a long and prosperous life." Ephai was now smiling and as he let out a childish giggle, Abner gave him his last words of consolation, "I am going to set you free, Ephai." And with that the general immediately pulled out his sword and stabbed Ephai through his torso delivering a quick death to the pitiful man.

As the soldiers subsequently took the body away, the conspirator still bore a smile of content upon his face. Abner followed behind the procession and made his way outside. Looking out toward the Valley of Elah, he could see that the Philistines did certainly occupy the hills of Sochoh, directly across from them. "We must not let Philistia gain anymore ground," he said aloud to Jonathan in a solemn tone. "They must not cross that valley. If they are able to do that, we will be as well off as Ephai. For each and every one of our hopes will then be dead."

Abner turned around to face the king's son and immediately noticed that the man was wholly preoccupied with something up in the sky. The general then looked down at his clothing as several white flakes landed there and immediately began to melt. He looked up and with a look of bewilderment listened to Jonathan proclaim with a laugh, "Snow..."

24

The waves of the Great Sea met the shores of Philistia with a crash and in with the morning tide came the landing of some daunting characters. Six days had past since the battle at Sochoh, and now Goliath along with a large faction of his cohorts had arrived. As their ominous sea-faring vessels were smartly moored, Goliath brandished his sword and stepped off starboard, into the sea. He plunged feet first into the uncharacteristically icy-cold water, making no effort to swim for it. The giant of a man instead took a deep breath and stretched his sword toward the heavens as he waited for his head then his skyward pointed arm and weapon to submerge below the waterline.

Not surprising to the men who looked on, the tip of Goliath's blade sank slowly down yet was still prominent above the ripples before it was already rising once again. The muscular arm of Goliath emerged next and then the face and body of the giant surfaced, dripping with anticipation. As he sauntered out of the water and onto the beach of his homeland, the giant planted his sword into the sand then turned towards his fleet. Next, he motioned for his warriors to follow with the hailing of his head and the roaring of his voice.

These particular Philistines were accustomed to such dramatics, for they were a breed apart from their resident counterparts, which had been born and raised on the soil of their shared homeland. Most of these warriors had instead spent the majority of their lives in Greece. Taken away as children to be trained and raised for the purpose of warfare, they were somewhat barbaric in their mannerisms. In the animal kingdom, they would have been considered not lions but feral dogs whose fighting tactics were both vicious and raucous. Goliath hence continued his beckoning yells as, horses, servants, boat loads of weaponry, as well as enough supplies to maintain a small army were simultaneously launched into the water and then onto the shore. Before long, all twelve ships that Goliath commanded on this journey of recompense had been unloaded and were made ready to begin the trek inland.

As Lahmi, the nephew of Goliath, had soon learned from some of the locals, they wanted to head towards Elah. "Our fight awaits us, in that valley," Lahmi explained to his uncle who sat regally on the beachhead upon a crude throne of drift-wood, which had been fashioned for him by some of his servants. "The valley has become known as 'The Shadow of Death', because of its recent reputation of what it offers those who occupy it."

Goliath nodded his head and confirmed the implication, "The waging of war has already begun then." He glanced up at Lahmi and spoke with a voice of intrigue, "Tell me more about this peculiar name, 'The Shadow of Death'. Sounds like our kind of place."

Lahmi went on to explain what additional information he had learned and how Elah had become the holding line for the Israelites. "Each day as the sun begins to set and the fighting comes to a cease at Elah," Lahmi repeated the words of the local residents, "a dark shadow is cast upon that place. And down the slopes of the hills, in the stretch of that dark valley, the bodies of fallen soldiers lie lifeless, piled atop one another. The faces of the men are often left frozen in eerie silence, which mimics the echoes of battle cries and the intensity of the afternoon's warfare. The bodies of warriors are left densely packed throughout the area, and in their clutches, as well as littered on the ground, is the added danger of razor sharp weapons. These are more than capable of impaling or cutting the bodies and limbs of those who attempt to navigate through the heaps of casualties within the dim light of the shadow-cast valley. All efforts are thus made to evacuate the area by late afternoon, and the fighting of the day ceases long before the sun makes its final descent into night. With the dawning light of the next morning, the men of Philistia, and those of Israel as well, commence with the clearing away of the valley floor. The entire scene is then played out all over again. They say that it has been this way since the first day of the fighting."

Goliath listened keenly to what Lahmi had so vividly described. He then stood up and walked over to his much younger nephew. Lahmi, a giant in his own right, who had stood towering above the mighty Adino after the two had been introduced in the desert by Bacchus, was himself dwarfed by nearly two feet when standing next to his uncle. And the obvious physical endowments of Goliath did not stop there, for the musculature of the latter was extremely overdeveloped so that he appeared nearly monstrous and not fully human at all. He placed a club of a hand on Lahmi's shoulder, looked over to the gates of Ashkelon, and spoke in a deeply commanding voice, "It has been over thirty years since I have seen my country. Tell the men that tonight we drink and celebrate in this magnificent city of ours. For within a few days we too will tread in this Valley of Elah, and the Shadow of Death shall loom upon many of us."

Three more days went by with the scene at the battlefront continuing in the aforementioned manner. Both sides were feeling the angst that comes with the demise of so many of its forces, but despite its losses, the spirit within the camp of the Philistines remained at an all time high. The five kings of the Pentapolis had already received word that Goliath and his reinforcements were on their way.

To the delight of the giant and his warriors, before they had even reached the camp of their countrymen, they were made aware by a messenger that a cessation to the fighting had been arranged with Israel for the next seven days and a ceremony in honor of their arrival had likewise been scheduled. "This will make for an additional week of celebrating and drink for me and my men," Goliath boasted in response to the announcement. He brought his chariot to a halt and then spoke to the messenger in a solemn tone, "We are already so wearisome from the making of merriment and lack of sleep."

"Shall I ride ahead and give word of your refusal to my king?" the messenger questioned Goliath in a concerned manner.

Goliath looked over to his nephew and then back at the messenger. With a devilish laugh he responded, "Nonsense, tell your king that I accept his offer. Me and my men will get enough sleep when we are lying in our graves. Ha ha ha ha!!!"

Goliath and his impressive entourage thus arrived to Ephes-Dammim later that same day in grand fashion. The men were ushered to a platform where the five kings of Ekron, Gath, Ashkelon, Gaza, and Ashdod sat upon their royal thrones. As the procession came to a halt, everyone in attendance bowed to the kings. The only two left standing were Goliath and Lahmi. Just as Lahmi prepared to bow down in reverence to the kings, he was stopped by Goliath who held him up at the shoulder and loudly proclaimed his reasoning, "In Greece we are but servants, but in these lands, the lands of our fathers, we are our privy to royal lineage. We bow to no man whilst here."

Most in attendance were surprised by the words of Goliath, but the kings of the Pentapolis remained calm and poised.

"That is right," the king of Gaza confirmed. He looked over to the other crowned men whom he sat amongst and returned their nods of consent. "You, Goliath, have returned to the lands of your ancestry. You rightly hold claim to the title of your forefathers. We recognize your lineage, which belongs to that of Og, past King of Bashan. But he was sadly defeated by a champion of the Israelites. All of this was discussed by the five of us just this morning. We likewise have come up with a solution for you to remedy the past and in doing so reclaim not only the title of your fathers but also their lands, which is now occupied by Israel. Join our ranks by leading us to victory. Realize your destiny and become a king amongst kings."

Goliath considered what was told him for a drawn out moment. He then walked up to the king of Gath. Looking down at the man, he drew his sword. "I gladly accept the gauntlet," he responded with an air of conceit as he held his sword high in the air and begged applause from the crowd. When the cheers had died down the giant continued in his braggart manner, "And after I have defeated these miserable Israelites, I will likewise accept my coronation. Finally, my birthright will be restored. Thus, let us celebrate the victory that I will soon bring to Philistia." As Goliath finished this last pronouncement, the king of Gath motioned for the wine to be served. Goliath took the large goblet, which was brought to him. He held both of his arms high in the air with the drink in one hand and his sword in the other. The giant then turned back to face the kings of Philistia and confidently pronounced his words, "Let us drink to Dagon, god of earth."

"Let us drink to Goliath!" the king of Ashdod proclaimed as he raised his own goblet. And with that, a loud cheer rang out once more throughout the camp of the Philistines.

A faint echo of those cheers reached all the way to the camp of Israel. Already suspicious of the Philistine's request for a seven day cessation in fighting, Abner and Jonathan discussed the possible meaning of it all as they stood together atop the hills of Azekah and looked out towards the camp of their enemy. "What do you think was the motive of this seven day pause?" Abner asked Jonathan apprehensively. "Do you think that it is this cold-spell? My soldiers give me reports that besides the short snow-flurries we get each day that the valley has pockets of ice formed on it every morning, which has only made it a more perilous place for battle."

"Although this cold can be a hindrance to an army's morale, I don't think that their motives for this seven day truce are that simple," Jonathan responded as he purposefully breathed out a cloud of steamy vapor into the chilly air. "Still, it is obvious that like us they are hurting, and have thus organized a rally to encourage their disheartened men. We have both lost a lot of soldiers and in a short time. Nobody, including my father, could have foreseen this war escalating to this level of intensity so suddenly."

"Yes, had they not attacked us first, and so suddenly," Abner affirmed, "we would have had more time to build our forces to the requisite amounts needed to take on the army of Philistia. And that is what worries me. Surely they realize that they vastly outnumber us at this point."

"Perhaps they do not know the truth about our numbers," Jonathan offered. "We have all of the soldiers that allowed us a sweeping victory over the Amalekites. We have the sword of every man of Judah. If only our forces from the north would now arrive, we would then be a much more potent force. The Philistine kings surely know of my father's edict. If they even thought that are troop levels were near full capacity, they would have to reconsider facing off with us in all out battle. They have probably thus decided to call this short truce in an attempt to begin negotiations with us."

Abner frowned as he spoke in a worrisome tone, "I don't think that it is quite that simple either. We can fend them off for the time being, but I fear that the philistines are planning something, something big. Your father's messengers have reported that King Saul and all of the royal guard should soon be arriving from Gibeah, but that will not be enough to hold this position indefinitely. I will feel somewhat better with the king here, but if my suspicions are correct about Philistia's plans, we will still eventually need Adino to pull through for us and coax every possible man from the north to also join us."

"Yes," Jonathan responded in kind. "With the Council behaving so stubbornly, Adino needs to pull through for us and gather the Northern Tribes. He is our greatest hope."

Just then a messenger from the king's guard arrived with a letter for General Abner. As he opened it, Jonathan inquired if it was from his father, "...Does he mention when he will be here?"

"No, it is not from the king," Abner answered in an astonished tone as he silently read some of the letter's contents. "It is from none other than Adino. It speaks of a strange plot..."

25

Word of many ill fought battles concerning Israel had reached the ears of Adino over the past years. He was always saddened to hear of these as he continued his duty with Samuel. Yet, he likewise always felt that Israel would prevail and all the while knew that he was doing his part by protecting the prophet. That is why it was with great remorse that Adino listened to the accounts of the tragic battles which were currently taking place at Elah. This time, Adino feared that Israel may not pull through, especially if he was not successful in his recently promised efforts to assemble all the tribes.

He thought of this as he fervently continued his attempts to gather the warriors of Israel. Recruitment had begun the very moment that the mighty man had left from his opportune meeting with Doeg, by then a fully deputized conscript of Saul's. As he walked down the steps of the palace, he and his men were met by the sons of Zeruiah. Recognizing the three as Abner's men, Adino immediately told them and the rest of his own troop to circle their horses. He then tossed a scroll through the air. "You are all about to hear the newest purpose of our mission," he said with a leer and a glimmer in his eye.

The parchment, complete with the king's seal upon it, was caught by Micah who answered Adino with a smirk and a wag of his finger. The entire group then excitedly listened to the reading of its contents:

> 'By order of King Saul.., Adino Ben Hachmon is hereby given full charge and authority to enforce imperial law, which without delay requires all men of warring age to report for duty in the king's army. Enforcement of this edict includes the right to arrest any and all detractors...'

Micah looked up with a smirk after reading the rest of the scroll and amusingly spoke to Adino, "Yeah, you've really gotten us into the mix this time, my friend..."

The mighty man nodded his head contentedly before pausing for a moment. He looked over to the three new arrivals and then reached for his father's lists of valor in order to confirm their names; "Joab, Abishai, and Azahel. I am glad to see that Abner kept his word by sending you here."

"We are honored to join you," Joab confirmed. "And by the way, Abner does send his regards."

"Yes, I will thank Abner the moment that I see him," Adino proclaimed in an appreciative tone. He once again referred back to his manuscripts, "You are all confirmed as men of renowned. And yet, you are just the beginning of those whom I plan to assemble in order to carry out this imperial commission." Adino put away his list along with the parchment from the king and spoke confidently to all the men once more, "This mission of ours begins immediately. And although we have been given authority to arrest those who are unwilling to join Israel's efforts against the Philistines, we will rely upon a less divisive method of marshalling up the troops..."

Adino had cleverly decided to begin his recruitment efforts

in the name of the king within the boundaries of his own homeland. In Judah, the mighty man could stand upon his reputation and family's influence to guarantee success in gathering troops for the king's army while simultaneously beginning to build a small force of elite warriors under his own command.

The hunt thus led him on a path throughout the lands of Southern Israel, and with plans to use his father's manuscripts as a continued guide, Adino and his troop of thirteen first traveled to the village of Beth-Arabah. There, the Eznite hoped to personally enlist the help of a well celebrated warrior from the region by the name of Abi-albon.

As Adino arrived into the heart of the village with his men, they were met by a group of nearly six hundred warriors, part of the defensive militia of the region. It was the first time that Adino would have the opportunity to present his case directly to a large faction of his countrymen. Yet, because Adino did not know how the men of the region would react to his new delegation, and they themselves did not know the true intent of the mighty man, there was plenty of tension in the air.

As the two groups met, Abi-albon spoke first, and with an aggressive tone, "We have already heard that you, Adino, have taken the side of the king and are putting men into jail for not following his edict."

"I haven't arrested anyone at this point," Adino explained to all the men of Beth-Arabah as the two factions brought there horses to a halt in front of the village square. Adino continued in a cordial tone, "Still, that is a right that my men and I have been granted by the king."

"But what if we refuse to join your cause?" Abi-albon asked looking over to his men who all appeared as anxious as their leader over the anticipated answer. He looked back at Adino and continued with a frown, "Will you attempt to exercise this sovereign right of yours by arresting us? I respect your endeavor, son of Zabdiel, but do you think that we will go to the king's prison without a fight?"

"Listen, I am not here for either reason," Adino said rationalizing with Abi-albon and the rest of the men from Beth-Arabah as he dismounted his horse and approached their spokesman. "Honestly, I do not wish to arrest you or to fight with you." The mighty man made his clarifications to Abi-albon in a low tone. He then quickly made his way to the top of an elevated pergola, which was located in the middle of the town's square. From there he could be seen and heard by all those present. "Men of Judah, I need you to hear me out," he announced loudly, getting the attention of everyone present. "I am here because I took a commission from the king for a cause that I sincerely believe in."

"And what is that cause? Going to war with an enemy that we cannot defeat?" a voice yelled out from the crowd.

"No! That is not the case," Adino immediately responded in an authoritative voice. "The king and his advisors have determined that with the sword of every man in the land, we can be victorious. But if we do not all stand together, that most certainly will not be the outcome. This is likewise the cause that I have taken up and my motivation for speaking with you today, to see to it that our country operates in one accord."

"Yes, but what of the issue of the elders?" another voice chimed in. "They have not given us the command to fight. How can we ignore custom and make decisions without their guidance? Why does King Saul demand this of us?"

"Forget the matter of who is giving you the order to fight or not to fight for a moment," Adino answered back. "Right now, there are men of Israel stationed on the borders of Philistia in the lands of our own tribe, Judah. They are the ones who are relying on you. Think of them at this moment and ask yourselves, if you were in their situation would you want your countrymen, your brothers, cousins, and kinsman alike to wait for an order from the king or from the elders before joining you on that battlefront? If you were them right now, would you expect others to take up this cause only for the sake of someone else's bidding? I say no. You would instead be expecting those left safely at home to now take up their swords, to gather with you, and to defend this nation that we call Israel simply for the sake of our future, for the sake of our children's future." Adino could see by the nods of many of those present that his words were beginning to strike a chord with the group. "I ask you this," he continued. "Out of all the tribes, which has the greatest to lose if this campaign is a failure? What if the army of King Saul is defeated?"

"The Philistines will overrun our borders first," Joab loudly answered from amongst the crowd, espousing Adino's argument.

"This is true," Adino continued. "They will overrun the borders of Judah and take away our lands, just as they have done in times past."

"What he professes is absolutely correct!" a voice familiar to the locals yelled out. The man who made this last proclamation then made his presence known by walking up and joining Adino on the small platform. This was Ari, the aged uncle of Abi-albon and one of the most respected elders of the region. Shrewdly, Adino had consulted with him first, before attempting to talk with Abi-albon and the rest of the villagers. Ari spoke to Abi-albon directly, "As you already know, my nephew, I have fought alongside this man's father on many occasions. And I have fought alongside Adino as well. Political affairs aside, in time of war, we only have one another to count on. Without that, we have nothing. I have therefore given Adino and his cause my blessing. He is right to ask for your help and all that of Israel's."

"Well said," Adino responded as he turned to the crowd. He then gave his final argument, "In days past, our families have fought together and bled together, making their blood as one on the grounds of the battlefield. And today we should forever remain loyal to that creed, loyal to one another. In order to win this war, it is necessary for you to join your brothers out on that battlefront. This should be the only call to arms that you need, the call to stand and fight amongst your countrymen and against a common enemy who have long been a thorn in our side. Tell me now, who amongst you is prepared to answer that call? Who will join their countrymen who are already stationed with Abner at Sochoh, with Jonathan at Azekah? Who will fight for God, for Judah, and for Israel?"

Abi-albon looked around at the men of his village who now likewise stared back at him wondering what his response would be. He then looked upon the face of his uncle who gave him a nod, signaling his favorable response. "I am with you Adino," the respected warrior subsequently declared. "Your cause truly appears to be a noble one."

It was evident that his attitude was shared amongst the men of the village, and with the sanction of these three great men, Adino, Ari, and Abi-Albon, all the warriors of Beth-Arabah at once declared their intentions to join their tribesmen on the border of Philistia.

The momentum of Adino's crusade was now in full swing, and as the village made immediate preparations to leave, Adino called for Abi-albon to join him in private. "You are listed here as Abiel, father of strength, and the valiant one," Adino commented as he referred to Zabdiel's list. "It says plenty more of your exploits and this is the reason that I have chosen you. There are not many men that could be considered your equal."

"Coming from the likes of you, Adino, I take that as quite the compliment," Abi-albon replied. The valiant man then went on to ask about the exact role that Adino had in store for him.

Adino replied in kind with what he had already told the other men currently under his personal command. "I am gathering a small group of select warriors who can be relied upon to help recruit the rest of our countrymen. If you see the importance of this charge, as do my men, then I ask you to personally join us as we travel throughout the rest of Israel and make ready our nation for war."

Abi-albon thought for a short while before responding. He then gave his answer in earnest, "Your reputation as not only a mighty warrior but also a man of honor precedes you, Adino. I will thus count it a privilege to do as you ask and to ride with you. Whatever you orders may be I will follow them."

The remaining men of Beth-Arabah were then sent to Abner and Jonathan at the battlefront as promised to Doeg by Adino. These were likewise the first troops to arrive and supplement Saul's army in Sochoh and Azekah, thereby beginning the optimistic attitude of those at the battlefront throughout the first week that they occupied the entire region of the Elah Valley.

During the following days, Adino and his troop had similarly increased in numbers as they traveled next to Tekoa in order to recruit the men from that district. There, Adino had used similar tactics to call another prodigious man of war by the name of Ikkesh to ride with him and his men. It was said that this man often took up the cause of those who were too weak or frail to stand for themselves; he was a warrior with a steadfast mind and a soft heart.

After conscripting the loyalty of Ikkesh, Adino then circled his troop and traveled in a northeasterly direction where he was able to recruit men from two of Judah's oldest families, the houses of Zerah and Baanah. Their men of warring age were gathered and sent to Abner while their champions Maharai and Heleb stayed on with Adino. These two had grown up together and had proven their loyalty to one another on many occasions.

"I would die for that one," Heleb said of Maharai. "He has been a real brother in war. I know he would do the same for me."

"Yes, and I have almost gotten the chance to prove that allegiance on more than one occasion," Maharai rejoined with laughter.

"We swear that same loyalty to you now, Adino," the two announced in one voice.

Azmaveth was then enlisted into the group. With a battle-name meaning 'Strong as Death' this long locked man of brawn was known for his many deeds of conquest over the Moabites in which he had displayed seemingly immortal strength.

Next, from the hill country of Judah, the sword of a valiant son of Sharar, known as Ahiam the Mountaineer, was procured. He had traveled far and wide during his many exploits. Known for his ability to climb the loftiest of heights, he could also track a man over rock, falling snow, or any other rough conditions or terrain.

Rounding off the enlisted militias of Judah were those from the regions of Giloh, Carmel, and that of the Arbites. Their men of distinction were of course each gathered into the company of Adino.

Finally, two brothers from the preeminent house of Kiriath-jearim, named Ira and Garib were called upon. These were the last two of Judah's men of renowned from Zabdiel's list to be recruited by the mighty man.

Thus, in little more than a week, the extraordinary band of men led by Adino had more than doubled to a force of twenty one. With control over this growing faction of phenomenally skilled fighters, Adino's commission from the king was simul-taneously validated as word of his recruiting efforts traveled throughout the lands of Israel. Success in implementing Saul's edict appeared promising.

Once more, this is why it was with great remorse that Adino first learned that not only had the fighting already begun, but the first battles had resulted in devastating losses for Israel. With news that the Philistine forces were building fast, Adino intuitively understood that there were still many areas to visit and many more tribal militias from Northern Israel to call to arms.

With all of Judah already at the battlefront, it was thus necessary to now take his venture out of his own tribal lands and head toward the territories of the other eleven tribes. As the men set up camp during their last evening in Judah, Adino let them know where their journey would now lead them, "Our first stop on our travels north will be the house of Dodai from the tribe of Benjamin. He and his entire family are strong men, recognized as having great battle-skill and volatile temperaments. While Judah is esteemed for its many gallant families, the house of Dodai, along with the rest of the Benjamites, are known for their rowdy sons and warriors.

Keep this in mind when we get there. We don't need to be getting into any scraps or cause any hostilities. Remember, although they are a relatively small faction, the Benjamites carry a lot of sway throughout the northern tribes. If we can convince them to follow Saul's edict, the rest of the north may very well respond positively as well and hopefully in short order." After Adino finished updating everyone, the camp turned in for the night. But although Adino was very tired, he did not sleep well. Instead he tossed and turned, dreaming his familiar dream over and over again.

When the men awoke and walked out of their tents the next morning they were all very surprised to see that a fresh layer of snow had fallen during the night. For most of them, this was the first time that they had seen a landscape of pure white. The ride north was therefore a tranquil one indeed, filled with plenty of opportunities to enjoy the pallid, yet wondrously blanketed scenery.

26

The dust rolled in a whirlwind behind Adino and his troop of warriors as they entered Dodai's lands. By now they had left the snow and cold weather far south of them.

After passing through a long drive that meandered through the hillsides, they eventually crossed over a small stream and through a forest of olive trees. In the distant pastures there were grazing sheep and cattle; among these were men tilling fields in the middle of the afternoon heat. Finally they came to the family's main compound and were surprised to see a throng of men gathered in the courtyard, some of which were engaged in groups of animate conversations, while others practiced swordplay and wrestling.

In the distance, Adino took notice of many gathered around the fires of the family's metal-workers eagerly waiting an opportunity to test a new forged weapon. Standing amongst the lot of them was Eleazar, son of Dodai, easily recognized by his long red hair and beard. This was the warrior that Adino had personally come for.

The mighty man dismounted and began to walk towards Eleazar, but his efforts were stopped short by the beckoning of another man's words, "Your arrival makes for perfect timing." The voice was raspy and came from the peripheral entry of the main residence. A lean man with the face of a gracefully aging lion came out to greet Adino. This was Dodai the elder, and despite his graying whiskers, his physique gave him a youthful appearance. "My servant's advised me that your chariot was approaching," Dodai's voice growled in a pleased manner.

Adino greeted the elder tribesman with a hearty embrace and gave kind regards on behalf of his father and grandfather, whom he knew to have always maintained a closely-knit relationship with the house of Dodai. "I see there is no sloth in this domicile," Adino said as he glanced around once more at Eleazar and the busy company of men. "I am on an urgent mission in the name of the king."

But before the mighty man could continue, Dodai cordially interrupted, "Hold off until we get inside." He then gave hasty orders for some his servants to bring the rest of Adino's men and their horses some fresh water. "Make yourselves comfortable gentlemen," he remarked with a smile. "What's mine is yours." He then led Adino inside.

The home was built more in the fashion of a fortress than an abode, with many servants and even the presence of a number of armed guards. Adino was brought a refreshing drink as Dodai continued, "We have been anxiously awaiting your arrival."

Adino was surprised to hear what Dodai was saying until he was led further into the dwelling and into a large room where there waiting for him was the prophet, Samuel.

"King Saul has stifled our efforts to gather with the other tribes without an overseer, but for now he can't stop us from coming together as a family," Dodai quickly told Adino alluding to the fact that many of the Benjamite elders were likewise present.

"That is right, and I am simply here as an invited guest," Samuel added as he rose to greet Adino.

"An esteemed guest indeed," Dodai acknowledged. He then led the two men out of the room and onto a back verandah overlooking his manicured land-holdings. "We can talk here without interruption," he assured them.

"But prophet, what of the king's orders for you to remain at Ramah?" Adino immediately asked with a look of concern.

"I am having to learn how to navigate my way through the countryside un-detected these days," Samuel declared as he took a seat on a nearby iron bench. He shook his head as he continued, "For there are some troublesome issues at stake right now, ones that I must do my best to take part in." The prophet looked up at Adino and motioned for him to take a seat of his own. "Don't look so distraught," he said with an encouraging smile. "Ramah will be there for my return, but I had to come here in order to help avoid a serious dilemma. You see, I am of a truth afraid that we are on the brink of civil war even while we are engaged in heavy fighting with our enemy the Philistines."

"Civil war, you say? How or what is this all about?" Adino questioned, again in a very alarmed manner.

"I will let Dodai explain," Samuel said as he gave a nod to their host.

"As you may or may not have heard, Adino," Dodai began, "I was nearly arrested alongside Eliel of Manasseh not too long ago as we attended the assembly for the Council of Seventy. Had my son Eleazar not been there to put a stop to things, I would be sitting in prison even now. The man who would have put me there, Doeg, seems ostentatious enough. Yet the king has put much trust in him."

Adino seemed all the more troubled at the mention of Doeg's name. "I have met this man that you speak of," he offered. "In fact, I personally dealt with Doeg while in Gibeah over the issue of receiving my latest designation as a deputy of the king. Tell me. What does he have to do with the mention of Civil War?"

"That is what I am trying to get at," Dodai continued in an

informative manner. "This man has become extremely powerful in a very short time, powerful enough to give directives in
the name of the king, and powerful enough to confer authority
to others such as yourself. In addition to a number of other
titles, including that of Supreme Advisor, we have just
recently been informed that the king has also bestowed upon
him the position of Chief Magistrate over the Council of
Seventy. We hear that this Doeg now has plans to issue many
edicts in the name of the king and to force the hand of the
Council. He has called a meeting to accomplish this. Therein
lies the crux of our problem. The tribe of Manasseh has made
many attempts to have Eliel released from prison, all the
while enjoying no success. Now Manasseh has threatened to
lead an all out attack on Gibeah if Eliel is not released in time
to attend this latest Council meeting."

"Surely this is just a bluff on their part," Adino quickly
surmised. "I mean with everything else that is going—"

"—It is no bluff!" Samuel interrupted rather anxiously.

Dodai gave the prophet an affable nod to demonstrate his
consensus over the significance of the situation before
concluding his account, "Baran, son of Eliel, was here for a
visit along with a group of his tribesmen. They have asked for
the assistance of my house and that of my own son, Eleazar,
in solving this problem."

"And what did you tell him?" Adino inquired in a bothered
manner.

"That is when the decision was made to summon me,"
Samuel answered as he stood and walked over to Adino.
Patting the mighty man's shoulder he then offered some
condolence, "You needn't worry. You will be able to bring
resolve to this predicament, my friend." Adino gave him a
look of surprise after this last statement whilst Samuel merely
smiled and nodded as he continued, "Word of your success in
harvesting swords for the battle reached me even as your
adventures in Judah unfolded. Hearing the route you were
following and knowing that this would likely be your first

northern stop, I made this journey to meet up with you as well as to dissuade Baran and the rest of Manasseh from acting in a rash manner."

"Baran listened to reason at first," Dodai quickly pointed out. "He and his men waited here several days but eventually grew restless. With the Council meeting scheduled to take place two days from now and no established solution, they left early this very morning without giving us any word of their latest intentions."

"Yes," Samuel retorted, "Having myself only arrived a short while ago I did not have the opportunity to speak with them, but from the looks of things, they intend to act. It is tragic because their response can do nothing more than divide the country further. They have already caused some turmoil in the heart of Eleazar, who likewise feels the urge to act."

"That would explain all of the anxious men gathered outside," Adino offered.

"Yes, with the possibility of a tribal retaliation upon the prison along with the overall hostile environment of Gibeah at the moment, my son insists on escorting me and the rest of our tribal elders to the Counsel meeting," Dodai said in a regretful manner.

"Perhaps that is not such a bad idea," Adino pointed out.

"No, that won't entirely do," Dodai responded. "Eleazar is too hot headed. He would be looking to cause trouble, and as Samuel points out, actions such as this can only make the matter worse. Besides, this Doeg has already given explicit directives against any such measures. We are to arrive alone for the Council meeting, unarmed and unguarded.

"So what is the solution," Adino asked.

"We have all heard of your delegation to gather the tribes in the name of the king," Dodai said in a hopeful tone.

"...Along with your subsequent success throughout Judah to gather a compelling troop of your own," Samuel then complemented. "I am glad, Adino, to see that you have your priorities in line. It appears that your latest commission from the king allows you to accomplish two directives at once, very efficient indeed."

"And that is precisely why Samuel has recommended that it be you who helps us get out of this whole predicament," Dodai rejoined, "which you can do by going to King Saul in the prophet's stead."

"But what influence do I possibly have over the king?" Adino questioned back. "I wasn't even given the opportunity to speak directly to him during my last visit to Gibeah. As I have already pointed out, I dealt only with this Doeg, the Supreme Advisor to Saul, when I received my royal commission."

"It doesn't matter if your commission was obtained from the Supreme Advisor or the king himself. You have proven your worth," Dodai answered. "With the exception of talk over the war, the success that you have achieved at rallying the militias in Judah is the most widely spoken of topic throughout Israel. Trust me; with the losses at the battlefront, the king and his Supreme Advisor both know exactly how valuable you are at the moment. King Saul will listen to you as an ambassador of the people and it is our hope that he will receive yours as a voice of reason and authority."

"An ambassador?" Adino questioned and then gave out a laugh. "This whole situation is becoming much too complicated for me. Now then, I know how to lead men. I know how to wage war. But diplomacy is not exactly my specialty."

"You must go strong-man," Samuel then directed in a compelling tone. "Consider this a significant part of my commission to you. For, it is my hope that you and your men will be able to diffuse this situation by escorting the elders of Benjamin as far as the city walls. Once there you would part ways, thereby respecting the orders of the Supreme Advisor."

"In the scheme of everything else that is happening now, what would be the purpose of such a task?" Adino asked in a pensive tone.

Samuel responded convincingly, "As Dodai has pointed out, you do not have the same hot temperament as his son, and Eleazar has already made it clear that he will not be dissuaded from at least traveling to the vicinity of Gibeah with his father. He claims that he will simply wait outside the city gates just in case he is needed, and this is where your expertise can come into play. You say that you know how to lead men? Well, like many others, Eleazar is a man that needs direction, someone who knows when to act and when not to." Samuel gave a smile to his host who once more returned his sentiments with an approving and gracious nod.

The prophet then quickly turned his attention and instruction back to Adino, "You will stay there in the backdrop in order to monitor the situation, to make sure that no more troubles arise, that Manasseh doesn't attempt to carry out their foolhardy plan, and that this nation of Israel does not fall apart. Remember your purpose, Adino. You are to gather those that will hold together our nation. Most importantly, you will use this trip as an opportunity to gain audience with King Saul, something that I am no longer able do. Once in front of the king you must act the part of an emissary—a mender of bad-will. And do not let me hear that you know nothing of diplomacy. I have gladly heard of your diplomatic methods of gathering the men of Judah. You must now use that ability to keep the peace and work-out the situation in Gibeah."

"This could not be unfolding at a less opportune time," Adino ruefully declared. "Nonetheless, I will go at your behest, prophet."

"Yes, I am afraid that your quest to gather the forces of Israel must be put on hold for the moment," Samuel told Adino with an equally remorseful pang in his voice.

"If your decision is final, Adino, I would be happy if you would follow me inside," Dodai directed. As they entered back into the company of the elders, Dodai then made a quick declaration, "Elders of Benjamin, the man who stands beside me is known by most of you. He is Adino, the warring Eznite, who has accompanied Samuel in times past and now gathers men to fight in the name of the king. He has likewise agreed to help us and Manasseh in our time of need. I can't speak for the elders of the other tribes nor solicit their Council at the present moment, but I believe that I speak for everyone here when I pledge in kind the support of our families for any and all of his future causes. Once these Council dealings are over with, my son and those of my house will indeed join our countrymen at Elah." Dodai then turned to the mighty man as he finished his sentiments, "This I can promise you, Adino. We are with you. Consider it an act of recompense for your loyalty and the first sign of the north's resolve to win this ill-chosen war with the Philistines."

The men in the room then each thanked Adino for all that he had done and pledged their compensatory support in like manner.

"Come now, Adino. I will introduce you to my son," Dodai finally said. "I have already explained that you might be accompanying us to Gibeah..."

After saying his goodbyes to Samuel and ensuring the prophet his best efforts, Adino made his way outside alongside his host. There, Eleazar was waiting along with a crowd of his edgy warriors. They stood opposite Adino's own troop of men. As he followed Dodai out to meet Eleazar, the mighty man noticed that the red-haired man not only stood taller then the entire crowd, but he was also as rotund as any two or three of the others put together.

Dodai was quick to make the introductions. He then excused himself, saying that he would like the two groups of men to get to know each other while he paid a visit to the stables in order to ensure that the proper preparations were being made for their trip into Gibeah."

"So, you are the great Adino, are you?" The ruddy man arrogantly questioned as his father departed. He then stroked his long beard and assumed an investigative posture. "Perhaps you have heard of my name and reputation as well?"

Adino responded in his usual collected manner, "I have indeed heard great things about you, my large friend. I also believe that we once fought together, at the battle of Ekron and Gath." Adino then introduced his group of prodigious warriors one by one. "...Many of these same men fought at the battle of Ekron and Gath as well," he said before introducing the three sons of Zeruiah. "Perhaps you can remember some of their great feats?"

Eleazer briefly considered Adino's question. "That was many years ago, but still I remember that you were there," he said as he pointed at Joab, "and you were there; as were you," he added as he pointed at Abishai and then Azahel. He then walked up and jabbed his finger into Adino's chest and spoke in a surly tone, "And it was you, the one called Jashobeam, who led the fight on that day." Eleazar then made a broadcast in challenging manner, "But who will take orders from whom on this upcoming journey of ours?"

Adino began to see where the conversation was leading and quickly perused the surrounding environment. He noticed that amongst the gathering of men, there stood the remains of an ox-drawn grinding mill and a stone watering basin.

Eleazer rotated his neck back and forth and rolled his shoulders as he stretched his prevalent trap muscles. "I don't know about you," he said motioning for his men to clear some space, "but neither I nor any of my warriors are willing to follow just anyone into a possibly dangerous situation. I have to know that the man in question is worthy of respect. And I am wondering if you have perhaps lost some of your zest after all these years, Adino." With this last word, Eleazer, unsheathed his intimidating sword as his warriors respectfully cleared out and made some room for the anticipated contest. Seeing that reasoning with Eleazar was not an option, Adino gave similar instructions to his own men.

Eleazer tossed his long red hair behind his shoulder before

suddenly lunging forward with his sword extended. Adino swiftly reached over his back and grabbed his holstered and readied, glimmering-sharp blade. With classic poise he brought it down in a precise defensive stance and exactingly deflected Eleazar's wily attack. In the same moment, Adino stepped aside and twisted his sword round and round, clanking and clashing the weapon out of his opponent's hand in a series of methodical movements.

Adino spoke to Eleazar in an appropriately composed manner, "Your fighting methods, while convincingly forceful, are untamed and sloppy. We will have to work on that, my friend." Then, as he walked over to pick up Eleazar's sword, he instantly felt the crushing tackle of the Benjamite on his back. The jarring force sent his own sword soaring through the air as his lungs crushed under a potent bear-hug. Adino felt his feet lift off the ground as he gasped for air and fought off his body's urge to give up consciousness. Mustering just enough strength to wriggle down and plant one foot in the soil, he instantly deposited his powerful elbow into Eleazar's abdomen and unsympathetically catapulted the man overhead and into the hardened earth.

The two men now both gasped for air simultaneously as Adino glanced over at Eleazer to see if his efforts had been convincing enough to arrest his opponents attack. The answer came quickly as Eleazar jumped to his feet and once again ran head first in full tackle-mode, but this time the attack was anticipated while Adino stood under the iron rods hanging from the traction wheel of the old wheat-mill. As Eleazer drew closer, picking up speed with every step, Adino reached up, grasped the heavy iron dowels of the mill with both hands, latched them onto the solid stone water basin, and tossed the entire contraption in the direction of the oncoming power-house.

The thudding sound that came next as the heavy stone crashed against Eleazar's skull and body while knocking him off his feet was enough to make everyone, including Adino, wince with pain. Eleazar once again stood up, took two wobbling steps, and then uttered some unintelligible words. With the fight taken out of him, he then fell backwards and reluctantly took a seat on the ground. As his upper torso and head spun around in a dizzied manner and his eyes opened then closed, the son of Dodai tried to register consciousness. Everyone gathered around to see if he was alright.

After a few moments of this, Eleazer shook off the blow and gave out a spirited chuckle. "Ha, ha, ha... Now that's a man that I would follow into battle," he said alluding to Adino and his extreme immobilizing tactics. Adino rushed over and helped the man up as Eleazer gave a proud, beaming smile, rubbed his head, and sportingly bellowed, "I definitely did not see that coming".

"You don't lack spirit. I'll give you that much," Adino announced.

As the two men brushed off the dust from the short scuffle, Dodai called out to them from the distant stables, "If you two are done playing, I have plenty of work for the lot of you. We must make ready for our trip..."

27

The elders of Israel sat quietly throughout the room anxiously shuffling in their seats as Doeg over-dramatically raised his fist in the air and made his first declaration, "I say that this day each of you will pledge your loyalty to the king. I have personally just returned from a trip to Beersheba. While there, I oversaw the capture and arrest of a priest by the name of Jehoiada. His seditious actions had gone unnoticed for quite some time. But I recognized him for what he is, a teacher of progressiveness, and a perpetuator of falsehoods. He has taught the people that the king is just a mere man, a contemporary of the populous, and perhaps chosen by circumstance. All lies!

The king is much more than this. He is a divine instrument of God, and it is this same divinity that has allowed him to appoint me as a delegate of justice during this time. Until you all realize these facts you will likewise know of no peace in your homes or those of your tribesmen.

This Jehoiada sits in prison now, but his sentence will soon be delivered. And mark my words; justice will be delivered to this man, this priest. He will be made to realize his own mortality. Any of you who cares to share the same fate are welcome to do so by not agreeing to give the immediate order, upon returning to your homelands, for every man of warring age to heed the edict of the king and to report and fight against the Philistines.

As stated at the last assembly, the king is now completely repealing the right for you to send whomever you wish to serve in his army while holding onto choice men to serve in your own tribal militias. This useless tradition ends now! Any tribesman of warring age who is currently not serving under the command of one of the king's generals will follow the lead of Judah and report immediately. And they will remain part of the imperial army until released from duty by his majesty's seal. Furthermore, the punishment for disobeying the king's edict will be imprisonment and possible execution..."

Dodai sat this entire time listening to the continual rants of the Supreme Advisor with quiet contemplation. As planned, Adino and his group of men had escorted Dodai along with the rest of the Benjamite elders to the gates of the city. The entire affair transpired without incident.

Once in Gibeah, Adino had given instructions for all of his men, including Eleazar and the rest of his contingent to stay back and out of sight. "Also, stay off of the main road," he warned them. "We do not need to attract any unwarranted attention." Meanwhile, the mighty man entered the city alone and followed well behind Dodai's lead. Before proceeding to the palace with a request to see the king, he wanted to personally witness the elders safely entering the assembly-hall. Adino took notice that this was not the customary grand courthouse of the Council but was instead the hall used by and for the ranks of the king's guard, as barracks and headquarters. The mighty man waited out of site for a short while until he was satisfied that everything was peaceful. He then consulted with one of the soldiers standing watch outside of the hall, "Is the king present at this assembly today?"

The guard gave Adino a bored look and told him that the Supreme Advisor and Chief Magistrate, Doeg, had taken charge of the meeting in the king's absence. Saul was reportedly too ill to attend. Adino attempted to find out more information but was told to get a move on. He thanked the guard for the information anyway and politely headed off. Once he was around the corner, he pressed his ear to one of the doors and listened carefully.

He could hear the persistent ranting of Doeg on the other side, "...The king has been much too easy on every one of you. He has allowed you to think that you still hold some kind of authority. Well, as Chief Magistrate, I am here to tell you that the king is neither a puppet nor a figure head. And to prove this, he has gone over an entire list of new laws that he expects you to abide by. So get a little more comfortable, we are going to be covering each topic in full detail. This should have all been addressed in our last meeting, but the unruliness of some of the Councilmen completely disrupted everything. I trust that this will not be an issue this time around." Doeg looked around at the many soldiers currently present as he made this last remark. He then spoke again in autocratic fashion, "You are all immediately required to collect two fold the taxes, which are already now due to King Saul by all the inhabitants of your lands. I have made some initial calculations from the rolls that you have provided to me, and make no mistake, a full one fifth of every man's fields and one fifth of his vineyards shall be accurately accounted for as they are surrendered, starting the moment that you return home..."

"Uh hem!" Adino turned around to see a soldier standing in front of him. "Can I help you with something?" the man asked in a stern tone after clearing his throat.

"Oh, not really," Adino replied, thinking of a quick excuse. He was doing his best to act in the same nonchalant manner that he had told his men to behave in if they were spotted in the area. His order was to act humble, cordial, and naïve. "I was merely curious as to what sort of wood this door is made out of. It is rather nice wouldn't you say? And very sturdy too, I might add. I couldn't even tell if there is anybody on the other side. I mean, I definitely couldn't hear anybody on the other side. Maybe there is, maybe there isn't. I don't know…"

"Uh huh," the guard replied in a smug tone. "Move along, and don't make me tell you twice."

This last comment sort of perturbed Adino, but he ignored it and did as the soldier demanded. It was a very good thing that the likes of Eleazar was not around. As he walked away, the mighty man thought of the fact that besides Dodai, both his father and grandfather were present behind the closed doors of the assembly. He would like to have seen and talked with them, but that would have to wait.

Next, Adino headed for the center of town, and toward the palace. Once he got there, he approached its entrance but was immediately turned away by the guards who abruptly stopped him and informed him that the king was ill. Orders had been given that he would not see or talk to anyone without proper authorization. "What did that mean?" Adino thought as he left the palace.

In order to get to the bottom of things, he then decided to speak with one of the guards over at the Council's court entrance, which was also the only way in or out of Gibeah's prison yard. "How are you?" Adino asked, starting the conversation off with a cordial enough greeting, but the guard at the entrance of the court merely gave him a quick glance and then assumed his previous posture by merely standing in a locked position looking forward. "You know, you might want to relax a little. I mean, do you always take your duties so seriously?" The guard ignored this last comment of Adino's as well, without even looking at him. "I am getting nowhere with this," Adino thought to himself. But then the mighty man said something that got him more attention than he had bargained for, "Listen, I am just here to see about Eliel of Manasseh." With this, the guard suddenly drew his sword and called over two more soldiers. "Hey, I am just trying to visit an old friend," Adino said as he backed away, "I can come back another time."

"Maybe you should take your request to the king," the voice of a woman suggested from behind Adino.

Adino was slightly agitated over this obvious inane suggestion and began to answer back in a snide manner, "Yeah I am sure that I can just go knock on his door and—" but he suddenly disregarded his sarcastic remark as he turned around to catch a glimpse of a beautiful and captivating woman who now stood in front of him. It was Zephaniah of Endor.

"So tell me. What interest do you have with this Eliel?" she asked in a suspicious voice.

"As I was saying, he is a friend," Adino replied having regained his train of thought. "And besides, I am really just trying to save everyone before there is any real trouble."

"And, as I was saying, you should take it up with the king," the woman once again suggested in a polite manner.

Adino all the while made his next statements without expecting a serious reply, "Yeah, well in times past I was able to enjoy audience with the king with no problem, but that doesn't seem to be the case anymore. I've already been informed that he isn't taking any unauthorized visitors, and I know that his Supreme Advisor is busy at the moment as well. I really don't know who else to talk to over the matter."

But Zephaniah did reply and in a serious tone nonetheless, "I'll see what I can do for you."

"Wait a minute," Adino said in bewilderment. "You think that you would be able to get me in to see him? I am sorry. What was your name again?"

"The name is Zephaniah, and as the king's personal physician and relied upon advisor, I have come to know the king quite well. If it is that important for you to see your friend, Eliel, I will do my best to get you in to explain your dilemma to King Saul."

"You mean right now?" Adino asked again, still hardly believing that he was finally starting to get somewhere after being snubbed by the guards all afternoon.

"You ask way too many questions," the woman from Endor remarked as she laughed in amusement over Adino's astonishment. "Listen, you wait here, and I will go and make the arrangements this very instant."

"Finally I get a break," the mighty man said aloud as he watched the woman walk down the road, briefly stop in order to talk to one of the guards, and then casually saunter directly up the steps of the king's palace and through its doors. Adino took in a deep breath and thought of what it was that he would tell the king in order to get Eliel released. But his plan-making was suddenly cut short by the sound of a multitude of horses approaching.

Adino looked up to see a horde of men riding hastily in his direction. He recognized them instantly and then remembered what Eleazar's father had told him about Manasseh's reaction to Eliel being locked up during the assembly. Adino thought of the reason why the guards were acting so apprehensive earlier and came to the conclusion that they must have known of a possible assault from Manasseh. "So that's what they were anticipating," he said under his breath.

Fortunately for Adino's cause, this was no all out assault. It was instead merely a large group of men from Eliel's tribe, here to demand the release of their senior Council member. Adino also realized that the small amount of men showing up was probably a temporary situation. If their attempts to have Eliel released were unsuccessful, the entire militia of Manasseh could be marching on the city within a few days. As Samuel had suggested, this could definitely lead to unrest and possible civil war.

The horses approached as the guards made ready by calling in reinforcements. Soon the king's forces easily had the men of Manasseh outnumbered. In the middle of it all was Adino who quickly raised his hands out to each party and signaled them to hold off their attacks as they came together in front of the court. "Listen, listen up! There needn't be any trouble here today!" he yelled as several men from Manasseh dismounted their horses with their swords drawn.

"This has nothing to do with you, Adino," Baran, the leader of Manasseh's men said as he stared down the guards.

He and Adino knew each other through their parents. They were merely acquaintances, but Adino was familiar enough with this man to know that he was somewhat level headed and could thus be reasoned with. Likewise, Baran knew that Adino could be trusted for his word. And that is exactly what the mighty man was counting on when he made his next statement, "Baran, I know that you and your men are here to get Eliel out of prison, but listen to me. We might be able to accomplish just that without taking this problem any further and getting people hurt."

Baran kept his angry gaze on the guards for a while as he seemed to contemplate the offer. "What do you have in mind?" he asked, not breaking his unrelenting stare.

"In just a short while, I am going to be speaking with the king about releasing Eliel," Adino offered. "So if you hold off and don't do anything rash you could very well be leaving here peaceably."

"Eliel is our elder Councilman and is currently supposed to be attending the assembly as the senior-member of Manasseh," Baran said in a fuming voice. "Furthermore, if Manasseh is going to adhere to any directive for us to join the war it will come from his input at the assembly."

"Alright, like I was saying, we will get him released, and he can go to the Council meeting. Then we can talk amongst ourselves about whether you and your men will be joining the campaign. Everyone will be happy," Adino responded in an easy and calming voice.

Baran then turned to speak with his tribesmen over the matter as Adino gave an affable smile and waved his hand over to the guards who had been standing-by, watching the whole negotiation. They were as anxious as Adino to find out Baran's reply and honestly preferred not to fight, but if Baran persisted they would have no choice.

"Alright, we will wait, for now, to see if you can get him released peaceably," Baran said as he turned back to Adino. "If so, we will escort Eliel to the assembly without giving any further trouble."

Adino tipped his head to the man who returned the gesture respectfully. He then breathed easily hoping that Zephaniah would come through with what she had promised. Just then, from the back of the horses, a ruckus broke out. Adino could see men being shoved aside followed by angry outbursts. "What now?" Adino thought to himself. Then he spied the source of the problem. It was a youthful man, solidly built, with a look of determination on his face, which likewise told the men of Manasseh to steer clear. He was indeed an unfamiliar person in the city, but had he been in the company of any of the villagers from his own remote region, he would have been properly recognized as "The Lion Killer", son of Jehoiada. For this was none other than Benaiah come to save his father. As the young man broke through the crowd and made his way to the front of the Manasseh horde, Baran and his men looked quizzically at Benaiah. They then turned their gaze toward Adino, wondering what he would do about this new situation. "Can I help you with something?" Adino inquired in a calm manner.

"Are you the captain of the guard?" Benaiah quickly asked.

"I am not with the guard at all," Adino explained.

"Then no, you can't help me, now kindly step aside," the stranger replied gravely. "I have no quarrel with you, only with the men holding my father prisoner."

Adino looked at Benaiah and almost laughed out loud. From the look on the young man's face, he definitely wasn't there to do any talking. The mighty man questioned the young man anyways, "Are you thinking of taking on a troop of, oh I don't know, let's say one hundred soldiers that are standing behind me at the moment, all by yourself?"

"If I have to…" Benaiah said in a convincing enough tone.

Adino thought of complying with the request by stepping aside. For just once that afternoon, he could be the spectator and watch what he thought would make for a pretty entertaining match. But then he remembered his purpose there and tried to talk Benaiah down, "Look kid, why don't you go back to wherever it is that you came from and nobody will get hurt, alright."

"I am no kid. The name is Benaiah, son of Jehoiada, and that is who I have come for. I have already wasted enough of my time at the jailhouse in Gilgal, where it took me several days just to learn that my father wasn't even being held there. Needless to say, the journey here has been one of frustration and my patience have since worn thin. So step aside, old man. I won't repeat myself another time."

"Old man?" Adino repeated in an incredulous voice. "Come now; I am hardly an old man." He shook his head, and then, for the sake of his delegation, he tried to reason with Benaiah once more, "Listen, let me explain what you've just walked into and maybe, since I am in a good mood, I will see what I can do to help you out. In a few moments an attractive looking woman is going to exit from that structure over there." Adino looked to his right. His actions were mimicked by Benaiah so that both men now stared at the guarded entrance of the palace. "Do you know what that structure is?"

"It looks like a royal palace to me," Benaiah responded.

"Precisely, and I have been lucky enough to gain an appointment with the indisposed king," Adino explained. "I am going to be speaking with him about arranging for the release of a friend of both mine and the unhappy group currently standing behind you." Benaiah turned to look at the angry mob as though it was the first time that he had even noticed them. "If you calm down and behave yourself, maybe I can do the same for your father. Jehoiada wasn't it?" Adino finished just as Zephaniah emerged from the palace and continued walking toward them. "See, I told you. There is the woman I spoke to you of."

Benaiah thought it over for a brief moment and then uttered his decision, "Fine, but I am going with you."

"What? Listen, I was fortunate enough to arrange a meeting for myself. I can't have you just traipsing in there with me," Adino retorted.

"It is either that, or I stay here and continue this conversation with the guards," Benaiah insisted as he pulled his sword out and rested its tip on the ground in front of him.

Zephaniah arrived. Undaunted by the added company she spoke nonchalantly to Adino, "The king will see you now."

Adino gave a quick look at Benaiah and realized that it was perhaps too dangerous to leave this young upstart behind. It could lead to trouble, which was something that the mighty man did not need anymore of at the moment. "Do you think the king would mind if I bring a friend along?" he asked of Zephaniah while still looking at Benaiah who stood resolutely in front of him staring-down the prison guards.

She looked the both of them up and down before answering in an indifferent manner, "Not at all. Bring him along if you wish. I am sure that any friend of the mighty Adino is a friend of the king." With that, the three made their way to the palace.

Adino now shook his head in disbelief over the sort of demands that he was having to put up with in the name of diplomacy. "So you know of my reputation?" he asked in a beaming manner of self-confidence as he looked arrogantly over to Benaiah.

"Not really," Zephaniah said spoiling his brashness.

"But I believe that you just called me by my name," he said attempting to correct her. "And I don't remember having told it to you."

"One of the guards at the palace had recognized you earlier and asked me if it was you, the mighty Adino, who I had been speaking with at the assembly gates," she explained. "I told him that I didn't really know exactly who you were, and then he reassured me that it was indeed you after getting a better look from the distance. I was just repeating what he had referred to you as. I actually thought that the 'mighty' part was a tad humorous. That is why I repeated it." After Zephaniah's last comment, Benaiah was now the one sporting the patronizing expression as he looked back at Adino with a smirk.

But unbeknownst to both the men, this woman of Endor knew exactly who Adino was. It was the very reason that she had made the arrangement for him to see the king in such a hurry. Remembering Doeg's worries that Adino's meddlesome antics could somehow drive a wedge into their plans, Zephaniah decided to take matters into her own hands. "I just ran into Samuel's companion, Adino, out by the prison gate," she had told the king shortly after leaving Adino to set up the assured appointment. She walked up to the king's throne and immediately provided Saul with a medicinal dose of the elixir that he had become accustomed to.

"What did you say to this agent of mine?" the king asked in a drowsy voice.

"I told him that you would see him," Zephaniah replied.

"Excellent you shall certainly send him in to see me," Saul instructed…

28

"Enter the king's courtyard," Zephaniah said to Adino and Benaiah as they stopped outside of the large doors preceding its interior.

"Are you not going to accompany us?" Adino asked suspiciously.

"No, I will wait for you out here," the woman of Endor retorted. "King Saul will make a more candid audience without the presence of me or any of his other advisors."

A guard unlatched the entryway and allowed Adino, followed by Benaiah, to approach the king, who sat in regal fashion high upon his throne. The only other individual in the room, the royal page, loudly announced the mighty man's entrance, "Adino Ben Hachmon to see the king!" The man then made a courteous exit, leaving the courtroom in hollow silence.

Saul sat up. Although he was a bit groggy, his interest had been sparked. "Ah, Adino," he said with a smile. "You know that I have always liked you. You have brought such consummate devastation upon our enemies, the Philistines." The king wore a devilish look upon his face as he reached over and palmed his scepter. His demeanor was cunning and collected, lending a chilly atmosphere to the room as he spoke, "It has been quite a long time since we had the opportunity to talk, so I want you to tell me straight away, and of course for my own indulgence in the nefarious nature of man, what was the exact reason that you volunteered yourself to my Supreme Advisor? Was it revenge?" Giving no time for Adino to respond, Saul then began to confide in the mighty man, "It seems that the two of us have more in common than I realized. And yes, how I do remember your history with the Philistines. That affront that they brought upon you, and what they did to your family so many years ago, it has no doubt caused you much pain."

This last statement of Saul's sent pangs of sorrow through the core of Adino, and for a moment he wished that the true reason for him volunteering to aid in the king's cause was revenge. For, that was something he knew plenty about.

"Philistia has caused me much sorrow in the past as well," Saul divulged, "sorrow that has itself never been properly dealt with. That is the very reason why I once had much hope in you, son of Zabdiel. When you took your plight to the battlefield in the past, I declared you a mighty warrior and foresaw your ability to lead my armies to victory. That was also why it was with such great disappointment I had to witness you abandon your true calling, as one who should wage war, and instead accompany Samuel. And as what? His personal guard? Ha, ha..!"

With this last comment, the king laughed aloud for quite some time. After a while of vindictively musing over the matter, he then continued his monologue with manic enthusiasm, "The prophet has always been too cunning to ever really require such a necessity. Still, he took you away from me, Adino, for his selfish purposes. I realize now that he has always enjoyed stealing my glory. And although I was fair with Samuel and his whimsical requests in the past, I will no longer allow him to stand in my way!" The king was very pleased with himself as he made this last declaration and gave out another baleful chuckle. As his laughter finally died down, Saul spoke to Adino once more with an air of solemnity, "I see that you have no intention of letting the prophet stand in the way of your own plans for retribution. Certainly, it makes me glad that my decree has finally brought you to your senses and roused your vengeful spirit."

After seeing the delight that the king took in having someone such as himself as an ally, Adino decided to play along. "You are right. This recent edict of yours has reignited a fire in my soul," he claimed in an attempt to convince Saul of his antipathy for the Philistines. "I have been truly honored with the opportunity to serve you by gathering the men of Judah. I am also glad to report that the Benjamites will be heeding the stipulations of your edict shortly, and I have good reason to believe that Manasseh will also comply once their Councilman is released. And that is why I am here," Adino stopped himself short and pondered the king's genial attitude. It was not entirely obvious, but there was something a bit odd about Saul's behavior. The mighty man looked over at Benaiah who returned his confused expression with an encouraging nod, which compelled Adino to continue, "Because I have come here with the hope that you might be willing to indulge my interest in a small matter." This last comment gushed from his lips as the mighty man attempted to shake off his apprehension.

"A favor from Adino, whatever could it be?" the king questioned in a sly tone as he stepped down from his throne and walked towards the two men.

"I would like for you to set Eliel free," Adino said unflinchingly. He then noticed that Benaiah had not given up his coaxing demeanor. Understanding the young man's motivation, the mighty man began to ask about Jehoiada, but he was suddenly cut off...

"—Come now, Adino," the king quipped. "You have won favor with me, but who do you think that you are fooling? Whose side are you on anyways? Traitors such as Eliel shall be given no pardon. Now tell me. Who has put you up to this? Could it be the likes of Samuel?"

At some point, on his way to see the king, Adino had decided that if all else failed he would try and reason with Saul by telling him exactly what was going on throughout Israel. Adino saw this as his moment of truth. "Your kingdom is falling apart around you," he abruptly declared. "You have this new Supreme Advisor who acts on your behalf, but the decisions that he makes are costing you the support of the elders of Israel. Furthermore, throwing respected men in prison and usurping the authority of both Samuel and the elders isn't—"

"—I am the only authority in this nation!!" The king suddenly screamed at the top of his voice after hearing Samuel's name. He then quickly turned around and walked up the stairs taking a seat back on his thrown once again. Saul then buried his face into his palms and began to utter something under his breath as if he was having a drawn out conversation with himself in order to regain his composure.

Benaiah leaned over to Adino and whispered, "I don't think that the king is doing quite alright." Adino looked back at Benaiah and shrugged his shoulders as the two men were forced to merely stand there, awkwardly waiting for the king to coherently proceed.

"Forgive me," the king finally said as he once again looked up at the two of them. He spoke in a calm voice once more, "What I meant to say is that I have decided that Doeg is more than qualified to understand the nature of his position as he advises me on the various affairs taking place throughout Israel. Now, I know that things are not going completely according to plan at the moment, but once the elders understand their rightful position everything will return to normal, and our war efforts can then continue with hopes of success." Saul had returned to his senses but after a short while he began his strange antics once more. Apparently having no knowledge or recollection of what he had already said, the king began repeating his earlier sentences almost verbatim, "I have always liked you Adino. You have brought such consummate devastation on our enemies, the Philistines. It has been quite a long time since we had the opportunity to talk, and I have been wandering something every since I was first told that you had volunteered to help enforce my edict. Was it actually revenge that started you on this mission of recruitment..?"

As the king continued with his repetitive dialogue, the idiosyncratic behavior tipped Adino off that there was definitely something wrong with the king's ability to rationalize and that this was probably the very reason why Saul had appointed this new Supreme Advisor to begin with. He also realized that the king's decision was probably for the best, because in his current state, Saul was in no position to run his own administration. After gaining an understanding of all of this, Adino suddenly took notice of a commotion taking place outside of the palace.

He nudged Benaiah, signaling him to take a look out towards the courthouse. It appeared that a great many soldiers had descended upon that place and were now in the process of arresting all of the men from Manasseh. Then, as the king once again buried his face into his palms and began to laugh hysterically, Adino took notice of the sound of many boots approaching from down the main corridor of the palace. "We have to get out of here," he whispered over to Benaiah.

"No!" Benaiah insisted trying his best to keep his voice at a whisper. "I have to tell him about my father."

"Well, all I can say is good luck, my friend," Adino hurriedly stated, making no attempt to argue at this point. He then took off in a sprint towards the door.

"You can run all you want," Saul said brusquely as his manic mood died down and he looked up toward the ceiling with his palms held up in repose. The king then closed his eyes and uttered his next words with contentment, "But your arrest is required this day as well. I was warned of your betrayal in advance, Adino. And the voices, they are never wrong on such matters!"

Benaiah looked at the king who continued on in a whispered incantation. The young man shook his head. "Wait," he yelled as he made a dash for the exit. After hurriedly reaching the main corridor of the palace, Benaiah looked in one direction to see Adino fleeing around the corner and dragging the reluctant Zephaniah behind him. He then peered in the opposite direction to see a large group of soldiers filing towards him with their weapons drawn. "Wait for me," he yelled out once more as he chased after Adino. Eventually Benaiah was able to catch up and assist Adino in restraining Zephaniah who would not give up her struggle to break free from her captor. The small but scrappy woman was giving quite a fight as she wriggled herself out of Adino's grip several times and then grabbed at his face with her long nails.

"Don't resist too much," Adino warned while holding a hand over Zephaniah's mouth and lugging her along. "I already consider you dead weight as it is. I would hate for you to prove me entirely correct."

Down one corridor and then a next, Adino led the way through the halls of the palace. With the guards chasing after them, it was impossible to find a safe escape-route until all of a sudden someone called out to them, "Quick, this way to safety." Adino complied without question and followed in the direction of the voice, which led them through the winding hallways and toward a dark and narrow subterranean stairway. As they dodged down into the stairwell, the three of them barely escaped the pursuit of what seemed to be an endless procession of soldiers. Adino continued holding his hand over Zephaniah's mouth until their pursuers had all funneled by. He then questioned her, "Where do these stairs lead?"

She mumbled something back, but with Adino's hand still clasped over her mouth it was impossible to understand what she was saying. After Adino peaked out to double check that there was no one else coming, he finally released his grip.

"This leads under and out of the palace," Zephaniah repeated in an irate tone.

They hence proceeded immediately down the steps and through a passageway, which sure enough traveled the length of the palace and far past the walls of the city. Once they reached the end of the tunnel and were convinced that no one had followed, each of them took a little while to catch their breath.

"Now then, that did not go how I had hoped that it would at all," Adino said, still breathing heavily, as Benaiah and Zephaniah both looked at him in exhaustion.

29

A dino and his two new companions sat in a shallow ditch outside of town. The mighty man looked around only to realize that the escape passage that had conveniently led them to safety had also put them a long way off from being able to help anyone. After mulling this fact over for a while he looked over at Zephaniah, who by now had given up any attempts of putting up a struggle. He spoke to her gruffly, "Start talking."

"Talking about what?" she responded in an astonished voice.

"About your obvious role in all of this!" Adino came back in an even more slighted tone. "You have a lot of nerve. How is it that you were so willing to get me a meeting with the king?" he asked in a suspicious manner. "You obviously set me up."

"Is this how you always react to someone who has just done you a favor?" Zephaniah questioned. "And I am not just talking about getting you in to see the king on such short notice. How about some thanks for letting you know about the tunnel?"

"Yeah after we were already tipped off by someone else," Adino declared in a smug voice.

"You're impossible," she said while shaking her head. "If you hadn't put your clumsy hands over my mouth I probably could have been a lot more help and a lot sooner for that matter."

Benaiah broke up the bickering by offering his take on the situation. "Yeah, whose voice do you suppose that was?" he questioned. "It was mysterious enough. And as far as the condition of the king, he was acting completely irrational. I don't think that he is really well at all. I mean that was an utter waist of time trying to talk with him."

"Exactly!" Adino acknowledged Benaiah's point of view before directing his suspicions back to Zephaniah, "What do you know about the king's odd behavior?"

"Alright, I apologize for getting you in to see the king when he was having one of his—" she paused for a brief moment while searching for the correct expression, "—when he was having one of his peculiar episodes."

"Having a peculiar episode? The man is a complete maniac!" Adino said in an astounded manner.

"Yes, yes. You are both right," Zephaniah finally admitted. "The king is not a well man, and that is the reason why he originally contacted me. Let me explain my role in the matter. I am from Endor, a small village with a long history of practicing divination. My family in particular is known for its knowledge of this art."

"Don't you mean sorcery or witchcraft?" Benaiah asked bluntly. He was very familiar with the strange practices of the rural countryside.

"Call it whatever you wish, but the fact is it is a very effective method to deal with ailments akin to the king's," the woman explained. "And it is also what has won me his trust."

"So you are merely trying to help him out with his illness, huh?" Adino asked in a skeptical tone.

Zephaniah defended herself, "It is part of my responsibility as a necromancer to use my powers to help others. Just because people like me are dubbed witches doesn't mean that we are evil or conniving." She then hesitated for a little while before blurting out a confession, "That is why I must tell you, Adino. I knew all the while who you were and your past role as the guardian of Samuel. Simply put, I wanted to get you in to see the king so you could witness his current condition. And now that you know about it, perhaps we can work together to do something for him. Believe me, with this newly appointed Supreme Advisor controlling things, Saul needs our help."

"Unbelievable!" Adino exclaimed in an exasperated tone as he looked closely at Zephaniah, trying to determine her level of sincerity. He then glanced over to Benaiah who simply retuned his look with an uncertain expression. It was difficult indeed to believe that there was any malevolence in this young beautiful woman. She had, after all, already been helpful, and her closeness to the king could very well prove to be a strong benefit in the scheme of things. "Alright, going against my better judgment, I guess I will have to trust you for now. The only thing I want to know is how much more are you willing to help out?" Adino questioned.

"I am willing to help in anyway that I can," Zephaniah responded.

"That is good to hear, because right now I can use all the assistance that I can get," Adino replied. "So listen, you two, I don't want to concentrate on the negative. What we need is an immediate plan that will help us figure this whole mess out."

Zephaniah suggested that they should all make their way back into town as quietly as possible in order to spy out the current situation. And this is where she was indeed helpful, for she not only knew her way through the dark passages of the palace; she also knew every side alley and path that could lead them back to the center of town without being detected.

It was decided that it would be best for Adino and Benaiah to conduct this mission together after the sun went down. They would be using a quickly drafted map drawn up by Zephaniah as their guide. In the meantime, Zephaniah was to return to the palace and try and find out whatever information she possibly could about the king's next move. "Find out what this Supreme Advisor is up to while you are at it," Adino suggested as the sun set.

This inclusion was very pleasing to Benaiah who spoke out suddenly, "Yes, his name is Doeg. The same man who had my father arrested. I would certainly like to get my hands on him! I'd make him sorry that he ever—"

"—Yes, Doeg is a very bad man." Zephaniah interrupted. "And I will certainly keep an eye on what he is up to."

Hence, the two men waited until it was completely dark and then donned cloaks before making their way back into Gibeah. As a group of soldiers crossed the intersections in front of them, Adino and Benaiah quickly ducked into an alcove. They had thus far made it deep into the city without detection, and the high walls of the prison were already in site. "From here on, we will have to be extremely careful," Adino whispered as they stood still waiting for the soldiers to pass. "There is sure to be a lot more of them as we draw closer to the center of town." He peeked out of their hiding place before signaling Benaiah, "They are gone. Let's go." They made their way toward the prison, stopping only when they were able to see the single entrance to its yard, the Courthouse's heavily guarded gates.

Sure enough, the number of soldiers along the entire perimeter of the prison was impressive. These same soldiers stood around casually enough, chatting with one another and nonchalantly passing the time. Their relaxed attitude was a result of the confidence that they had in their large numbers. A sizable contingent of men would probably think twice before attempting to take on such a force. So the idea of Adino and Benaiah being able to do anything at this point was almost laughable. Adino pulled his hood down in a resigned manner and shook his head. "Now what are we going to do?" he said out loud.

"I say we go for it" Benaiah suggested.

Adino looked at him wondering whether or not he was actually serious. "I am here to prevent a civil war not start one," he told the spirited young Benaiah as they once again traversed the open streets.

Suddenly a man yelled out to them, "Stop right there!"

Adino did not immediately turn around, but he knew that the voice he heard was that of the same guard who had caught him snooping by the doors outside of the assembly earlier that day. And this time the obtrusive soldier was not alone. Instead, he was accompanied by a group of other soldiers along with the Captain of the Guard, whom he seemed to be busy reporting Adino's presence to at the moment.

This Captain of the Guard was in fact the same high ranking, scar faced man who had recently become Doeg's number one henchman. "You two, turn around and show your faces!" he demanded. Adino slowly complied, followed by Benaiah. The captain instantly drew his sword and stood his ground for a short while as he and Adino sized each other up.

"I told you they'd be here," Zephaniah said as she stepped out from amongst the soldiers. "Arrest these men, captain, and throw them into the prison with their friends," she ordered.

"Why you..." Benaiah said as he started after Zephaniah, but his efforts were stopped by Adino who quickly held him back.

"Hold off. We'll deal with the witch in due course," the mighty man said as he pulled his cloak off and threw it to the ground.

"But she is a traitor," Benaiah complained.

Zephaniah let out a wicked laugh. "...Ha, I believe the word you are looking for is spy, you pitiful fools. I was never on your side to begin with. You two are as gullible as they come," she said while continuing with her ridiculing laughter.

"Mark my words, Zephaniah," Adino answered back in a stern voice, "I will some day see you pay for your treachery."

The captain of the guard meanwhile stared at Adino and Benaiah, and then, without a word, he approached. At first he took brisk steps, but soon his saunter gave way to a darting rush forward.

Reacting to the captain's hasty approach, Adino did not stand still. Without even drawing his weapon, he likewise made a hasty advance. These fierce men charged at each other with their muscles flexed and their eyes locked, like two rams preparing to joust. Both Benaiah and the small group of soldiers looked on in anticipation of the collision, but then a strange thing happened. The only clash that took place was that of the captain's sword clamoring against the ground as he dropped it in order to embrace an age old friend. As chance would have it, the two men had a long history between them. In fact, it was Adino who had guaranteed the captain's position within the king's guard many years prior.

"Shammah, my old friend!" the mighty man gladly announced as the two embraced and patted each other on the back. "It has been some time since we last met."

"And a long time since first meeting at the old rock quarry, from which came the stones that helped build all of this," the captain happily replied as he looked around the city walls and gestured toward the heights of the prison and palace in the distance.

As Adino took a good look at his friend, he was surprised to see the large scar across Shammah's face along with how poorly the man had aged.

"I will tell you that story later," Shammah said noticing Adino's focused gaze. "We have a lot of catching up to do."

"Captain," the soldier who had previously alerted Shammah to Adino's presence spoke up as he and the rest of the soldiers approached, "should we apprehend these men? We have been given orders to—" In a move that even surprised Adino, the soldier voice was quickly silenced as he was flattened out with one swat from Shammah's hand. Then, immediately picking up on Shammah's cue, both Adino and

Benaiah did their parts to take out some of the other men. But despite their quick reaction, they were unsuccessful in stopping the flight of Zephaniah and a couple of the other soldiers who did not stay to fight but instead ran off straight away.

"Follow me. We had better find a safe haven for the time being. Zephaniah will surely be making a report to the Supreme Advisor in short order," Shammah announced to Adino and Benaiah. "By the way, who's the kid?" he then asked of Adino as they headed off in the opposite direction of the prison.

"I am Benaiah son of Jehoiada," the young man brashly answered for himself.

Shammah gave him an amused glance and then looked back at Adino who returned an acknowledging nod as they both smirked over Benaiah's bold attitude. They ducked and shuffled around corners in order to avoid the king's soldiers. The captain then quickly led them to a residence on the outskirts of town. They arrived out of breath and looking a little conspicuous as they proceeded to glance over their shoulders in anticipation of their pursuers. "They won't know to look for us here," Shammah explained as he knocked on the door.

An old woman answered and immediately asked Shammah if everything was alright. She then quickly invited him and his two companions inside. The captain tried to be reassuring as he explained that everything was fine and that he had just wanted to pay a visit to her husband. But the old woman was wise enough to know that something else was afoot. "My husband is away on a trip. But I thought that you were aware of this?" she replied in a deliberate tone as she peered at the three of them. "Nonetheless, you and your companions are welcome to stay as long as you want. I will get you something to quench your thirst." As the woman left them, she closed the door behind her, giving Shammah the privacy that he required in order to speak openly.

"I helped her husband deal with some issues with the local judges. They have felt a debt of gratitude ever since," Shammah briefly explained.

Adino once again perused his friend's scarred face as he spoke, "Well it seems as though you have maintained your prominent position. But what has the price been along the way?"

"You are very perceptive," Shammah replied as he rubbed his scar once more in remembrance of what it signified. "The both of you might want to sit down and let me explain…"

30

As Benaiah and Adino both made themselves comfortable, Shammah began his story, "First of all, let me just say that I am ashamed of my actions over these last several years. I have intimidated the weak for no good reason, I have burned down the houses of innocent men, and I have imprisoned the guiltless all on the orders of the king and his diabolical designs. It wasn't always this way though. You know that, Adino. There was a time when I knew right from wrong. But on the one occasion that I was able to come to my senses and question the no good deeds that I was committing, I was taught a hard lesson. I was given the wound that produced this scar on that day, and I learned that acting on my own accord would come with consequences.

It is somehow appropriate that this mark is on my face though. It represents my reality and the notion that I have become an ugly remnant of the man that I once was. I attempted to keep my prominent ranking at all costs, but it is time that I remedied my ill behavior. I have heard of your many achievements of late, and I know that by taking your side, my old friend, that I am doing the right thing."

"Well your actions back in town certainly prove which side

you are on now, Shammah. Whatever you have done in the past, we can leave there. Agreed?" Adino said as he looked at both Shammah and Benaiah.

"Not so fast. I am not finished," Shammah respectfully admonished. "I have something to confess to your companion. Hear me out, Benaiah son of Jehoiada. It was me that oversaw your father's arrest. I know that he is a good man, and I regret having had any part in his detainment."

Benaiah had been listening to Shammah in a relatively composed fashion, but this last statement cut him to the quick. His first impulse was to rush at this man and gain a reprisal, but before he could react, the meeting was interrupted by the kindly old woman who had returned with some refreshments for them. As she past out some drinks and a platter of sweetbread, Benaiah suddenly thought of his own mother. He thought of her kindness and her caring nature. He then thought of his father's pardoning spirit, and all at once, he regained his composure. As the woman left the room, Benaiah somberly asked two questions of Shammah, "Tell me then, what is the reason that my father was arrested? And more importantly, how do we get him set free?"

Shammah explained the situation, "Your father is quite the historian and storyteller, I hear. He purportedly speaks of King Saul and his place in Israel's history quite often. Unfortunately that is exactly what has gotten him into trouble. Jehoiada is basically being used as an example of what is to befall any priest who utters the name of the king in public, and it makes no difference if the instance is for the sake of good. You see, the problem all began when Saul became paranoid that everyone was speaking ill of him behind his back. He soon started claiming that the problem stemmed from the priesthood, the teachers of the people. He told his previous lead advisor, Jephthah, to investigate the situation. And although Jephthah found no wrong in it, his replacement, the Syrian, took a different view on the matter. On an extreme mission to alleviate the paranoia of the king and to prevent the priesthood from blaspheming the sovereign's name, Doeg decided to find and impugn one prominent figure amongst the priesthood. When the palace priest was caught and then threatened for engaging in such practices, he implicated your father as his greatest inspiration when it came to using such methods. Apparently this same palace priest had at one time studied under Jehoiada and was often encouraged by him as a young man. I don't think that he honestly wanted to hurt your father, but once he said that many of the other priests could attest to the matter and of his teaching methods, Jehoiada's fate was sealed."

"My father is a great historian and does indeed love to include stories of inspiration in his teachings," Benaiah acknowledged after hearing Shammah's account. "But he is of course innocent of any attempts to undermine the king. Yet, after seeing the condition of Saul, I am not surprised to hear of his delusional credence to the existence of such conspiracies."

"Yes, that brings me to your second question," Shammah replied. "As far as getting your father or anyone else out of prison for that matter, this will be a complicated undertaking. You see, the king is not really who we will need to deal with at all."

Both Adino and Benaiah reacted with a confused look after this last statement. "What exactly do you mean?" Adino questioned.

"It is quite an extraordinary story," Shammah declared. "Let me back up a little and give you a complete explanation for the king's eradicate and most outlandish behavior, which you no doubt got a taste of today. It all started with the introduction of two very unsavory characters, this Doeg and his cohort Zephaniah. Their services were retained by the king not too terribly long ago. And I was there to witness it all.

I had already taken notice that Saul's behavior was growing increasingly eccentric over the years, but after his rebuke by Samuel at Gilgal and the prophet's assertion that his majesty's kingdom had been finally torn from him, Saul was perhaps the worst that I had ever seen him. Following that event, the king sat on his throne for days. To most he appeared to sit in silence, but from my close point of view he was anything but. I could here Saul mumbling unintelligible words over and over, under his breath, as though he was talking with someone or something for that matter. Saul's next decision was soon to take him to an added state of madness as he turned not to Samuel or his God for help with this oppression but instead seemed to invite the very progeny of Belial to his bedchambers.

He had ordered the summons of Doeg and Zephaniah in a whispered voice to me from his throne, along with the beckoning of his then lead advisor, Jephthah, whom I have previously spoken of. This Jephthah had already made plans to visit the king that day as he was leaving on one of his infrequent trips to visit his family. The innocent man merely wished to pay his departing compliments to Saul as he always had done in the past, but he never made it home. The king's bedchamber was where he enjoyed his last moments as a free man. Saul had already sentenced him that morning. 'Jephthah is guilty of sedition,' the king said to me concerning his long trusted advisor. Saul also told me that Jephthah was to be put into prison and to completely disappear without witness. I was merely to watch for the signal, a tilt of the king's head, before carrying out the arrest.

But this malice of Saul's did not go unrequited. His treacherous deeds were soon to be repaid by the very ill-sought advisors who he had chosen to take over for Jephthah. You see, the scheming on the part of Doeg and Zephaniah indeed began the moment the two arrived to behold the ailing condition of the king. The plot was launched by the ever conniving Doeg who immediately understood the power that Zephaniah held over Saul as she administered him a remedy, which was probably nothing more than a harmless concoction of healthful herbs at that time. But the ingredients of Zephaniah's brew were to soon change.

As the king made it to his chambers that afternoon he was suffering from a terrible headache and very groggy to the point that he had collapsed on the floor in the middle of his room. Upon arriving, Zephaniah immediately rushed to his aid and with the help of Doeg got Saul to his bed prior to the king completely passing out. Then, before his Majesty could recover and regain clarity, Doeg quickly and nervously put forth a proposition by first asking Zephaniah if the king knew the precise ingredients of the tonic that she usually gave to him. Doeg spoke in a whispered voice right there in front of the ailing king. In his state, Saul was unaware of what was being said, but I heard plenty from right outside the door.

At first Zephaniah answered Doeg in an insulted tone. She claimed that the recipes of her medicinal tonics were a combination of complex ingredients never written but instead passed down by word of mouth by the women in her family. The knowledge of their constituents had allegedly been revealed to only a privileged few.

Doeg slyly claimed that he understood. He then took notice of the fact that Zephaniah had brought many concoctions with her and asked if she always gave King Saul the same one.

Zephaniah naively responded that it depended on what was ailing the king at the moment. But her naivety was short lived after Doeg pointed out the fact that she alone had gained the king's trust enough to administer his remedies. He hinted at the fact that she could easily give him any tonic that she wished. Imagine subduing the power of a king, manipulating his emotions, and his wits with your soothing potions, Doeg told her.

I could then only hear the two of them whispering for a short while. I suspect that a strong potion of sorts was subsequently given to the king for the first time as an experiment. He was only able to regain consciousness long enough to temporarily break up their scheming and explain his desire to promote Doeg and Zephaniah to high authority amongst his advisors. The king then quickly dismissed them and was fast asleep even before they left his bedchambers.

Once outside, and with the doors closed behind them, the two immediately continued their scheming, but they were not alone; I listened intently from the darkness of the palace corridors. Doeg commended Zephaniah on the potency of her 'medicine', suggesting that they each take note on just how long the king was indisposed. He then snickered, saying that perhaps next time they should try a completely different remedy, one that would perk him up a bit. Doeg then asked if such a preparation could be made, something to heighten Saul's senses.

Zephaniah chimed in asking if Doeg was suggesting the use of something to intensify the king's fervor and trifle with his phobias. She quickly admitted to have seen such hexes used on lesser men but never a king.

After they departed, I personally watched over Saul, taking into account the fact that he remained sleeping for the entire evening and most of the next day. When the king awoke, he was all the more confused, hardly remembering Doeg and Zephaniah's visit at all.

They have manipulated him in a similar manner from that first day. Carrying out their scheme has been all the easier considering that the king is of a truth oppressed by a legitimate ailment and believes that the powerful potions of Zephaniah to be his only redemption. The fact of the matter is that lately the king spends most of the day in a tonic induced coma, lucid only for brief moments between stupors and mania under the influence of Zephaniah's medicine. Half the time he doesn't even know who or where he is.

And not long ago, he suddenly began making claims of being haunted by a spirit, which has made Doeg much more cautious with his handling of the king. The first of these incidences, Adino, coincided with the day that you first came to the palace to declare your allegiance to Saul." Shammah took a short while to give a chuckle over the incident and also to respond to the surprised look Adino was now giving him. "Yes, I was there, my friend," he continued, "In the backdrop of the incident, but I was there nonetheless, watching as always. It was no coincidence that you were given entrance into the palace that afternoon, where you were directed to see Doeg? I would have loved to have seen his expression when he opened up his chamber doors to the likes of you."

"Then it must have been you also that called out to us in the corridor as we were being chased by the soldiers," Benaiah immediately deduced.

Nodding his head and smiling all the while, Shammah continued explaining everything, "It was seeing Adino that inspired me to actually begin taking action around the palace. After you left that first day, I swiped some of the witch's remedies. Then, I secretly consulted local mediums over the probable ingredients of the elixirs and have found a consensus on the combination of their constituents—gall and some very powerful herbs I have been told by several medicine-women."

"And what did you do when your suspicions were confirmed?" Benaiah asked, surprised by the brazen actions of Doeg and Zephaniah. "Why not have the two of them arrested immediately?"

"That's just it," Shammah explained. "Who would do the arresting? I once had control of the king's guard within the city, but Doeg has since used his position as Supreme Advisor to take away most of my authority. Meanwhile, I have become nothing more than a glorified herald for the scrawny tyrant. All the men of the king's guard have been instructed, by Saul himself no less, that Doeg's authority outranks my own. If I had attempted a move to have him arrested, it would be I that would suffer the consequences, not Doeg. The king trusts him completely and whatever Doeg says goes around here. That's another reason I decided to operate covertly for so long. I figured the longer Doeg and Zephaniah believed me to be their moronic henchman the more information I could collect. But now that they know that I have betrayed them, it will not be possible for us to break up their plot from the inside."

"Then we must take the facts directly to the king!" Benaiah said excitedly. "We can not continue to allow this."

Shammah just shook his head as he spoke despairingly about the matter, "It is impossible. The king is never left alone. Doeg and Zephaniah take turns watching over him and tending to his so called condition. They dictate where he goes, who he sees, everything. And all the while they play the part of his majesty's most loyal servants. What's more, I overheard Doeg telling Zephaniah that once they have every-one convinced that the king is truly mad, the position of Supreme Advisor could easily be converted to the highest office in Israel, usurping that of the king himself. It is no doubt the very reason that he has orchestrated all of this, including the war that we are now in with the Philistines. He knows that keeping all the high ranking military officers as well as the king's son, Jonathan, on the battlefield and away from the politics of Gibeah is a key element to his rise to power and eventual succession."

Adino had remained relatively silent this whole time, but he now spoke up, "You saw the condition of the king yourself, Benaiah. Do you really think that he could be reasoned with?"

"Exactly my point," Shammah interjected. "There is nothing that we can do and no one to turn to. Doeg controls the king and his guard. Just today, he issued diktats to the Council of Seventy as their Head-Magistrate. He practically already controls the entire country at this point. And now that he knows that someone like Adino is onto him and that I have more than certainly told everything, Doeg and Zephaniah will both be extra careful while protecting their hold upon Saul."

Adino drew out his sword and looked down its edge with one eye. "There comes a time when diplomacy must be forgotten," he said in a stern voice. "I know just the person who can deal with the likes of Doeg. But for now we must concentrate on the matter at hand. Before addressing the fact that the Philistines are lined up on our border, we must consider the elder-tribesman of Manasseh and the reality that many of his would-be rescuers still sit in prison along with him now. There likewise appears no chance of them being released. When word reaches Eliel's homeland, an attack on Gibeah could very well be mounted by our own countrymen. This must be avoided at all costs. We must get the men of Manasseh as well as your father released, Benaiah."

"Help me get my father out of that prison in one peace and I will forever owe you a debt of gratitude," Benaiah responded straight away.

Adino then paused for a moment and thought the situation out. He looked at Shammah. "Who holds the keys to the prison cells?" the mighty man asked with a smirk.

Shammah said nothing but instead reached down his shirt and pulled out a wooden key which was hanging around his neck by a braided cord.

"And do you have at least one messenger who would act on our behalf and deliver a message for us?" Adino questioned, receiving a nod of assent from Shammah. "Good, then the situation will work itself out."

"I don't get it," Benaiah said in a puzzled tone.

"It's simple," Adino stated. "We will simply walk in and set the prisoners free."

"But how?" Shammah then inquired.

"The question is not how, my friend," Adino told him. "The question is who. Who will possibly stop us now that I have decided that the time for action has come..?"

31

Through the fog of the cold morning air, Adino led a group of over twenty men into town. He had sent instructions for the warriors that he had gathered to procure for him the largest tree that they could possibly find and to cut it down. With it they were to meet him on the outskirts of Gibeah. These men had followed his instructions unquestioningly and now entered into town with him. They did not rush forward on their horses but instead sauntered in at a slow, even pace. Forming a tight pack, they rode in on the main thoroughfare heading directly towards the grand façade of the Council's courthouse and assembly-yard.

In between the group, being carried with ropes, which they held tightly over the top of their shoulders, was the massive trunk of the tree. They had found it standing alone on the lowland valley outside of Gibeah, and it was to make for an ideal battering ram against the gates that stood between them and the prison.

On the outskirts of the town, both soldier and civilian alike stepped aside as the pack meticulously advanced and Adino called out to the citizens, "Hear me out. I, Adino Ben Hachmon, once known as Jashobeam, the warring Eznite, have proven myself trustworthy over the years as a man of my word. And I pledge to you my word to today; we have no desire to fight against you or any other of our countrymen. We only desire that men no longer be wrongly imprisoned and that justice reigns throughout Israel, not evil tyranny. The captain of the king's guard is here alongside me, and he too upholds my position..." Adino's loud plea continued as his squad drew closer to the prison. Meanwhile, mounting groups of the king's soldiers began to encircle them on both sides of the lane but did nothing to stop their advance. The soldiers instead began to murmur over Adino's sound reputation and to contemplatively give consideration to his petition.

The fact that Adino's men were outnumbered by more than a hundred to one by the king's reinforced guard did not seem to bother any of them at this point. The expressions on their faces remained staid and undaunted as they traveled all the way to the heart of the city. Adino was the first to dismount as they reached the steps of the court with the trunk in tow. The guards in front of them nervously stood their ground as the mighty man warned them, "We are setting the prisoners free one way or the other. If you don't want to get hurt, step aside and open the gates or else—"

"—Or else what?" a voice called out from the top of the lofty court walls. It was Doeg, who had hastily called for an early dismissal of the second day of the assembly after he was given report that Adino and his men had entered the city. At the moment he stood behind the protection of the grand structure's small head-beam, atop the guard's footbridge. He was surrounded by archers who even now aimed their arrows at the men down below.

"Or else we will let this old tree trunk do the talking for us," Adino confidently responded as he looked up at Doeg.

"This really is a magnificent structure," Doeg answered back. "It has been built to last for hundreds of years. Do you think that you and a few men can break through its gates? Come now Adino I thought that you were smarter than that."

As the Supreme Advisor spoke, his voicing echoing throughout the streets of Gibeah, the inhabitants of the city began to come out and fill the central-square. This was an event to witness. Amongst the crowds were all of the Council elders who likewise stood in astonishment as they considered what Adino and his men were now attempting to do.

"No, Adino," Zabdiel faintly said under his breath from his position amongst the crowd. He began to make his way toward his son, but Hachmon quickly stopped him. The gray haired man shook his head and motioned for Zabdiel to merely look on.

Doeg continued his taunting, "I must give you credit, Adino. I never suspected that you would become such a worthy adversary in my rise to the top." With this last comment, Doeg opened his arms out wide into the air while dramatically conveying his towering locale and intended pun. "Believe me though; from up here I can see that men like you really are quite small."

The crowd was growing larger by the moment. Adino looked around to notice that the rest of the king's advisors had come out to see what was unfolding. He addressed Doeg once more, "And the king? I see that he is not standing beside you at the moment. Where does he fall in the scheme of things?"

At this point, Doeg wasn't about to admit that he had complete disregard for the king, at least while he stood in front of the citizens of Israel along with both the Councilmen and all of the king's advisors. He instead played up the claim that he had gained the complete confidence of Saul. "Ah yes, the king," Doeg said looking out to the crowd and taking on an officious air. It was the crowd whom he now addressed while answering Adino's question, "It is a pity that the king has not been feeling well lately, but he has put his trust in me nonetheless during these difficult times. In fact, King Saul was just telling me earlier this morning how proud he is of my accomplishments and that no matter how much his own health declines that he would like for me to continue carrying out his vision and plans for Israel. I likewise commended him on the success of this campaign against the Philistines. We will be victori—"

—Doeg's speech was suddenly cut short as the tree trunk, held quickly by Adino and his men, was used as a battering ram and smashed into the prison gates. Doeg and the rest of the guards that stood with him were nearly knocked off of their platform. Adino's men drew their battling ram back, ready to go at the gates again, but Doeg yelled out to them, "Stop, stop you fools. What do you think you are doing?"

Adino looked up at him and questioned, "Will you open the gates or do we have to repeat our efforts and find out just how strong they really are?"

Doeg paused just long enough for the men to take a few steps toward the gates once more. "Alright, stop already," Doeg repeated his earlier entreaty while considering the fact that he was standing in a vulnerable spot directly above the gates. Another good strike may not only break through them it could very well knock him off of the ledge. "Guards, open the gates," he ordered. And no sooner had he given the command then they were indeed opened.

Adino was the first to enter the court followed by Shammah who ran toward the prison yard and quickly began to open the large wooden locks on each of the cell doors. Benaiah followed close behind, quickly running to each door and calling for his father. Meanwhile, every one of the prisoners began yelling for their doors to be opened. The entire affair became a melee as the excited prisoners waited for Shammah to set them free.

Amongst the excitement, Doeg waited for the right moment to yell his next orders. Just as the last of the prison doors were being unlocked, he called out, "Charge those men." With his arms flailing in the air, he shouted the order as loud as his shrill voice allowed. All at once, a river of soldiers advanced on the rescuers forcing the entire group of men beyond the court's entrance and into its yard. Doeg then yelled orders for the gates to be closed, and in an instant, Adino and all of his men found themselves trapped within the confines of the quad located anterior to the prison cells.

The laughter began slowly and grew louder, "ha ha ha! Ha ha HA HA! You fools! How dare you think that you could come up against me. Just look at you. Your trapped." Doeg's voice resonated throughout the courtyard as he now stood on top of the interior half of the footbridge looking down at everyone.

Adino stood amongst his men and the prisoners who all simultaneously looked up at the arrogant Doeg in disgust. Their battering-ram was left outside. They were undeniably shut in without any reasonable contrivance with which to escape. With a calm voice, Adino asked his captor what was to happen next, "...Surely you don't plan on keeping us in here indefinitely."

"Not at all," Doeg responded. "Despite your valiant effort to emancipate these prisoners, you and the rest of them shall all die now." Doeg then gave the order for the archers standing alongside him to launch their arrows into the courtyard and exterminate every man within its interior. This last directive immediately sent all of Adino's men along with the rest of the captives fleeing for cover. For, not one man amongst them possessed a shield at the moment, and in the middle of the courtyard they stood no chance of survival. Many of the men ducked back into the holding cells, while others lined up under the narrow walkway where the arrows were being shot down from. Quickly darting underneath the same platform, Adino and his men were likewise safe for the moment, but it was a very tight fit. Some were unable to keep their bodies completely under cover and subsequently received wounds to their feet and legs. At least a few of the prisoners were mortally wounded in this manner as the barrage of arrows continued raining down upon them from the platform above in a vertical trajectory.

All the while, the previous crowds of spectators, out in the streets in front of the court, became anxious over what was happening on the other side of its walls. With their blocked view, the people had no sure way of knowing what was taking place, thus they began to speculate amongst themselves. Then somebody began to yell out loud, "They are killing them. The archers are killing them all." This outburst caused a mixture of emotions from the crowd who could do nothing but wait in anticipation of the outcome. Meanwhile, Adino and most of his men, including Benaiah and his father, stood silently trapped under the narrow footbridge opposite the multitude of onlookers.

The trapped group of men all looked at the ceiling above them and then to Adino who himself could do nothing at the moment except wait. Before long, the shower of arrows stopped and the intermittent voices of conjecture began to ring out from the crowd of spectators:

"What happened?"

"Are they dead?"

"Of course they are dead."

"They must be, after being trapped in the open courtyard."

"The archers have killed them all."

Then there was silence once more. Adino peaked out. His head snapped back underneath the cover of the roof just in time as another barrage of arrows began their assault. Then archers appeared on the distant rooftop at the opposite end of the prison yard. The soldiers now had a straight shot at them all. Their arrows came in a bombardment, overwhelming Adino and his troop. For a moment he thought of giving the order for them all to retreat toward the distant prison cells, but he refrained with the knowledge that crossing the open court-yard would have been a death sentence at this point.

The arrows now came from all directions sending everyone lined up under the court's interior platform seeking some form of cover, but there was little shelter to be had this time. The only place to find protection was behind the columns which held up the walkway above. Here the men scurried and were now required to move constantly back and forth on either side of the columns depending on the direction of less danger. The sheer amount of arrows flying through the air at any given moment made the task of avoiding death a tough prospect.

The scene once again became silent out front. Zabdiel and Hachmon waited amongst the crowd. Their worried expressions were mimicked by the other bystanders. Then a low rumble began to disturb first the air and then the ground below them. As they stared at each other and then the court's imposing façade, it slowly became evident that the entire structure was shaking. The men standing on top of it, including Doeg, scampered about to escape from it. It was coming down.

For, as the arrows from the distant wall flew towards them in the moments prior, Adino noticed something odd. In his peripheral vision, he saw Benaiah pushing against the column in front of him.

The young man spoke first to Jehoiada, "This is my destiny, father." He then began whispering the same prayer that his boyhood hero, Samson, had said before bringing down the Philistine temple at Gath, "Oh Lord God, remember me I pray thee, and Strengthen me I pray thee, oh God. Oh Lord, remember me I pray thee. And strengthen me I pray thee, oh God. Oh Lord, remember me I pray thee, Strengthen me I pray thee..." Over and over, Benaiah said these words.

Admiring the young man's instinctive response to react to this grave situation with such trust and faith in his God, Adino placed his own hands on the massive stone column in front of him and began to repeat the same incantation, "Oh Lord God, remember me I pray thee. Strengthen me I pray thee, oh God. Oh Lord, remember me..."

Following the lead of these two, all of the other strongmen, which Adino had so appropriately gathered for an occasion such as this, planted their hands upon the great pillars. And with one voice, they called out to their God whilst pushing against the pillars with all of their might.

Unbelievably, after just a short while of this, Adino noticed movement from the column that he was now straining against. It was slight yet definite, giving hope to everyone. All of their prayers thus grew louder and the efforts to damage the integrity of the structure by pushing against the heavy stone pillars increased. The swaying of the columns, which had begun with a prayer, was then multiplied many times and a furrow of movement began throughout the roof above them, the converse Doeg and the king's archers did tread. A number of small cracks began to form in that structure and then a thousand such fissures caused the ceiling to begin to slough apart in sheets, which fell hard and fast to the ground. That's when the earth began to shake and Doeg along with the archers frantically trampled each other in an attempt to flee from the faltering footbridge. The men underneath pushed harder and with all of their strength as the rest of the prisoners ran from under the covering. By this time, the thick dust that rose up from the crumbling edifice temporarily halted the assault of the archers from the distant rooftop as they looked on blindly and with awe. Next, the columns began toppling one by one, and Adino yelled for his men to run to the center of the courtyard and to safety. Then, all at once, the entire front wall of the court's façade fell to the ground with a deep undulating thud. Yet, unlike the temple, which had consumed Samson and his Philistine enemies, there was miraculously not even one man injured in the wreckage this day. As the dust cleared, the citizens who had come out to witness the fate of Adino and the rest of his men cheered loudly as their silhouettes appeared amongst the settling dust and each one of them emerged from the rubble unscathed.

Some would later say that the massive tree used to batter the gates of the courthouse moments prior had been enough to weaken the entire structure so that such a feat could be accomplished. Others knew it to be the power of the Lord, which had been bestowed upon His faithful as they called out to Him. Yet, whatever the achievement would ultimately be attributed to, it was clearly understood that each person who helped bring down the walls of the courthouse in Gibeah that day were without a doubt all mighty men of renowned...

Adino mustered the prisoners, and with them he left town straight away. It was then that the voice of Doeg was heard. He had survived the building's collapse and was now yelling for assistance, "Somebody get me down from here!" All the while, he stubbornly clung to the side of one of the remaining walls, upon a narrow ledge at the top of the court's towering heights. Like all of the archers that stood amongst him, he hadn't fallen to his death with the collapse of the structure's grand façade but was instead able to jump safely to an adjacent landing at the last moment.

After taking some time to get down, with the help of the king's soldiers, Doeg immediately called for a company of men to be put together, "I want every available man here ready to go after those treasonous cowards. And if we have to chase them to the ends of earth, we will find them!" Doeg then made his way to the king's chambers alone.

On the northern turret of the palace he heard the eerie voice of the banshee once more. It was unmistakably coming from the king's bedchamber. When he got there, Doeg expected to find Zephaniah, but instead, he merely found the king lain out on his cold floor in a similar posture that he had been in when the two had first met. "Zephaniah!" Doeg called out, but there was no answer from her. He perused the room to find that she was nowhere in sight.

The king mumbled some incomprehensible words and reached out for a small goatskin bag across the room from him. The witch's preparations, Doeg recognized. "Zephaniah, I need my tonic," the king sputtered. "The voices, they have left me and must not be allowed back. Zephaniah, I need your help now!"

"Oh be quiet you old fool," Doeg told him as he walked over to retrieve Zephaniah's potions. "Is this what you want?" he said to the king in a taunting fashion as he picked up the bag and turned to face Saul.

The king comprehended Doeg's presence for the first time and called out to him, "Doeg, my trusted advisor. Please, bring me my tonic. I need it to stop the pain, to stop the voices from returning." He grabbed his head, writhing in agony and then hunched into a ball upon his knees.

Doeg walked over and stood above him. With a disgusted look, he began to search through the various contents of the sheepskin. He pulled out one of the tonics and then coldly spoke to the king as he bent down, "You asked for it..." He pulled Saul's hair and head back and then poured the entire contents of the potion down Saul's throat.

The sound of many boots approaching the room startled Doeg. He immediately stood up and headed for the door in a feisty manner. But the door burst open on its own before Doeg could reach it and in came a troop of the king's soldiers. "What is the meaning of this? You fools. I didn't summon you. Get out!" Doeg shouted.

The reason for the sudden company of soldiers then became apparent as General Abner followed by the king's son, Jonathan, entered the room. Doeg continued yelling his orders, "What are you doing here? This is the king's headquarters! You have no jurisdiction here. I, as the king's Supreme Advisor, am the only one—"

"—For the time being, the king's guard will start operating under my authority," Abner declared as he cut Doeg's blabbering short. He then took out a letter and alluded to its contents as Jonathan quickly saw to his father by escorting him from the floor to his bed. "When a messenger brought me this letter, I could hardly believe its contents. But now I see that Adino's concerns were surely justified," the general said as he gave a nod over to Jonathan who was already rubbing down his father's brow with a cloth. He then read calmly from the message that Adino had sent to him,

> '**If you do not arrive and take matters into your own hands, I will no doubt have to take drastic measures to avoid a possible coups in Israel. I believe there is now underway a legitimate plot to overthrow the king...**'

Abner peered out of one the turret's transoms and down at the rubble below where he scrupulously scanned the destruction of the Council's court. He spoke to Doeg in a continually calm voice, "I must admit that had it been anyone else that sent this message I may not have come at all. But I've learned that Adino is truly a man of his word." With this last statement he turned back around and peered at Doeg.

"This is preposterous," the Supreme Advisor complained. "You have no proof. It is Adino that is the guilty party in this..."

But Doeg quickly stopped giving excuses as Abner marched up, grabbed him by his scrawny neck, and lifted the Supreme Advisor completely off of the ground as he spoke to the spindly man with severity, "We will let the king decide your fate." Abner then threw Doeg across the room and gave orders to the guards, "Take him away."

The rest of the afternoon was spent nursing the king back to health, explaining to him what had happened, and searching for Doeg's co-conspirator, the witch of Endor. But Zephaniah was never found. Reportedly, she was last seen leaving the city as the walls of the prison came tumbling down.

As for Doeg, he was thrown into the prison for the time being. His sentence would later be delivered by the king. By most accounts, a somewhat lenient punishment was given. Doeg was not sentenced to death, but he was instead 'promoted', as Saul put it, to the position of Royal-Stable-Keeper. With hundreds of horses to tend to, this was a demanding job indeed. His duties would include cleaning the stables from sun up to sun down everyday of the week, without the use of any form of tools, and without cessation. In addition, he was not only forced to sleep amongst the animals but was also made to eat with the horses, fending for himself over the little bit of grain that was fed to them along with the grass of the fields. "I may one day see fit to put him out of his misery," King Saul was known to say. "But for now he is exactly where he belongs, amongst the filth that doth soil his hands and filleth his nostrils with stench."

The Syrian was to thus toil many years in the stables where he was recognized by the locals as the great Doeg, one time Supreme Advisor to the king, and consequently, thereafter, the Royal-Stable-Keeper of Israel...

PART V

AND THE STRONG BOW DOWN

32

The king along with Jonathan and Abner left two days after that remarkable occurrence at Gibeah. They made the hasty journey back to the Elah valley and arrived there by sunset of the last day of the fighting's cessation. Saul, having seemed to have completely recovered and returned to his senses once he was no longer under the care of Zephaniah and her potions, was eager to begin the negotiations with the Philistines in order to end this short lived but costly war. As reported by both Abner and Jonathan, a desired end to their losses could be the only reason that this seven day armistice had been requested by Philistia. But little did they know that this was not the motive of Philistia at all. Little did they know that Philistia's champion, Goliath, was that very evening preparing to wage war.

As the sun rose the next morning, there was an eerie silence throughout the valley of Elah. It stretched over both the Philistine and Israelite armies like a blanket. Saul was thoroughly briefed on the circumstances that had led up to their current situation and the role that Adino had played in busting apart the plot between Doeg and Zephaniah. The king was also told how, as a result of one surprise campaign, the Philistines had pushed their way into the land of Israel but were successfully stopped at what had now become known as this valley of death.

"You are looking at it," Jonathan explained in a cheerless voice to his father as they each peered out across the Elah Valley. "By evening it will be a litter of soldiers, a valley of death for both their men as well as ours."

"That is if we have not reached a truce by that time," the king responded in a hopeful tone. His sentiments were being shared throughout the Israelite camp, which was not quite finished licking its wounds, despite the seven day break. There was one encouraging sign, which was the fact that the weather had warmed enough for all the ice on the valley floor to melt. This had allowed the down-trodden spirits of the men to thaw a bit as well. The early morning hours were thus spent in hopeful anticipation as the Israel command finished drawing up the terms for a peace agreement. King Saul and a group of his officers had diligently worked on the endeavor for most of the night. "We will not, however, deliver our terms first," Saul insisted. "Instead, we will wait for the Philistines to come to us."

"The sooner this is all over the better, father," Jonathan stated. "I do not think that this is a time for hesitation."

Saul replied with a sympathetic voice at first but his tone became increasingly irate as he spoke, "There is nothing I want more than to return to Gibeah where reparations can be made to both my administration and our great capital, but I will not be made to look like a weakling at this point by begging the Philistines for mercy. I will not bow down!" The momentary outburst came as a surprise to those present. Each man stood silent, ill at ease to offer any rebuffing words. Still, although no one had voiced their opinions, Saul could easily read disapproval in their eyes. Understanding everyone's alarm, and slightly mistrusting his own rationality at the moment, the king paused briefly and then gave in, "You are right, son. It is my fault and my own lack of judgment that has gotten us here. We will send our conditions for peace." Everyone in the headquarters breathed a sigh of relief as Saul continued speaking in a reticent tone, "And I want this Adino found. He should be commended for his valor. Surely, I will find a permanent place for him within my new administration." Saul paused again, honestly taking another moment to reflect upon the situation. "Yes, I want this strong man always close to me."

The conditions of the truce were therefore redrawn. In an effort to show true diplomacy, everything was now kept as simple as possible on the part of Israel; if the Philistines would simply agree to give up their newly gained territory, thereby recognizing the pre-war borders, the fighting would be over. Royal messengers rode on horseback to take the stipulations across the valley. All there was to do now was wait for Philistia's reply.

King Saul sat on the bench of the valley looking across the wide expanse in the direction of his enemy's camp. His officers anxiously joined him. Meanwhile, word of the war's end quickly spread across the camp of Israel, sending waves of excitement over Azekah. Again, all there was to do now was bide time and hope for a favorable response. Unfortunately, the messengers returned sometime later stating that the Philistines had graciously received their message but then sent them away with no answer.

The afternoon arrived, and still there was no answer. The day hence wore on slowly. Finally, as the sun began to make its descent, the answer came. To the dismay of King Saul and his entire camp, the Philistines marched down from their stations at Sochoh and began to align in full battle array at the base of that same hillside.

"What shall we do, father?" Jonathan asked nervously.

"We have no other choice," Saul answered glumly. "I suppose that we have our reply. Prepare our forces for battle." Hence, the two armies were soon separated only by the dusky expanse of the valley floor.

As the last rays of sunlight ominously stretched over the hills, a deep voice then arose from the gathered multitudes of Philistine warriors. It was taunting and insidious, "Why do you gather for battle, oh Israel. Have you not already plead for the mercy of Philistia? Have you not already asked us to accept your terms of peace?" Then the source of the bellowing voice revealed itself. It was a man, but none ordinary. This was immediately evident as soon as the giant, Goliath, walked out to the center of the naturally formed arena. The site of him standing on that valley floor was astounding to behold. For every inch of his ten foot frame was covered in thick, heavy bronze armor, from his shins to his head. And upon this armor was the image of Dagon.

In front of him came twelve men rolling out a cart made generally for horses to pull, but because of the length of the various weapons, which it held, the cart had to be guided by the sides and not the front. It included an arsenal of deadly weapons and also one-hundred-plus pound spears, along with various other javelins and swords. Three of the men then unloaded from the cart an enormous shield, which they carried out to Goliath. Next, in a display of his awesome might, the giant picked up two of the spears in one hand and hurled them at lightning speed, splitting the thick trunk of a lone tree, which occupied the valley floor.

Then the giant turned to the army of Israel, held his burdensome sword high above his head, and yelled out once more, "I have come to offer our terms of peace." He turned around in order to enjoy the cheers of his countrymen. This terrible man of war then let the applause die before continuing, "I deliver peace in the form of a challenge to the men of Israel. For, I have heard that you are a nation of a great God and many strong, many mighty men." The giant turned towards his own army and begged applause before once again addressing the forces across the valley. "Here is my decree," he said and then paused for a moment to look at the army of his enemy. "You look a little thin today," he remarked alluding to the fact that Israel's numbers were far less than that of his own countrymen. He let the moment pass, enough time for King Saul and the rest of Israel to consider the reality of his words. Goliath then continued in a strident tone, "Am I not simply a Philistine? I am not a mighty man, a servant of your God, of your great king, Saul? Please, I beseech you, choose a warrior for yourselves and then let him come down to me. If he is able to fight me and then kill me, then Philistia will be your servants. But if I prevail against him, and instead kill him, then you shall be our servants as you once were to Egypt!"

This last remark of Goliath's sent an undulation of spirited recourse across the entire army of Israel and a true challenge was felt in the heart of every man of that nation. Then, after Goliath had finished issuing his proposal, he turned around in circles, showing the men of Israel his remarkable physique and impenetrable armor. "I will wait for your reply on the morrow," he announced before walking off the field of battle and towards his own camp. He was promptly followed by all the forces of Philistia.

Not knowing exactly what to think of this strange decree or how to answer it, King Saul gave the command for his own army to likewise return to Azekah. Once there, the question of who this Philistine man was and where he had come from laid on everyone's mind.

In an attempt to subdue his father's annoyance, Jonathan immediately pointed out the fact that this was not really that bad of a prospect. "We are, after all, missing the necessary forces to wage all out war with Philistia at this time," he said in a poised voice. "A fight between champions may be our best prospect."

"Yes, yes, I realize that," the king responded in an irate tone. "The question that is on my mind is how can it be possible that there are giants in the army of our enemy and my officers know nothing of their existence? This has put us in a most precarious predicament."

Remembering Adino's account of the giant, Lahmi, whom the mighty man had purportedly met in the desert, Abner spoke up, "The one man who may not only know the most at this time about these giants but also the best method of facing off with one is not here, my king."

"Adino," the king acknowledged. "But surely there is someone else who can fight."

The answer from all of Saul's advisors was the same, a resounding "no one, if we expect to actually win."

"No one?" the king yelled. "I know of our strength. Where is Joab or his brothers? Where are the sons of Dodai, or the son of Agee, or of Baanah, or Ribai? Where are the sons of the many elders of Israel? All of those valiant men with reputations of bravery and strength? This Adino Ben Hachmon," the king finally yelled, "where is he now, whom I long ago declared mighty amongst men?"

Jonathan stepped forward and informed the king about the situation, in an attitude of remorse, "As far as the warring aged champions from the north who are relied upon to stay back in order to head up their homeland militias, I personally made attempts to muster the Council elders before we left Gibeah with hopes to implore each of them to return to their homes where they could give the orders for these tribesmen of theirs to join us. But as you already know, the elders abandoned that place in a hurry once the walls of the court were destroyed, in fear that the wrath of Doeg would be released in their direction. We have yet to hear any word concerning their current stance or status.

Judah meanwhile is the only complete tribe amongst us, but Adino has indeed used all of their renowned men in order to enlist the help of others for this very cause, this war of yours. They, like Adino, are not presently in our ranks and are completely unaccounted for. These same men were last seen and likewise involved in the incident at Gibeah. From that place—with the same reasoning as the elders—did each of them quickly flee."

"I can hardly blame them," Abner admitted. "Adino and the sons of the elders are perhaps the finest and most faithful warriors in all of Israel, yet they must believe themselves wanted for sedition after what occurred at that place."

"Yes, yes, that is it," the king suddenly acknowledged. "They must be informed that their deeds have been recognized as noble, not as seditious. They must be told to come back, that I need them, that all Israel needs them. We must send out messengers. Someone must come and face this giant." Then the king boldly announced, "I will lure one of these men back to my battlefield. Put out a decree that any of these men who will step forward and fight this Philistine will receive not only the hand of one of my beautiful daughters but will remain free from taxation for himself and all of his family for their entire lives."

With this plan in mind, preparation resumed throughout most of the evening, and a consensus on how to proceed, on the part of Israel's high command, was finally reached: Messengers would be sent out the next day, one to the Philistines in order to accept the challenge put forth by Goliath, and many others to search out and find Adino or any other brave warrior who could defeat this giant; lastly, everything possible would be done in order to find out more about Goliath and whence he had come...

33

All of the required measures were carried out the next day. Acceptance to Goliath's challenge went out with the provision that Israel would be given forty days to choose their champion. Saul and his officers all agreed that this would be more than enough time to procure the aid of a worthy opponent for the giant. Seven messengers were therefore sent throughout Israel in search of a candidate.

Yet, the morning was not entirely without incident. Soon there came a recognizable voice rising from the valley below. It was Goliath who had come out in full battle gear to issue his challenge all over again. His taunts could loudly be heard throughout the camp of Israel. "Forty days or eighty, it does not matter," he howled. "Any man that you send to me will be defeated. I will break the back of Israel and crush your spirits and you will know on that day Philistia is your better. So send me your champion. Let him walk down to me with his tail between his legs…"

This bantering would last all morning, day after day in the same manner as Goliath did his best to unnerve the army of Israel. And his strategy seemed to be working. King Saul was sorely afraid each time he heard the voice of the monstrous man. After a week, he finally summoned his officers, along with his son, Jonathan, and inquired of them, "Why does he torment us in such a manner? Do we not have any answers about where this giant comes from?"

Abner stepped forward and explained what he had been able to learn, "It appears that he is originally from Gath. However, he was taken to the lands across the Great Sea when he was just a young boy. There he was trained to be a warrior. His record of success in battle is unparalleled. The last known giant that successfully waged war against us was indeed back in the days of Moses; Og king of Bashan, the last of the Raphaim and the race of giants. This Goliath claims to be a descendant of the same man."

King Saul shook his head. "Well then obviously Og wasn't the last of anything. Tell me, who have our messengers contacted thus far that would make a good match for this giant?"

"We have heard no word from our messengers," Abner replied. "But I assure you that they are doing their best to carry out their mission. They will; they must find our man."

Adino all the while, a world apart from the battle front, a world apart from knowing exactly what he should be doing at this point, took a seat in humble fashion within a house at Ramah. His group of men had not disbanded. They had instead accompanied him as he sought the advice of Samuel. The mighty man thus sat at that table of his mentor and friend. He questioned why he had to get involved with the calamity at Gibeah.

"...You question your role in helping your nation?" Samuel said in reply to Adino's words.

"Have I helped?" Adino then asked.

"Your accomplishments at Gibeah, well known throughout the country by now, should have taught you all that you need to know about yourself," Samuel explained. "Tell me, what is it that you have you learned from it?"

Adino peered out the window at the group of men whose help he had enlisted. He thought hard before answering Samuel's question. Then, as he gazed at Benaiah and thought of the inspiring role that this young man had played, it came to him, "I have learned that together, with the help of these men, which I am now aligned with, that we have great potential; that through our God, we have strength enough to do the impossible; that I should never question my..." As Adino finished his sentence Samuel chimed in and spoke in chorus with him "...ability to accomplish anything again."

"That is it, Adino. You now understand why you needed the detour through Gibeah," Samuel assured him. "I hope that you also understand that your delegation is not over."

"I have gathered Israel's mighty men as you instructed," Adino said in an obliging tone. "And after what we have already been through together, they have assured me that we will always fight for the same cause. They are ready to do as I bid them."

"Are they?" Samuel questioned as he rose up and put the strap of the ram's horn around his neck. "Let us see about this claim of yours," he declared as he led Adino outdoors and to the crowd of warriors, who up until this point had been waiting patiently in the front courtyard. They all stood immediately to their feet. The respect that they had for Samuel, and Adino both, could be seen in each of their expressions. "Come forward please," Samuel requested. "Each one of you, I want to see the best that this country has to offer." Whilst the men did as Samuel requested by lining up in front of him, the prophet passed by each one of them and looked into their eyes. He then turned, walked over to Adino, and gave him a nod before continuing, "This man here tells me that you have all pledged your loyalty to him. If this is true, then there are some things you each must understand. As the chosen of God, a young shepherd was anointed some time ago in Bethlehem. He is David, son of Jesse. Adino witnessed the occasion first hand and was told by me that this same young man will one day become king."

Samuel paused to allow this news to sink in and for the surprised expressions to subside. He began to pace back and forth in front of the group as he continued, "This will not occur for many years and will likewise involve no injustice to our currently reigning king, whom David will love and honor. Saul, however, will not respond in kind. The Bethlehemite, David, will thus require loyal men to follow him, to protect him, and to perhaps die in doing so. Adino has agreed to this cause and if you are willing to do the same, to become the next generation of King-Makers alongside him, I ask you now, strong men, to bow and receive your own anointing."

Because they trusted the prophet and had already seen the strength that they possessed as a group, none of the men needed more persuading. Benaiah was the first to kneel, followed by Eleazar, Shammah, the son's of Zeruiah, and the rest of the mighty men in attendance. They each respectfully bowed and accepted their commissions.

When the improvised ceremony was over, Samuel spoke to Adino once more, "I hope that you have not forgotten that you have accepted a charge given you by your king as well. You must keep this pledge. Saul needs the support of the north. So you must now ride, and do not stop until you have reached the tips of our borders. Rally every man and every sword that is available. For the course is set. All out battle with our enemy is now inevitable."

With the prophet's declaration, Adino and the mighty men once again made immediate preparations to make the journey north. But before Adino left, he addressed an issue that had been on his mind for quite some time. "Samuel, please tell me your thoughts concerning a dream that I have continually had since before I can remember," he requested with a furrow upon his brow. "This dream is wicked, I believe…"

As Adino finished his explanation of the dream with the tree, the men who would attempt to cut it down, and the lion, Samuel sat quietly pondering its details. "Strange indeed, I have to admit," he replied with a gaze of contemplation. "This is of a prophetic nature, though. I am sure of that. The only thing that is not peculiar about it is the fact that you are the one that has seen these images."

"What do you mean by that?" Adino asked.

"Are you not the King-Maker?" Samuel replied.

Adino smiled and gave a wise response, "I believe that it is you who is the King-Maker, my friend." He then paused and thought about what Samuel had inferred. "It has something to do with our next king then?" Adino surmised. "It has something to do with the young man from Bethlehem? The son of Jesse?"

"You are on the right path, Adino," Samuel offered with a glimmer in his eye. "It has much to do with that. It has much to do with this young David. And it is funny that you mention him. I have had him on my mind quite often lately..."

Two days after the group had left, one of the royal messengers arrived in Ramah. He quickly dismounted his horse and explained to Samuel that he was looking for Adino and his group of cohorts. The messenger then explained the situation at the battlefront, giving the details of Goliath and his challenge. He left immediately upon being told in which direction Adino and the rest of the men had traveled. As he rode away Samuel spoke under his breath, "You will not catch them though, but worry not. They will arrive in Elah in plenty of time. As for this Goliath, God has already appointed an unlikely champion to meet him on that valley floor..."

34

The morning sun glistened as it stretched over the quiet countryside just outside of Bethlehem. Far away from the battlefield, the only noticeable disturbance in the solitude of this place was the brushing sound of birds' wings. Two small pheasants circled the breezy sky as their sturdy wings cut through the air and created the turbulence that allowed them to soar. Down and down they descended, each one perching atop the lofty branches of an olive tree. As they attentively looked out across the valley, a hunter's sling rapidly spun round and round in the distance before releasing two stones simultaneously. They were aimed with keen accuracy in the birds' direction. It was an impossible long range shot, but the trajectories did in fact both reach their marks in deadly, rapid succession. The pheasant perched on the lower branch was hit first, and before it fell two feet, the other realized the same fate.

The birds had not yet hit the ground, before the lone hunter, David, anointed son of Jesse, ran to retrieve his prize. As he reached the base of the tree, in search of the two birds, a voice yelled out his name, "David, David where are you?" It was his sister, Abigail, who had brought to the pasture with her loaves of bread and a variety of cheeses. After finding him, she instructed David that their father wished for him to take the treats to his brothers and to the captains of the king's army in the distant valley of Elah. It had been many weeks since Jesse had heard word of what was taking place at the battlefront and he desired a report from the region.

David gladly exchanged his pheasants for the cheese and bread and told his sister that in short order he would bring back news of the battle, along with word from his brothers. With that, the young man took off in a sprint with the intention of retrieving his horse. He was anxious to see his brothers and to likewise learn how his countrymen were faring in battle.

By the time David arrived in the valley of Elah, Goliath had been issuing his frightful challenge to the army of Israel for well over a month. In fact, this day was also the deadline for producing a warrior to fight the giant. And although messengers had been sent out to all of the elder's family's, none of their renowned warriors had responded to the king's summons. So, without a champion on the side of Israel, the entire army was again being made ready to wage war against the Philistines.

David quickly delivered the gifts to the officers and went out to find his brothers amongst the divisions gathered at Azekah. As he found his brothers and greeted them, the booming voice of Goliath once more rang out and over the ranks of Israel's men, "I see that there is not one man amongst an entire army of dogs who will step forward and fight me. And still you cowards prepare for battle? Will you go out against an army when you who can not even step forward to fight one man? I spit on your weakness and on the dirt of your entire spineless nation."

As David heard Goliaths challenge he looked around at the despondent men who now prepared for battle with their heads down low. "Who is this man that has the nerve to challenge the people of Israel?" David questioned. "What is the matter? Does he not know of our strength and of our God? Am I the only one who just heard what he has said..?" David continued to loudly offer his complaints and disbelief over the giant's insults.

"Be quiet, David," his oldest brother, Eliab, told him. "You have no right to talk concerning the matters of soldiers."

David ignored his brother's rebuke and began to inquire from others in the area about the intentions of this irreverent man. They told him how Goliath was a giant who had been issuing the challenge for forty straight days and also how the man who was willing to fight him would receive the honor of marrying one of the king's daughters as well as tax exemption for his entire family.

"I will fight him," David immediately announced to the further annoyance of his brother.

"I told you to be quiet. You don't even—"

"—I said I will fight him," David spoke over his brother's voice in a louder tone, which stirred up some interest from some of the officers in the area.

They immediately looked up to see who had just uttered those words with such confidence. This was because over the past several days, with no success in convincing anyone to fight Goliath, King Saul had issued an extreme order, "At this point, I will send forth the first man that steps up and says that he is willing to face off with this Philistine. I don't care who it is or what reputation he has. Just bring me a willing soul!" In addition, anyone who was able to find a challenger was promised a significant reward by the king.

So when David repeated the declaration, "...I will fight anyone who stands in the face of Israel and shouts out challenges, which insult my God," he was quickly approached by the group of officers.

"Are you serious?" the ranking man asked as he admiringly considered what David had just said.

"Of course I am serious. I am not afraid," David said as his brother resignedly shook his head.

With that, the officer immediately escorted David to the king. Upon being presented, he received nothing more than a disparaging laugh from the likes of Abner, but the king was willing to consider any takers at this point. With David standing before a crowd of officers and court advisors, the king double checked his intentions, "You say that you, a shepherd, can defeat this terrible Philistine warrior? I don't see how that is possible. This man is a true killer. From what I understand, he has been trained from the time he was much younger than yourself in the art of fighting. He has never been defeated in a match." The king considered the prospect for a moment and then deliberated the possibilities aloud, "Still, you are the first and only man who has volunteered to fight. What choice do we have at this point?"

David reasserted his resolve, "I have always protected my fathers flock. At times a wild animal would come in the night and snatch away one of the sheep. I would then go after the wild beast with the intention of slaying it and delivering the sheep from its mouth. (*)- Thy servant has slew both the lion and the bear; and this uncircumcised Philistine shall be as one of them, seeing he hath defied the armies of the living God."

"Bring out my armor," The king said immediately. David's words had been enough to convince him. When the armor was brought out, King Saul himself stood and took the honors of bearing the brilliantly made gear for the brave young man. "This is the finest made armor in all the land. Not even the wealthiest of the Philistines have for themselves such magnificently made battle-gear," the king said in an assuring voice. But as he helped David into the heavily fashioned armor, it became apparent that it was too large a fit for the young man. Still the king persisted until David stood completely encapsulated in the oversized suit. "Alright, that's it," the king encouraged, "now practice your movements."

David tried to walk, but his efforts were excruciatingly slow as he picked up his foot and awkwardly thrust it forward in an unnatural step. He gracelessly repeated this as the king perplexingly looked around to ascertain the response of those present. With great tension in the air, nobody dared to question the king's endeavors at this point, and as he continued to encourage David, all of Saul's officers gave a nod of their heads in artificial approval of the embarrassing display.

The king went on with his instructions, "That's it, keep moving. Now turn around towards me." Once again, David did as he was told. He clumsily inched his way around to face the king. "Now walk towards me," Saul continued. "Yes, yes, closer, very good." As David struggled to take his steps, the king signaled for his sword to be taken to the young man. He then persisted with the futile exercise, "Now, reach out and grab the sword."

David slowly turned his head trying to determine the location of the sword through the heavy bronze helmet's slotted eyeholes. He then reached out as its handle was placed into his flailing hand. But, despite his efforts to wield the sword, it somersaulted out of his grip and onto the ground. King Saul tried to contain his anguish and to think of an alternative solution while burying his face into his cupped palm.

Then the voice of David unintelligibly echoed beneath the bronze visor. The king looked up at him and gave a gesture for the sword bearer to remove the stifling helmet. With the head piece removed, David repeated his earlier statement, "I said, I don't think that I will need any armor, my king."

With this last proclamation, Abner followed the familiar actions of the king and buried his own face in his hands as he anguished over the bleakness of the situation. "Perhaps we should go ahead with our plans to call off the fight," he suggested.

But the king was amused with the prospect. "You mean that you would go into battle without the protection of any armor against the giant and his arsenal of weaponry?" he asked in a contented tone.

David answered again, "I have never worn armor such as this and have no need for it, because (*)- the Lord that delivered me out of the paw of the lion, and out of the paw of the bear, he will deliver me out of the hand of this Philistine."

The king considered David's courage. "Magnificent," he blurted out in a somewhat envious yet respectable manner. "Someone help him out of that gear..."

35

The stage for the fight was thus set. Goliath would be the first to walk onto the valley floor. Alongside him was Lahmi. Before the giant commenced with the challenge, this is what he spoke to his nephew, "What I have to say to you is not out of misuse of the drink or of fear for my life in the coming battle. Instead, I speak as a man confident only of what I can understand, as one full of his own humanity. I am likewise a man who has never known the anguish of defeat."

Goliath spoke proudly to Lahmi as they started the walk toward the battlefield. The roar of the crowd was almost deafening at this point with thousands upon thousands of Philistine soldiers screaming the name of Goliath. He was accustomed to such incidences. The giant soberly continued in a manner that was so sincere it surprised his nephew, "In the scheme of it all, I have only attempted to witness the pleasures of life. I have thus sought enjoyment while contemplating the meaning of misery. Yet, thanks to our gods, I believe that I will never know defeat or the anguish that accompanies sincere yearning. What I speak of is truly sardonic. Because, while I have known the love of a woman, of all the pleasures of life, of the good wine, I still have no knowledge of a true god. I believe that although we speak of them, we truly only create them in our minds. If I am wrong about this and there is a real god in Israel, let him protect my adversary today. Let it be me who dies on that battlefield. Otherwise, I am, as always, destined to win..." After this poignant speech to Lahmi, Goliath once again began his shouting and exhibition of vicious intentions for Israel.

The army of Saul then began to part allowing David to walk out alone toward the giant. With a staff in one hand and his trusty sling in tow, David boldly made his way toward the center of the valley as thousands of men from the two armies looked on.

Goliath then yelled out, "Send me your best man, and I will snap his bones with my might." He then took one of his beam-like spears and bent it in his grasp until it snapped in two. "You see that, you miserable army of puny men. Today I mock your God and will make an example of his weakness." He paused for a moment to let the cheers subside before yelling out at David who still approached from the distance, "That's right, come closer. I like to look at the face of a man before I kill him."

David suddenly veered to his left and walked in a southern direction for a couple hundred yards before stopping to pick something up out of a small brook that flowed there. "What's wrong? Have you changed your mind? You swine of Israel. Come over and fight me like a man," Goliath continued his ribbing.

King Saul and his entourage of officers looked on nervously, wondering what David was up to. Then David turned around and this time ran straight ahead in the direction of Goliath. As he drew nearer, the young man could hardly believe the size of the giant, but regardless of the unequal difference in their stature and outfitting, David unhesitatingly approached. He stopped only when he was within close enough proximity for the two to look each other in the eyes.

The giant began a loud over exaggerated laugh once he

saw David. He then turned around to face the kings of Philistia and the rest of his countrymen who stood watching from
the sloping hills above. "What is this?" he yelled back to
them. "Are there no men in all of Israel? I challenge them to
send me their best warrior, and they send a boy?" The giant
then turned around and once again faced David. Just as his
shield bearers began to run out in front of him, Goliath
grabbed one of the men by the shoulder, yanked the shield
from his hand, and gave him a swift foot in the back, which
sent him tumbling over the rough soil. "I won't need this you
imbecile," he said while taking the shield and hurling it at
David who quickly ducked to miss it. The giant continued his
banter, yelling loud enough for all to hear, "Why do you carry
a stick in your hand? What do I look like to you, some sort of
a dog? Why don't you throw your stick and maybe I will go
and fetch it for you." Goliath gave another staged laugh and
turned around with his hands raised in the air begging some
attention from his audience who accommodated him with
accolades.

This time, as the giant turned around, he quickly reached
over his shoulder, grabbed his javelin, and with great precision hurled it at David's head. The young man was quick to
move out of its path while performing a duck and roll. He was
instantly on his feet, and repeating his defensive moves. He
dodged two more of the spears, three, and then another
barrage, which Goliath aimed at him with fatal intentions.
The giant became agitated with David's successful moves and
spoke out once more as he reached for his sword, "You
scrawny boy. Just wait until I drive my sword into your flesh. I
will skin you while you still breathe and feed your tissue to the
birds of the air. Then I will take your carcass and give it to the
beasts of the field."

David had grown tired of the giants threats. So, he grabbed
one of the smooth stones that he had retrieved from the creek-
bed moments earlier and made his sling ready. He then began
twirling the sling around and around as he yelled back at

Goliath so that all of the men from the two armies gathered that day in the Valley of Elah could similarly hear him, "You come at me with your mighty arsenal, complete with sword, spear, javelin, and empty threats. (*)- But I come to thee in the name of the Lord of hosts, the God of the armies of Israel, whom thou hast defied. This day will the Lord deliver thee into mine hand; and I will smite thee; and take thine head from thee; and I will give the carcases of the host of the Philistines this day unto the fowls of the air, and to the wild beasts of the earth; that all the earth may know that there is a God in Israel. And all this assembly shall know that the Lord saveth not with sword and spear: for the battle is the Lord's, and he will give you into our hands."

And when David was finished saying this, he released the stone from his sling, and it flew through the air with imperceptible speed and accuracy and sank deep into the skull of Goliath. The giant immediately dropped his sword, took two wobbling steps, and then fell to the ground to the disbelief of all who looked on.

Then David walked over to the Philistine, picked up the giant's mammoth sword, and raised it high into the air with both hands. He swung it down with all his strength thereby decapitating the giant. A thunderous cheer rang out from the army of Israel as David picked up the Giants head and held it out first for his own army to see and then for that of the Philistines.

Although fear was immediately struck into the hearts of the Philistines over the words and actions of David, the Kings of Philistia, seeing the apprehension of their armies, gave the order for their cavalry to charge. These mendacious kings thus forsook the edict of their champion, Goliath, and yelled the orders for their horsemen to first run down David and then to proceed on to the rest of Israel's army.

Saul watched in horror as the mounted cavalry began a slow trot in David's direction. "He will be killed," the king uttered in a trance like daze as his officers asked what should be done.

"Should we rally the soldiers or order a retreat sire?" Abner begged.

The king remained stunned expressing his incredulity, "The decree of their champion was that they would surrender if he was beaten."

"Sire, I need to know what order to give the men?" Abner once again pleaded.

But before the king had time to respond, there appeared on the right flank of the valley a magnificent haze of dust and flying debris. This cloud was the result of a tempest, which blew intensely over the desert-sand and was spawned from the hooves of many furiously driven horses. From the haze of that dust, there suddenly appeared a small succession of mighty warriors and out in front of them was Adino. As the dust cleared even further it became apparent that they had not arrived alone. For following them was a charging cavalry made up of thousands of brave warriors. The northern militias had arrived.

Being the first to descend upon the scene, Adino quickly dismounted his horse and dashed in beside the young champion just as the Philistine assault arrived. All the while, David had stood his ground, screaming at the oncoming forces of his enemy as he held onto the sword of Goliath, "Come on you Philistines. I have beaten your champion today. I refuse to now taste defeat, for the battle truly is the Lord's..." David therefore fought on, not believing the fortunate fact that the group of his countrymen, led by Adino, had arrived just in time to join him. He looked on as Adino used unrelenting tactics to help deflect the first oncoming barrage of Philistines.

With his powerful arms flexed ready and his feet dug determinedly into the ground, the mighty man grabbed the neck of the first oncoming horse and instantly brought it to the ground. Then this man of war used his magnificent strength to rip the Philistine soldier from his saddle. He slung the man around at the ankles and used him as a human projectile to dismount the following horseman. It was then that he clasped onto his sword and held its lion-faced handle high into the air. Soon Adino was going to work, delivering a barrage of fatal swings against his enemy. His feats were just the first of an all out exhibit of brute strength put on by his team of men.

Eleazar and Shammah having likewise witnessed Adino's inspiring war tactics each took to dismounting cavalrymen in the same manner, pulling down horses and tossing grown men through the air with grunts and battle cries. As they fought against the first wave of Philistines sent their way, David too held his own until there were no more blows to be dealt. The valley floor had quickly become a litter of wounded horses and defeated Philistines.

Then, without any order being uttered by King Saul or his officers, the rest of the army of Israel rushed to join their countrymen in battle. The Philistines were overwhelmed and went into an immediate retreat. But Israel followed and drove them over the hills and back to their own lands. By nightfall their enemy was vanquished and the men and women of the nation celebrated. They praised the feats of David who had defeated the giant and led them into battle as King Saul ordered a feast to be given in the young man's honor.

Everyone at the feast praised David, even the king. But amongst the crowd that gathered around him that night, David desired most to meet those men who joined him at the center of the valley and who had fought against the Philistine cavalry so valiantly. Thus, Adino and the other mighty men presented themselves before David, and he was once again impressed with their astounding brawn.

Adino spoke for the rest of the men. "David, son of Jesse, we arrived today to fight with you and for the sake of your highly regarded honor. We now swear to you our personal loyalty, the loyalty of our households, and that of our tribesmen. We pledge ourselves to all that you would endeavor upon from this day forward."

David was surprised. After all, the week before he had been a mere sheep herder, the youngest son, and the last in line for his father's inheritance. He wondered silently over the words that Adino spoke, thinking how he was now perhaps the most celebrated man in all of Israel.

King Saul meanwhile realized that this situation was something that he could benefit from. Adino and his warriors were after all men from powerful families, and they were now vowing allegiance to this young man. Thus, after Adino's announcement, the king stepped forward and made an announcement, "Men and women of Israel, here stands your champion." The crowded room filled with applause as King Saul raised the hand of David in support of his triumph. As the lengthy applause died down, Saul continued, "I have decided to make him a captain over men in the hopes that he will continue to lead us in the successful defeat of our enemies."

The crowd gave a deafening cheer with this last announcement. David was then raised on the shoulders of some of the men and paraded around the room. As the procession circled back around, David was set down next to Adino. He shouted over the noise of the merriment toward the mighty man, "I still haven't learned your name?"

Adino's longtime friend, Shammah, who stood adjacent to him, gave a shrewd look of surprise and spoke up, "Let me make the introduction. My young captain, the man standing before you is the legendary Adino also once known as Josheb-Basshebeth, the mighty-one, Jashobeam..."

36

After the defeat of Goliath, the first undertaking of King Saul was to test the prowess of his newly formed team of warriors led by the young but able-bodied David. Besides possessing the loyalty of Adino and those known as mighty men, David was also given charge over one thousand soldiers, many of whom were hand picked by him. The king planned on putting this group on the offensive. They would be sent to head up an attack against the remaining armies of the Philistines who had now reassembled in the region of Gath.

In order to promote his own reputation as a mighty leader and soon to be all conquering king, Saul arranged for this first offensive to begin in grandiose style. A military procession was therefore organized with the king watching from above the city square on the lofty balcony of his palace.

The celebration would include the procession of the king's guard, including the company of David, who were to pass through the crowds as they rode out of the city and on their way to battle. It was announced well in advance, and on the day that it was to begin, the square of the city was crowded with throngs of the nation's citizens.

The king looked out at the people and arrogantly boasted over his own popularity, "You see, they have come from afar to witness my strength and to bask in the power that I, their king, doth possess."

Abner and Jonathan were indeed amazed over the king's apparent esteem in the eyes of the nation and both congratulated him on his accomplishments. The parade of men was accompanied by scores of musicians and entertainers that intermittently filed down the center of the city to the cheers of the crowd.

Then the king rose and walked to the edge of his elevated stage as trumpets blew to quiet the crowd and initiate Saul's intended address to the people. But just as King Saul was prepared to speak, inadvertently out filed David, and after him, riding in adorned chariots, were his mighty men.

Their arrival could not have been more perfectly timed to give the mistaken impression that the trumpets were being sounded in this group's honor. And the crowd responded with loud cheers, which drowned out the isolated voice of the king.

"What is the meaning of this?" the king complained to Abner.

"It appears that the crowd cheers for David and his men, my king." the response came back.

"Preposterous. Sound the trumpets again," the king fumed.

As the trumpets were sounded louder and louder, the cheers of the crowd grew equally boisterous for David and his men. In frustration the king finally decided to make a dash for the lower wing of his palace so that he too could make a celebrated entrance into the crowd. But by the time Saul made his appearance onto the square, the majority of the crowd had already made its way out of the city gates. They followed David cheering his name and throwing wreaths of flowers after him.

The king returned to his palace. His many officers and advisors all diverted their eyes as he passed them on the way to his thrown. Saul then summoned Abner. "Why do they love him so? What does this Sheppard boy have to give them?" he asked.

Later that same day, David and his mighty men engaged the Philistines in battle west of Adullam and instantly pushed the Philistines back into retreat. So overwhelming was their attack that by mid-afternoon on the third day of battle, tens-of-thousands of those besieged enemies had withdrawn all the way back to the interior of Philistia, leaving the region between Azekah and Gath for David and his men to occupy.

Their victory was confirmed by a messenger from the King of Gath who stated that there would be no more Philistine assaults into Israel as long as David did not attack any further. He was do doubt in fear of David's ability to lay siege to and occupy the whole of Philistia itself.

Thus David stationed his men in the area known as Ephes-Dammim where the Philistines had previously gathered with their champion Goliath and returned to Gibeah in order to find out the wishes of King Saul. As he drew nearer to Gibeah, word of his great victory over the Philistines and the fear that he had struck in them had already reached the city's inhabitants. A crowd began to gather around David as he approached, and by the time he entered through the city gates the people were lining the streets, singing and dancing with delight over the young man.

The city once again resembled the celebration that the king had intended for himself a few days prior except this was an unplanned festivity and all the more lively because of it. As the king and his court came out to the second-story terrace in order to see what all the noise was about, they witnessed the people gathering around David in great merriment and once again throwing flowers and garlands through the air in his honor.

The king and his entourage had already returned indoors when the women of the city began to sing, play their tambourines, and dance. But as Abner hurried to close the doors that led outside, he paused to listen for a short while. He then yelled for Saul to come quickly. "They are singing of your greatness, my king," Abner announced excitedly.

As the king stepped out onto the terrace, sure enough, he could hear the women singing in his honor:

> "Saul has slain his thousands
> We know his strength and might
> Saul has slain his thousands
> We know his strength and might..."

The chorus grew louder as it was sung over and over throughout the streets. It was a true delight to the king who began to clap his hands along with their mantra, but he suddenly cut himself short as the next verse began. It rang in his ears over and over again:

> "And David has slain his ten thousands
> In the dark, he is our light
> And David has slain his ten thousands
> In the dark, he is our light...
> David...ten thousands...ten thousands
> David...He is our light...David...David...
> David...David...David...David!!!!!!"

The king could take no more and practically tore down the palace door to get back inside and away from the singing and shouting of the crowd. As he passed Jonathan, who was on his way to see what all the commotion was about, he began to sweat profusely and shake with rage over his resentment. Seeing the state that his father was now in, Jonathan offered to see the king to his chamber. He took Saul by the arm.

"Don't touch me! DO NOT TOUCH ME!" the king bawled in a maniacal holler as palace servants and guards all looked to the ground in order to avoid his wrath. Realizing his mad appearance, the king regained his composure, patted down his hair, and straightened out his garments. "I am fine! I've always been just fine," he claimed after clearing his throat. He then spoke calmly to Jonathan, "I will be in my throne room."

As David entered the palace, Jonathan was there to warn him of King Saul's growing resentment over his popularity. While he escorted David to the king's court he explained the matter, "I can't deny that your triumph over such a formidable force was astounding. My father, with all his armies, has never had such a rapid victory. Yet, you seemingly accomplished it with ease and with just a small force."

"It is not the quantity of soldiers that wins battles," David interjected. "It is their quality that determines the outcome. The men that fight for me are not only the most skilled of warriors; they are also loyal to the point of death. More importantly, they fear the God of Israel and look to Him for their strength."

"Well said," Jonathan responded. "I must admit that that is the one thing that is in your favor; your sanction, it is from God. And you continually seek after his heart. Once again, my father does not know of that sort of devotion. That is why his enmity grows. I on the other hand believe that you will one day be the greatest of leaders. That is if you can avoid the ploys of your adversaries." Jonathan opened the doors to the king's antechamber and whispered, "His condition grows worse by the day."

David did not know what to make of Jonathan's last few statements, but the way these words were spoken, in a hurried and hushed tone, just before they entered the king's chamber was foreboding enough to cause David to speak to the king in a cautious manner. "Your servant, David, has news for you, my king," David declared in humble fashion as he knelt before Saul."

Saul sat on his throne brewing over his thoughts. He looked around the room and then he gazed at David. But his stare went through the young man, and he spoke in an aloof manner all the while behaving as though he did not recognize David. "Who do the people in the streets sing of?" the king asked.

"They sing of your greatness, my king," David assured him.

"No!" the answer came back sharply. "They sing of the greatness of David as they usher him out to war and back home again. They love him." The king paused and then looked around the room. And then, as though he was speaking to some sort of unseen spirit or ghost, he continued, "I wanted to love him also. Have you seen him?"

David did not know how to respond as he finally stood from his kneeling position. Then suddenly, Saul's stare came into focus with that of David's. The king seemed to notice the young captain's presence for the first time and his demeanor changed.

"Why do you kneel, my son?" Saul inquired. "Come closer and tell me of your triumphs."

David approached Saul in an apprehensive manner and gave him a kiss on each cheek.

"I am proud of you, David. Tell me. Tell me," Saul begged.

To the delight of the king, David began to tell of his success against the Philistines. Saul listened intently, and after learning about the King of Gath's appeal to David, his eyes sparked with gladness. "You say that he was willing to make a pact with you as long as you did not advance any further?" Saul questioned in a pleased manner. "Then that is what you and your brave men must do. I want you to attack as far west as possible."

David thought of the danger involved and then gave his answer in a confident manner, "The King of Gath will pay tribute to you by week's end."

Seeing the zealousness of David and the impossibility of the situation, the king continued, "You will be outnumbered greatly. I will tell you what. You know that I have promised my daughter's hand in marriage to you already for your victory against the giant. When you return from your conquest, we will hold the ceremony." As a small ensemble of musicians entered the king's courtroom and began to set up their instruments, the king then changed the subject, "In the meantime, I would like you to do me a favor."

"What is it my king?" David responded.

"My headaches grow worse every day. I hear that before your warring days you were esteemed as one of the greatest musicians in the land of Judah. Will you join this group of musicians and play for me now, in order that my soul should be soothed?"

David readily agreed and took his place amongst the instrumentalists at the harp. As they played, the king savored the soothing melodies and seemed to drift off to sleep. But then suddenly, he awoke. Once again, his stare was remote and his eyes began to follow an invisible phantom that floated around the room. "No, you will not have me! You will not have my soul!" Saul's sudden yells halted the music as David and the rest of the room looked on with bewilderment at the senseless behavior.

"What is the matter my king?" David questioned. "What do you see?"

Saul stared in David's direction but was oblivious to his presence once more as he continued to rebuke an invisible tormentor who seemed to be located between the two of them, "Get away! You can not touch me!"

And with that, the king picked up a javelin that was located near to where he sat and hurled it through the air in the same direction of the perceived threat. David had to quickly duck out of the way as the javelin was hurled within inches of his head. He then decided to make a quick exit as another javelin was menacingly launched toward him by the king. David narrowly escaped just as Jonathan and Abner came running to see that he was alright.

"You must leave here," Jonathan cautioned. "He is up to his old antics. Do not frequent the palace or attend any function where my father is present. I will talk to him and try to calm him, but I am afraid that he has it in for you."

And so it was, David did his best to steer clear of Saul while simultaneously receiving the honor of marrying the king's daughter, Michal, as promised for his defeat of Goliath. And Michal loved him dearly, but her love was rescinded by the growing hate of her father towards David. At the same time, the elders of Judah and that of the rest of Israel became increasingly pleased with David's success in war. Along with his pure character, they loved him for his ability to lead from the front. Still, the king became foul, and his enmity grew over David's success.

As the months past and David led his men to continued triumph, Saul's mind began to grow increasingly mad with thoughts of how to rid himself of this young man. Thus, trifling conspiracies were launched by the king against his own son-in-law. And after a number of failed attempts to inconspicuously bring demise to the young champion, King Saul finally went completely mad. He no longer tried to hide his hatred, and one day, thinking over the situation, while cantankerously sitting in the presence of his court, the king yelled out, "He must die. I want David's head on a platter before me..."

37

Despite the perfidy of the king, Adino and the rest of the mighty men who had vowed to support David remained loyal. And, as written in the Books of the Kingdoms, these mighty men guarded the son of Jesse throughout the many years that Saul pursued him, engaging in many battles and exploits to assure his protection.

And over those years, Adino would often visit Samuel at his home in Ramah where the prophet had lived in exile since the days of King Saul's edict. On many of those occasions the mighty man would converse with Samuel over those series of strange dreams that he continued to have. He tried to explain the dreams in great detail, telling the same story over and over, "There is always the mammoth tree, the men who gather to subdue it, and the lion who only watches from the distance..."

Samuel never offered much explanation concerning the meaning of the dreams but always assured Adino that they were indeed of a prophetic nature. This intrigued Adino all the more until one day he told Samuel that he believed that he finally understood their meaning. It was one of their last conversations.

"Tell me then, what have you come up with?" Samuel

begged as he lay on his bed. A graying old man, he was too old to travel from the confines of his humble home.

"Everything in the dream is symbolic," Adino rationalized. "The men who gathered on that secluded field represent the men of our nation, perhaps the twelve tribes of Israel. I never took the opportunity to count them," he admitted as Samuel listened intently.

"Yes, that sounds reasonable," the prophet said, "but what of the tree and the lion? What do they represent?"

Adino continued, "It is really quite simple. You see, the dreams started back in the days that I gathered the warring men of Israel, just before David slew the great giant. So if the men from the dream do indeed represent the tribes of Israel then the tree represents an enemy of theirs, which they were afraid to go up against, a giant enemy nonetheless. Just like the giant Goliath."

"I see," Samuel said smiling at the rationalization. "The lion is the only mystery then."

"Not quite," Adino explained. "I admit that it was the most difficult piece of the puzzle, but I now believe that I can explain the lion's presence as well. Up until recently, the lion in the dream remained in the distance, merely watching as it lay down. Yet, lately the creature has stood up in my dream and began a slow approach toward the tree as if stalking it." Then Adino pulled out his sword and rested the tip of its blade on the floor so that he could display the prominent handle on the opposite end as he finished. "See there, it is the symbol of our tribe, the lion of Judah. The beast symbolizes the tribe of Judah or more specifically, the lion in the dream represents the champion of our tribe, David, who came forth from Judah to slay the great giant after no one else did and to be the one who would lead us into consummate victory over each of our enemies."

Samuel was really quite pleased with Adino's clarification on the dream and as he reached over and patted the hand of the mighty man, which still rested on the swords handle, he reassured him, "You seemed to have figured it out for yourself. Having done so, you will have the dream one more time and then no more."

Shortly after that occasion, Samuel died, and the entire nation of Israel mourned for him, coming by the thousands to attend his burial. The ceremony took place on the grounds of his home there in Ramah. King Saul attended that day and wept for the great man, whom he declared the last and greatest of Israel's High-Judges, a prophet respected by all the tribesmen and elders alike.

There was likewise another unexpected person who attended the ceremonies that day, one that drew the attention of Adino almost immediately. The heavily veiled individual kept a distance from the likes of both the king and his soldiers while attempting to blend in with the crowds. The ploy may have been successful had not Adino's intuition tipped him off concerning the identity of the veiled personage.

The mighty man first took notice of the situation because it appeared that whoever this was, they were paying less attention to the services that day and instead constantly staring in his own direction from behind that dark shroud. Adino thus kept a watchful eye out and noticed that when the opportunity presented itself, the person broke off from the multitudes and fled through a dense patch of forest in an attempt to flee Ramah completely undetected.

But the mighty man followed closely, calling out as he grabbed the absconder by the shoulder, "I told you that your day of reckoning would come, witch."

The mysterious figure turned around to reveal that it was indeed Zephaniah of Endor. The dowdy veil covered her face, but Adino could nonetheless see Zephaniah's distinctive features underneath. The one thing that he noticed which had changed was her hair. It had become streaked with many gray strands. This last fact surprised Adino somewhat as he considered her relatively young age.

"You did once say that you would see me pay for my

treachery, Adino. And it appears that you were precisely correct," the woman said in a besmirched tone. "If you only knew how soon I was made to pay. For, my punishment came swiftly. You see, I did not make a clean escape from the evil web that I had foolishly helped weave for King Saul. No, instead I found myself caught in the middle of that luring and evil trap, which I had set for another. And I have thence become haunted by the very spirit which once oppressed Saul. It apparently left its royal host the same day that Doeg was arrested. The foul being followed me out of Gibeah and has become a shadow of mine ever since."

"Is this indeed recompense for what you have taken part in?" Adino asked with a doubtful expression. "You believe this haunting, as you call it, is your penance?"

"I know that it is," the witch declared. "For it is the most malicious of beings that haunts me, and unlike other familiars, this spirit will not yield to my control. It desires to possess my mind and body instead and wearies me because of its persistence daily." Zephaniah made these last claims with a panicked voice but her timorous disposition soon gave way to exuberance. Adino even believed that he perceived a sudden smile sprout under the veil as Zephaniah made her next statement, "In fact, it was this familiar spirit that insisted on me coming here today. I have to admit though; I was very willing and interested in attending the burial of Samuel, the prophet of the Almighty."

Adino tried to get a closer look at the woman's face as he leaned in towards her. "And what interest would a spirit, or demon, have with the likes of a prophet of God?" he asked while circumspectly placing a hand upon his sword.

"Oh no, you don't understand," Zephaniah said attempting to clarify her position. "I said that I wanted to come and witness the passing of a prophet. My familiar came to see someone else entirely."

"And who might that be?" Adino asked.

As the answer was uttered, Zephaniah voice seemed to

change, becoming deep and reverberating, "We came to see the face of the one that dreams of the great prophecy. We came to glimpse upon the antecedent of the King-Makers."

This decree sent a chill up Adino's spine and for a brief moment he thought that he had witnessed a complete transformation in Zephaniah's appearance. Behind the veil flashed a contorted and fiendish face with hair that shone completely white. An evil cackle accompanied the next words, which were spoken in the same chilling voice, "We came to see you, Adino, ha, ha, ha..."

The revelation and provocative intonation caused Adino to close his eyes tightly and shake his head in shuddering fashion as he attempted to rid himself of the unnerving sensation that had suddenly overcome him. Upon opening his eyes only moments later, Adino realized that he now stood alone in the mere presence of falling leaves and a forest of trees. Zephaniah had once again made her escape.

As the mighty man emerged from the woods, he thought of the words spoken to him by Zephaniah's so called familiar. Could she possibly entertain such a spirit, and if so, why would it have such a profound interest in him, Adino Ben Hachmon? And had it really alluded to his reoccurring dream, the one that he had explained to no one except Samuel? "You will have the dream one more time and then no more," the prophet had said.

Adino finally made his way back to the front of the funeral procession and left his thoughts of mysticism and dreams for another day. He instead paid his respects to Samuel and shared sentiments of love and honor in memory of the great prophet along with the rest of the nation.

Likewise beloved for his service to Israel, Adino would eventually become chief among captains and attain the highest admiration from Israel's next king, David. And as Adino grew older, he too would take his place amongst the elders.

Yet after telling Samuel about the meaning of his dream, after being confronted with its significance by the demon in the woods, he never did dream of it again, not even once as Samuel had professed. The years thus past and the mighty man grew older and gray.

Then on a stormy night, not long before his own death, Adino dreamed about the rolling hills of the valley for the last time. Only on this occasion, he was not soaring through the skies up above like a bird of prey. He instead stood atop one of the adjacent hillsides looking down at that menacing tree below in the distance. And this-time the tree too had changed. It seemed peaceful and had lost its threatening appearance. In addition there were no men come to destroy it with their axes and swords. It occupied the valley floor alone. Then Adino looked over to the grassy meadow to his left. It was vacant save the long golden stems of the grass, which blew in the quickening wind.

Suddenly something got his attention. There beside him on his right side was the lion. Adino examined the creature more closely and suddenly realized that this was not an actual lion at all, but instead, it was merely a man wearing the pelt of a lion, headdress and all. Then the man stood up, and looked over towards Adino. He was very tall, and his eyes were bright as light. They seemed to burn like the flames of a fire. In his hand he carried a sword, but it was unlike anything that Adino had ever seen. For, surrounding its blade was also the burning flame of a fire. The man said nothing but instead looked out at the tree as he began walking towards it. Adino did not follow, but simply watched from the distance observing the unfolding event.

After finally reaching the proximity of the tree, this intensely somber individual stood under its branches and then discarded the lion's pelt onto the ground along with his sword. Then suddenly, a terrible thing happened. The once unassuming tree immediately took on its former lifelike appearance as it limbs sprang to life and attacked. With one great assault of its long branches, it instantly impaled the man and raised him high up into the air as the flash of a lightning bolt struck down from the heavens in the distance.

Adino instantly awoke and sat up after being awakened by the deafening roar of thunder outside his window. He spoke aloud although he was alone in his dark room, "Samuel, I was wrong about the dream."

At that moment, he all at once remembered Bacchus and the intriguing claims that the strange little man had made in the desert concerning his father's ability to interpret dreams and to read the stars. Adino, along with many of his servants thus packed up and left Israel that very morning. They headed for the East. There, he would find the home of the Magi and study their ways. He would learn the meaning of this dream. But being a man of ripe old age, Adino also understood that this long and demanding journey East would take a toll on him. He knew that he was destined to never again return and see his homeland of Israel again.

Josheb-Basshebeth and his life's exploits would nonetheless go down in the records of antiquity, and he will forever be remembered as the mightiest of David's men, those men of old, men of renowned...

THE END

www.ingramcontent.com/pod-product-compliance
Lightning Source LLC
Chambersburg PA
CBHW031053260626
47172CB00001B/53